FURY *of* ICE

D0675636

The characters and events portrayed in this book are fictitious. Any similarity to real persons, living or dead, is coincidental and not intended by the author.

Text copyright © 2012 by Coreene Callahan
All rights reserved.
Printed in the United States of America.

No part of this book may be reproduced, or stored in a retrieval system, or transmitted in any form or by any means, electronic, mechanical, photocopying, recording, or otherwise, without express written permission of the publisher.

Published by Montlake Romance
P.O. Box 400818
Las Vegas, NV 89140

ISBN-13: 9781612182957
ISBN-10: 161218295X

FURY *of* ICE

Coreene Callahan

To my beautiful girls.

Acknowledgments

My thanks to the amazingly talented people at Amazon Publishing for all their hard work and support, especially my wonderful editor, Eleni Caminis, whose insights never cease to amaze me. And also to Jessica Poore and Nikki Sprinkle. Working with each of you is pure delight.

To Alain: thank you. You are the absolute best!

To Kallie Lane—friend, fellow writer, and critique partner extraordinaire. Thank you for all the breakfast brainstorming sessions, late-night phone calls, and encouragement. I would be lost with you.

As always, a huge thanks to Christine Witthohn, literary agent, friend, and teammate. You rock, sister!

Mom and Dad, I love you. Thank you for everything, but mostly for just being you.

And last but not least, a heartfelt thank you to my readers for falling in love with the Nightfury Dragon Warriors as much as I have and sharing your enthusiasm with me. I love hearing from you and enjoy fielding your questions, even when I can't answer them for fear of giving too much away!

I raise a glass to all of you!

Chapter One

The globes swayed, bobbing like jellyfish against the cavern's ceiling as Rikar flew beneath them. White scales gleamed in the low light, throwing starbursts of iridescent color across stalagmites and uneven stone walls. He didn't notice the rainbow. Didn't hear his claws scrape granite or the water rolling off his wing tips go splat on the landing zone's floor. His focus was absolute. Only one thing mattered.

He was going to kill the male. Open him up like a can of sardines. All while making him sing like a canary.

Lucky for him, he didn't have far to go.

The rogue was chained seven stories beneath Black Diamond, the home Rikar shared with the other Nightfury dragons. That the enemy was within easy reach should've pleased him. But nothing could bliss him out tonight. The battle—the retrieve and retreat routine—had FUBAR written all over it. Yeah, a total catastrophe from beginning to end. The only good thing about it? Bastian had his female back, had pulled her from enemy claws in the nick of time.

He should be happy about that. Throwing high fives with his fellow warriors and yakking it up, reliving the action over tequila shots and lime wedges. But, that was a definite no-can-do. Not tonight. Not when another female was missing.

Right. *Missing.*

Wishful fucking thinking.

Rikar's stomach fisted up hard. The Razorbacks had taken her. He knew it like he was standing there, four paws planted on stone, horns on his head tingling, anguish pumping through his veins with every beat of his heart. Now she was in the hands of his enemy, at the mercy of Ivar, leader of the rogues.

With a growl, he tucked his wings and stepped over the beat-to-shit Honda in the middle of the LZ, trying not to think about what the bastards were doing to her. But God help him, he couldn't turn his brain off. Couldn't breathe without his imagination firing up, planting terrible images in his mind's eye.

Christ, he needed to get her back. Had to locate the Razorback lair and pull her free before…

Rikar swallowed the burn at the back of his throat. What a total mind-fuck. The need. The obsession. The pain.

He'd only met the female once. Had spent a couple of hours getting his ass kicked by her in a friendly game of pool. Okay, so he was lying. He'd done a little more than that. But he refused to think about the feeding or how good she tasted. Rikar shook his head, and water flew as he tried to forget. His behavior. Her acceptance. The fact his frosty side wanted more, another go-round with a female that drew pure power from the Meridian. From the energy source that fed Dragonkind.

Which made him…what? A sicko? A male without honor or conscience? Yeah, without a doubt. The female he didn't want to remember, but couldn't forget, was missing.

Was probably in hell right now, suffering at the hands of a Razorback, and what was he doing? Dreaming of her in ways he shouldn't be.

Angela Keen. She of the gorgeous energy and hazel eyes. God, he wanted her back. He wanted her safe. He wanted the clock to spin in the opposite direction and undo the last three hours. Maybe then he could've prevented his enemies from taking her at all.

Angela.

Her name whispered through his mind. A shiver rolled through him, rattling the spikes along his spine as he pictured her face. With a violent swipe, he tried to erase it like their resident computer genius deleted info from computer hard drives. But memory was a tricky thing: hard to control, impossible to ignore. And as the power of recall got busy planting images inside his head, Rikar accepted the truth. He wished he'd stayed with her that night, taken all she offered and given more in return.

Which was just plain wrong. In every way that mattered.

Wind rushed in from the tunnel mouth, kicking up dust and the smell of damp earth. A second later, green scales flashed in his periphery. Rikar shifted, moving from dragon to human, getting out of Venom's way as the big male set down. Poised on his back paws, his buddy wing-flapped, sending water flying and air rushing, making the light globes bump into their neighbors seventy-five feet above their heads.

Rikar conjured his clothes. Leather settled against his skin, feeling like home as he stomped his foot into his boot and headed for the entrance into the lair. He glanced over his shoulder at his friend. "You coming?"

"Hell, yeah." Scales undulating over thick muscle, Venom indulged in another total body shake. Man, with a move like that, the male looked more like a dog than a dragon. "No way I'm missing the show."

Show. Right. More like a beat down with death as the endgame.

Under normal circumstances, it would've bothered him that Venom knew what he was thinking. Not tonight. Rikar didn't give a shit. Transparency was the least of his problems. A female was involved. So, yeah. The Razorback would hurt until he gave up the goods. End of story.

Upon approach, the cave wall rippled. As the magical doorway glimmered in the low light, Rikar breathed deep, preparing for the electrostatic jolt, then stepped through what had been solid rock moments before. The hair on the nape of his neck rose, reacting to the spell that surrounded Black Diamond and hid their lair from outsiders...human and Dragonkind alike. His boots connected with smooth concrete on the other side of the portal. Thank Christ. The inside of the lair smelled a whole lot better than the cave, like pine floor cleaner, fresh air and...

Home.

He closed his eyes, taking a moment to center himself. A second was all he needed. As the aftershocks of the magical doorway faded, he strode up the slight incline of the double-wide corridor, following the round lights embedded in the concrete floor. The only source of illumination, the runway took him past the medical clinic. He glanced through the sliding glass doors as he passed, looking for his commander. Empty. Not a soul in sight: nothing but an examination table, state-of-the-art equipment, and a shitload of silence.

Rikar shook his head. It made sense. No matter the scrapes and bruises, B was no doubt with his female: holding her, soothing her, making love to her. All life-affirming activities, ones his best friend no doubt craved after what had gone down in the Port of Seattle.

A strange sensation settled in the center of Rikar's chest. His heart hurt as it sank deep and poked around, stirring up all kinds of debris.

Rikar frowned. What the hell was that? Jealousy?

Nah, couldn't be. He was happy for his friend…really. A male of worth like Bastian deserved the best. And Myst? Man, she was exactly what his commander needed. Still, the awful feeling pressed in, twisting him up tight. He upped his pace, refusing to acknowledge it, not wanting to believe he envied his best friend.

Bypassing twin elevators and the gym, he heard Venom move in behind him. The sound of their footfalls became one, echoing together, two males moving in unison toward one purpose. Answers. Rikar wanted them. And like the upstanding male that he was, Venom would back him up.

Good thing too. The next hour would get messy…in more ways than one.

Chapter Two

A steady hum hung in the stale air, the sound's a soft accompaniment to the elevator's rapid descent. Smooth and uninterrupted, a ride in the Otis would've been perfection any other time. But not now. Not tonight. Never again. Angela Keen would forever equate the small, steel box with a cage…

And boatloads of pain.

Squeezing her eyes shut, she tried to forget the last few hours. Nothing good lay in those memories. Minutes or hours ago, it didn't matter. The past needed to stay where she'd put it, locked in a box at the back of her brain.

Along with her fear.

But panic had her by the throat, making it hard to breathe. She forced air into her lungs, rebelling against captivity…against fate. And God. Anyone who would listen as she twisted her hands, searching for a weakness in the flex-cuffs. It was a no-go. There wasn't any give. No defects in the plastic. No fault in the way they'd been used.

And she should know. How many times had she cuffed perps just like this on the job? A hundred times? Two hundred…a thousand?

Man, what a joke. A helpless homicide detective.

All that training—the martial arts classes, shooting qualifications, and survival courses—and for what? To find herself out-muscled and trapped. Nothing but a POW in a war she hadn't known existed until just hours ago.

Dragonkind. Holy hell, who would've guessed?

Not her. Not the rest of the planet either. As far as she knew, the human race was oblivious that monsters with claws and scales lived among them.

She swallowed, fighting the pitch and roll of her stomach, wishing she'd been spared the knowledge. But the truth had a bad attitude. Getting in her face. Hitting her with another dose of reality as the guy holding her prisoner nudged her from behind. She shuffled sideways—paper slippers sliding on her feet, hospital johnny brushing her knees—desperate for more distance between her and the guard at her back.

The rat-bastard.

Yeah, the name had a nice ring to it. Then again, maybe "black-eyed son of a bitch" was a better fit. Asshole Razorback sounded good too. Well, whatever she called Lothair, it wasn't "friendly." The guy carried mean like a baseball bat and knew how to wield it.

"Ready to see your new home, female?" the rat-bastard asked, shifting closer, making her lean away, his boots scraping the steel floor while her heart pounded. "You'll like cellblock A. It's cozy. And you'll have company."

Angela's stomach twisted into a knot. Thus far she'd avoided talking to Lothair. She couldn't stand his proximity, never mind the sound of his voice, but...

She couldn't let that intel go. If other women were imprisoned in the Razorback complex, she needed to know.

"How many?" As the question left her mouth, she winced. God, she sounded raw. Like the victims of violent crimes she talked to every day. But then, she guessed that description fit her to a T now. And just the thought made her want to sit down and cry. "How many are here?"

"Two so far. With more to come." He hummed behind her, his pleasure so obvious Angela wanted to turn and take his head off. Too bad she didn't have a weapon. "High-energy females just like you…good breeders. Good feeding, better tasting than the whores downtown. Hmm, yeah. I can't wait for another taste of you, sweetheart."

Angela clenched her teeth, refusing to react to the endearment. Lothair was smart, ruthless with a slap-happy helping of brutal. He wanted her to remember the feeding, to relive the press of his mouth against her throat, hard hands on her body, the awful suck and draw and…

Uh-uh. No way.

She refused to go there. Didn't want to relive a second of the violation or dwell on the fact Lothair had taken something vital from her. What? She didn't know exactly, but the awful experience wouldn't leave her alone. Kept reminding her until her eyes burned with the threat of tears. She blew out a shaky breath and pushed the panic away: compartmentalizing the pain, moving the memory to a different mental zip code while she brought another front and center. One she couldn't quite touch but knew was there…buried in her mind, surrounded by some sort of impenetrable wall.

R. She remembered a name that started with R. And something else too. Pale blue eyes: beautiful, concerned, shimmering in the darkness. She clung to the visual and how it made her feel—safe, sane, strong enough to cope with whatever came next.

Which needed to be a swift kick in the pants.

Feeling sorry for herself wouldn't help. Resourcefulness and a quick mind, however? Yeah, those were vital. She was tough, skilled, and able to set the parameters of what she allowed to hurt her. And as she set up mental roadblocks and retreated behind psychological barricades, she glanced over her shoulder. Brown eyes met hers, the color so dark the pupils blended with the irises. Leveling her chin, she made herself a promise. "I'm going to kill you, you know that?"

He laughed. "I'd love for you to try, she-cop. Please… try."

The murmur was eerie, like the creak of frozen tree limbs in winter, the sound of isolation and mass murder. And as fear slithered along her spine, Angela smothered a shiver to keep it from surfacing. The sadist SOB would love that. Oh, yeah. Nothing got him off more than the sight of her afraid. She'd learned that the hard way in the examination room. She quashed the memory. Her experience with him proved the bastard liked her cowed to the point of subservience. He was diabolical, really. Brilliant with a capital B. Lothair was a tactician with brutal focus: accessing her weakness, using it against her, revving her imagination into the danger zone.

God, what was taking the elevator so long? She needed out. Away from the bastard pushing her buttons because…

She could smell him. Feel him staring at her even though she wasn't looking at him. And as his eyes moved over her—ever watchful, always waiting—her stomach pitched. Muscle tightened over her bones, preparing to let fly. It would feel so good to hit him. Just wind up and send her elbow into his face. To feel the crack as she broke his nose and heard his roar of pain. But she'd already tried that, and trapped in an elevator with a pissed-off guy was the last place any sane woman wanted to be.

"You thinking of running when the doors open, she-cop?" Uncoiling like a poisonous snake, his voice slithered through the silence, making her scream inside her own mind. He nudged her with the toe of his boot. "Come on. Make it interesting. Run."

Angela swallowed her rage along with an unwise retort. She couldn't fight fire with fire. Words wouldn't get her anything but more bruises. The best strategy was silence. Her nonreaction would drive him nuts. Maybe even piss him off enough to make a mistake and hand her the information she needed to break free.

"What? Nothing to say? You done fighting?" He leaned in, getting too close, winding her tight, provoking without touching. "Such a pity. I like a little fight in my female."

Fight. Right. What he *liked* was a live punching bag, one that cried and begged for mercy. No way would she give him the satisfaction. Or an easy victory.

Flexing her hands, Angela worked the blood back into them. As her fingertips tingled, she got ready. The quiet creak and sway of the Otis told her they were almost there. Yeah, she might be praying for rescue, but that didn't mean she should sit back and wait for it. She had skills, carried a mental toolbox full of fighting techniques and tactical knowledge. She needed to use it—stay focused, pay attention, find a way out.

Which was a great plan…in theory. The only problem? The beatings and medical procedures had sapped her strength, and now, nausea ate her from the inside out. Wave after wave washed in, eroding her confidence, devouring the place where know-how lived. And as bile threatened the back of her throat, she tasted the vile protein shake again. Angela huffed. Protein shake, her ass. She hadn't landed in Spa-land, and the green drink they'd forced down her throat hadn't been jammed full of antioxidants. Drugs. The aftertaste washed over her tongue as the medicine sloshed in the pit of her stomach.

The elevator slid open with a soft ping.

Lothair pointed, motioning her through the entrance into...

Where exactly? The descent proved she was underground, in some sort of facility. But the structure was far from new. Paint peeled, leaving bald patches on the walls in some places and latex curls hanging from cinder block in others. And the concrete floor? Worn as though the passageway had been well traveled, but not maintained.

Angela stepped out of the Otis and into the corridor. The paper slippers slid on her feet, catching on the uneven floor as fluorescents buzzed, making her head ache, but at least the air was fresher down here. A continuous click-click-whirl sound rattled through the corridor. Angela glanced up at...

Thank God. A steel grille. The place had a ventilation system. Maybe she could—

A big hand clamped down on one of her biceps.

She jerked, wrenching her arm out of Lothair's grip. He smirked, planted his palm between her shoulder blades, and pushed. As she cursed and stumbled forward, calling him every name she could think of, he kept up the shove routine, herding her ahead of him until they came to steel bars. Straight out of a prison, the barrier was old, but effective, blocking the corridor in both directions.

Lothair shoved her sideways, away from the electronic keypad. Her shoulder collided with the wall. Angela barely noticed. She was too busy to bother with the pain. Her focus was pinpoint sharp, glued to the digital screen and…

Bingo.

The idiot.

He hadn't blocked her view. And as Lothair's fingers got busy punching in the access code, she paid attention, squirreling away each number and…

Gotcha.

Man, the bonehead was clueless. She had the access code. Now all she needed was to make sure she could find her way out when the time came. A problem for most people, but not her. She controlled the swing vote, had an ace up her sleeve, so to speak: a photographic memory that provided perfect recall.

Thank God the Razorbacks didn't know that. A blindfold would've been the kiss of death for her.

The steel bars retracted with a clang, echoing through the deserted corridor. Well, "deserted." It was all relative, really. She was here along with Mr. Asshole, after all.

Lothair shoved her again. "Move it."

"Screw off," she rasped, her throat raw from that awful drink.

"There you are," he said, sounding pleased. "The spirited female I know and love…back at last."

He had no idea. Payback wasn't fun, and after what she'd suffered the last few hours, Lothair was first on her hit list. 'Cause, yeah, given half a chance? She would pump him full of lead. Blow his head off without hesitation.

Too bad her gun had been lost in the firefight. At the precinct. Where her partner had been blown through a plate-glass window.

Angela blinked back tears. Oh, no…Mac.

She'd thought of her partner countless times since the explosion and her capture. Had prayed and pleaded… *Please, God, let him be all right.* Whether or not *he* heard her she didn't know. All she could do was hope.

Hope. Pray. And beg.

Holding in a sob, she walked past cinder-block walls and under bare lightbulbs. Lothair hummed behind her—like he knew what she felt and loved the show. She ignored him, her mind fully occupied with Mac.

Please, don't let him be dead.

She could handle a lot: the torture and pain, the humiliation and imprisonment. But a world without Mac? No way she could go there and survive what she knew was coming. He was the big brother she'd never had, the only family she acknowledged. The only one who cared enough to come looking for her.

Rounding a corner, the empty corridor gave way, branching in two different directions. Angela wanted to go right. She saw tools down there: lying on the concrete floor, leaning against dingy walls, stacked on top of half-open boxes. Two men, looking empty-eyed and exhausted, glanced up, then looked away as though afraid to acknowledge her. Desperation hung in the air around them. Hers? Theirs? She didn't know. Maybe it was a combination of the two, but as her mind sharpened, her body responded, hitting her with a shot of adrenaline.

The nausea evened out. Her heart picked up the slack, thumping hard as she scanned the dilapidated hallway, looking for the fastest route, the likeliest weapon with the deadliest potential. Lothair was big, too strong for her to outmuscle. But, maybe, just maybe, she could surprise him. Deploy the blitz attack so many murderers used to down their victims. One sharp blow to the head. One hard slash to the throat, and she'd be free, sprinting back toward that keypad with the access code riding shotgun.

Lothair veered left.

Angela lunged right, kicking out of her slippers, forcing her legs to work, her gaze on the box cutter no more than ten feet away.

A growl sounded behind her. Heavy footfalls followed, pounding out a terrifying rhythm.

Panic grabbed hold, making her run flat out. Something white flashed in her periphery. Clear plastic. And inside? Loose powder. She grabbed a handful as she sprinted past. Three feet from the tool, Lothair grabbed her hospital gown from behind. Angela twisted, flung her bound hands wide, and opened her palms. The fine dust flew, hitting Lothair in the face.

With a roar, he reeled and, heavy boots sliding, lost his grip on her. She slid into a stack of boxes. Cardboard toppled, but she didn't retreat. All she saw was the weapon she needed to stay alive. Time slowed. Sound came from far away, like voices through water as she reached out. The cutter's metal handle touched her fingertips, then slid between her palms. Her teeth bared, she spun, raising the tool like a knife. She slashed, striking out with an upward arc. The blade struck, slicing through skin to meet bone. Lothair howled as she cut his cheek wide open.

Blood arced in a violent splash, spraying across the wall and the front of her gown. Angela didn't care. Victory was seconds away.

She raised the cutter again. All her focus on her captor's throat, she plunged forward. He countered, blocking the strike with his forearm. Pushed back by the thrust, Angela pivoted, ducking beneath his arm. She aimed for his ribs.

Air exploded from his lungs as she slashed him again. "Fuck!"

Black eyes flashed fury. Angela didn't slow. She deployed skill instead, kicking out with her foot. Bull's-eye. She nailed him in the balls. He squawked, cupping himself as his knees hit the floor. She thrust hers forward, hammering him again. His chin snapped up, and his head whiplashed. A sick crack echoed as the back of his skull slammed into the cement wall.

Breathing hard, she watched him crumple, the makeshift knife raised in defense. One...two...three seconds passed. He didn't move. And she didn't wait.

Galvanized into motion, she leapt over his body. The instant her bare feet hit the floor on the other side, she let loose, legs pumping, heart hammering, hope lighting a fire deep inside her. A window. She had a narrow slice of opportunity before the other Razorbacks realized Lothair hadn't returned.

She needed to run hard. Think fast. Make every second count.

Her life depended on it.

Chapter Three

Rikar slowed his roll, pausing in front of a reinforced steel door to punch in his access code. As his fingers did the walking, his inner beast stirred as though the bastard knew what awaited him on the other side. An hour with a Razorback. Nothing but a Razorback.

Oh, thank you, God.

A quick hand flex. A little neck action—rolling his chin against his chest, stretching out the tense muscles bracketing his spine—and he was ready to go. To cause pain. Inflict suffering. At one with his frosty side.

A rarity among his kind, a frost dragon whose blood ran cold, he was fortunate that his magic never abandoned him. The power was always Johnny-on-the-spot. Night or day—in and out of dragon form—it simmered in his veins, wanting out of its cage, begging to be used.

Most males weren't so lucky. Their magical abilities diminished in human form. But he was different. Bastian, too. His best friend was the only other male he knew who could command his magic in both forms. Maybe that was the reason they were so tight, bonded in a way he found difficult to describe, never mind understand.

Right now, though, the mystery didn't mean much. He had a job to do. And what do you know? His frosty side was on board with the plan, juicing him up, chilling him out.

His mouth curved as frost rose. As the chill got thicker, the temperature dropped, and Rikar exhaled, thankful for the deep freeze. The cold evened him out, settled him down, made him remember his purpose.

Angela. Why the hell couldn't he find her?

He should've been able to…had tapped into her and fed on the energy she drew directly from the Meridian. Which meant he was linked in, so attuned to her life force that tracking her should've been the work of minutes. Instead, he had nothing. Zippo on the leads front.

Rikar cranked his hands in tight, praying for a miracle. For the rogues to screw up and let the cloaking shield they held around Angela slip. He needed thirty seconds tops to lock onto her signal. But that wouldn't happen now. Not with dawn approaching and the deadly UV rays that arrived with it spreading over Seattle.

Twelve hours. Twelve freaking hours before he could go back out. Before he could hunt, maim, and interrogate Razorback soldiers. And in the meantime? He had his very own plaything locked deep inside Black Diamond.

"Rikar, man." Venom took a step back and turned his face to the side, like someone forced to stand too close to an inferno. "Could you lay off until we get in there? I'm getting frostbite over here."

"Suck it up, Ven…or find a parka." Yeah, that and a bomb shelter. His frosty side was just getting started, and as the air fogged, ice spread, turning the door frame and wall into an arctic wonderland of white. "It'll only get worse."

"Great." The grumble in his voice unmistakable, his buddy pulled a long-sleeved shirt over his head. "I'm gonna end up a frigging ice cube before this is over. Theraflu, here I come."

Rikar's lips twitched. Thank God for Venom. The male never failed to pull something out of his hat. And that *something* was either wicked funny, off-color, or just plain cool. Which always chilled Rikar out, parked his instincts long enough to put intellect in the driver's seat. Man, he needed that right now. Walking into the interrogation center in snarl mode wouldn't get him the information he wanted. Or a map...with the longs and lats of the Razorback lair.

Pinpoint accuracy. Lethal precision. A successful raid, and...bam! Angela would be home safely. Was that too much to ask? He swallowed past the lump in his throat, hoping beyond hope that it wasn't.

Rikar threw Venom a grateful look and grabbed the door handle. The security system beeped, releasing the electronic locks. With a tug, he pulled the heavy door wide. Even toned down, his frosty side made itself known as icicles formed, clinging to the handle before he let go and stepped over the threshold. With a curse, Venom scrambled—shitkickers sliding on the icy floor—to avoid touching the freezing steel and muscled the door aside with his shoulder.

Completed less than a month ago, the interrogation center was a thing of beauty. Secure, state-of-the-art, surrounded by miles of granite, the facility sat one level below the underground lair. A prison with attitude, the cell capacity maxed out at seven prisoners. Not that he wanted that many rogues anywhere near Black Diamond. Especially now, with B's female in residence. But planning equaled preparedness.

Or so he'd been told repeatedly by Gage.

Their resident gearhead-slash-architect-slash-engineer and…well, all right. So the male was a jack-of-all-trades in the "build something" department, and now that the facility was completed? He was glad Gage had pushed Bastian to build the prison.

But that didn't mean he liked the magic surrounding it.

The electrostatic current pulsed in the air, attacking his central nervous system, drawing him so tight his skin felt like it was shrinking. The nausea hit next, making the back of his throat burn.

And wasn't this fun? Uh-huh, so not a picnic. Just steel walls, concrete floors, and dimmed halogens marching down the middle of twelve-foot ceilings.

Rounding a corner, Rikar tensed as the current grew stronger, boxing him in until claustrophobia reared its ugly head. No surprise there. Enclosed spaces weren't his thing. Venom, though, didn't mind tight quarters, liked riding the elevator to reach the main house above the underground lair.

But shit, even his buddy was squirming under the strain, shuffling his feet as he growled, "I hate this place."

"Almost there," he said as much for himself as for Venom.

He hoped voicing the fact out loud would settle him down. No such luck. The rush beneath his skin grew worse the deeper he walked into the center. As sensation screamed along his spine, he jogged down the steps. The descent was fast, controlled, his focus on the door at the bottom of the single staircase. Another security measure. One way in. One way out.

Halfway down, he punched the code into the keypad with his mind. The electronic locks clicked. With a mental push, he swung the door wide a second before he crossed the threshold into the wide open space on the other side.

He released the breath he'd been holding. The electrostatic bandwidth stabilized, throwing all its energy around the prison cells that ran down the left side of the narrow room. He checked the first as he strode past it, searching for the purple-eyed Razorback.

Empty.

The second was too. Which made sense.

Bastian would want the rogue in the largest pen. Farthest from the door, the extra space would give them more elbow room for all kinds of yakkety-yak and nasty—

Something moved in the shadows. Rikar's head snapped to the right.

Green eyes shimmering in the gloom, his best friend stepped into the light. He tipped his chin. "Anything?"

Rikar dialed back the frost factor. Bastian wasn't stupid. Truth be told, the male knew him better than anyone. Under normal circumstances, a big plus. Right now? Not so much. His commander would guess his intentions in a heartbeat if he wasn't careful. Which would KO his shot at the Razorback. B wouldn't turn a blind eye. Not when he'd gone to such lengths to cage the bastard. And not before Bastian got the information he needed to keep his mate safe.

Rikar shook his head, indicating a negative.

A muscle twitched along B's jaw. "Fuck."

No kidding, and the understatement of the century. Angela was out there somewhere—alone, afraid, vulnerable—and what did he have? A shit storm in the making. He refused to let Bastian shut him down.

Did it matter that he loved the male like a brother? Respected the hell out of him? Normally followed his command without question? No. Not even a little. He needed the Razorback to squawk. So as much as he hated the endgame, he would take B out of the equation to have his way.

Stopping alongside his best friend, he looked inside the last pen. The corners of his mouth tipped up. Satisfaction, it seemed, came in size extra large.

Built lean, but loaded with muscle, the rogue stood at least six foot eight in his bare feet. Thank God. Just by looking at him, Rikar knew the male owned fighting chops. Enough to challenge him. Which lit him up, added that special sauce to the dish he was about to toss into the Razorback's pan.

Bastian's eyes narrowed on him. "We gonna have a problem?"

Rikar shrugged off his internal flinch. He hated that soft tone. The low pitch was a shade shy of melodic and, when B used it, a smart male got out of the way.

"Nah," he said, lying his ass off. Backing up the BS with a head shake, he geared up. Distraction time. He didn't want to tip his best friend off, so in the spirit of the *me-me-me* crap he had going on, he threw out the only question guaranteed to shift B's focus. "How is Myst?"

"Exhausted, but okay." Bastian scrubbed a hand over the top of his head. The action spoke volumes, of the worry he suffered for his mate and the relief of bringing her home safely. "I finally got her to sleep fifteen minutes ago."

Fantastic. He'd missed his window by a measly fifteen minutes.

The irony, right? Now he was stuck in a place he didn't want to be. He made the hard decision anyway. Bastian would be pissed, but maybe if he left the rogue alive, it would all wash out in the end. Okay. So, that was a long shot, but what else could he do? Honor wouldn't let him leave Angela and—

Ah, hell. That was a big, fat lie.

Honor had nothing to do with it. What drove him was much more powerful than that. It was predatory and instinctual, territorial and terrible. Somewhere along the line, his dragon half had decided Angela belonged to him and, no matter how much he disliked the admission, biology wasn't something Rikar could fight.

Silence grew, sliding against the steel walls as Bastian studied him, no doubt working all the angles.

Venom stepped into the void—thank fuck—and up to the energy barrier stretched across the front of the prison cell. Flying in the face of physics, the thin electrostatic current was stronger than steel, yet invisible, giving him a clear view of the male imprisoned on the other side. As their gazes locked, the rogue snarled at him: amethyst eyes flashing, fists flexing, veins popping against the electronic collar around his neck. Rikar studied the metal band, imagining how it would feel against his skin. Not good, that was for sure. But worse than that was the knowledge that once secured, the thing would blow your head off if you crossed the magical threshold into the free zone.

A trap. Perfect. Absolute. Diabolical to a male who valued his freedom.

Raising his hand, Venom brushed his fingertips against the invisible wall. The barrier shimmered in the low light, rippling like water in a pond. His buddy's ruby-red eyes glowed, flashing aggression as he glanced over his shoulder. "He say anything yet?"

"No." B stopped giving Rikar the evil eye and switched focus. His too-shrewd gaze landed on their prisoner. "We got a name, though."

Rikar raised a brow, asking without words.

"Forge."

"Good to know," he murmured and…made his move.

His feet left the ground before his brain told him to go. He rocketed through the barrier into the cell. Electricity lit him up from the inside out. Rikar ignored the pain and Bastian's curse. He had one purpose: reach the Razorback before his commander downloaded the launch code and went nuclear on his ass.

Unleashing his frosty side, ice exploded from the floor, slammed into the walls and ceiling, sealing the entrance into the cell. The thick barrier shut his friends out and him in with a rogue he couldn't wait to get his hands on.

Frost cracked, coating steel and concrete. Rikar roared across the space, breathing white clouds of air on each exhale.

His best friend pounded against the ice barrier. "Goddamn it, Rikar!"

Dropping into a fighting stance, the rogue met him with raised fists. Rikar dipped beneath and swung left, unleashing an uppercut beneath the male's chin. Bone met bone, cracking through the quiet as the rogue's head snapped back. Rikar hit him again, his knuckles connecting with the fucker's rib cage.

Air exploded from his lungs, but no lightweight, Forge countered. Spinning on bare feet, he brought his elbow up, nailing Rikar in the temple. With a snarl, he absorbed the blow as he drove the Razorback into the back of the cell. He needed to hurry. B would give him a minute tops. After that he'd shift into dragon form, use his freaky electropulse exhale, and blow the lid off his interrogation.

"Where is she?" Drilling him again, Rikar cracked the male with a right cross. Blood flew, streaking across the rogue's face as a cut opened beneath his eye. "Where's your lair?"

Forge answered with a growl. Blocking a punch, the Razorback hammered him with a strong jab. Rikar's head snapped to the side. His teeth scraped the inside of his mouth. Blood washed over his tongue. Rikar swallowed and pivoted, kicking out with his foot. His shitkicker connected. The rogue's knee buckled, sending him to the floor in a messy sprawl.

Rikar raised his fist again. "Tell me where."

"I'm not that easy, asshole," Forge said, the Scottish brogue rolling in his voice.

The thick accent ramped Rikar up. Fury roared through him, unleashing violence in an uncontrollable wave. "You fucker. She's a female…an innocent."

"So was mine."

A shadow passed over Forge's face a second before he rolled, avoiding the next strike. With a slick move, the male gained his feet and, fists raised, circled right. Rikar moved left, eyes narrowed and heart hammering, searching for an opening. Christ, Forge was skilled. Giving as good as he got. But the ice worked against him. The slip and slide hampering his ability to dodge. Losing his balance, Forge's guard fell. Rikar punched through, knuckles taking punishment as he hammered the enemy with body shot after body shot.

A roar sounded from outside the cell. Shit. B was in full dragon mode. And about to enter the fray.

Working fast, Rikar lunged forward and grabbed hold. His hands slipped beneath the collar around the rogue's throat. He squeezed, cutting off his enemy's airway as metal tore at the backs of Rikar's hands. Blood rolled between his fingers. Rikar didn't care. With single-minded focus, he tightened his grip and shoved the rogue hard. Thrust off balance, Forge's feet slid. He went down, shoulder blades slamming into concrete. Rikar went with him, landing on top of the male's chest.

Losing air fast, Forge struggled, fighting the vulnerable position. Without mercy, Rikar squeezed the male's throat, crushing the life out of his opponent. "Tell me…tell me how to find her."

Both of his hands wrapped around Rikar's wrists, Forge twisted, easing the pressure on his windpipe. Denying him the answer he needed. Craved. Couldn't do without.

Rikar snarled. "You son of a—"

The ice wall exploded, throwing chunks of ice inward. The sharp shards blasted his back, and…

God forgive him. He'd failed.

The rogue wouldn't give up the goods, and as B's midnight-blue scales flashed in his periphery, hope shriveled, leaving a hole inside his chest.

Angela. His female was in trouble. Was being hurt and…

Christ. He couldn't stand it. Wouldn't survive as seconds ticked into minutes…into hours and days. With her held captive. Suffering God only knew what.

Moisture gathered, pooling in the corners of his eyes as his best friend came through the hole in the ice wall. Shifting to human form, B moved like an organized hurricane, grabbing hold of Rikar. One forearm against his throat, the other clamped across his chest, his commander yanked, hauling him up and backward. As his hands slid from the rogue's throat, Rikar roared, the anguished sound filling the corners of his heart along with the room.

His female would die in a Razorback prison. There was nothing he could do to stop it.

Chapter Four

Swedish Medical's ER was a frickin' zoo, and the noise was messing with Mac's head. Not that he had much to screw with in the first place. The explosion had fried his circuits, and after going a dozen rounds with unconsciousness, his brain was doing cartwheels. End over end. Minute after minute.

Motherfuck, would the spinning ever stop?

Fighting his stomach's one-way evacuation plan, he clutched the mattress edge and rolled onto his side. The hospital bed creaked with his movement. Man, the thing wasn't made for a guy like him. For the Olympic-size headache slamming the inside of his skull? Yeah, okay, maybe. But not for a six-foot-five homicide detective with a bad attitude and no time to waste.

The whole situation was bullshit. All of it. The waiting. The noise. The fever and dizziness. The fact his captain had planted him on a hospital gurney in the middle of Baghdad. Okay, so that last bit wasn't fair. It only seemed like he'd landed in the middle of a war zone, but he didn't care. His partner was MIA. Had been taken by—

Jesus, had he really seen what he'd *seen*?

Mac rubbed the center of his forehead, bringing the visual into focus. The split-second snapshot didn't seem like much, but…definitely. He'd gotten a good look before the scaly SOB airlifted him through the window. A dragon. With sharp claws, black scales, packing a whole lot of pissed off and breathing a boatload of poison.

Or radiation. Whatever.

Mac didn't know what he'd been hit with. Neither did the doctors. Even after all the stupid blood tests.

Which was a problem.

His partner needed him, and where was he? On injured reserve, sitting on the sidelines while Seattle's finest searched for Angela—his kid sister by silent agreement if not blood. His throat went tight. God, had he said the entire situation was BS yet? Yeah, a total frickin' farce. He knew Ange better than anyone. Understood her in ways she didn't understand herself. Knew her haunts, preferences, where she went to hide when she craved time alone.

And what had his captain and the team of idiot doctors done? Ass-planted him…with a rent-a-cop outside his door.

Mac snorted. Like that would make him stay put.

Swallowing a groan, he swung his legs over the side of the bed and sat up. The room went topsy-turvy. His stomach sloshed, then leveled out as his brain came back online. Thank Jesus. Yeah, the pain might still be there—thumping against his temples, cramping his muscles—but at least he was mobile. Operational and combat ready, because he couldn't stay here. Where no one gave a damn about Ange. About the fact she was out there somewhere: alone, without her Glock for backup.

So to hell with the doctors. With tests and CAT scans. Getting out of Dodge was priority one. Not his health. And not the dickheads who expected him to put himself first.

Now if only he could find his boots.

Busy looking under the bed, he missed the squeaking approach of nurse's shoes. Metal screeched against metal, making him wince as the curtain surrounding his bed got yanked aside. The squeak of rubber shoes went silent. "Detective MacCord…what do you think you're doing?"

Hell, she was back, and the last thing he needed. Nurse What's-her-name was a slick operator. A liar with big blue eyes and no scruples. "Of course, detective, you're free to go anytime," she'd said. "Just a few more tests…"

Yeah, right. She blah-blahed with the best of them and then screwed him over. Exhibit A? Conan—the genius with a security badge on his shirt—eyeballing him from the open doorway.

The nurse hesitated a second, then stepped into his little patch of heaven. He watched her from his periphery, not looking directly at her, but keeping her in his sights. "Did you hear me?"

"Loud and clear."

"Well?"

Ah, eureka. There they were. Pulling a stretch and grab, he hauled his black steel-toes out from under the bed. The action spoke louder than words, and as she gasped, he stomped his feet into his boots.

"You can't leave. We haven't finished running tests." Her voice came out clipped and hard, like a battle commander's in the middle of a firefight. "Get back into bed."

Ironic, wasn't it? On any other night, he would've jumped on board that party train: shagged her hard, made her scream with pleasure and beg for more. But not tonight. He didn't have time to play nice. All he wanted was out.

Sweat dripped off the tip of his nose and hit the floor with a splat. Taking a steadying breath, he pushed away from the bed and stood. His legs protested a second, thigh muscles twitching before he caught his balance. The dizziness—the weakness and nausea—was a bitch, but that was the least of it. Other things were bothering him too. Like the fluorescents above his head. The bright light hurt his eyes and made his temples pound. And his skin? Way too sensitive, as though he'd been sandblasted while drifting in and out of la-la land.

Rolling his shoulders, he cringed, hating the scratchy feel of the jeans and cotton tee he'd pulled on that morning. "Where's my jacket?"

"Detective MacCord, you're not well," Nurse Pain-in-the-Ass said, her voice cajoling now instead of steely. Good plan. Not that the tone switch-up would work. He was leaving whether she liked it or not. "Please…just a few more—"

He pivoted in her direction, nailing her with the full force of his gaze.

She blinked, then sucked in a quick breath. "Oh, my God. Your eyes. They're…they're…"

Mac's brows collided. His eyes were…what? What the hell was she talking about?

The nurse backed up a step. Then another, staring at him like he were some kind of freak show. He reached for her, his gaze glued to her face. Panic flared in her eyes a second before she spun and ran for the exit. The instant she cleared the door frame, she yelled, "Doctor! I need a doctor over here!"

"Goddamn it." Guess his leather coat would have to wait.

But *he* couldn't. The nurse would be back with reinforcements. And as much as his job called for it, he didn't like knocking people around unless they left him no other choice.

Moving like an enemy tank, Mac rounded the end of the bed and headed for the door. Rooted between the steel doorjambs, Conan the Brilliant jacked up his pants. The security guard's badge winked in the bright light, flashing silver against the navy-blue uniform. Mac wanted to roll his eyes. He made twin fists instead and, without slowing, met the baby rent-a-cop's gaze. "You really wanna fuck with me?"

Yup. That did it. Mr. Tough Guy moved, just slid right out of his way. As Mac passed, he nodded at the guard, acknowledging the crappy position he was putting him in. The kid would probably lose his job over letting him go. Or at the very least end up with a reprimand in his file.

"Sorry, man. My partner's in trouble."

Conan nodded. "Go left…out through the loading docks. I'll tell 'em you went the other way."

"You're a peach."

"With an ulterior motive." Putting his feet in gear, the kid trailed him down the double-wide corridor. As they dodged patients on gurneys and medical personnel, he raised his voice to be heard over the din of the ER. "I want a recommendation that'll get me into the academy this spring."

Pausing at a bustling hallway intersection, Mac's mouth curved. Well, well, well. Maybe the kid wasn't so dumb, after all. "Bring your creds to my office…I'll consider it."

"That way." Right on his ass, the kid pointed to a set of doors dead-ending one of the corridors. "Laundry's through there. It'll lead you straight out. Good luck, man."

Without looking back, Mac punched through the double doors. Five minutes later, he was outside and around the side of the building. Chilly autumn air washed over him. He clenched his teeth, trying to keep them from chattering, and rubbed his bare arms. But the cold persisted, sinking deep, rattling his bones until...

Jesus. Where was he? Canada?

It sure felt like he'd landed in his northern neighbor's playground. The only thing missing? About three feet of snow. Not that he had time to be grateful for the lack of thick-white-and-fluffy. He needed to get across town, to the shipyard where he moored his boat. The hospital wouldn't keep Captain Hobbs in the dark for long. When hospital staff couldn't find him inside the facility, a phone call would be made and...boom! His boss's temper would explode.

So, home first to grab his backup weapon, then he'd get good and ghost. After all, his captain couldn't give him hell if he couldn't find him.

A cab ride—and the world record for dry heaving—later, Mac crossed the deserted parking lot and approached the shipyard's entrance. Surrounded by a twelve-foot chain-link fence, he got within ten feet before the motion sensors went live. Industrial-grade halogens clicked on, flooding the security gate with light.

Mac flinched and, turning his face away, stumbled sideways. God, that hurt. Which was beyond strange.

Normally, the light-bright routine didn't bother him. Tonight, the brilliance tunneled into the back of his brain, making his head scream. Gravel crunched beneath his boots as Mac's shoulder bumped the warehouse wall flanking the walkway. Using it to prop himself up, he spread one hand against the cold steel, planted the other on his knee, and doubled over, fighting another case of the gags.

Frickin' hell.

The nausea was killing him. And as the pain got worse, his muscles cramped, knotting so tight he couldn't catch his breath. Sucking air in through his nose, he blew it out his mouth, trying to unlock his lungs. The in-and-out routine helped and, after a minute, he pushed himself upright and squinted at the keypad mounted next to the gate.

Seven feet. Just seven more feet and he'd be inside, walking into the place he called home.

Slamming his internal gearshift, Mac put himself in drive, forcing one foot in front of the other. He punched his password into the keypad. A motor hummed and chains clanked as the gate retreated, sliding sideways. Not waiting for it to open fully, he slipped through and staggered down the concrete steps, each footfall quiet even though his body was in riot mode.

Force of habit. The necessity for silence had been drilled into him in basic training, then solidified by his time with SEAL Team Six. No matter how badly injured, he never made a sound.

Keeping to the shadows, he headed for the fourth pier, passing nautical relics along the way. A working museum of sorts, the shipyard was the place old tugboats came to get a makeover. Kitted out with the best of everything, the tidy marine complex hummed during the day, shipwrights working on the tugs in hopes they would sell. And man, did they ever. Bigwigs paid a fortune to possess one of the beauties. The fact the yard was owned by a guy who owed him a favor?

Well now, that was just his luck.

Hoity-toity marinas weren't his thing. But here, away from nosy boaters and polite society? Yeah, the shipyard was home, and he loved living on his boat.

He'd never understood it, but he needed to be surrounded by water. Craved the smell of salty air, the rolling wash of ocean tides…the wet, inky depths beneath his home. And his daily swim? Pure heaven. Just a hop, skip, and a jump away.

Taking a sharp left, he strode down the ramp onto the wooden finger dock. Metal groaned under his weight, but he adored the rock-n-sway as the water reacted, throwing brine into the air, making the dock move beneath his feet. And, hmm, there she was, sitting right where he'd left her.

His Sarah-Jane. The forty-seven-foot Chris-Craft motor yacht he knew and loved.

Restored to perfection, she was his girl. She knew it too, gleaming in the moonlight, showing off her curved lines and polished teak railings. Slowing his roll alongside her, he unzipped the canvas doorway and hopped aboard. The instant his feet touched down, the ocean took over: Zening him out, suppressing the sick feeling, allowing him to take a full breath. Yeah, the urge to puke still circled, but at least dry heaves took a backseat, letting him move without cramping up his abdomen.

Crossing the open-air sitting area at Sarah-Jane's stern, he dug the key out of his front pocket. The padlock disengaged with a snick. With a quick flip, he opened the door into the main cabin. Not wasting a second, he walked down the narrow staircase and headed for the galley. Stepping around the kitchen island, he grabbed the oven handle. Springs creaked as he yanked it wide and reached inside.

Easy as pie, the Glock 19 slid into his palm.

Mac's mouth curved as he ripped the gun from its duct-taped cradle. Straightening, he flipped open the breadbox sitting on the counter. His hand closed around the magazine he always kept hidden there. Tilting the Glock in his hand, he rammed the clip home, heard the click—felt the satisfaction—as he chambered a round. After giving the weapon one last check, he shoved it, muzzle down, against the small of his back.

All right. Almost there.

Pulling a drawer open, he palmed twin five-inch blades. Sheathed in black leather, he strapped one to each forearm, handles facing toward his palms. Their cousin—a seven-inch KA-BAR—got slipped inside the neck of his steel-toed boot.

Now he was good to go.

Kicking the oven closed, he glanced out Sarah-Jane's side windows. Nothing moved except the ocean, the soft laps against boat hulls the only sound in the shipyard. But with dawn an hour off, it wouldn't be long before workers clocked in and ruined the serenity. Not good on any level. He needed a place to bring Ange if—no, not *if...when*—he found her, and the traffic from boat to boat might prove a problem.

So...

That left plan B. The cabin on his small, but private, island.

And wasn't that a kicker?

He never took anyone there. Ange didn't even know about it, but today was a new day. A shitload had changed in the last few hours, so what did it matter that his secret hideout was about to become not so secret anymore? He couldn't take her home. Not if he was right about the thing that had taken her.

Jesus. Dragons. Who would've guessed and…why wasn't he more surprised? The question was an excellent one. And the fact he couldn't answer it should've freaked him out. Instead, all he found was acceptance…and a crapload of subtext and mental flashbacks.

He'd been dreaming about dragons lately. A lot. And one in particular. A blue-gray dragon with webbed claws, smooth scales, and sharp fangs. One who loved the ocean and swimming as much as he did.

Weird. But maybe it explained why seeing one hadn't come as such a shock. His brain had already downloaded the file. Now he was just sifting through the rubble, looking for clues, acting on his ability to perceive things other people couldn't, all while operating on an instinctive level that wasn't ruled by intellect. Or logic, apparently.

With a sigh, Mac shook his head and, moving slowly to avoid the toss-n-tumble in his gut, made for the stairs. He needed to get out of the shipyard before the sun rose. His captain would send a patrol unit looking for him. Probably try to haul his ass back to the hospital, but as he cleared the stairway and came up on deck, he got hit with a wave of…

Mac blinked to clear his vision. All he got was static buzzing in his ears, the sound hissing like a radio with its wires crossed. Sweat trickled between his shoulder blades, then ran down his spine as another wave slammed into him. He backed up a step. Then another. God, something wasn't right. The clawing sickness was shifting, becoming more…something else entirely.

White light flashed behind his eyes. Pain hit him like a body shot, cracking him wide open, twisting until his vision went dark. A scream lodged in his throat, his muscles twisted, knotting up so hard he felt one snap. With a "fuck me," he stumbled sideways toward the side of the boat. Just as his hand connected with the handrail, agony took him over. He hit the water with a splash and, as cold, salty liquid filled his mouth and nose, he pictured his partner.

Angela.

His baby sister was in trouble, and there was nothing he could do to help her. He was already drowning, the pain tearing him apart.

The steel bars barely made a sound as Angela slid them closed behind her. Crouching low, she listened, straining to hear beyond her hammering heartbeat, and twisted her hands to get a better grip on the box cutter. A shiver rolled through her as the flex-cuffs bit into her wrists. She wanted to cut through the plastic and free her hands, but time wasn't on her side. If she took the minute she needed, she might get caught. So as much as it killed her, she would wait. When she was safe in the elevator, she'd slice through the cuffs. For now, she needed to swallow the fear and keep a hold of her impromptu weapon.

But, man, the metal handle wasn't cooperating.

Slick with Lothair's blood, it kept sliding between her palms, defying her will to control it. Angela tightened her grip on the cutter and scanned the hallway stretched out in front of her. Empty. Nothing but peeling paint and uneven floors. Her luck was holding. For how much longer? She didn't know.

"No sense sticking around to find out," she murmured to herself.

As crazy as it seemed, talking to herself helped. Hearing each word kept her straight and moving, instead of scared and paralyzed. 'Cause, yeah, inaction wasn't an option. Later, when she found a way out of the madhouse, she would rant, rave…cry, scream…whatever. But she couldn't give in to the pressure threatening to geyser inside her. Not right now. Not when she still had a chance.

Glancing over her shoulder, she stared through the bars and listened hard. Nothing. No shout of alarm. No moans of pain. No sound at all.

Pushing to her feet, Angela sprinted down the corridor, each of her footfalls light. Fluorescents flashed overhead, the long tubes buzzing, pointing the way to the elevator. Breathing hard, she paused at the mouth of the corridor. Bingo. One Otis, dead ahead, waiting with tarnished steel doors to take her to freedom.

Her heart thumped a little harder as she closed the distance, reached forward and—

Oh, God…no. The miserable sons of bitches.

There wasn't a button. Just a blank cement wall. Nothing she could push to bring the elevator down to her level.

"Shit," she said, mind whirling as she tried to think. Where to go? What to do? How much time did she have left before Lothair came to and found her gone? "Double shit."

Panic clogged her throat for a second. The cop in her shoved it aside. She didn't have time for BS. There must be another way out…a rear entrance or something. No way the Razorbacks would build a bunker without a backup plan. The bastards weren't that stupid.

Pivoting on her bare feet, she looked left, then right. The corridor stretched in both directions. Yeah, the Otis might be the center of the underground complex, but something else lay deep in the maze. So now, the million-dollar question…which way should she go?

Instinct told her to head right.

Angela listened without hesitation. Intuition was a tool, one that always needed to be heeded. Her partner had taught her that and—as much as it sometimes annoyed her—Mac was rarely, if ever, wrong.

Sending another silent prayer his way, she ran hard, searching for a door, another elevator, anything that might lead her out of the underground warren. Another intersection. Another decision. She kept to the right and—

"Thank God."

Her chest so tight she could hardly breathe, she stared at her salvation. Doors. At least a dozen of them marching down the double-wide corridor. Six to a side, the same color as the walls, each blended into its surroundings, as though the Razorbacks hoped to hide them with a coat of paint.

Grasping the cutter with her teeth, Angela freed up her hands and checked the first one.

Locked.

Crap.

By the fifth, desperation took hold. Tears in her eyes, she moved onto the next. The knob chilled her palms as she grabbed hold. Praying hard, she twisted and…

The lock disengaged with a snick.

Her heart went loose inside her chest as she cracked the door and peeked inside. A solitary light flickered, casting eerie shadows across pale walls. She scanned the room. An old table with mismatched chairs. A bank of cabinets with a sink and stove. A fridge. But other than that? Not a soul in sight. Thank you, God. With one last look in either direction, she checked to make sure the corridor was still empty, then slipped inside the small kitchen.

Working fast, she grabbed the box cutter and attacked the flex-cuffs binding her wrists. She nicked herself once, twice, a third time while she looked around. Her gaze locked onto the ventilation shaft. Up near the ceiling, it sat just above the top of the fridge.

And wasn't that a blessing? Escape route complete with a makeshift ladder and launching platform.

All right, so climbing up a steel tube wasn't her first choice. But beggars couldn't be choosers. She wanted out and a cramped ventilation shaft was better than nothing.

Grabbing the tea towel hanging on the stove, Angela wrapped it around her cut wrist. She didn't want to leave any trace behind—not a single clue—for the bastards to find. If they saw any of her blood, they'd know exactly where she'd gone. And how to find her.

After hiding the mangled flex-cuff under the sink with the cleaning supplies, she hopped onto the counter, then climbed on top of the fridge. On her knees, one eye on the door, both ears wide open, she attacked the vent screws with the tip of the box cutter. Around and around. One screw then the next. The last bolt dropped into her hand, and her bottom lip trembled. Her hands took up the cause, shaking so hard she struggled to get the grille off the wall.

"Steady," she whispered.

Taking a deep breath, she tried again. Jackpot. The vent cap came away in her grip.

Not wasting a second, she turned her back to the wall, lifted her legs into the hole, and walked backward on her palms. When her elbow connected with the lip of the shaft, she reached out and grabbed the metal grille from its perch on top of the fridge. Flat on her stomach, she backed all the way in, set the vent cap back in place, and put herself in reverse.

Her eyes burned with unshed tears. She'd done it. Had made it inside. Now she needed to find her way out. Must locate a vertical shaft and climb to freedom before Lothair and the Razorbacks came looking for her.

Chapter Five

Bastian's chokehold was more effective than a WWE wrestler's. A lethal combination of hard male hands and amped-up aggression. Rikar struggled anyway, muscles straining as he got dragged away from his target.

With a snarl, he stayed locked on, face forward, all his attention on the Razorback. The bright blue of his gaze lit the rogue up, painting a bull's-eye on the back of his skull. Not that the fucker noticed. Nah, not Forge. The bastard was too busy rolling to his feet, trying to get his balance on the slippery floor.

Thank Christ for small favors.

No way he wanted to make it easy for the male. Bastian was doing a great job of that already: getting in his way, pulling him off, denying him the satisfaction of eviscerating the rogue.

All he needed was one more go-around. Just one more.

Another fist to the head. A couple more shots to the kidneys, and Forge would buckle. And if the male didn't, all the better. Rikar craved a fight. Wanted the knuckle-grinding, body-bruising brawl that would make him hurt on the outside as much as he did on the inside.

Maybe if the pain was bad enough, he'd forget. Would be able to close his eyes and not picture Angela's face.

With another roar, Rikar rotated into a body-torquing twist.

"Rikar—"

"Get out of my way!"

"Listen, brother…just listen to me."

No time for that.

He didn't want to hear a thing his commander had to say. Not now. Not ten minutes from now. But man, the male was strong…and clingy as hell, like an octopus wrapped around its prey. Switching up his strategy, Rikar unleashed his magic and lost his muscle shirt. As the cotton disappeared, B cursed, hands sliding on Rikar's icy skin, struggling to hang on. Fucking A. He was almost free. His best friend wouldn't be able to hold on much longer and—

Bastian lost his grip.

Baring his teeth, Rikar lunged forward, boots getting traction on concrete, his gaze locked on the bastard across the cell.

"Rikar…don't!" B's voice came from far away, through a tunnel filled with blind rage and pinpoint focus. He understood the command, but couldn't stop, not until the rogue lay broken, nothing but a bloody mess on the floor. "Jesus fucking Christ."

Rikar ignored the warning. Big mistake. B wasn't a lightweight in a fight or anywhere else. He was commander of their pack for a reason. A growl rolled in behind him. The scramble came next: the scrape of heavy footfalls, the rush of oncoming air.

Rikar didn't slow. He had one shot. One chance to wrap his hands around the rogue's throat and—

He grunted as Bastian tackled him from behind. Strong arms cranked down hard, wrapped him up tight, body slamming him off balance. His feet left the floor.

Oh, shit. He was airborne and headed for a hard landing.

Twisting midfall, protecting his head, he collided with the floor shoulder-first. Pain knocked the air from his lungs as Bastian landed on top. Without mercy, his best friend sat on him, knees digging into his ribs, hands pressing him down as they slid toward the opposite wall. Rearing, Rikar let his elbow fly. A sick crack echoed as he connected, nailing Bastian in the side of the head. B hammered him back, making his cheek throb and his conscience sting.

Good Christ. What the hell was he doing…hitting his best friend?

The question made him hesitate. The split second was all his commander needed. Shifting right, B flipped him onto his stomach, pulling a quick grab-and-wind on his arm.

"Get off me!" Pinned with his elbow folded back almost ninety degrees, Rikar bucked the hold. "Get the fuck—"

"I'm sorry…I'm sorry, my brother, but I need him." His chest pumping, each exhale coming on short bursts of frosty air, Bastian said, "Rikar, man, I *need* him."

Like a bomb detonating inside his head, the plea in B's tone shredded him. Fuck. It wasn't fair. None of it. Not the fact Forge would get a free pass for Angela's abduction. Nor that his friend was right.

His commander's female would die if Forge didn't explain Dragonkind's ability to energy-fuse with a female. The rare bond B shared with Myst was sacred, so rare all knowledge of it had been lost over time. And like it or not, the SOB hailed from the Scottish pack—the only one who knew how the energy exchange worked…how it saw a female safely through pregnancy and birthing one of their kind.

Rikar's throat clogged, tightening with tears he refused to shed.

He couldn't stand it. Ivar. Lothair. It didn't matter. Neither would show Angela any mercy and, as he planted his free hand, trying to dislodge Bastian, desperation went nuclear. The detonation stripped him bare, laid him low… made his chest ache and his heart hurt.

Closing his eyes, Rikar stopped fighting. His bruised cheekbone throbbed as it touched down on the cold floor, and he rasped, "He's hurting her, B. He's hurting her and I can't…Christ help me…but I can't…"

"Jesus…I'm sorry." His voice rough with regret, Bastian eased his grip, then released him. Hitting his haunches beside him, Rikar accepted the warm, heavy weight of his best friend's hand as it landed on his shoulder. The touch didn't help or bring comfort. He was off the reservation, out in dangerous territory…the hell of the situation too much to bear. "Rikar…you're the best tracker we have. You'll find her. We'll get her back, I promise, but—"

Movement flashed, light glinting off the steel walls of the prison cell.

"I wouldn't advise it, Forge." B's hand stilled on the back of Rikar's head. A heartbeat passed before his best friend glanced up, nailing the rogue with a glare. "Stay put. Or I'll blow the collar and your head off."

The threat stopped Forge cold. Upper lip curled off his teeth, he paced away, putting the width of the room between them.

"Ven?" Soft and low, Bastian's tone said it all. He wanted backup, was through with the bullshit.

"Here." Like a giant watchdog, Venom moved into view, ready to help: to hurt, to give whatever B needed.

Wrung out, still belly-down on the floor, Rikar huffed, grateful for his buddy. Despite their commander's wishes, Venom had stepped off and stayed out of the way, giving him a shot at the Razorback. Now, the male would catch hell…be on B's shit list for a while. And man, how upstanding was that? Very. Big in a way Rikar appreciated. So, yeah. Venom would be getting his fair share of "you're the best, buddy" from here on out.

With a gentle squeeze, Bastian let him go and pushed to his feet. "Get our boy out of here, Ven."

The command made Rikar cringe. Terrific. He'd just had his wings clipped.

Not that he blamed Bastian. His behavior didn't warrant inclusion, and his commander had every right to be pissed off. As executive officer of the Nightfuries, B expected more from him. Control was valued by their pack; the lack of which couldn't be overlooked. He'd crossed the line. Defied a direct order with deliberate intent when he attacked Forge, but…hell. He'd hoped for more on the back end: information mixed with a mitt full of satisfaction.

Now he had less than nothing.

Rikar shook his head. Stupid. He was an idiot, plain and simple. One that deserved exactly what B was giving him… exile from the interrogation center.

Pushing himself upright, he settled into a crouch and tossed a Hail Mary pass in a losing game. No way Bastian would change his mind, but he tried anyway. "I'm good, B… in control. Just give me another—"

"I dinnae know where they took her." The thick brogue rolled, Forge's quiet tone moving like a steamroller through the room.

Rikar wasn't immune. The admission flattened him, along with his fellow warriors. The proof? Bastian stood unmoving, his gaze locked on Forge, astonishment on his face. Shitkickers rooted to the floor, Venom didn't look much better. And him? His jaw had come unhinged, hanging open like a freaking Venus flytrap.

And still, they stood there, frozen in time. Silence rising to meet their incredulity.

Twitching under the scrutiny, Forge stared at the floor. "If I knew…I would tell you."

Rikar shook his head, trying to wrap his brain around that one. Christ. What the hell did he mean? Forge was a Razorback. How could he not know where he lived…where Ivar and the others slept every day and flew away from each night?

It defied reason.

Which naturally set off every internal alarm he owned.

As the thing got busy shrieking, his eyes narrowed. A deflection. The rogue was playing them, tossing out tidbits like chum into shark-infested waters. Excellent strategy. Stellar, really. Especially since Rikar's bite had always been bigger than his bark.

Forge kept his head down and his senses sharp, waiting for *Frosty* to come at him from across the room. The pale-eyed male was on edge, ready to attack without provocation or warning. Any other time, he would've been on board with the plan. Relished the challenge. Enjoyed the fight. Given as good as he got.

But not today.

He understood the Nightfury's pain: could see the devastation, felt it as keenly as he did his own. That kind of anguish ate at a male and didn't go away. Ever.

Which was the reason he'd opened his flippin' mouth.

Big mistake. Frosty wouldn't give him any brownie points for honesty. Neither would Bastian. Hope, though—nasty beast that it was—sprang eternal. It whispered in his ear, made him believe volunteering a little information would create goodwill. Get him what he needed while setting the Nightfuries back a step.

Wishful thinking? Probably.

But what other choice did he have? The bastards had his newborn son.

So, what did that make him? A first class fool? A real dumb-dumb imprisoned in, well…shite. He didn't know where they'd brought him. After getting zapped with electricity in the shipyard, he'd been unconscious most of the flight. And joy of joys, he'd woken up here, surrounded by a formidable energy field, strapped into a fancy new necklace. The steel collar was brilliant. Diabolical in a way Forge could appreciate…if it weren't around his own neck.

But then, he hadn't expected any less.

The Nightfuries were a smart bunch, skilled with an extra dash of cunning. Proof positive? The three males staring at him from across the cell with varying degrees of pissed off. Rikar was the most dangerous, though. Too angry to care how much damage he inflicted, the male would tear him apart to obtain the information he wanted.

Forge didn't blame him. It was a sound strategy, and had his female been—

Bloody hell. Caroline.

As her name whispered through his mind for the thousandth time, Forge curled his hands into fists, looking for an internal escape hatch. None appeared. The door to his grief was sealed tight. He couldn't get out. Couldn't get away or forget. The female he'd promised to protect was dead. And it was his fault. His need for acceptance—the naive belief he deserved a new start—had killed her.

The truth sank deep and the hurt expanded, becoming a physical pain in the center of his chest. Breathing around it, he lifted his head and met Rikar's gaze. "If I could spare your female the pain, I would. I dinnae hurt females, warrior. And I've never been a Razorback."

"Bullshit." His front teeth bared on a snarl, Rikar stepped toward him. "You live with them. Break bread with them. Believe what they believe."

"I wulnae lie," Forge said, telling the truth even though it killed him to admit it. He'd flirted with the rogues, trying to decide whether he belonged in their midst...yearning for a place to call home. In the end, he'd turned away, unable to stomach the Razorbacks' endgame. "I've gone a round or two with Ivar, but—"

"Where is he?" The Nightfury commander's quiet tone raised the fine hairs on Forge's nape. Green eyes shimmering in the low light, Bastian stepped forward, putting himself front and center. Bloody hell. Wasn't that something to respect? A male with brass balls and the skills to back them up. "I want to know everything...the fucker's plan...all the details along with a map to their—"

"And I want my bairn." The demand came out low, harsh, the vocal equivalent of opening a can of whup-ass. The truth, though, was far more dangerous. He was riding a fine line. If he walked too much one way, Bastian would blow the collar, and he'd never get to hold his son. "You want tae know more? Bring him tae me...along with your female, Nightfury. I have questions only Myst can answer."

Bastian's eyes went from glimmer to glow in a heartbeat.

"No...fucking...way," Rikar said, answering for his commander, the words far more lethal for their softness.

"You want answers, Frosty? Give me what I want, and we'll all get what we need. You...your female. Bastian... the information he needs tae protect his mate. And me? My bairn." Walking the line, Forge twisted the noose, using every bit of leverage he held. "Not too much tae ask, is it now, Bastian?"

"B?" The biggest male shifted. Ruby-red eyes trained on him, Venom circled in behind his comrades, protecting them while being shielded in return. "How about you let me rearrange his face?"

Silence rose in the wake of the male's offer, and Forge got ready. As he waited, time slowed. He counted off the seconds, each one cranking him tighter.

"Rikar's got first dibs, Ven."

"Outstanding," Rikar growled, shitkickers already in motion.

Forge dropped into a fighting stance.

Bastian stepped in between them and pressed his palm to Rikar's chest. As he held his warrior in check, the glow in his eyes faded, and all of a sudden he was looking far too thoughtful and not nearly pissed off enough. Forge saw the wheels turning. Shite. The bastard was a quick study, far too savvy to be fooled by sleight of hand.

"What's your game, Forge? The takedown in the shipyard…your imprisonment? Way too easy." Giving his warrior's shoulder a squeeze, Bastian put his feet in gear, coming within striking distance, daring him to lash out. "You want to know what I think?"

"Dazzle me," he said, feigning a nonchalance he didn't feel, wanting to hit the Nightfury so badly his knuckles ached.

"You wanted inside our lair." One corner of Bastian's mouth curved up. "All that pain…the loss of your freedom. For what? An infant? One who is being well cared for…one my mate loves and has accepted as her own?"

Forge's heart clenched. *Loves and has accepted.* Fuck him, but that was the best news he'd ever heard. Myst Munroe loved his son, which meant she'd protect him from all comers. Nightfury warriors included.

Relief hit him like a sledgehammer, sent him sideways so fast he hung his head. Bad move. Forge knew it the instant his chin touched his chest. The position left him vulnerable, unable to see his enemy, never mind defend himself. But…God. He couldn't help it, and as he struggled to hold back the tears, he murmured in Dragonese, grateful for the gift of a mother for his wee son.

"Good to know, isn't it, warrior?"

Jesus Christ. Again with the soft tone. The melodic son of a bitch didn't know when to quit.

"Aye, it is." Raising his head, Forge got back with the program, plugging the Nightfuries with a don't-screw-with-me glare. "Doesn't mean I'll tell you anything, though, does it? Not until I see him…hold him in my arms and make sure for myself. So get your—"

Steel clanged against steel. As sound exploded, reverberating against concrete, a male yelled, "Rikar!"

Heads swiveled, including Forge's, as a dark-skinned male skidded to a halt in front of the magical barrier guarding his cell. Doubling over, he planted his hands on his knees, breath sawing in and out of his chest. "Jesus, you guys…I couldn't reach you through mind-speak down here. Not with the energy field in place and…shit, but we got problems."

The Nightfury commander cursed and headed for his warrior. "When don't we, Sloan?"

"Always…but not this kind." Pushing himself upright, Sloan glanced at him for a split second, then refocused on his commander. "You know the male cop?"

"Angela's partner?"

The new addition to the party nodded. "The hospital did a bunch of blood tests. The results just came in. He's gone active."

His brow furrowed, Rikar stared at his comrade. "What the—he's one of us?"

"Yeah…and changing fast," Sloan said. "If he gets anywhere near a female—"

Venom growled. "How much time before sunup?"

Sloan checked his watch. "Forty-nine minutes."

"Twenty minutes to reach him. At least that to find safe shelter for the day." Bastian glanced at his XO. "Doable?"

"It'll be close." Rikar tipped his chin, pale eyes glowing, room temperature dropping as he ran for the exit. "But I'm on it."

Forge didn't doubt it. Frosty had fast and deadly written all over him. Add that to the heft of male muscle hauling ass out of his cell? Shite. The Nightfuries knew what they were about. Good thing, too. No one—himself included—wanted a fledgling Dragonkind male wandering around the streets of Seattle.

Chapter Six

Warm steel brushed the sides of her shoulders as the walls pressed in, narrowing as the ventilation duct headed up another incline. The cramped quarters made Angela's breath come fast and the air feel thin. She couldn't get enough oxygen. Her imagination? The truth? She wasn't sure. All she knew was a raging case of hyperventilating hovered seconds away.

Her lungs contracted, pushing her toward panic. Belly down, Angela hit the pause button on her forward shuffle. Closing her eyes, she forced her rib cage to expand and plastered a sign on her frontal lobe. One that said…

No freaking out allowed.

Later. She kept telling herself that, using the word as a catalyst…as a reward for pushing forward. 'Cause, yeah. Once she made it out of here, was safely home with a gun in her hand and the deadbolts flipped, she'd let herself go, indulge in a full-blown breakdown. But not right now.

Later.

It was hard to keep going, though. To hold it together, ignore the scrapes and bruises, the nausea and fatigue. Ravished by the drug, her blood was delivering the medicine with each pump, pushing it deeper into her muscles until it tingled along her spine. Rat-bastard Razorbacks. Whatever they'd pumped her full of was doing its job and, as exhaustion crept closer, the pain got worse, making her want to slow down, rest for just a moment. No harm, no foul. Right?

Wrong. The second she gave in—laid her cheek down on the warm metal—she was dead with a capital D. No passing go. No collecting two hundred dollars. No way out.

And wasn't that a lovely thought? Uh-huh, a real barrel full of laughs.

But no matter how much she hurt, she needed to keep moving. Anger became her ally in the dark, handing her a lifeline, helping her embrace the idea of payback. Vengeance. Her get-even gene cranked over, giving her strength where her body had none.

Different scenarios rose in her mind as she dragged herself another few feet. Coming back with a grenade launcher. Blowing the underground bunker to kingdom come. Or maybe she could use C4, make sure the boom-boom factor hit record levels. Hmm, definitely C4. Mac was good with the stuff. He'd make sure the fireworks went off better than the Fourth of July.

Yup. No doubt about it.

She'd stepped up her game, moved past dating, and was now married to the idea of premeditated murder. She'd never understood it before, the kind of rage that brought a man to the brink. What sent him over the edge into unrelenting violence. Well, she knew now. Twelve hours ago she would've toed the company line and said "vigilante justice" should never be condoned. Now?

Everything had changed. And not for the better.

She was army-crawling through an endless shit hole, for God's sake, a hot, dark place full of creepy-crawlies and cobwebs. Angela wiped another one from her face, hoping the spider that built it wasn't stuck in her hair. Pausing, she did a quick tousle-and-swipe through her pixie cut. The last thing she needed was a pissed-off spider without a home.

What she wouldn't give for a pair of infrared goggles. Or a flashlight. Hell, a candle. She didn't care what kind of light source came her way just as long as she saw what was coming. Eight-legged freaks included.

Stupid. Her. Them. The situation. All of it was beyond sick.

"Stinking Razorbacks," she murmured, holding onto her voice to keep the panic at bay.

Feeling her way through the dark, Angela elbow-walked up the ventilation duct's incline. Sweat made her skin slick, and she cursed as she slid, losing ground on the metal. Gritting her teeth, she slapped her palms against the vent's side walls. Her nails raked against steel, screeching as she dung in. The eerie sound echoed, raising the fine hair on her nape, but she didn't stop. No way could she give up. If she tumbled back down, she wouldn't have the strength to make it out alive.

Bending her knees, she planted her feet, bracing one against the side wall and the other against the floor of the shaft. Her toes cramped, protesting the pressure. Angela ignored the pain and, with a crablike shuffle, crawled inch by excruciating inch to the top. At its mouth, she felt around, getting her bearings. The shaft ninety-degreed into a T. She grabbed for the corner, felt sharp metal cut into her palm and blood flow, and still she pulled, heaving herself into a wider ventilation corridor.

Jackpot. She'd found the main duct. Decision time. Which way should she go...left or right?

Crouched with her knees pressed to her chest, Angela looked both ways. The darkness was absolute. She couldn't see a—

Holy hell. What was that? It was lighter at one end of the tunnel. Not by much, but enough for her to see the blackness morph into fuzzy gray. Angela stared at it a second, disbelief warring with hope. Yeah, definitely. Light was coming from somewhere down there.

Uncurling her limbs, she slid onto her belly. Pinpoint focus and the push-pull combo of her hands and feet propelled her forward. Reaching the right spot, she glanced up.

A vertical shaft.

With a twist, she played the contortionist. Her muscles squawked, protesting the pull. Angela ignored the sting and, exhaling a shaky breath, looked up the duct, searching for the...

Bingo.

There it was. Proof positive. The darkness faded near the top, becoming lighter by the second. Her heart skipped a beat, then settled into a slamming rhythm, hammering her breastbone. Was this it? Had she found her way out? Would it bring her to ground level and freedom? Avoiding sharp metal corners, Angela examined the trajectory again. Looked good. Seemed solid. So...

Only one thing left to do.

Her hands flat against the side walls, Angela stood, pushing her body through the mouth of the vertical vent shaft. She took a moment, sent a quick prayer heavenward, asking for strength and luck, then started to climb.

Pulling his wings in fast, Rikar set down hard. His talons slid, gouging parallel tracks in the asphalt inside the shipyard. Ignoring friction burns on the pads of his paws, he scanned the area. Not a soul in sight. Perfect. He didn't need any witnesses, human or otherwise. Not if he wanted to get MacCord out in one piece.

Cloaked by magic, invisible to the naked eye, he swept the scene again, waiting for his comrades to land. Industrial. Quiet. Nothing but steel-clad warehouses and chain-link fencing. The shipyard's security screamed "stay out," the setup complete with bright lights, barbed wire, and bad attitude. Well, all right. A whole lot of pissed off he could handle. The sound of ocean waves crashing into the breakwater, sending spray twenty feet in the air as docks bobbed and wood creaked? Rikar rolled his shoulders to loosen the tension. Yeah, not his favorite thing.

Christ, he hoped Sloan's intel was good. The last thing they needed was a wild goose chase. Not with dawn twenty minutes away. But…shit. A boat? The male lived on a fucking *boat*? Rikar grimaced. What kind of dragon did that?

The soft snick of claws sounded behind him.

Glancing over his shoulder, Rikar nodded as Bastian tucked his midnight-blue wings and shifted, moving from dragon to human form. As the leather trench coat settled across B's back, covering him from shoulder to knee, he stomped his foot into one of his shitkickers. The thud-thud echoed, bouncing off boats, skimming the choppy surface of the water as Venom landed on the closest warehouse.

Perched like the angel of death, the big male leaned over the steel edge. Ruby eyes flashing, horned head swiveling left to right, his green scales glinted as he mind-spoke, *"Go to it, boys. I'm the lookout."*

"There aren't any Razorbacks in the area, Ven."

"A pity." Folding his wings against his sides, Venom kept his eyes on the sky. *"Would've been fun to kick some more tail tonight."*

Rikar snorted.

B shook his head, then glanced at him. "So, what are we looking at here?"

"My guess?" Following his commander's lead, Rikar transformed and conjured his clothes. "A water dragon."

"Thought they were a myth."

"I've never met one either, but it makes sense, B." Giving the area another visual sweep, his eyes narrowed on the fourth finger dock. The Chris-Craft didn't fit...was out of place in a shipyard full of tugboats. "If what Sloan dug up is right, the male likes water...was with the SEAL teams for seven years."

"Sloan's never wrong," B said, an unhappy look on his puss. "And there isn't a dragon alive...prechange or not... that *likes* water."

No kidding. Just standing next to the ocean gave Rikar the creeps.

Which, naturally, pissed him off.

Fear wasn't in his bag of tricks. He rarely felt it, but right now...knowing he was not only headed toward it, but about to climb on board a freaking motor yacht? Rikar grimaced. The memory was so not going in his photo album under the "happiest moment" of his life.

Rikar put his feet in gear anyway and jogged toward the Chris-Craft. Had he been into boats, he would've said she was beautiful, all curved lines and sleek body. But he wasn't, so he scowled at the bitch instead, silently cursing the male who'd brought him to the shipyard.

The urge to turn around and walk away thrummed through him. The problem? He couldn't leave the male vulnerable, prey to something he didn't understand. Supposition? Maybe, but Rikar didn't think so. MacCord had been raised outside the safety of a pack, without any knowledge of his Dragonkind sire. But had his father known about him, the male would never have left his son alone in the human world.

It simply wasn't done. Ever.

Add that to the fact Angela cared about him, and yeah, Rikar was on the hook. No way could he leave MacCord to suffer and expect his female to trust him.

Ammunition. He needed ammunition—proof of his worth—when he got Angela back. Something to hold up and say, "See? Look at what an upstanding male I am." If he walked away from the male cop now, she'd shoot him down without giving him a chance. Not something he wanted to think about, never mind experience firsthand.

Reaching dock number four, he ignored the ocean sway and leapt over the gangplank. His feet landed with a thud on the dock. An instant later he slid to a stop alongside the Chris-Craft. "MacCord!"

His voice carried across the water, ricocheting off boat hulls. Nothing came back. No answer from the male, just the groan of ropes and the soft creak of wood.

"I'll look inside." Grabbing the handrail, Bastian vaulted through the unzipped canvas and onto the boat. "You search the tail end."

"Asshole," he said, growling at his friend as he drew the short end of the stick.

He didn't want to go anywhere near the stern. There was no doubt a swim platform back there. One he'd have to step on, get closer to the water in order to—

Rikar sucked in a quick breath. Fucking hell. What did MacCord think he was doing?

More in the water than out, the male clung to his boat: eyes closed, hands gripping teak trim, cheek flat against the swim platform. Terrific. The situation was beyond FUBARed. Trust a water dragon to actually immerse himself in *water*.

Gritting his teeth, Rikar made the leap. He landed on the platform, boot treads slipping on wet wood, a "fuck me" locked in his throat. Off balance, he grabbed for the metal ladder bolted to the boat's stern. His fingertips caught and held, saving him before he took a nosedive into the ocean.

Good thing too. Otherwise, there would've been a skating rink around the Chris-Craft, not choppy, blue water.

A death grip on the ladder, he hit his haunches and cupped the back of MacCord's head. The male flinched, groaning as Rikar connected with his life force. Energy glazed his palm, telling him how much time they had. Christ, the cop was close to the *change*. So close, they needed to move him now. And get him a female fast.

"B!"

Like an apparition, Bastian appeared at the railing. "You got him?"

"Yeah, and we gotta go."

MacCord stirred. The male raised his head, nailing him with shimmering aquamarine eyes. "Fuck…off."

Despite the urgency, Rikar's lips twitched. He couldn't help it. Freaking MacCord…giving him attitude while weak as a newborn. "Give over, big guy. We're here to help."

The cop shook his head, trying to dislodge his hand.

Rikar ignored him and, releasing the ladder, grabbed him under both arms. With a snarl, the cop reared, fighting the grab-and-pull. Water flew, splashing all over the place, throwing the smell of salt in the air, making Rikar want to kill something. MacCord was his first choice. He thought of Angela instead, reminding himself how important the male was to her.

Bastian leapt from the boat onto the pier. Waiting for the handoff, he crouched at the dock edge as Rikar dragged the cop down the swim platform.

"D-don't. Get the f-fuck off." Half in the water, half out, MacCord struggled, legs kicking up spray, shivering so hard his teeth chattered. "The w-water…I n-need it."

"We'll get you more," Rikar murmured, hoping to soothe him. The *change* was never fun. It hurt like hell, and there were no guarantees. Some males didn't live through it even when they knew what was coming. But MacCord didn't have a clue, which made guiding him through it all the more dangerous. "I'll get you want you need, okay? Right now, we need to move."

At the end of the platform, Rikar pulled a heave-ho, transferring the male to Bastian. *"Ven…you're up."*

Claws scraped against steel as Venom took flight. *"Where we headed? Myst's?"*

"Her loft's our best bet. It's closest." With a grunt, B secured his grip and hauled MacCord out of the water.

"Windows?" Venom asked, circling overhead.

"Not secured," Rikar said, watching the horizon start to glow as he jumped dockside. Grabbing the cop's feet, he helped Bastian muscle the male to the gangplank, then onto shore. The sooner Venom pulled the grab-and-go, the better.

Ten—fifteen—minutes tops before the sun made an appearance. No time like the present to get the hell out of Dodge. *"We'll blanket spell the glass to block the UV rays when we get there."*

"Roger that." Wings spread wide, Venom dipped low, came in fast and…

He and Bastian got ready, legs braced, feet planted as they lifted the cop skyward. MacCord groaned, thrashing like a fish on dry land. And what do you know? Venom treated him like one. Front talons extended, he plucked the male out of thin air, the same way an eagle took a salmon from beneath the surface of the water.

Not wasting a second, Rikar shifted and launched himself skyward. Midnight-blue scales flashed as Bastian followed suit, taking to the sky behind him. Flying fast, soaring over skyscrapers and rooftops, Rikar kept one eye on the cop, the other on the horizon. A pinky-orange line formed, heralding the rising sun. Not that MacCord cared. Oh, no. The male was too busy swearing and…yeah. Now he was hammering Venom's talon with his fists.

Not the brightest move. Considering Venom's temper.

"Hey, Ven." Increasing his wing speed, Rikar flew alongside his comrade. *"Wanna play hot potato?"*

"No time…we're almost there," Venom growled, shaking his talon, and the shit out of MacCord. *"Otherwise, I'd toss the blockhead over to you."*

Banking right, Rikar followed his buddy, coming down through wispy clouds and cold air. Myst's building lay dead ahead. A five-story walk-up, the brick glowed pink with the coming dawn, tall, arching windows nothing but black holes in its face.

"Around back," B said, bringing up the rear. *"Fifth-floor balcony."*

Extending his wings to full capacity, Rikar caught air, using the webbing to slow his flight. As he rounded the corner of the building, he mind-spoke to Bastian, *"Sloan got something waiting for us?"*

"He called an escort service."

Venom huffed. *"A hooker?"*

"MacCord needs a female." Waiting for Venom to clear out of the way, Rikar circled left into a holding pattern. *"A professional…one we can pay to service him and mind-scrub after."*

Shifting to human form in midair, Venom dropped to the balcony below. As his combat boots connected with concrete, he ignored the cop's curse, tossed him over his shoulder, and headed toward the patio doors. *"Good plan."*

"I hope so," B said, the grumble in his voice coming through mind-speak loud and clear. *"Myst's not gonna be happy when she finds out I let MacCord use her bed."*

Rikar's snort turned into a laugh—the idea B was afraid of a female hitting his funny bone—as he transformed, boots touching down on the balcony.

Landing beside him, Bastian threw him a perturbed look. "Just wait until you have a female of your own to keep happy. You won't laugh then."

The thought sobered Rikar fast. Despite the teasing, he respected the hell out of Bastian for risking it all: for loving Myst without reservation, for being brave enough to trust that he could save her life when she went into labor with his son. Until recently, none of them had thought it possible.

Females always died birthing Dragonkind, without exception.

At least that's what they'd believed before learning more about energy-fuse. The bond allowed a male to feed his female healing energy. The divine connection was rare—a magical, emotional, physical force of nature—a pairing so powerful it joined a male's life force to his female's. Which was good news, except for one thing. Energy-fuse couldn't be forced. It wasn't enough to love a female, or for her to love a male in return. The link was a mystical one, and acceptance was required from the magic in a dragon male's DNA.

No easy feat. Their dragon halves were notoriously finicky. Like a master lock, the beast required the right key—or rather, the right female—for energy-fuse to take shape and form.

And as he stood staring at his best friend beneath an awakening sky, the truth struck with the force of a hammer. He'd give anything to possess what B had found. Acceptance. A shared life with a female he revered enough to think of always and, well...yeah. Even be a little afraid of on the reaction front.

Hell. He *was* envious. When had that happened? Black and white wasn't so *black-n-white* anymore. Somewhere along the line, he'd shuffled the crayons in his box, coloring his world ho-hum, pansy-ass gray.

And Angela? She was the bright yellow in a pencil case full of shadows, and as he walked toward the loft door—prepared to guide the cop through his change—Rikar knew what his life would be without her.

Cold. Dark. Nothing but gray.

He snorted. Just his luck. Trust a female to screw up a—

"Ah...Rikar?"

"Yeah, buddy?"

"Gonna need some help with Boy Wonder here," Venom said, sounding out of breath. A crack ricocheted as though an elbow had just met the side of someone's skull. With a grunt, Venom rasped, "Jesus, he's already—"

A growl rolled out onto the balcony. Someone shrieked. With a "fuck," Rikar dodged right, shoving B out of the way as a kitchen chair sailed through the open patio door. It smashed into the balcony wall, crumpling against concrete. Another crash was followed by a couple of thuds and the scrape of boots on wooden floorboards.

"Oh, my God!"

The female yelp of alarm put Rikar in gear.

As he sprinted over the threshold, Venom said, "Ah, hell...we have liftoff."

Oh, Christ. Did they ever...in the form of MacCord wrapped around a dark-haired female. Halfway across the loft, the male pinned her to the wall: hands skimming beneath her sweatshirt, mouth against the side of her throat. Score one for the cop. Nothing wrong with his instincts. His dragon DNA was roaring, searching for the energy every female possessed. And wonder of wonders, the pretty brunette was responding, relaxing for MacCord instead of pushing him away.

Rikar exhaled, relief replacing the air in his chest. He couldn't have asked for better. High-energy and willing—a rare combo for a male in transition—the Meridian pulsed in her aura, lighting her up from the inside out, giving MacCord the connection he needed to jump-start the change.

"Fuck." Bastian growled, sounding more disgusted than pissed off. With another curse, he slid the glass door closed behind him and unleashed a spell, blanketing the interior of the loft as the sun crested the horizon. "Myst is going to skin me alive."

Rikar added his magic to B's. The windows went dark, blocking the UV rays. "What for?"

Pivoting, his best friend reached out and pulled a framed photo from the wall beside the door. Eyes bright, two females smiled from behind the glass. The blonde Rikar recognized. B pointed to the brunette in the picture, the one MacCord was now kissing. Ah, make that undressing. "Rikar...meet Tania Solares. My mate's best friend."

Shit on a swizzle stick. Had he said FUBARed earlier? Well, not even close. They'd officially crossed into goat-fuck territory because when Myst found out they'd used her BFF as MacCord's main course, none of them would get out unscathed.

Chapter Seven

Downed by a scrawny female. How fucking embarrassing.

Lothair rolled his shoulders, his pride stinging more than the gash on his cheek as he imagined his sire's reaction; the laughter as it echoed in the high court of his home. The shame brought him low, slowed his pace in the deserted corridor until he stood unmoving, staring at cinder-block walls, seething inside.

Derr`mo, he wanted to kill the female for that alone. For bringing the memory back. Making him recall cold winter nights in a frozen Great Hall where his brother played the golden boy. His sire's right hand always and forevermore.

Favoritism at its finest. Hurt at its most lethal.

It shouldn't matter. Not now when his father was half a world away, and Lothair was full-grown. A warrior with purpose. Well-respected. Feared for his skills. A valued member of the Razorback pack and his commander's XO. Still, the old wound made him ache in ways he didn't want to think about, much less acknowledge.

Good thing family was easily discarded and simple to replace.

Ivar was his family now. His brother in every way that mattered. Thank God. Any more time spent in Russia with those bastards, and he would've gone postal, wiping out an entire branch of the Archguard. Not a good idea, considering where Ivar's funding came from and his boss's political aspirations.

So, sure. He'd toe the line and bury the past. For now.

And job number one? The breeding center and finding Angela Keen. Stupid she-cop and her box cutter.

He couldn't wait to get his hands on her. To give her what she deserved…a slow, agonizing death. Except he couldn't put her six feet under. The female was high-energy, too valuable an asset to their breeding program. To Ivar's clinical study, the chromosomal DNA mapping, and drug testing. Lothair didn't understand the complexities of the science, but man, the endgame was sweet. All the high-energy humans he could stand…a fuck-fest for him and his fellow warriors in a quest to breed the first Dragonkind female.

But first? He needed to find and cage them. Not an easy proposition. High-energy females were rare, and Ivar wanted six guinea pigs to start. Which meant none could be wasted. So, yeah. Angela-of-the-box-cutter would stay alive. Didn't mean he couldn't beat the snot out of her, though. Drain her energy to the point of death. Make her suffer so badly she begged him to end her life.

And hmm, coming from the she-cop? Begging would be good. Very, very good.

Upping his pace, his footfalls echoed, bouncing off stained cement and bare lightbulbs, each boot thud quiet, familiar, nothing but ordinary. Now if only his body would get with the program. But the blood just kept coming. Rolling from the gash on the side of his face. Soaking through his waistband, running warm and wet from the wound on his rib cage. He wiped more from beneath his broken nose and silently cursed the pain.

Punching through a set of double doors, he crossed the medical suite, heading for the supply cabinet and the mirror above it. Tarnished by time, age spots ate at the polish, spoiling the reflective quality, impeding his view as he stopped at the counter and tilted his head. Jesus Christ. He'd been sliced wide open. Blood dripped down his jaw, then let go, free-falling into a dingy sink basin well past its expiration date.

Drip-drip…splat. Drip-drip…splat.

The bitch had nailed him so good his dragon half was struggling to keep up. The steady pump of his heart pushing plasma out faster than his rapid-fire DNA could repair the damage. The drip-fest made his mouth curve up at the corners. The female was skilled, possessed a whole lot of kick-ass he hadn't expected.

Well…bully for her. Score one for the she-cop. *Prisoner Number Three* was now on the scoreboard. Too bad she was playing a game no female could win. Even at her best, she was no match for him. Add that to the fact he never made the same mistake twice, and the she-cop was plumb out of luck.

He flipped open an upper cabinet, looking for butterfly bandages. Grabbing the box, he dumped the entire load on the chipped countertop, then cracked open a bottle of hydrogen peroxide and picked up some gauze. As he cleaned the wound, the sound of heavy footfalls echoed, coming closer to the medical suite by the second.

Lothair snorted. *Suite.* Right. The name didn't come close to describing the place. The old clinic was just that…

old. An ancient relic too long in use: yellowed, full of aging equipment, peeling paint, and worn concrete floors. Nothing like the space in their new lair.

Still under construction, the state-of-the-art facility was modern, efficient, and best of all, comfortable. It had everything the warriors under his command needed: bedroom suites, a myriad of living spaces, the computer center, a kitted-out laboratory for Ivar and his science experiments... and the cherry on top of the Razorbacks' sundae—the new, but as-yet unfinished, cellblock A.

Which explained why he was here, didn't it? In a run-down rats' nest. In the middle of nowhere instead of home, kicking back with a glass of vodka in his hand.

Stupid humans. Slow-ass, inefficient insects. Ivar's worker bees had screwed up. Dug in the wrong direction, delaying construction by weeks if not months. Now he was stuck guarding female prisoners in the old cellblock until he could transfer them to the new. Not a big deal under normal circumstances, but Angcla—super cop, Wonder fricking Woman—wasn't *normal.* The fact he needed stitches, and shc wasn't in her cage, was all the proof he required.

The nasty little viper.

A skidding sound rose from the corridor outside the clinic. An instant later Denzeil pushed into the examination room. The twin doors flapped closed behind him. With a quick inhale, the male stopped short, his focus on the side of his face. "*Schizer...*are you all right?"

"Never better." Done with the gauze, Lothair looked away from his warrior, returning his attention to the mirror. Picking up a small Band-Aid, he started at the top of his cheekbone, closing the slice one butterfly at a time.

Denzeil's reflection appeared over his shoulder. His brows cinched tight, D watched him apply the white strips for a second and then reached out. Lothair tensed as his comrade grabbed his T-shirt and yanked it up to examine the cut along his rib cage. "Man, she really did a number on you. Need some help?"

"*Nyet,* I'm good," he murmured, ignoring the mother-hen routine along with the warrior's interest. He wasn't into males, unless a female was involved. A threesome with Ivar was one thing. Like him, the boss only swung one way, which made taking turns with a female all about her. Not about either of them. With Denzeil, though, sex wasn't so cut and dried. "What did you find, D?"

Taking the hands-off cue to heart, Denzeil dropped his shirttail and took a step back. With a sigh, he crossed his arms and leaned back against the examination table. "Nothing. There's no sign of her. It's like she poofed her way out of the lair. The others are still searching, but—"

"Call 'em off." Yup…wicked skilled. Lothair's lips twitched. The redhead impressed the hell out of him. "She's already aboveground."

"Not good," his warrior said, a growl rolling in his thick accent. "The boss isn't gonna be happy."

Probably not. But the situation would be rectified, cleaned up before Ivar ever got wind of it. No cause for alarm. No need to give the boss man a heads-up, either. At least not right now. Injured fighting the Nightfuries at the Port of Seattle, Ivar didn't need any more bad news. Especially on the female front. They'd already lost one high-energy female to Bastian and his band of bastards tonight. No sense stirring the pot or the Razorback leader's temper. The she-cop wouldn't be on the loose for long.

"Keep your yap shut, D. I'll tell Ivar myself." His hands paused in midair, he met Denzeil's gaze in the mirror, a warning in his own. "We clear?"

Denzeil glanced away, breaking eye contact, ass-shuffling on the cracked vinyl tabletop. "No problem, boss. Your call."

"*Da*, it is," he said, enjoying the male's reaction. Fear—the ability to instill it in a full-blooded warrior—was better than any drug on the market. "I'll retrieve her at sunset."

Surprise flared in Denzeil's dark eyes. "You've already—"

"Fed from her?"

Hmm…had he ever.

She'd tasted good, the white-hot energy she drew from the Meridian so delicious it made his heart pound. Better still? Her defiance. She'd fought like a wildcat, struggling as he forced the energy connection: drew her deep into his veins, took without mercy, wounding her soul-deep, leaving bruises on her soft skin.

Lothair's mouth curved as he relived the feel of her. Hot, tight, and oh-so-unwilling.

He could almost love her for battling so hard. Almost, but not quite. Revenge was more his style and, unlike the two females already locked in their cages, the she-cop deserved his retribution in spades.

Too bad he was grounded by sunlight, shut down by ultraviolet rays and his light-sensitive eyes. Not that it mattered. He was a patient male. Half a day. Just twelve hours before he went after her, became hunter to her prey. He could hardly wait for sunset. The moment he took flight over the forest, she wouldn't stand a chance. He was linked in now, connected to her in a way no other male could match. Like a beacon in the dark, her energy called to him, leaving a trail he could track.

A growl rose in his throat as Lothair applied the last butterfly, absorbing the pain, letting it sink deep to fuel his rage. The slice to his face hurt like hell, but not half as much as Angela would when he got a hold of her.

Mac was surrounded by endless waves of dark hair. The thick strands filled his hands, curled around his forearms, cocooning him while he nestled in, nuzzled deep, needing more.

So good. She was so damned good. Nothing but soft, willing curves and white-hot desire.

With a groan, he licked her pulse point, feeling the buzz along his spine as he pressed deeper between her thighs. She sighed—the sound half hum, half plea—and shifted beneath him, rocking her hips into his. More. She wanted more, and Mac wanted to give it to her. Except…

He knew he should let her go, that she couldn't be real. Nothing in reality came close to how amazing she felt in his arms. And any second now he'd wake up. Drunk. Alone. With only the memory of her face and a hard-on to keep him company.

But goddamn, everything about her felt *real*: her heartbeat, the small hands in his hair, the taste of her on his tongue, her scent on him, his on her, and yeah, the relief. Her touch banished the pain, made the world fade and him float until all Mac knew was her. Then again, that was the point. A delusion wasn't a *delusion* unless you believed it.

Breathed it. Made it your own. All the better to fuck you with, my pretty...cue the witchy laugh.

Mother of God, he was losing it. Making up a fake woman. Imaging hot, sweaty sex with a beautiful stranger. Except she wasn't a stranger. Not really. He'd dreamed of her for days, ever since he'd seen her at the SPD precinct.

Tania. Her name was Tania, and oh man, he didn't want to wake up. Or let his fantasy lover go. She belonged to him in the dreamscape like sugar belonged in cookies. Inseparable. Undisputed.

His.

Mac growled, the need to get closer and something more prickled beneath his skin. The sensation drew him tight, and muscles coiled, preparing for...what exactly? He frowned, revolving around the mystery, trying to unravel it, but his thoughts tangled, leaving his mind blank and his heart empty. Something was coming. He could feel it rumbling toward him, gaining speed by the second and—

A heavy hand curled around the nape of his neck.

Mac twitched. That wasn't right. He never invited other guys into his dreams. And imaginary dream woman or not, he didn't want the bozo anywhere near Tania. With a quick twist, he shielded her with his body and tried to shrug out of the touch.

"Easy, big guy," a deep voice said, tone soothing. "B...we good to go?"

"Furniture's cleared." Footfalls came from far away, the soft thuds throwing red flags inside Mac's head as a second voice joined the first. "Is he ready?"

"Any second now. She fed him well. His energy levels are good...stable."

"Calm before the storm."

Jesus Christ. A third guy? This was the strangest dream he'd ever had, but weirder than that? He heard the sheets rustle, felt the mattress dip as someone climbed on beside him.

The third guy murmured, "I'll grab him. Get the female out of here."

Aggression rolled through him, pumping him full of "oh, no, you don't." If one of them tried to touch Tania, he'd rip him a new asshole. Imaginary or not, she was his, and right now? Way too vulnerable, so relaxed Mac knew she was fast asleep.

The mattress shifted. A second set of hands touched his shoulder. Mac let loose.

Punching his fists into the sheets on either side of Tania, he thrust up, back and…oh, yeah. Instant liftoff. The 180-degree spin put him on the balls of his feet, face-to-face with Dickhead at the end of the bed. Surprise flared in shimmering red eyes an instant before Mac hammered him with a right cross. The guy's head snapped back, throwing the idiot off balance and over the side of the mattress. As he hit the floor, the other two cursed.

Keeping himself between Tania and them, Mac swiveled, fists raised, teeth bared, desperate to do damage. To ignore the onslaught of returning pain and keep her safe… away from the bastards tag-teaming him. He set his stance and—

Motherfuck, too late.

Brutal and quick, the frosty-eyed SOB moved in, nailing him with a quick jab. As his head cranked sideways, hard hands dragged him off the bed and into a full nelson chokehold.

"You touch her and I'll kill you." Muscles straining, pain gnawed on his bones as he reared, fighting the lockdown. "I'll rip your fucking—"

"Settle down, MacCord." Breathing hard, the bastard hauled him into the center of the open-plan loft. Upended furniture lined the walls beneath blacked-out windows. Alive with movement, the glass seethed, rolling from frame to steel frame. As his "holy shit" meter went red zone, the guy forced him to his knees. "No one's gonna touch the female. We just want her safe and out of the way."

The assurance struck a chord, and he stilled, relief warring with a boatload of "really?" But something in Full Nelson's voice—the undercurrent in his tone, the absolute confidence—told him not to worry. They weren't interested in Tania. Crazy conclusion? Maybe, but Mac didn't think so. His spidey senses were on overload, tingling, picking up a strange vibe. One that said *trust this guy.*

"Mac," he rasped, testing the waters, giving a little to see what came back at him.

"What?"

"It's Mac. No one ever calls me *MacCord.*"

"More with the attitude." Full Nelson huffed, the laughter underneath the exasperation unmistakable. He eased his grip without letting go, giving Mac enough slack to lift his head. "You know what, Ven? Give me some time, and I might actually like the big dummy."

"Not me." Dickhead—Ven…whatever—wiped the blood from his mouth and rolled to his feet. "The blockhead rattled my cage."

"You deserved it," Mac said, grinding out each word as agony closed the gap, gluing his knees to the floor. His gag reflex kicked in. He fought the dry heaves, breathing with lungs that felt like they'd been poured full of cement. "Goddamn…what's wrong with me?"

"The change." Full Nelson released him. As his hands slid away, he moved around front and crouched, nailing Mac with pale peepers. "You go head-to-head with a dragon lately, Mac?"

He nodded.

"Not sure why the magic in your blood was dormant…" The guy paused, a furrow between his brows as he shook his head. "Call it a sleeping giant…but whatever the reason, contact with the Razorback triggered you. Now your dragon DNA is kicking in."

What the fuck? *Razorback? Dragon DNA?* Was the guy insane? Except…

He couldn't get the black-scaled bastard out of his head. The SOB had blown him through the two-way in IR One with his freaky exhale, and he'd been sick ever since.

Mac frowned so hard the center of his forehead stung. "Who…"

Losing the battle with his stomach, he squeezed his eyes shut, slammed his palms on the wood floor, and dry heaved.

"I'm Rikar, and you're Dragonkind…just like me. Like us."

On all fours now, he shook his head. "No…way."

"Look at your hands, big guy," Rikar murmured. "And then tell me no."

Fighting his stomach and a bad, bad feeling, he opened his eyes as Rikar gave him a gentle push, throwing him off balance. As his spine touched down on the cold floor, Mac raised his hands, a scream locked in the back of his throat.

Scales.

Interlocking blue-gray scales.

Like a disease, the nightmarish weave spread over the backs of his hands, up his arms, wrapped over his shoulders, heading straight for his heart. Cold and deadly, the sensation slid deep, chaining him to the floor. Immobilized by invisible bonds stronger than steel, his roar of horror turned to screams of agony as his bones snapped: hands morphing into paws, fingers into claws.

Exhaustion gnawing on him like a bone, Rikar sat down on the floor beside the kitchen island. Leaning back, he propped himself against the cabinetry, brushing shoulders with Bastian, and stretched his legs out in front of him. As his muscles unlocked, his bones cracked, protesting the long hours, hard work, and cramped conditions.

"Jesus," B murmured, rolling his chin against his chest.

"Yeah." Not much more Rikar could say. Getting hit by a Freightliner carrying a heavy load at full speed would've been easier than the last few hours.

The quiet, though, was nice. No more cursing. Or screams of pain. Just silence, and a whole lot of relief.

Done with a shoulder roll, Rikar refocused on the cause of his condition. He blew out a long breath. Man, the male was big and...yeah. Unlike any dragon he'd ever seen.

Sleeping like the dead, Mac lay curled like a cat in the center of the large loft: his face tucked behind one wing, his tail wrapped around the whole. Blue-gray scales glimmered in the low light, the interlocking dragon skin polished to an almost shine, protecting the male like armor, the mean-and-hard outer shell a characteristic shared by all of Dragonkind. But the weird thing? His scales were almost perfectly smooth, lacking the ridges and valleys of most males. Rikar frowned, his gaze wandering along Mac's sleek hide and muscled flank. Maybe all that smoothness helped him swim, made him more water-dynamic or—

"Jeez, Rikar," Venom said, footfalls quiet as he paced another circle around Mac. Ruby gaze roaming, he studied the male, examining him like a scientist would a new species. Which, come to think of it, wasn't far from the truth. "Blockhead's got some serious blade. And get a load of all that ink."

Bending one leg, Rikar propped his forearm on his knee, attention straying to Mac's tail. "Blade" didn't begin to describe it. Lethal was a better word, considering the nine-inch paper-thin ridge that started behind the horns on his head. Sharp as a razor blade, the narrow, steel-gray strip gleamed like a knife edge, running between his shoulders and along his spine before spreading to both the top and underside of his tail. And the tip? Dagger quality. Rikar shook his head. Nope…not the usual spikes for Mac. Christ, he could cut another male in half with that thing. A single sideswipe and…

Wham. Game over. Add that to the webbed paws, sleek skin, and Mac had water dragon written all over him. The magical tattoo, though—the Celtic-esque swirl of dark blue lines covering one half of Mac's torso—baffled him. He'd never seen a male with ink like that before.

Chasing an itch, Rikar rubbed his back against the raised edge of a cabinet door. "Stop calling him a blockhead, Ven."

"Feeling a little possessive there, buddy?" Meeting his gaze over the top of Mac's shoulder, Venom raised a brow.

Rikar glared at the male, his message clear. *Back off.* So he was feeling protective? Big deal. Getting Mac through the change hadn't been easy, and he'd been the primary: connecting to Mac through mind-speak, guiding him through seven hours of hell, through the energy shift and the physical change that came with it. Just like a sire would for his son. The fact he felt invested in the male's welfare now didn't make him a pansy. It made him normal. Right?

Man, he hoped so. His work with Mac was nowhere near done. As a fledgling, their boy was vulnerable right now and would be for a while…until he learned the basics. How to shift from human to dragon form. How to control his new body and curb the increased strength that accompanied it. How to fly and fight. So, yeah, Mac was headed into some serious training: boot camp, dragon style.

"Hey, that's cool." With a shrug, Venom turned his palms up in the universal gesture of *whatever.* "You got him through the change. You can feel however you frigging want."

"Gee, thanks, buddy," Rikar said, sarcasm dripping from each word.

"Lay off, Venom." With a sigh, Bastian crossed his shit-kickers, leaned his head back, and closed his eyes. "Give our new boy the respect he deserves. He did well…came through strong."

Pride filled Rikar's chest to bursting and…fucking hell. Maybe pansy-ass pathetic applied to him after all. And as Rikar scrambled to plug the crack in his defenses—one Mac had slipped right through—he covered the breach by changing the subject. "We got…what? Four hours to sunset?"

"Give or take," B said. "Get some sleep."

Good plan. After the fight in the Port of Seattle, his search for Angela, and Mac's transition, he was running on empty. All of them were, and sleep deprived was no way to start the new night. Not with a pack of Razorbacks on the loose. Not when he needed pinpoint focus to track, find, and kill the males who'd taken his female. After that? He'd retrieve her. Hopefully in one piece without—

Rikar murdered the thought. He refused to picture scenarios that might never come true. Facts. Strategy. He must deal in what he could control, whom he could pursue, what locations held the most promise. And as he stretched out flat on the floor, Rikar sifted through a list of possibilities. Nightclubs. The university. Outdoor concerts. All-night coffee shops. Art galleries. Anywhere a rogue would go to find a female and feed.

Interrogating the enemy wouldn't get him what he needed…the location of the Razorback lair and by extension, Angela. The idiots were too afraid of Ivar to ever give up the goods. None of them would crack. So where did that leave him?

Nowhere. In butt-fuck country with only one option.

Tracking one of the rogues. A tricky play? Absolutely. The enemy was as aware of him as he was of them. Shadowing a male without being detected wouldn't be easy. Hell, he didn't even know if it was possible, but…

What other choice did he have? If he didn't free her soon, Angela would—

A tingle slid over the nape of Rikar's neck.

Sucking in a breath, he jackknifed off the floor. As his feet touched down, he squeezed his eyes shut and concentrated, struggling to connect. Static buzzed inside his head, washing in and out as he hunted for the signal. Christ, had he imagined it? Was thinking about his female making him feel her when—

His head snapped to the side. There it went again. Whisper soft, the sensation slid down his spine, lighting his senses on fire.

A heavy hand landed on his shoulder, gripping him through his leather jacket. "Whatcha got, Rikar?"

"Angela."

Bastian's palm shifted, cupping the back of his head. "You locked on?"

"Fuck." Rikar flinched as the pinging beacon hammered his temples. "I can feel her…B, she's out from under their shield. I can *feel* her."

"Where?" Venom rolled up on his other side. "Where is she?"

Gritting his teeth, Rikar bowed his head, sifting through mental static. The telepathic flight took him out of Seattle toward the Canadian border. "North of the city. Somewhere in the redwoods." With a full-body shiver, he tracked her elevation, coming up over mountain tops. "Shit…I gotta go. I need to—"

"Sun's up, my brother." His best friend's hand flexed, tightening on his nape. Taking a step back, Rikar tried to shake off the vise grip. He should've known better. A move like that never dissuaded Bastian. Instead, his commander stepped into him, putting them chest-to-chest. "You go now…you get fried."

"The rogues—"

"Are grounded until nightfall…same as us," B said, his reasonable tone pissing Rikar off. "If you can feel her, she's in sunlight where they can't reach her."

His hands flexed into fists, Rikar shook his head. Fuck him. He knew Bastian was right, but…God. He didn't want to wait. Angela was out there, alone, vulnerable, probably half-frozen in cold mountain air. If he didn't leave now, the Razorbacks might reach her first.

He swallowed, trying to stuff his fear for her down deep. It didn't work. The worry kept circling, taking potshots.

"Rikar, man, we're a team," Venom murmured, jumping on B's bandwagon. "We wait for sunset, then go after her."

Applying gentle pressure, Bastian forced him to raise his chin. As Rikar opened his eyes, he got nailed by his best friend's shimmering gaze. "You can't help her if you're dead. We'll get her back, but we do it together."

Together.

The word—the show of loyalty—should've made him feel better. Stronger. More confident about staying put until the sun sank low and night took over. But as he ran his hands over his skull-trim, breaking B's hold, a gaping hole opened inside him. One filled with hope and a raging faith that he'd retrieve Angela unscathed. And as both rose, clogging his throat, tying a knot around his heart, Rikar called himself a fool. Hope was for idiots, and faith for the dying. He clung to them anyway, like a drowning man would a life preserver.

Chapter Eight

The cold nipped, damp autumn air sinking bone-deep as Angela crested another rise. Thick forest behind her, more of the same in front, she suppressed a shiver and paused at the center of the bluff, appreciating its smooth, dome-like top. Big contrast, a welcome one from broken branches she'd stumbled over most of the afternoon. But even better than the smoothness? Sun-warmed granite beneath the soles of her bare feet.

God, that felt good.

Settling into a crouch, she pressed her palms flat against the stone, absorbing more heat, and searched the sky. Way off to the west, the sun sank closer to the horizon. Stupid Razorbacks. Trust them to build a bunker in the middle of nowhere. With nothing but rock and brush for miles around. She should know. Her sore feet told the story. Scratched, bruised, cut in places she didn't want to think about, the tale was a sad one. A woe-is-me-I-need-to-kick-someone's-ass kind, and it wasn't getting any better.

Blowing out a breath, Angela pushed to her feet. She stood weaving a moment, the light breeze making her sway like a bulrush in the wind, exhaustion dangerously close.

Temptation called, urging her to lie down and rest…if only for a second.

She shook her head. No time for that. Nothing to do but keep running. She needed more distance between her and the enemy.

The rat-bastard's name skated through her mind. Angela picked up her feet and the pace, avoiding the bluff's crumbling edges, and scrambled down the slope on the other side. As she rounded a boulder the size of her Jeep, she paused on a ledge. Seven, maybe an eight-foot drop to the ground below. Under normal circumstances the distance wouldn't be a problem. But today she wasn't looking forward to it. Her feet hurt like hell, and the landing wouldn't be fun.

Angela leapt anyway. Her knees rebounded, slamming into her chest, knocking the air from her lungs on impact. With a curse, she lost her footing, went sideways and…

Crap. Another hill. Another spine-grinding fall down an unforgiving slope.

Her heart kicked, hammering her breastbone as loose earth crumbled beneath her heels and she fell backward. She dug her elbows in, protecting her back, desperate to slow her slide down the hillside. Good plan, one that worked like a charm until a raised tree root entered the game, smashing into her tailbone. As she gasped and fought forward momentum, she wished she was a little more mountain goat and a lot less human.

Yeah, hooves and a crapload of sure-footedness would be helpful right about now. 'Cause, man, she was running out of places to bruise.

Too bad there weren't any trails to follow.

She'd given up hope of finding one hours ago. Of stumbling upon helpful hikers. Of catching a ride on a hunter's ATV. The bush was too dense, a thick, inhospitable landscape only the most experienced would brave. And only then with the right equipment—warm clothes, food, water…a rifle. And as she continued down the never-ending descent, skirting tree trunks, tripping over rocks and sticks, she wished herself home for the thousandth time. Maybe if she prayed hard enough God would hear her…have mercy and teleport her inside her condo.

Or the nearest police precinct.

Definitely. The cop shop was a better choice. At least armed, she stood a chance. But here? Surrounded by forest and frosty air? She gave herself a two-in-ten shot at survival. Bad odds, but she had to try. The second she lost faith, she'd quit…find the prettiest redwood, curl up in a ball underneath it, and die. Or get eaten by a mountain lion.

And my, oh, my, what a lovely thought. Right up there with getting recaptured by Lothair, only over much quicker, with a lot less brutality.

Angela ground to a stop at the bottom of the hill. She scanned the terrain, taking cover behind a fallen log. Quivering with fatigue, white puffs of air sawing out of her mouth, she reached out to steady herself. As her hand settled on rotten wood and wet moss, she tilted her head and listened hard. Nothing. No sounds of pursuit, just bursts of birdsong and the creak of tree limbs.

She checked the sun again, using its position in the sky to gauge the time. An hour—maybe two—before the light faded, and she'd be forced to find shelter for the night.

"Keep moving…you're doing all right," she murmured, adding a rah-rah-rah-go-Angela to the mental mix. "Just keep moving."

As the cheerleader inside her head got busy shaking her pom-poms, Angela rubbed her upper arms, wincing with each pass of her battered hands. Not that her fingertips hurt much anymore. Like a gift, numbness had set in, her body throwing out endorphins, easing the scrapes better than a pantry full of ibuprofen. Add that to the adrenaline rush, and…

Bam. She had a little more fuel in her tank. Enough, maybe, to get her to a highway. A rest stop. Somewhere safe.

God, she hoped she was headed the right way. Without a compass, she couldn't be sure, but…yeah, south was the best bet. Civilization lay in that direction. She was almost positive. Wanted to believe it like she wanted her next breath. If she kept running, somewhere along the way she'd see lights through the trees, spot a lone house, run into a small town.

Which meant break time was over.

She needed more distance between her and the Razorback bunker. Lothair was a vindictive son of a bitch. No way would he let her go, not after she'd taken a chunk out of his pride and left him for dead. Too bad she hadn't thought to check. If she'd just taken a couple more seconds…

But no. She hadn't finished the job and slit his throat. And she knew—just *knew*—the lapse in judgment would come back to bite her.

Her hands curled against the rotten log, pushing moss under her fingernails. She couldn't think about it. Not about *him*. Or the fact he'd left her alone all day. It didn't make any sense. Why hadn't he come after her yet? Was he playing some sort of game?

Probably. She knew his type. The bastard enjoyed the thrill of the hunt too much to pass up a challenge. Add that to his sadistic nature and...yup. Mystery solved. He'd let her run, hide, play cat to her mouse while she struggled to stay alive. Wait until she was half-frozen, out of gas, too exhausted to fight. And then? He'd hurt her again. Force her to—

No...no. Don't go there.

Angela shook her head, banished the memory. The past was the past, no matter how recent. She must concentrate on the here and now. On the fact she was strong, well trained, and, for the moment, free. No reason to lie down and die. Nothing in God's playbook said Lothair would win. Or she couldn't make him pay for hurting her.

The thought gave her courage. Got her moving, but as her feet obeyed, carrying her around the fallen log, she glanced over her shoulder. The bogeyman was real. And as the creak of tree limbs shivered through the quiet, Angela searched the shadows: looking for dragons, expecting the snatch-and-grab, her heart nothing but an awful throb inside her chest.

Go. Go. Go.

She broke into a sprint, racing between tree trunks. As she passed the last one, the ground leveled out. Damp with recent rain, wet leaves slipped beneath her soles, kicking up the scent of decaying earth and old sap. But the rotten smell came with benefits...softer ground cover. Easier on the feet than the pine needles she'd crossed over at higher altitude.

Slowing her pace, she snaked between low-lying cedars. She ignored the grabbing pull of wooden fingers, her focus on a break in the forest where the prickly undergrowth thinned. The setting sun hung low, slicing between trees, painting the branches with an orange glow. She squinted and got a clear shot of open terrain. A clearing and—

Water. She could hear the gentle rush and lap. A glacial lake? A river, maybe?

Angela prayed for the latter. A river, after all, went somewhere. And where water traveled, people set up shop, building towns and houses close to the shoreline.

"Please, please," she whispered, running toward the lip of the clearing.

Five feet from her target, she veered right behind a mound of rock. Recon time. No sense blowing her cover. At least, not before she knew what lay beyond the tree line.

She saw the blue Chevy first. Tireless, circa 1950, half buried in the dirt, the rust bucket listed to one side, a twisted axle raised as though it waited to shake her hand. Angela grazed it with her fingertips as she moved past, brushing rust chips from the cold metal, making sure it was real.

Hallucination had never been her style, but she was beyond cold, way past tired. So yeah, checking seemed like a solid plan. Especially with fatigue setting in, blunting her normally sharp senses.

Rubbing her eyes, Angela forced herself to focus and—

"Oh, thank God."

A cabin. Nestled between two ancient pines.

Small with crooked eaves, moss had moved in like it owned the place, growing between chinked logs, rambling over old shingles, making a meal of the wooden porch steps. The signs of neglect were everywhere, and as she scanned the terrain, she picked up other details. The crumbling chimney top. An abandoned, weed-ridden garden. Another old car, built in a long-forgotten decade, sat beside it. The cabin's roof looked solid, though, and the windows? Unbroken.

Within seconds, Angela was halfway across the clearing, her footfalls silent on the compacted dirt of the little-used trail. Reaching the steps, she slowed down. Rotten in places, the treads were slick with recent rain. She tested each board, taking the steps one at a time until she reached the narrow landing. Her breath caught as she reached for the handle: hoping, praying, making all kinds of impossible bargains with God if only…

Metal squawked as the knob turned.

Angela nearly fell over and, after sending a *thank you* heavenward, wedged her shoulder in tight and pushed. It cracked open, wood groaning, hinges squeaking, the door bottom scraping against the cabin floor. One, then two inches grew between the warped frame and the door edge. Not nearly enough for her to slip through. Angela thrust again, bloody feet sliding on slick boards, her strength disappearing as fast as the setting sun.

"Come on. You…" Angela pushed harder. "…stupid…" With a curse, she hammered the door again, putting all her weight behind it. "…thing."

The last shove did the trick, and her feet left wood. She had an instant of "oh, crap" before she hit the floor. Pain arced, stealing her air as the body slam rattled her bones. Facedown in the dust, she wheezed, seeing spots, the threat of unconsciousness nanoseconds away. As her vision dimmed, self-preservation kicked in. She couldn't pass out. Refused to give in, but…

Goddamn. She hurt…everywhere.

As the agony expanded, the urge to close her eyes and stay down came with it. Man, it was persuasive, murmuring in hushed tones, tempting her so softly she wanted to listen. To relax into oblivion and let herself fall. To sleep and forget about the wide-open door, wild animals, and asshole dragon guys. The problem? Her body might be fried, but her brain was still online, working well enough to know succumbing to exhaustion was a bad idea. So, yeah. Much as she yearned to cop out, she needed to get up.

Right now.

Gritting her teeth, Angela pressed her palms to floor. One minute. She just needed sixty seconds to catch her breath, and she could get up, start moving, make her tired body work.

The water wasn't far. She heard it lapping at the shoreline. From the sound alone, Angela guessed the river snaked past the cabin's back side. With a groan, she pushed into a crouch and raised her head, forcing her mind to work. A boat. Maybe whoever owned the place kept a canoe out back. Something sturdy enough to float her down river and into civilization.

Now all she needed was some luck. She was sick of running, tired of looking over her shoulder. People. She needed to find someone to help her. No matter how tough, she wouldn't last much longer. The thought got her moving.

Shivering in the dark, Angela struggled to her feet and searched the shadows. Nada. The place was empty but for a single chair sitting kitty-corner in front of a shallow fireplace. From its shape, she guessed a wingback. From its smell? She knew it had seen better days.

Angela headed for the rear entrance and—

Great. All that effort for nothing.

The back door stood wide open, dirt and leafy debris piled high between the jambs. Angela glared at it while she made a mental note—always check the back door before body slamming the front one open. Good advice. All right, so it came a little late, but as she glanced out the opening, she found it hard not to be grateful. At least she could run straight down to the shoreline. No walking around the cabin. No extra muscle required.

Forcing her stiff legs to work, she half walked, half shuffled to see the river beyond the threshold. The moon peeked through high clouds now, lighting the surface of the water, making it look like a ribbon of black silk.

Angela snorted. *Black silk?* She really must be losing it if she was getting poetic. Completely off her rocker if she—

A tingle swept the nape of her neck. Her head snapped toward the front door. Something wasn't right. The buzzing sensation lit her up, screamed along her spine, telling her to run. To hide. To head straight for the river's edge.

Adrenaline punched through as she crouched low. Listening hard, she stared through the open front door, straining to see in the dark. The thump-thump of heavy wings sounded overhead, and Angela's throat closed. Oh, no. He was here. The bastard was—

"Here, kitty-kitty-kitty." The soft growl slithered through the night air, polluting her with fear. A soft snick came next as claws touched down in the front yard.

Without thought, Angela bolted, launching herself off the back porch. As she touched down, branches snapped, giving away her position. She didn't care and refused to stop. Lothair was right on her heels. She could feel him in the mountain air, rising in the dark. The awful prickle of awareness exploded down her spine, and panic picked her up, instinct urging her to run faster. Zigzagging through the underbrush, each breath a harsh rasp against the back of her throat, Angela kept her eyes on the water.

"Come out, come out, wherever you are."

The terrible voice singsonged in the moonlight, sliced through the quiet, and Angela tried not to cry. Tears fell anyway, leaving twin tracks on her cheeks.

Rikar broke through the cloud cover, coming down like a vengeful God, wisps of fog curling from his wing tips. The blowback washed out behind him, bending trees in half as he skimmed evergreens and redwoods, his night vision so sharp he saw every blade of grass. Up ahead, the forest thinned, then stopped short, running out of ground as rock tumbled off a cliff into the river below.

Banking left, he leveled out, following the river's snaking turns. Another tight turn. More of Angela's energy. His magic responded, rising so fast frost gathered, coated his scales, rattling the spikes along his spine. Locked on, his sonar pinged and information whiplashed, narrowing the target zone.

The riverbank. She was somewhere close to the water's edge.

"Good girl," he mind-spoke to her, trying to touch her mind. Shit. He hoped she understood…was picking up the instructions he threw at her despite the distance separating them. *"Angela…get into the water."*

He sensed her shift, increase speed, the struggle in each pumping stride. Rikar reached deeper to connect, throwing more mind-speak her way. *"Come on, angel. You can make it."*

Thump-thump-thump.

Her heartbeat rushed at him, throbbing through cold mountain air to reach his own. His went jackrabbit inside his chest as he clung to her bio-energy, pushed her harder, knowing what chased her. He might not know "who" exactly, but he felt the fucker. His dragon radar picked up all kinds of trace, giving him an impression of big-dark-and-ugly, but beyond that?

He wasn't getting much. And unlike Bastian, he couldn't dissect a male's strengths and weaknesses from a distance. Too bad. He could've used the skill tonight. Especially since B hadn't made the trip.

What a freaking nightmare. Nothing was going as planned.

FUBAR number one? Mac.

As a fledgling, he couldn't be left alone, and not many were qualified to take care of him. Venom wasn't an option. Not after calling the cop "blockhead" all day. The warrior was as likely to roast their new boy as help him. And Wick? Rikar snorted. No way he could trust the male. Their resident sociopath wasn't fit for babysitting, no matter the circumstances. So, yeah, that put B on the hook, waiting at Myst's loft for Mac to wake up.

"Rikar, man." Venom flipped in midair, rolling in on his left side. *"Lay it out…talk to me."*

"Half a mile out." Rocketing around another bend, Rikar's wing tip skimmed the surface, throwing up spray. Water turned to ice, free-falling with a splash into the river. *"ETA…thirty seconds."*

"How many?"

"Can't tell."

Venom cursed. *"Where the hell is Wick?"*

Like he knew? Christ, the warrior might be lethal in a firefight, but his punctuality sucked. Which meant they were going in light, one wingman short of a fighting triangle. *"No time to wait. Split wide right. Go in on the blind side…divide and conquer."*

"Wicked," his buddy said, a whole lot of pissed off in his tone. *"You divide. I'll conquer."*

"Watch your six."

As his buddy hoorahed, a deep growl came out of nowhere, *"Rikar…right flank."*

Speak of the devil. Backup, coming in hot.

Black, gold-tipped scales nothing but a blur, Wick separated from the gloom, rocketing toward them like an arrow tip. Unfurling his wings, he slowed his flight, settling beside Rikar's right wing.

"About time you got here." Ruby eyes shimmering, Venom glared at the male.

"Fuck off," Wick said, using his favorite greeting.

Venom smiled at his best friend, showing fang. *"Love you too, man."*

The familiar exchange settled Rikar down. Trash talk before a fight always focused him, cranking his dial to lethal. And this time, the stakes were higher than ever. Angela needed him, and he was still too far away. Moments from becoming her shield…from getting between her and harm's way.

But he was close. So fucking close. Just one more bend. Another few more seconds.

Please, God. Let me make it.

A scream echoed, ricocheting off the surface of the water.

The horrific sound wound him tight then let go, sling-shotting him around the last curve. A quick snapshot laid out the scene frame by frame. Angela. Her desperate scramble backward across the beach: bare feet churning, chest heaving, tears rolling down her cheeks. Lothair's bared fangs, his hiss and pursuit.

Rikar growled. The bastard was toying with her, flicking at her with razor-sharp claws, letting her get up only to pounce and bring her down again.

Rage grabbed hold, narrowed his vision and...

Boom!

He lost control and ice exploded. The snap-crackle-n-pop rolled in an arctic wave, freezing the river solid below him. With a snarl, Rikar tucked his wings and set down fast. His claws dug in, ripping up ice, throwing out frost as he slid sideways, skating toward the beachhead. Lothair's head snapped in his direction, and Rikar clenched his teeth. Stupid. He was a freaking bonehead, blowing the one advantage he had: the element of surprise.

But Christ, he couldn't stand it. Seeing Angela's torment and tears. Watching her flinch and scream as she fought for her life.

Black scales glimmering under a full moon, Lothair crouched like a cat and hissed at him, refusing to leave his prize. Perfect. A downed dragon made for a big bull's-eye. And the Razorback was right in the kill zone, locked in Rikar's crosshairs, the best kind of target. The trick now? Hammering the asshole without hitting his female. If he didn't time it just right, the rogue would use Angela as a human shield.

Rikar's eyes narrowed. No way he could chance it. He needed a load of visual interference...right now.

The sound of his claws sliced over ice as Rikar whipped up a blizzard. As snow blew in with hurricane force, providing cover, he zeroed in, waiting for just…the right…moment and—

"Angela…move right!"

His command ripped through the blanket of thick-white-and-fluffy. He saw her flinch a second before she obeyed, scrambling toward a huge boulder. Talons open wide, Lothair reached for her. Rikar inhaled hard and exhaled fast, launching his arsenal.

With a growl, the bastard dodged, somersaulting into a backflip. The ice daggers struck like automatic gunfire, ripping a path up the beach as, paws still in midair, Lothair's spiked tail whipped full circle. The sharp tip caught Angela, flipped her over, sent her into a whiplashing spin. She screamed in pain. Rikar roared as the smell of her blood filled the air.

Oh, God…no. "Angela!"

His shout echoed, giving voice to his fear as he watched her tumble across the frozen sand like a rag doll. Claws digging into ice, he hauled ass, stretching his limbs, running like a cheetah to reach her. *"Venom…cover me!"*

"Go!" The deep growl belonged to Wick. The male streaked overhead, moving like a black-and-gold lightning strike. *"Grab her and get out."*

Rikar didn't hesitate.

Neither did Wick.

Blue-orange flame shot from the warrior's mouth. The ball of poison gas exploded against the night sky. Scrambling in full retreat, Lothair unfurled his wings and went airborne, leaving his hostage behind on the ground. With a clear line of sight, Rikar slid sideways onto the shoreline. The second his talons left ice, he tucked his head and rolled, shifting to human form midrotation.

Bad move? Absolutely.

He was more vulnerable without his scales, but…shit. He needed his hands to help his female. To find her wounds and stanch the blood flow. And as he sprinted toward her—shitkickers sinking in snow and sand, heart hammering his breastbone—he prayed she was still whole and breathing. He would never forgive himself if she died.

Reaching her side, he dropped to his knees. She lay belly down, red hair matted with sweat, face hidden behind her out-flung arm. He checked her vitals, her spinal column, working fast, one eye on the sky as dragons roared overhead. Go Venom and Wick. The boys had his back, pushing Lothair away, giving him the time he needed to check Angela.

Nothing broken. Time for the gentle flip-over.

She whimpered when he rolled her. Oh, thank fuck. She was still alive, but…

Christ help him.

Blood ran from a gash on her temple, and that was nothing compared to her leg. The bastard's sharp tail had clipped her skin, slicing her thigh wide open. And oh, God…the blood. It was everywhere, all over her and on his hands, staining the blanket of snow beneath her.

A quick shrug-and-tug and his leather jacket landed beside her. His T-shirt came off next. With quick hands, he twisted the cotton into a makeshift bandage and wound it over then under, binding the cut. He needed to stop the bleeding and get her to Black Diamond…and Myst. A nurse practitioner, Bastian's female specialized in medical emergencies. She would know how to help Angela.

"Hold on, angel." He kept working, wrapping the cotton around her leg. "Come on, Angela…hold on for me."

She stirred at the sound of his voice. As her eyelashes flickered, her hazel gaze lit him up, tugging at his heartstrings. But her voice? Shit, she undid him as she whispered, "You…"

"Yes, angel…it's me." Unable to help himself, he cupped her cheek, held eye contact even though he knew he shouldn't. He didn't have time to waste. "Angela, baby, I need to move you. It's gonna hurt, but hang tight for me. I'll get you help."

"R." Pale skin aglow in moonlight, she shivered violently, making him afraid for her. "You're…my R. I r-remember you."

Hers.

Jesus fucking Christ. He *was* a pansy. A freak for craving her ownership, for wanting to be claimed by a female he'd done nothing but hurt. And as he wrapped her in his leather jacket, protecting her from ice and snow, and cradled her close, Rikar cursed himself. His nature. The plague of his kind.

His obsession with her would end badly. He knew it, but somehow didn't care.

He wanted her. And she needed to live. If she didn't, he would never have a chance to convince her of his worth…to make her crave him as much as he did her.

A long shot? Without a doubt. But as Rikar shifted, unfurled his wings, and leapt skyward with her curled like a kitten in his paws, he reminded himself he never took the easy route.

Yeah, he'd always been a long odds kind of male.

Chapter Nine

Both arms bent, hands tucked behind his head, Forge lay flat on the floor, staring up at the ceiling. Not that there was much to see. No cracks or pockmarks, just grainy gray concrete surrounded by a whole lot of cold, hard, and mean. He snorted. Aye, without a doubt. The Nightfuries got full marks for thoroughness. The place was rock solid. A prison's prison.

Not that it mattered. He'd been in worse places.

Granted, the decor had always been a wee bit better, but otherwise? Nothing but more of the same in his sea of ordinary. Which was what he kept telling himself. Make-believe, after all, was one of his specialties. Too bad the mental escape hatch he usually slipped through wasn't working. The dumb thing was locked up tight, its sign flipped to "closed," giving him the psychological equivalent of *piss off, asshole.*

Uh-huh, that about summed it up. Which left him with nothing, except bucketfuls of irritation and…oh, aye, time. Time to marvel at his stupidity. Time to curse his dumb-ass plan. Time to scratch at the steel choker clamped around his throat.

Jesus, the thing was brilliant. A real ode-to-the-prisoner without the song and dance. A shame, really. At least the music would've entertained him. As it was, the only sound he got was a beep every fifteen seconds. Well, that and a pinpoint flash of red light. Dog collar complete with LED features.

Beep-beep, flash. Beep-beep, flash.

Bloody hell, it was like Chinese water torture, only worse. The metal chafed, making him twitchy as claustrophobia circled just below the surface. Forge glanced at the standard-issue prison cot against the back wall. Maybe, if he flaked out on it instead of…

Nah. No good. He preferred the floor, and honestly? Didn't deserve any better.

His female's death proved that, and she'd been strike two. Strike one? Forge clenched his teeth, killing the wayward thought. No way he wanted to go there. The memory was long gone, buried beneath a mountain of mental debris, just the way he liked it. His family was ancient history, and old wounds were better left untouched.

But Caroline?

God, he couldn't get her face out of his head. The gaping hole she left in her wake was still too fresh. No matter how many times he sidestepped it, the loss came with him, getting in his face, blocking his escape route. Not even ignoring the pain worked. Like an infection, the grief festered and blame bubbled up, pointing a bony finger at him.

Which was exactly where it belonged.

His chest tightened. Forge blew out a long breath. He wanted a do-over…another shot at doing the right thing. Of walking away instead of stopping to help her. Given half a chance, he would've left her there. Alone by the side of the

Highland road, propped against a broken-down car, cell phone in hand as she tried to get a signal.

But oh, no, not him.

Like an idiot, he'd come to the rescue, changed her flat tire, watched moonlight dance in her dark hair and...aye, played the empty-headed fool smitten by a pretty lass. Now he was nobody's hero, just a male full of regret yearning for a life already lost.

Forge gave the ceiling a break and closed his eyes. A picture of Caroline rose, making his heart hurt. He ignored the awful ache and stayed with her, unable to give her up even in death. And as he followed her in his mind's eye, memories of their time together sent him sideways, and he drifted, allowing her warmth to draw him deep into the daydream.

So beautiful. She'd been magnificent with her sky-blue eyes and winsome smile. The scent of her, the taste of her on his tongue...God. She was like the blood in his veins. A part of him he couldn't lose. Not that he hadn't tried, but the heart always remembered what the mind yearned to forget, and like a ghost, she haunted him. Taunted him as he recalled the softness of her skin, her moans of pleasure as he'd slid between her thighs and taken her as his own.

God forgive him.

He was sick for thinking of her that way, for wanting her as much now as he had when she was alive. Caroline deserved better. A shrine, maybe, for putting up with him, for giving her life so that their son would live.

Unfair. It was so fucking unfair.

His brows drawn in tight, Forge shook his head. A mistake. Somewhere along the line, he'd made a huge mistake. Otherwise he and Caroline would be energy-fused, locked in a cosmic bond—mated for life, instead of separated for eternity. Oh, aye, it was easy in theory. One Dragonkind male. One human female. Put the two together and… eureka! Instant you're-mine-forever magic. Too bad reality was a bitch with an axe to grind. His dragon half hadn't bonded with the female of his heart, denying the energy-fuse and his ability to protect her from harm.

Now he was stuck in a cage with a pack of Nightfuries riding his ass. And if that wasn't enough, Rikar would rip his head off the next time around. No doubt with his commander's blessing if Forge didn't give the male what he wanted. Namely? The knowledge he possessed about energy-fuse. Which wasn't a big deal if he got what he needed in return. Question was…would Bastian reciprocate?

Forge pursed his lips, turning the problem over in his mind. Aye, it was a gamble, but allowing the Nightfuries to capture him had been a bigger one. And now that he stood waist-deep, he planned to wade into the deep end and see what swam out to join him.

Or drown him.

Either way, he needed leverage, a weakness to exploit. Which meant putting the female in play. Shuffling his shoulders against concrete, Forge grimaced, shying away from the plan. He didn't want to use Myst, but like it or nay, the strategy was a good one. Bastian's female held the key. The fact she loved and protected his son shouldn't matter, but…

Shite, it did. More than he wanted it to. But with his son in the mix, his options were limited to, well…fighting dirty.

So aye, much as he hated the idea, throwing a few cheap shots was on his to-do list. Might as well accept it and move on. The female would survive. All right, maybe a little the worse for wear, but Myst had her mate to soothe her in the aftermath. But his lad was an innocent in need of his sire. Which left him no choice. He would swallow his pride and abandon his scruples. Do whatever it took to get his bairn back, and in the end hope Myst forgave him for—

The soft click of steel echoed through the quiet.

Forge tensed but didn't move. Still flat on the floor, he cracked his lids, watched from beneath his lashes, and listened. A bumping thump. The scrape of plastic on metal. A soft curse and the subtle smell of—

Jesus Christ. Myst.

It couldn't be anyone else. Not with the whiff of pheromones headed his way. The perfume was subtle, but one Forge knew well. He'd lived with it for eight months, and although the fragrance was unique to each female, the scent of pregnancy—of renewal and growth—couldn't be denied. And Myst smelled beautiful, like female and fresh-cut lilies.

Forge's mouth curved up at the corners. Had he said leverage? Yes, indeedy, he'd hit the mother lode and found Bastian's weakness.

Soft footfalls scraped against concrete. The squeak of rubber against steel.

With a quick inhale, Forge popped to his feet. The instant his bare soles touched down on the cold floor, he put himself in gear and strode to the front of his cell. Getting as close as the invisible barrier would allow, he craned his neck to gaze down the wide corridor. He wanted to watch her approach, see her the instant she came into view. The muscles bracketing his spine flickered, coiling tight with anticipation. Had she brought his son with her? Was he even now snug in her arms?

Please, God...be merciful.

Holding his breath, Forge leaned a little closer. The collar zapped him and, with a curse, he took a step backward, still straining to see, hoping, praying and—

His heart contracted as a baby stroller came into view. Red with black trim, the domed canopy arched over the stroller's bed, shielding his son, but Forge knew he was there. Baby powder. The smell made his knees go weak. He locked them and stood stone-still, afraid if he moved the pair would disappear into thin air.

Silence expanded, interrupted only by the squeak of rubber tires on concrete.

"Hey," Myst said when she spotted him. Her voice drifted in the quiet, raising goosebumps on his skin.

Swallowing hard, Forge forced his chest to expand. He needed to keep his wits about him, but…shite. He could hardly breathe as he stared at her. She'd come. Myst Munroe, the female he owed but could never repay.

Forge tipped his chin in her direction. The lackluster greeting was the best he could do. He'd never once imagined she would visit and…Jesus, her generosity slew him where he stood.

Rolling to a stop, keeping her distance, she smiled a little. "Guess you didn't expect this, huh?"

Forge shook his head. Bloody hell. What was the matter with him? *Talk, motherfucker…charm her…make her feel your pain.* He needed an ally, and Myst was the best sort. A female who hated to see another suffer. But even as the instructions roared through his mind, his voice refused to obey. Surprise had him by the throat. And respect? Aye, a shitload of that was circling too, the male in him responding to the courage she showed.

He cleared his throat, trying to dislodge the lump.

She glanced at the collar around his neck, the beep-beep-flash loud in the silence. Touching her fingers to her own throat, Myst met his gaze and said, "I'm sorry about that. Bastian doesn't trust you."

His voice made an appearance…thank Jesus. "Smart male."

"The smartest."

"Enough tae know you're here, female…without protection?" The second the words left his mouth, Forge wanted to kick himself.

He shouldn't be growling at her. Not if he wanted her on his side, but the conscience he said he'd ignore reared its ugly head. He planned to use her, so aye, it was only fair he give her a fair chance…forewarn her in some way. And if snarling at her a little evened the playing field, he'd live with that.

Which didn't make a lick of sense. Stupid collar was obviously giving him brain damage.

"Nice try, Forge," she said, rolling her eyes.

His brows collided. *Nice try?*

"Really…it was." Pursing her lips, she tilted her head as though judging his performance. One hand on the stroller's handle, she kept the canopy between him and his son. Good plan if she wanted to drive him flipping nuts. He couldn't see a thing with the canvas in the way. "You get an A for effort on the tough-guy act, but I'm not convinced. You want to know why?"

A little baffled by her, but mostly charmed, he dialed back the snarl factor. "Sure."

"You would no sooner hurt me than cut off your own arm."

Forge opened his mouth, then closed it again. Freaking female. She was whipcord smart. Way too perceptive. Which didn't bode well for his game plan.

"So, let's make a deal, okay?" Moving around the side of the stroller, she pushed at the canvas, folding the canopy back. His throat went tight. Little hands. He could see his son's wee fists waving from between the folds of a blue blanket. "You cut the crap, and I'll stay a little longer. Maybe even introduce you to someone who'd like to meet you."

His gaze flashed back to Myst's.

She raised a brow.

He scowled at her. "That's blackmail."

"Yes, it is." Expression serious, she waited, let the silence build, wielding her advantage and his desperation like a weapon. "So…what's it gonna be? Will you behave or not?"

"I'll behave," he said, feeling like a chastened four-year-old after a full-blown temper tantrum. Not that it mattered. She'd brought his son, so…fuck it. To hell with his pride. "May I see him…please?"

Myst leaned down and gathered up the blue bundle. As she settled his lad in the crook of one arm, she murmured to him. The bairn cooed back. Forge exhaled, already fighting tears. Seconds ticked by, lasting forever as Myst adjusted the blanket and approached his prison cell. The barrier snapped, crackling in warning, and she flinched, stopping a few feet away.

"I'm sorry," she said. "I can't come any closer. The current will hurt him and—"

"I know," he said, the wait nearly killing him.

With a soft smile, Myst tilted her arms, and he got his first glimpse of a wee face. His heart went loose inside his chest, and as the damn thing flopped around, he lost the battle. Tears gathered, blurring his vision. God, he was beautiful, so perfect it made him ache from the inside out.

Wiping beneath one of his eyes, Forge studied his lad. Eyes wide open, he chewed on his fist, baby drool glistening on chubby fingers, dark Mohawk of hair shining in the low light. Unable to stop them, Forge's fingers curled. He wanted to hold him, feel the slight weight of him in his arms, and listen to each happy sound he made.

"Thank you," he rasped, his throat so tight the words came hard. "Thank you for bringing him."

"He's your son. You have a right to know him. Caroline would've wanted that." Tears in her own eyes, she stroked the bairn's cheek with her fingertip. "I named him Gregor."

He grimaced. "A human name?"

"Oh, for goodness sake." Making a sound of exasperation, Myst glared at him. "You guys and your stupid names."

"Stupid," he murmured, watching her closely. "Gregor is just as—"

"Say it, and I swear to God I'll find a gun and shoot you." With a grumble in her tone, she said, "His middle name is Mayhem, okay? So don't get your panties in a wad."

A smile tugged at the corners of his mouth. "Mayhem's good, strong…a warrior's name."

She stuck her tongue out at him. His grin broke free and, for the first time in a long while, he felt lighter somehow. Like he'd been touched by an angel, one who'd taken pity and lifted his burden, if only for a minute. The carefree moment sobered him and, as Myst returned his smile, shining light into his darkness, the urge to warn her took over.

"Myst," he said, his happiness fading into seriousness. "Your mate is right not tae trust me."

"Maybe. But you and I both know the truth."

His eyes narrowed. "And what is that?"

"I know you're not a bad guy..." She paused to drill him with her violet eyes. "...and so do you. Bastian's fair-minded, Forge. Make peace with him. Otherwise, you stay locked up here, away from your son and everything that's important."

Uh-huh. A pretty speech. Too bad he'd been there, done that, and didn't deserve a do-over. "You cannae save me, female."

"Doesn't mean I won't try."

Wonderful. Just what he needed...a female on a quest. Shite. He might as well add stubborn to her list of qualities. Though pigheaded might be a better word. Aye, definitely. He liked that one much better, and as he—

Door hinges creaked, metal clicking against metal.

"My lady?" Edged by urgency, the British accent floated into the cellblock. "Myst?"

Her arms still snug around his son, Myst pivoted toward the exit. "What is it, Daimler?"

"Oh, thank goodness...I found you." Twin tails of his tux flapping behind him, the male *Numbai*—a member of serving class to Dragonkind—pranced into view. Pointed ears visible beneath hair pulled back at the nape, Daimler danced to a stop in front of his mistress. "Master Rikar needs you, my lady. He's inbound with an injured female and—"

"Angela?" Forge asked.

The Numbai's gaze flicked to him a second before settling back on his mistress. As he opened his mouth to answer, Myst cut him off. "How bad is she? I need details, Daimler, and an ETA."

"I don't know. And ten minutes, my lady," Daimler said, answering each question rapid-fire. "Master Sloan's already in the clinic, setting up triage."

"Can I help?" The second the question left his mouth, Forge felt like an idiot. What the hell was he doing? Offering to lend a hand? Playing the hero? Jesus, he needed his head examined. Aye, that, and a swift kick in the arse to smarten him up. But even as he told himself to zip it, his mouth opened and, like a pathetic pea brain, he dug his hole a little deeper. "I've been trained as a paramedic."

His offer made Daimler's mouth fall open.

Myst wasn't surprised.

"Told you," she said, a smirk on her face. "Keep it up, Forge, and I'll make a good guy out of you yet."

"Bloody hell." Forge wanted to growl at her…he really did. Instead, he stood stone-still, fists clenched and heart aching as she strode to the stroller and settled his son inside. Out of sight, but never out of mind. "Myst, could you—"

"No," she said, tone sharp, her expression serious. "Play all the games you want, it won't work with me. You want out? You want more time with your son? Grow a brain and make peace with my mate. Otherwise, you'll stay exactly where you are for a very long time."

An ultimatum with teeth. Deadly, and oh…so…tempting.

Could it really be that easy? Hit one knee, bow his head, and swear loyalty to the Nightfury pack and…bam! Instant acceptance.

Forge shook his head. No way. Nothing was ever that simple. The visit today. Myst's warning. All of it smacked of conspiracy, one older than time. Show the prisoner something he wanted—would kill to possess—then take it away unless he gave up the goods. Bastian wanted information about energy-fuse; the ins and outs of how a male used it to protect his female through the *hungering* when the Meridian realigned, her pregnancy, and finally, the birth of a child.

The strategy was diabolical. And right up Bastian's alley.

As suspicion banged around inside Forge's head, his admiration for Myst grew. Aye, she'd brought his son, but not out of kindness. It was psychological warfare. She would never be his ally. He would never win her over. Even knowing it, however, didn't stop the urge to call out and beg her not to walk away with his son.

He almost did it. Almost opened his mouth and asked her to come back.

Almost, but not quite.

He was stronger than that, a warrior born and bred. So he killed the temptation to give in and swallowed the plea. But as the door clanged closed behind her, his cell got a little smaller, and the collar much, much tighter.

Chapter Ten

The murmur came from somewhere south of sanity, pulling Angela through thick mental fog. Floating inside her own skull, she kept her eyes closed and listened to the voice. A hint of an accent in the undertone, the timbre broke through the noise inside her head. She clung to each note. Listened to the pitch and swell. Let it hold her high. Away from the pain. Away from terror. Away from the unknown.

Except that wasn't right.

She knew who—correction…make that *what*—held her. Remembered the beach as she'd comc to, fclt thc swaying glide of flight and the hard scales against her cheek. Another dragon; white scales to the rat-bastard's black. That had to be a good sign, right? Heroes and saviors always wore white. Or did that only happen in fairy tales?

Angela frowned. She couldn't remember. Her brain was stuck deep in fluff and mental feather down. Not much made sense. Not the flight. Not the warmth of the dragon's scales. Nor the fact he held her gently in the cradle of his talons.

Maybe that's why she wasn't screaming. Wasn't struggling. Was just floating, lost inside her own mind while her white dragon in shining scales talked to her. God, it was nice; the depth of his voice, the words, and how safe he made her feel.

Which was just plain nutso. But sometimes, Angela decided, crazy made sense.

"Just a little further, angel," her dragon said, soft tone full of reassurance. And there she went again, falling into each syllable, taking solace from the sound of his voice. "Almost there."

Almost *where*? She shifted in the palm of his talon and cracked her eyes open. Yellow flashed up ahead, pushing a gentle glow through the darkness. Angela squinted. Was she really seeing that? Or were her eyes playing tricks, screwing with reality? Seemed like a good guess because that looked like a cliff wall. Or the inside of a tunnel, one with jagged outcroppings and narrow ledges.

His wings angled, the dragon swung around another corner. The light became stronger, illuminating a wide landing pad. An abrupt shift. A moment suspended above the solid rock outcropping, and then…

Touchdown. To the accompaniment of claws scraping stone.

All right. Now was probably a good time to start screaming. Or searching for a weapon. Anything to hold him at bay. But something malfunctioned, crossing her mental wiring. She didn't want to do any of those things. Didn't feel the need to, either. All she wanted was to hang onto the voice, to hear him talk to her some more.

"R," she whispered, a soft call for comfort.

"Shh, baby," he murmured. "It's okay. I'm gonna get you help."

Help sounded good. Excellent, really, because...God. Now that she was more alert, her leg hurt like hell and, as the pain poked at her like a bully with a sharp stick, each breath came a little faster. A little harder, one on top of the other.

With a whimper, she reached for him, needing something solid to hang onto as she opened her eyes. She expected to see a dragon. A man's pale gaze met hers instead, and wham! Sparks lit off, exploding into a kaleidoscope of color inside her head. The wall around the memory—the one she hadn't been able to touch—collapsed, and images flashed like playing cards. McGovern's bar. The cracking sound of billiard balls, the gorgeous guy making her laugh, helping her relax and drop her guard. His callused hands on her bare skin. The soft rasp of his whiskered cheek against her own...the unbelievable pleasure.

"Rikar." His name came out like a question, though she didn't mean it like one. She remembered now. "You're a... big...jerk."

Cradling her in his lap, his mouth curved. "Bang-on, angel."

Not true. Angela knew it, but man, if felt good to give him a hard time. The show of spirit meant she was still alive. And as her focus sharpened, her mind followed suit, turning over enough to give him heck for McGovern's and the fact she'd woken up alone...with a chunk of her memory missing. Something weird—and okay, half-wonderful too—had happened between them that night.

So, yup. Whatever the details, he owed her and would be the "jerk" for a while longer. At least out loud. In secret, she'd call him awesome. He'd come after her when no one else had. Fought like hell to get her back, away from the rat-bastard. Angela's throat closed, thankfulness ripping her wide open. If he'd been one minute later…if Lothair had…

She gagged as her stomach heaved.

"Angela?" He cupped the back of her head. Concern tightened his features a second before he pushed to his feet with her in his arms. "How we doing, baby?"

"I c-can't…b-breathe."

"Hang tight…one more minute."

His footfalls echoed at a fast clip, jarring her with each stride. Too tired to keep her eyes open, Angela let them drift closed. Bad idea. Without the cavern walls to ground her, she went topsy-turvy, her mind cartwheeling into thick, gray fog. The tumble spun her around, and unconsciousness circled like a shark looking for its next meal. As it sideswiped her, she told herself to be strong, but the siphoning pull seduced. Whispered in her ear, telling her to relax and forget. And as her chest rose and fell, each breath became more difficult than the last.

She wasn't going to make it. Her body knew it, and so did she.

"Rik-kar?"

He dipped his head, brushing her hair with his mouth. "Yeah?"

"D-don't leave me, ok-kay…p-please don't—"

"I won't, Angela." Her ear pressed to his chest, she listened to his heartbeat, each thump a lullaby, the last one she would ever hear. "Just stay with me. Baby, please…stay with me."

Angela tried—she really did—but as agony gathered she saw the shark swim toward her through the mind fog.

Sharp teeth bared, the dark shadow attacked, dragging her down before swallowing her whole.

Rikar cursed as Angela went limp in his arms. Hitching her higher against his chest, he held on tighter, afraid if he let her go he'd lose her. Zip. Bang. Gone forever...just like that.

Hurry.

The word banged around inside his head. He ran faster, sprinting across the LZ, each of his footfalls booming against uneven cavern walls. The light globes' bob-and-weave caught the beat, swaying against the ceiling, sending stone dust drifting in the damp air. A thousand sparkles lit off, each fine grain grabbing onto the dim light like leeches onto bare skin.

God, why had he landed so far from the lair's entrance?

A vast space, the LZ could launch four dragons at a time. And like a dumb-ass, he'd set down on the corner farthest from the door. But after the rough flight through storm clouds to reach Black Diamond, the need to check her with human hands—see her through human eyes—had overpowered him. Now Angela was in serious trouble, her bio-energy so low she wasn't even shivering anymore. Her body had tapped out, and even though he cocooned her with his magic—

Christ help him, it wasn't enough. And as her vitals took a nosedive, he felt her slipping away.

A howl of denial locked in his throat, Rikar slowed his roll. Not the brightest thing to do under the circumstances. He needed to reach the clinic, but he couldn't share his energy with her on the run. That was if he could feed her at all, but…shit. He had to try. If she took from him, she stood a chance. The question was: Would she accept the healing energy he offered?

He'd never shared his energy with a female before. Had only watched from the sidelines while Bastian fed his mate, and honestly? The exchange freaked him out. But afraid or not, there was no other play. Angela needed him. So yeah, no matter how tricky, he would deliver. Would crack himself wide open, bind himself to her heart, body, mind, and soul through energy-fuse if it meant saving her life.

Which was a total mind-fuck.

Energy-fuse was a forever kind of commitment, a mating bond forged without the possibility of separation. Once he connected and she accepted, he would belong to her. Life without possibility of parole.

Angela twitched in his arms.

"Fuck it," he said as desperation dragged him to the edge, then pushed him over.

Closing his eyes, he sank deep into the rawness of the Meridian's energy stream. Power crackled, making him tense as he connected to the uniqueness of Angela's bio-energy. The electrostatic current that fed his kind surged, rising in a wave to meet him. With a twist, Rikar looped the band, wrapping them in magical splendor, refolding the stream, blocking the life-giving flow. The magic whip-lashed. He grabbed its tail and reversed course, redirecting the healing current from him into Angela.

She flinched, fighting the intrusion.

"Please, angel…take it." Concentrating hard, he pushed the plea into her mind. *"Please, baby, let me feed you."*

A pause. Less than a heartbeat in time. She hummed, the sound warm, soft, and—

Rikar sucked in a quick breath. Sweet Christ. She'd linked in, accepted him, snuggling closer as she took what he offered.

Drunk on sensation, Rikar swayed. Widening his stance, he planted his shitkickers and…hmm, that felt incredible. And he wanted more. Needed to give her every last piece of himself.

Sinking to the cavern floor, he settled her in his lap. "That's right, love…take all you need."

Dumb-ass thing to do. Stupid on so many levels, but God, he couldn't resist her. Or deny his compulsion to feed her. Savage need ripped through him as energy-fuse grabbed hold. Undeniable. Powerful. Addictive. The magical bond rooted him to the stone floor, made him cup the back of Angela's head, press his cheek to hers, and align them temple-to-temple.

With a moan, she nestled in, brushing the corner of his mouth with her own. Warm breath on his skin. A flick of her tongue. A gentle grazing of her teeth. The pleasure of her in his arms.

God give him strength. No wonder B loved serving his female this way.

Unable to resist, he slipped his hand under the hem of her hospital gown and put them skin to skin, spreading his fingers wide across her lower back. Connected at three junction points—nape, temple, and spine—the Meridian amplified, marrying their energy streams. Rikar growled, relishing the rush as Angela drank deep, drawing him into her veins. Within seconds, her vital signs stabilized, each breath coming a little easier as her muscles unlocked and her heartbeat leveled out.

"There's my angel," he said in Dragonese, using the language of his kind to soothe her. "I see you now."

She whispered his name.

Tears flooded his vision as his throat went tight. Rikar accepted the gift, then put it away. No time to wallow in the intensity of the mating. Angela might be stable now, but she wasn't out of danger yet.

Pushing to his feet, Rikar skirted the beat-up Honda in the center of the LZ and jogged toward Black Diamond's underground lair. Ten seconds out, he banged on the magical door with his mind, triggering the energy shield. The powerful current crackled. Blue-white sparks flew, the snap-crackle-n-pop warning him to slow down.

Rikar ignored the hint. He could handle the pain of coming in too fast. His female's need took precedence and every second counted.

Upping the pace, he thumped on the barrier again. The cave wall rippled, shifting from solid stone to clear and wavy. Curled like a shield around Angela, he tucked his chin and braced for impact. He hit the energy shield head-on. The invisible doorway hissed then whiplashed, throwing the magical equivalent of a temper tantrum. Rikar snarled at it. The thing retaliated, sideswiping him with electrostatic shards, and sensation exploded into pain. Holding his breath, he gritted his teeth and waited for the shield to spit him out the other side.

One Mississippi. Two Mississippi…three Mississippi, four—

The portal released its grip and shoved, launching him like a human torpedo. Scrambling to keep his balance, boot treads sliding on concrete, ancient stone walls flashed in his periphery.

Thank Christ. He'd made it. Was now standing in the hallway of Black Diamond's underground lair.

He checked Angela. Breathing well. Heartbeat strong. Curled like a kitten in his arms, and none the worse for wear.

Putting himself in gear, he sprinted up the double-wide corridor. "Myst!"

The clinic's glass door slid open. Bastian's female stuck her head out. "How's she doing?"

"Stable, but hurt," he said. "Deep laceration to the right thigh."

"Still bleeding?"

"No, but—"

"We're set up and ready to go. Get her in here fast."

Like he wasn't hauling ass already? Still he didn't argue. No time. No inclination either. All he cared about was Angela. And having Myst on hand to play doctor was a gift. B's female could order him around as much as she liked, just as long as his female pulled through—hale, whole, with nothing but a shitload of healthy ahead of her.

Putting on the brakes, Rikar skidded into the clinic.

Set up like an operating room, medical supplies were lined up on top of a metal rollaway cart beside the stainless-steel examination table. Plastic crinkled as Myst cracked open one of the packets. An IV needle pushed from its depths as she got ready to pump fluids into Angela's bloodstream.

"Lay her down, buddy," Sloan said, hanging a bag of clear liquid from the IV pole. "Let Myst see what we've got."

Good plan. But as Rikar ran toward the table he'd been stitched up on so many times he'd lost count, his feet slowed, then got stuck to the floor. God, he didn't want to put her down. What if he let her go and—

"Rikar, man." Sloan frowned at him, throwing a load of WTF in his direction. "Get over here."

Breathing like a wounded racehorse, he shook his head. "I can't let her go…I promised. I…" Rooted like a tree in the middle of the clinic, he played a game of internal tug-of-war. The idea might be idiotic, but they were still intertwined, the fusion pulling thimblefuls of energy from him to give to her. And if his hands left her skin, Rikar knew—just *knew*—she'd crash. "I promised I wouldn't leave her. If I let her go, she'll die and…fuck…I can't…"

"Okay…no problem." Myst jogged over to his side. Cupping his elbow, she used gentle hands instead of force and pulled him over to the table. "You don't have to let her go, but you've got to put her down. I can't help her unless you do…all right?"

The words made sense. Logical. Reasonable. Perfect freaking sense. And yet, he clung to Angela like a dying man to life, unable to do as Myst asked. His fear for her was too great, and like a beast with big teeth, it had bitten so deep Rikar didn't know how to shake free.

Myst met his gaze. "Trust me, Rikar."

Trust. Christ, what a tall order. But as B's female squeezed his arm, his muscles unlocked, opening the protective cage around Angela. The second he relinquished her, Myst went to work: shoving him to the head of the table, telling him to hold Angela's head still, to talk to her, to soothe her, all while staying the hell out of the way. Her tone didn't brook any argument. Rikar didn't offer any. Instead he watched, tears clouding his vision as each cut and scrape was revealed on her pale skin.

The bastards. The fucking bastards.

They'd hurt her so badly. Used superior strength to hold her down. He could see the finger marks on her arms and throat. And God, the needle marks on the curve of her belly—just above her hipbones—almost killed him. But the worst? The bruises on the insides of her thighs.

Sinking to his knees at the end of the table, Rikar tucked his face against hers, put them cheek-to-cheek as he stroked her gently. His female. Even broken and bruised, she was the most beautiful thing he'd ever seen. And as he felt her flinch and heard her whimper, Rikar held her close and made a promise. He would avenge her. Lay waste to Seattle—burn the whole city to the ground—to find the Razorback lair and kill them all.

Lightning forked, stroking the underbelly of dark clouds. Stupid thunderstorm. The crash-bang was lighting him up like a firefly, illuminating his black scales, giving the enemy a clear line of sight and plenty to track. Lothair banked hard, maneuvering around another tight corner. The mountain terrain, all the narrow crevices and sharp peaks, should've helped him. Instead he was flying blind, looping like a circus animal between sheer cliff faces to evade the Nightfury warriors on his tail.

Another flash. More blue-white light.

Jesus Christ. The E&E (evade and escape) had gone from simple to goat-fucked in seconds. Lothair glanced over his shoulder. He caught a flash of green scales and shimmering ruby-red eyes. Venom was right on his ass. Terrific.

Nothing like the threat of getting hammered by poisonous exhale and then flambéed by fire to motivate a male.

Diving beneath a rocky overhang, Lothair flew in close, hugging the cliff face. He heard the hiss of breath, got a whiff of the Nightfury's special brand of poison. Derr`mo, it smelled nasty, like gasoline mixed with turpentine and rotten eggs. He needed to get the hell out of range.

Two more minutes, a little fancy maneuvering, and…

Poof. He'd be gone. But 120 seconds seemed like an eternity. Especially with Tweedledum and Tweedledee breathing down his neck.

The two males were like dogs with a bone: vicious, tenacious with bucketfuls of never-say-die. Literally. Which was a shame. Seeing them KO'd would've been fun after the clusterfuck of a night. Another high-energy female lost to Rikar and his band of bastards. Man, that stung. It really did. Enough for him to want to say "fuck the plan" and turn around long enough to hammer the Nightfuries riding his tail.

Too bad he wasn't stupid enough.

No way would he screw with Ivar. Disappointing the boss man never ended well for a male, so…yeah. He'd stick to the plan and buy Denzeil enough time to get the females out of the underground lair. Which left him on bait duty, swishing his tail, leading Tweedledum and Tweedledee on a wild goose chase through mountain passes.

But later. When the female captures were secure? He'd come back for revenge. To get what he was owed before the round ended and the bell went ding-ding-ding.

Another bright flash. More thunder.

Banking hard, Lothair flipped sideways, threading the needle between two cliff faces. His fast flight ripped stone from the mountainside. Shards of rock flew, splintering into long, jagged pieces. Lothair held his breath, listening for—

Yup. There it was. The curse he expected, and even better? A hiss of pain. He'd nailed the green-scaled bastard with a face full of fuck you. His night was looking up. Now only one thing left to do. Find Tweedledee. The black one with gold-tipped scales and a mouth like a toxic blowtorch wasn't behind him.

Making himself small, Lothair rocketed through another crevice. The rock face closed in, narrowing into a tight channel. His wing tip dragged along the granite rise. Lothair ignored the burn, absorbing the pain. Distraction wasn't an option. He needed to stay focused to stall for time.

His velocity nearly supersonic, his night vision flared, picking up trace: the arc of electricity, the dampness in the air, a slight disturbance in the magical shield guarding the lair's back entrance. Bingo. Tweedledee at ten o'clock, gold-tipped scales gleaming in the storm-flash, hanging like a gargoyle off the cliff face.

Hmm…clever plan. One on chase duty, herding him toward the kill zone. While the other waited with his finger on the trigger, an exhale away from blowing him out of the sky.

Lothair stifled a grin. The bastards deserved full marks. An A-plus-plus, because whatever else they were, stupid wasn't one of them.

He bared his fangs. Time for the grand finale.

The first raindrop hit, splattering his scales, sliding across the bridge of his nose. More followed as the sky opened like a gift. The hissing deluge blurred dark mountain edges, distorting sound. Lothair hummed and counted off the seconds.

The Nightfury exhaled.

Blue-orange flame flashed against rain-slick rock. Rocketing toward him, the fireball ate through the darkness, streaking like a comet with a furious tail. Muscle gripped his bones, and Lothair held his breath, timing it to perfection. An instant before the lethal mix of fire and toxic gas struck, he tucked his wings. Gravity took hold. He fell like a stone between the cliff faces. Fire hammered the mountainside. Granite exploded, raining down like shrapnel, rock mixing with rainfall. Like a wild animal, the jagged ground approached with a snarl.

Ten feet from contact, the air crackled, rattled the spikes along his spine.

A growl locked in his throat, Lothair shifted into human form, cloaking himself with an invisibility shield as he plummeted. A tug. A rough pull and…

Bam!

Magic grabbed hold and dragged him sideways. He hit the energy shield protecting their lair at maximum velocity. The barrier expanded then contracted, rippling like water before snapping like a rubber band. He catapulted into a cave, into a face full of dark, damp, and musty.

With a curse, he tucked into a ball and rolled. Sticks, stones, old bit of bones scratched at his skin. Lothair didn't care. The only thing that mattered lay outside…in the rain, hunting for any sign of him. Had they seen his freefall turned rescue? Had they detected the crack of magic in the air? Derr`mo, he hoped not. The storm played on his team tonight, an ally throwing out electricity like a whore gave out blow jobs.

So…yeah. Fingers crossed. Maybe he'd gotten lucky.

Heart thumping, Lothair landed in a crouch. Balanced on the balls of his feet, his eyes narrowed on the mouth of the hidden cave. Breathing hard, he waited, struggling to hear through the blood rush as he listened for sounds of pursuit: the scrape of claws against stone, the hiss of an exhale, and growl of dragons.

Foolish, he knew. The energy shield was solid. Not even the Nightfuries could break through it. At least not for a while. And he needed less time than that.

Sure, the bastards would eventually figure it out. But they'd spend the rest of the night scratching their heads, hemming and hawing before hammering their way into the lair. By then, he'd be long gone. Along with the female captives.

"Surprise, surprise, motherfuckers," he murmured, the chill in the air raising goosebumps on his bare skin. Still he watched the entrance, counting off the seconds. When he got to thirty, he relaxed and conjured his clothes. The idiots didn't have a clue. His mouth curved. Nightfury losers. "Have fun trying to find me."

His footfalls soundless in the gloom, he pivoted and strode toward the back of the cave. Skirting tall stalagmites, he approached the rear wall, reached out, and, curling his fingers around a small stone ledge, pressed down. The lever clicked. Metal shifted, the clink and grind sounding loud in the silence as granite slid sideways, uncovering a steel door.

With a flick, Lothair opened the keypad and punched in his code. Another series of locks. More clicking, and he was over the threshold. He hit the stairs running, his boots rapping against steel treads as he slammed the door and reengaged the electronic locks with his mind.

Down. Down. Down. The circular staircase went on forever, taking him into the bowels of the earth, closer to the underground lair. When he reached the bottom, he checked in with his comrade. *"Denzeil…where you at?"*

"On the move," the male said, sounding out of breath. *"Females in tow."*

"Keep it tight. I'll meet you in the garage."

"How soon?"

Lothair sprinted past the old clinic. *"A minute and a half."*

A female screamed, her terror coming through mind-speak loud and clear.

Denzeil grunted. The crack of knuckles sounded against flesh. A female voice begged for mercy in the background as Denzeil asked, *"Nightfuries?"*

"Clueless, but not for long." Lothair's lips curved, reluctant admiration for his friend's methods growing with each female sob. *"Get your ass in gear."*

"Ten-four."

Ten-four. Lothair fought an eye roll. Denzeil's trucker lingo drove him bat-shit crazy. The male might as well have said, *Breaker, breaker-one-nine, good buddy.* He shook his head, wind whistling in his ears, pace NASCAR fast. The male watched way too many reruns of *Dukes of Hazzard.* Still, terrible taste aside, Denzeil was useful most of the time, solid in the heart, if not always in the head. So, yeah. Guess he was living with the eighteen-wheeler crap.

Uneven concrete crumbling beneath his boots, Lothair skidded around the last bend. Boxes lay strewn in all directions: up against walls, in the middle of the corridor, stacked three high in some places. And in between them? A pool of congealed plasma and blood-spattered walls…his parting gift from the she-cop.

A whole lot of *get even* banged around inside his head.

Lothair pushed it aside. He needed to keep his head screwed on straight and stay focused on the exit strategy. But later? New plans would be made with payback in mind.

With a swallowed curse, he put the memory away and ran past the mess, leaping over an overturned box as he headed for a set of double doors at the end of the hallway. He hammered the wooden panels, punching through into the garage. Just in time too. The party had started without him.

Slowing to a jog, he watched Denzeil toss the second female into the trunk of a rusty Oldsmobile and slam the lid closed. The bang echoed in the large cavern, bouncing off the domed ceiling and smooth stone walls. It pissed him off. Angela should be there, crammed in with the others, coming along for the ride as his personal pet.

Fucking female.

Somehow, some way, he'd hunt her down. And when he did? No more Mr. Nice Guy. High-energy female—ideal for the breeding program—or not, he didn't care. Ivar and his order could go to hell this time around. The second he got his hands on the she-cop, he'd rip her heart out. Watch it beat in his palm as he raised it high. Like a trophy. Like the conqueror he was and always would be.

Chapter Eleven

Sitting in the backseat of a cab, Tania Solares rubbed the bridge of her nose, wondering what the hell had happened. The last thing she remembered had something to do with plants, a watering can, and a box full of Miracle-Gro. Not surprising, really. As a landscape architect, her job required all three, but not at…

She pushed the sleeve of her sweater above her wrist. No watch. Huh. She could've sworn she'd buckled up the faux snakeskin band before she left home, but boy, her brain was fried. And she felt frazzled, like she needed to hurry up for no apparent reason.

With a frown, she glanced out the side window. Rain streaked the glass, running in rivulets as thunder boomed overhead. Another storm. Another day in Seattle. As the tires splashed through puddles, washing waves of dirty water over the street curb, she watched storefronts flash past, neon signs blurred by rainfall. She shook her head. What the heck was going on? No way she should be riding around in the back of a taxicab so early in the morning.

Raising her hands, she rubbed the grit from her eyes. Clue number…she paused (well, she didn't know what number, but they were piling up and she could take a hint). Okay, so she was sleepy, like she usually was when she got out of bed each morning. But as far as she could tell, the sun had just come up, so…

Leaning forward, Tania rapped on the partition between her and the driver. "Excuse me?"

Tired brown eyes met hers in the rearview mirror. "Huh?"

"Can you tell me what time it is?"

"Ah, sure." Deep wrinkles got deeper as he squinted at the clock embedded in the dashboard. "Six-seventeen, miss."

Tania nodded her thanks and sat back. Six-seventeen a.m. Yikes, she was done for…already scrambled and the day had barely begun. Not a good sign. Particularly when her meeting with the bigwigs was scheduled for later this morning. Well, all right. At least she remembered *that*, but the lost hours worried her. No surprise there. She was always kind of worried, but the missing memory bugged her more than the usual stuff. She could almost touch it. Could see the hole with her mind's eye, but couldn't fill in the blanks.

Closing her eyes, she leaned back against the headrest. God. What was her problem? A brain tumor? Early-onset Alzheimer's? Okay, now she was just being a jerk. Twenty-eight was too young to be losing her mind, but really, what else could a girl do after experiencing…

What, exactly?

The question gave her a headache. As the thump-thump-throb caught rhythm, banging like a drum on her temples, she grabbed her handbag and plopped it into her lap. The monstrosity took up all the real estate, sagging over the tops of her tights as she rooted around inside. Finding a bottle of Advil, she popped the cap and downed two, hoping for some relief because she sure as heck wasn't getting any answers.

Why…why…why?

The continuous question circled, chasing its tail, making her hate the word all over again. She had every right. Her life was nothing but one big string of *whys*. The most recent casualty was Myst. Her best friend was missing. Taken. Murdered. Goddamn it, she didn't know what had happened. And guess what? Neither did anyone else…cops included.

Her throat grew tight as she thought of her best friend. The situation pushed past strange into downright frightening. Something bad had gone down at Caroline Van Owen's.

Chewing on the inside of her lip, Tania stared out the window, hands strangling her handbag as her imagination went wild. Maybe the pregnant girl's abusive boyfriend had come home. Maybe Myst had gotten caught in the crossfire. Maybe a flat tire had taken her off the beaten path on the way home and a serial killer had—

"Stop it," she whispered, staring at her reflection in the window glass. "Get a grip, you big scaredy-cat."

She tried. She really did, but…God. She was driving herself crazy, imagining all sorts of awful scenarios. Ones that involved chainsaws and wood chippers. And the cops on the case? Big jerks. Okay, that wasn't fair. Detective Keen was cool. Tough, sure, but as compassionate as they came. Her partner, though?

Frigging Detective MacCord.

The guy rattled her cage. For a plethora of reasons. None of which she liked, never mind wanted to admit. He tempted her to a dangerous degree, and not just because of the way he wore a pair of Sevens. All right, so she enjoyed looking at him, butt-gloving jeans and all. The man was gorgeous, and no one could fault a girl for noticing. No harm, no foul, right?

Tania nodded. Right. And had that been the end of it—just a healthy girl admiring a beautiful man—no problem.

But her attraction to him went beyond the physical. Something about him drew her. His vibe, maybe. Intangible. Confusing. Strange. Call it whatever you wanted, but he possessed that extra special *something* in spades. And foolish or not, she wanted to believe him when he told her not to worry...that he'd untangle the mess and bring Myst home.

Which burned her butt.

Twenty-first century women didn't rely on he-men with aquamarine eyes and a body that never said quit to solve their problems. A shame on so many levels. She liked the idea of leaning on him, of those strong arms around her. He would feel good and...

Holy crap. The whole attraction thing with MacCord needed to die a fast, horrific death. Along with her fantasies. God. Her imagination was so lit up, she swore she could taste him. Feel the softness of his dark hair between her fingers. Smell him on her skin. Hear his voice as he whispered her name, driving desire way past need into *must-have* territory.

Heat and pleasure. Pure and simple.

Oh, boy, she needed to get a grip. Especially since she planned a sneak attack later this afternoon. The detective needed a fire lit under him, and she was just the girl to strike the match. First things first, though, she needed a shower. Or maybe a swim. Thinking of MacCord made her sweat, which made her realize she wasn't just watchless, but sticky too: cotton T-shirt plastered against her back, damp tendrils of hair stuck to the nape of her neck.

Tania combed her hands through the rat's nest on her head. Jeez, what a catastrophe. What had she been doing? Running the Seattle marathon? Blowing out a breath, she rooted through her bag, found an elastic, and swept the entire mess into a ponytail before tapping the glass again. The taxi driver's head swiveled, one eyebrow raised. He nodded as she gave him the new address. The YMCA.

Yup, definitely. The gym and its Olympic-sized pool was the best bet.

She needed to stretch her stiff muscles and calm down before she headed to the police station for round two with Detective MacCord. Her lips curved as his face surfaced in her mind. It would be good to see him again. Especially if it meant upending his unhelpful butt. She wanted answers and her best friend found, so…

MacCord would just have to suck it up as she put the screws to him.

Chapter Twelve

Grabbing a chair from beneath the table edge, Rikar dragged it behind him as he crossed the recovery room. The metal feet bumped across the hospital-grade floor, protesting the rough treatment. Not that he cared. The pathetic excuse for a chair could squawk all it wanted. In the end, it was going right where he put it. Beside Angela's bedside.

He set the thing down with a thunk, then dropped into the plastic seat.

And groaned. Talk about uncomfortable.

He shifted, trying out different positions. Why? No freaking clue. Comfort wasn't in the cards. Sleep either. At least for the foreseeable future. But, man, he needed it. The past twenty-four hours were a blur, and he was whipped, in need of his own bed, a shitload of Zs, and yeah, something else too.

Food. Dragonkind style.

Rikar scrubbed his hand over the top of his head, fighting the hunger. No way could he feed now. Not with his frosty side on guard duty. Even without the daylight complication, his dragon wouldn't let him leave the lair. The territorial SOB had nailed his ass to the chair, keeping him chained in the recovery room. So forget about finding a female and tapping into the Meridian to get what he needed. The whole thing was a no-go. Especially since the only female he wanted lay curled on her side less than an arm's length away.

His gaze flicked over her. His chest tightened another notch. She looked so small in the king-size bed: blankets pulled to her chin, IV plugged into the back of her hand, dark lashes lying against her pale cheeks. He frowned, worrying about her lack of color, her stillness, if she needed another blanket, or maybe she was too warm…

Christ, his list went on ad infinitum. Not that he could help it. Bonded males were like that. Concern for their females came naturally, and after what Angela had been through, the needle on his worry dial was buried in the red zone.

Planting his elbows on his knees, he leaned forward, listening to the beep of the heart rate monitor, clinging to the steady beat like a lifeline. God, he'd almost lost her. It had been close out there. Way too close. Had he arrived an instant later…not left Myst's loft the second night fell, she'd be—

Rikar shook his head. No need to think about it.

But even as he told himself to leave it alone, his mind laid out possible outcomes like flash cards. As he pictured each one, he shuffled on the chair, wanting to get up and go hunting. To carve the Razorback into little pieces and watch him bleed out. He watched Angela instead, breathed with her, willing her chest to rise and fall even as his heart ached for her. For the moment she woke up and discovered the life she knew was over. No more police precinct. No more homicide division. Good-bye, normal. Hello, strange new world.

His brows collided as he laced his fingers between the spread of his knees. Maybe she knew already. Maybe, on some level—deep down in the place called female intuition—she understood what capture by the Razorbacks meant…that she was no longer safe in the human world.

Wishful thinking? Probably.

He wanted her acceptance: of him, her new life, all of it. And right now, fooling himself into believing she wouldn't fight the transition was fantastic fiction. The fantasy chilled him out, relaxing his frosty side, and as his tension eased, the headache hammering his temples moved to the back of his head.

With a sigh, Rikar dipped his chin, pulling on the stiff muscles bracketing his spine. As the knots released, slipping loose one by one, he groaned. Hmm, that felt good. Maybe a full-on stretch session was in order. Although, no way he'd follow Venom's example and hit the yoga mat. Screw the *hatha* shit. Wrapped knuckles and hitting the heavy bag was more his style. Still, a little Zen in his morning couldn't hurt, so—

"No!"

The sharp denial—half scream, half rasp—brought Rikar's head up. His gaze caught on Angela's face, and he lost his ability to breathe for a moment. Fine brows furrowed, she flinched, fists balled and legs churning beneath the sheet as she cried out in her sleep. A nightmare. After what she'd been through, he'd expected it, but the reality was far worse. Watching her fight an imaginary foe gutted him, and as he shoved the chair back and stood, he wasn't sure what to do. Wake her? Restrain her?

He shook his head. Holding her down wasn't a good idea. Lothair had done that and…fuck him. He refused to do the same.

"Angela…shh, baby," he said, hoping to soothe her. God, he wanted to touch her so badly, but instinct told him to keep his distance. At least for now. "It's all right. You're safe…you're safe now."

"My gun," she rasped, eyes moving rapid-fire behind her lids as she fought imaginary monsters. "Where's my…I need it…he's gonna—"

"No, angel. I'm right here." Rikar struggled to keep his voice even, but it was hard. He wanted to let loose, give voice to his pain, and put his fist through the nearest wall. But Angela didn't need his rage. Not now. What she needed was comfort and soothing, both of which he could provide…as long as he kept his frickin' head screwed on straight. "He can't get you. I won't let him. You're safe."

Her breath shivered in and out, the harsh sound one of fear and—

Fuck it. He reached out, her hitching sobs tearing him apart. Moving slowly, keeping it soft, he cupped her cheek. She went still a second, then turned her head, pressing her face into his palm. His breath caught as she nestled in, seeking more of his touch. He gave it to her, sliding one hand to her nape while he caressed her temple with his fingertips. "That's right, angel. Settle down. You're all right."

Her brows furrowed. "I want my Glock."

Her words came out slurred, and Rikar's lips curved. Christ, he couldn't help it. Relief had him by the balls. Respect for her had him by the heart. Anyone else would've said, *I want my Mommy.* But oh, no. Not his angel. Even pumped full of painkillers and gripped by nightmares, she was strong. Ready to defend herself from all comers. And in that instant, he decided. His magic flared as he conjured a Glock 19, standard police issue.

Still cupping her nape, he put the gun in her hand. “Here, love.”

She jerked as the cold metal hit her palm, then hummed and settled, curling onto her side, hugging his forearm to her chest like she needed both him and the weapon close. Which choked him up.

And there he went again…falling into pansy mode.

Shaking his head, Rikar gave himself a mental kick as footfalls echoed out in the corridor. Time to pull it together. One of his brothers was seconds away and—

The door handle cranked down.

He tried to untangle himself from Angela. With a whimper, she tightened her hold, fingers flexing on the gun, her arms around one of his, and Rikar dropped the tough guy act like a hot potato. Who the fuck cared what anyone else thought? He could handle the teasing, all the jokes about being whipped, wearing a leash…whatever. His female needed him, so yeah, his boys could go straight to hell.

He sat down on the edge of the bed. She snuggled against him, pressing her face up against the side of his thigh. Murmuring to her, he stroked his hand over her hair, listened to her steady breaths as she fell into a deep sleep.

Steel hinges sighed a second before the door swung wide. Sloan crossed the threshold, tray in hand, the smell of scrambled eggs rolling with him and…oh, hell yeah, cinnamon and brown sugar. His favorite. Bless Daimler. The Numbai knew how to “caretake” like nobody’s business.

Seeing his interest, Sloan grinned, white teeth flashing against mocha skin. “Hungry?”

Rikar stroked Angela’s hair again. As his fingers played in the short strands, he held his buddy’s gaze, daring him to comment about the cozy arrangement. “Whatcha got?”

Sloan snorted. "You know what I got. You're practically salivating over there."

Cinnamon toast. Mmm, mmm good.

Sliding the tray onto the small round table between the cabinetry banking the far wall and the bed, Sloan tipped his chin. "You want it over there?"

"Yeah. Bring the table." With a gentle twist, Rikar freed his arm, sliding it out of Angela's grip. She frowned, making a sound of protest. Which, of course, squeezed his heart so hard he gave her his left hand to hold before she stirred from the healing sleep. "I'm one paw short at the moment."

"I can see that," his buddy said.

His hand drifted over the nape of his Angela's neck, touching her soft skin, combing through her red hair. And Rikar waited…for the derogatory comment, for the warrior's derisive tone, for his reputation as a hard-ass to be challenged. But Sloan didn't say a word. Just kicked the other chair out of the way, picked up the table—tray and all—and walked the entire mess over. Rikar blinked, his eyes burning like a house on fire, his throat so tight he found it hard to swallow.

Christ. He hadn't expected that, but…man, straight up? Sloan was the poster boy for a worthy male, looking after him when most would've teased him about his need to stay with Angela.

Fine china clinked and utensils rattled as the table got set down with a thunk. Sloan whipped off the cover, and Rikar nearly melted into a puddle of gratefulness. He dug in instead, picking up a piece of cinnamon toast, shoving half of it in his mouth as he murmured a heartfelt thanks.

Sloan's big mitt landed on his shoulder, then gave him a squeeze. "How's she doing?"

"Better," he said around a mouthful. Polishing off the last of the toast, Rikar chugged chocolate milk to wash it down. When he saw the bottom of the glass, he picked up the fork and went at the eggs. Hmm…protein in a scrambled mess. Nothing better. "It'll take a while, but she'll heal."

Propped against the wall next to the bed, Sloan's gaze flicked to the gun in Angela's hand, then came back to him. He raised a dark brow. "You think that's a good idea?"

"It isn't loaded," he said, shrugging off his friend's concern. "She needs it to feel safe."

"The gun isn't doing that…you are." Lightning quick, his buddy leaned forward and snagged a piece of bacon off his plate. "You fed her, didn't you?"

The fork halfway to his mouth, Rikar paused. How much should he admit? All of it? None? The whole Bastian and Myst thing hadn't surprised anyone. B had been looking to hook up and sire a son. But with his frosty side in perpetual "fuck you" mode, no one expected him to ever feel for a female this strongly.

Silver clinked against the plate as he put his fork down. "Got a problem with that?"

"Not even a little one." One corner of Sloan's mouth turned up, like the bastard knew what he was thinking, and Rikar had the sudden urge to pop him one. "But if you have, you need to get into bed with her. Enough of the hand-holding shit."

Christ, there Sloan went again, smacking him in the face with the unexpected. *Get into bed with her.* Had the male gone freaking insane? No way Angela would want him curled up next to her. Not after what she'd endured, so yeah…

"Not a good idea."

"You want her to heal fast?" Sloan held his gaze, dark eyes dead serious. It was a challenge, pure and simple. "Ditch the leathers and get in. She'll relax deeper into the healing sleep with full body contact. And fuck, man. You're wiped. You need to sleep too."

Rikar's gaze strayed to Angela. He traced the outside curve of her ear with his fingertip, temptation circling like a son of a bitch. It would feel so good to slide in beside her…to pretend she belonged to him as he held her. If only for a little while. But that was just plain selfish. What he needed shouldn't matter. His dragon half, though, wanted what it *wanted.* And as the beast stirred, male need and territorial instinct mixed into a volatile cocktail. Rikar shifted on the mattress, aching to have her in his arms.

Wrong. It was so fucking wrong.

He rolled his shoulders, suddenly feeling like his skin was three sizes too small. "I don't think—"

"Then don't," Sloan said, pushing away from the wall. "Think of the benefits for her instead." His buddy's shit-kickers thudded softly, joining the beep of the heart rate monitor as he rounded the end of the bed. Grabbing the blankets, Sloan flipped them back, pouring more gasoline on Rikar's fire. "You settle in with her…share your energy? And she'll have less of a scar. Maybe nothing at all. All those bruises and cuts, buddy? Gone. And that's just for starters."

A little desperate now, Rikar shook his head. "She won't like waking up with me."

"She won't get the rest she needs if she doesn't." Holding his ground, Sloan rammed his point home with a verbal hammer. "She needs you with her."

"Fuck…" Rikar ran his hand over his skull-trim. Rubbing his nape, he stared at the smooth expanse of mattress Sloan had exposed beside his female. Exhaling hard, he stood and shrugged out of his leather jacket. "You're an asshole."

His buddy huffed, catching the leather load Rikar tossed at him. "Takes one to know one."

Didn't it always, Rikar thought as he ditched the rest of his clothes and slid in next to Angela.

Mac came awake with a suddenness that startled him. The stiffness hit him next and, as his cramped muscles screamed for release, he cracked an eye open. The brick wall wavered into focus. Next? All the upended furniture jammed beneath tall, arching windows. Three of them, black glass rippling in waves, like the surface of a lake.

Hmm, yeah. Water.

He could do with a little splash action right now. A steady front crawl across the marina would straighten him out. Well, either that or a chiropractor. Goddamn, what had he been doing all day…an excellent imitation of a pretzel?

With a groan, he closed his eyes and rolled his shoulders. First one, and then the other. His bones clicked in their sockets, protesting where sore muscles left off, aching like a son of a bitch. And God, his head hurt too. Pain thumped his temples, then slid around to hammer the back of his skull. Mac clenched his teeth on another moan. Sound wasn't a good idea right now. Not with his body one big throb of pain.

What had he been thinking? The feeling—and the morning-after regret that came with it—was all too familiar…tequila. Most likely an entire bottleful of Patrón. Although, why the hell he'd been hitting the good stuff was anyone's guess. Drinking to excess and blackouts weren't his usual MO. At least not anymore.

Mac shook his head, instantly regretting it as the hammering got worse, but something was way, way off. None of what he felt made sense. He hadn't been drinking. Mac frowned. Had he?

As the accusation circled, he tried to remember. Tidbits came at him, flipping into place inside his head. He labeled each one like evidence at a crime scene, retracing his steps. Last thing he remembered he'd been—

Jesus fucking Christ.

Angela.

Mac's head came up. Something rattled with his movement, and his focus snapped toward the windows. A blurry outline took shape. Mother of God. A dragon. Blue-gray scales glimmering in the low light, the thing stared back at him: unblinking, unmoving, its stare holding his. He went stone-still, not wanting to spook it. The horned head froze too, like it was waiting for his next move or—

Wait a second.

He blinked. The beast blinked back, aquamarine eyes fixed on him. He turned his head a little to the left. Yup, the dragon followed, mirroring each movement. As a load of WTF got rolling, Mac breathed faster, air sawing in and out of his lungs. The scaled chest rose and fell with his, the clickety-click of scales sounding loud in the silence.

Uh-uh. No way. His brows collided. That couldn't be him. It *couldn't* be, but—

The dragon's eyes were the same color as his, and a memory was chasing its tail inside his head. Leading the recall parade? A deep voice talking to him, echoing inside his head, helping him change into—

Holy shit. He was a dragon.

A sound of distress left his throat. The whimper sounded raw, on the edge of fear, but Mac didn't care. The weak-ass reaction could go to hell. Something bad had happened, and now, he was in monster territory. Not a big problem on a normal day. He dealt with the human variety all the time, but...

God help him.

He scrambled backward, away from the reflection. The scrape of claws on wood floors bounced around, echoing off brick walls, making the black glass swell and ripple. The clatter made him look down. He flexed his hand. A huge talon responded, curling and releasing on command. Jesus Christ. *That* didn't belong to him. It couldn't, but as he spread his fingers and stared at the webbing between the claws, he knew denial wasn't an option. He wasn't dreaming. The blue-gray dragon was not only real, he was *it*. It was *him*. One and the frickin' same.

His breath came faster. Twin tendrils of steam rose from his nostrils, freaking him out as viselike pressure roped his rib cage. One crank at a time, the band tightened until he couldn't breathe and the walls closed in. Claustrophobia lit him up, warning him to get the hell out before he got buried alive. His gaze swung to the patio doors on the other side of the loft. Could he make it? Would he fit through them like—

"It's all right, buddy." Hushed and even, the voice came from out of the shadows. Mac latched onto it as panic spun him around the lip of insanity. The sucking whirlpool tunneled his vision, narrowing his world until he couldn't see anything but blur. "Easy. You're all right."

"Out," he rasped, not recognizing his own voice. He sounded like a monster, all growl and hiss, nothing like his normal self. Pressed up against the back wall, he shook his head, and sensation tingled, slid across his temples, then up to surround the horns on…Jesus. The things were growing out of *his* skull. "I need…out."

"I hear ya, but not yet," the voice said, sounding a lot closer. "Hang tight, buddy…let me explain. We'll get you straightened out."

"Can't wait." Seeing spots now, a second away from hyperventilating, Mac clung to the only thing that mattered. Kept his sanity by focusing on Angela. As always, she helped ground him, driving the "holy shit" reaction to the back of his mind. He needed to find her…to make sure she was safe. "Ange…my partner…she's in trouble and—"

"Not anymore." Shadows morphed into the outline of a man. Raising his hands, the guy turned his palms up, a gesture meant to reassure. But it was the eyes Mac focused on. The shimmering green felt like a lifeline and, as he grabbed hold, the guy said, "Rikar's got her. She's safe, Mac."

Mac's brows collided. *Rikar.* He knew that name. Remembered the voice and the patience. The kindness over the hours he'd spent in hell. And God…right this minute? Big sissy or not, he needed to hear it again.

"Where is he?"

"With Angela. Protecting her…making sure she's okay."

Relief rolled through him. Which was just plain stupid. He didn't know this guy. Didn't trust him, but his cop instincts were squawking again, telling him that despite the blurry eyesight and the fucked-up situation, the guy was solid—for real in a trustworthy kind of way—and Mac wanted to believe him.

Claws clicked as he set his foot back down on the floor. "Where?"

"At Black Diamond…our lair." A little closer now, the voice came at him like a sidewinder through the blur. "It's solid, Mac. Our enemies can't track her there."

"Let's go," he said, needing more than reassurance. No way he would believe it until he saw her for himself. Add that to the bonus of getting the hell out of the loft's confining space, and yup, it was win-win all the way around. "I want to see her…to make sure."

"Sun's coming up, big guy."

Mac frowned, a big "so what?" rolling around inside his head.

Like a mind reader, the guy murmured, "One thing you need to know about our kind, Mac. We don't tolerate sunlight. You go out now? You'll get fried."

"Shit." Guess now he knew why he didn't sleep much. He'd always been that way, staying up all night, falling into bed when morning lit to catch a few Zs. It explained a lot, actually, and as the puzzle piece clicked into place, his brain came back online. Along with the mental focus, his vision evened out. He studied the guy standing in front of him. Dark hair. Green eyes. With the intensity of a lightning strike and the muscle to back it up, he looked human enough, but…yeah, not quite. "You're Bastian. Rikar's commander."

"Good…you remember." Dropping his hands, Bastian nodded, like he approved. "The change is an ass-kicker. Most Dragonkind males come out of it blank even when they know what's coming…even if they've been trained beforehand."

Dragonkind males. The words gave him pause. Why? He didn't know exactly because sure as shit, he was one of them. Frowning, he flexed his talon again, then glanced down and got a load of…good God, look at that thing. A tail, tricked out with razor-sharp edges: top, bottom, around the tip. Trying not to flip out, he curled the length around his paws, took a harder look. Wow. It looked lethal, and if it hadn't freaked him out, he might've thought it was cool.

Awe rose along with disbelief. He glanced at Bastian. "How…I mean…Jesus fucking Christ. I'm thirty-four. How could I not have known I'm not…"

"Human?"

His throat went tight as Mac nodded.

"You are…half human. Born of a human female and a Dragonkind male." Stepping up close, Bastian rapped his knuckles against his shoulder. High-pitched sound pinged, echoing as though he'd just struck steel instead of his fancy new skin. "I don't know how you were missed, but your sire didn't know about you. No way he would've left you in the human world if he'd known you existed."

The old hurt surfaced. It always did when he thought of his father, a man he'd never met…who'd never claimed him. Rescued him from a world where no one gave a damn what happened to him. But the idea that the man he'd dreamed of meeting hadn't abandoned him after all? Jesus, the knowledge filled the void, the empty corner of his heart where hurt had lived for so long.

Maybe it was bullshit. Maybe it wasn't. Mac didn't care. He liked the new version better than the one he'd lived with his entire life. His mother dead on a hospital operating table. No family to claim him. All the years spent at Sacred Heart Orphanage.

Home sweet fucking home.

"I know it doesn't make sense to you right now, but had your sire known…" Bastian trailed off, and the pause spoke volumes. The guy understood exactly what he felt. What he relived day after day. All the pain he buried deep, trying to forget. "He would've come for you."

Tears burned the back of his throat. Goddamn it. He'd turned into a frickin' sissy, drawing comfort from a man he didn't know. But Bastian provided it without hesitation. No doubt about it. The guy was tight in the head, solid in the heart, and man, if he didn't pull it together in the next three seconds, they'd break into a bawling rendition of "Kumbaya." Sniffle-sniffle-sob-sob.

Mac cleared his throat. "Look, I'm—"

A tingle swept the back of his neck, rattling the razor blade along his spine. Mac tensed, his spidey sense putting him on high alert. As he watched and waited, a shadow flew in, landing on the balcony beyond the patio door.

What the hell was that? He thought they were alone, but more had joined the party. Now all he sensed was anger. His eyes narrowed. Yup, definitely. A load of pissed off was coming down the pipe in his direction. Shifting right, he stepped around Bastian and into a crouch. Getting low seemed like the thing to do…the best bet when under attack.

With a muttered "fuck," Bastian slapped a palm to his chest. "Ease up, my man. Nothing doing."

Bullshit. Something was definitely "doing."

The patio door slid open. Light exploded through the opening, blinding Mac. With a curse, he squinted, trying to get a read on what was coming at him. A no-go. All he could see was a bright band of sunlight on the horizon. Frickin' eyes. Stupid daylight. Like he needed an eyeful of spots right now?

Bastian pivoted, planting himself between him and the door. "Anything?"

A dark silhouette crossed the threshold, shook its head. "Lothair went to ground…found a wormhole or something. And we ran out of time."

"Fucking rogue." With a growl, the second guy walked into the loft behind the first. The lock clicked as the glass slid closed behind him, shutting out the sun. Thank God. Now all Mac needed to do was clear the dots floating in front of his eyes. As he blinked rapid-fire, guy number two said, "We'll find him come nightfall. Send his balls back to Ivar in a basket."

Surprise lit across Bastian's face. "Good to know, Wick."

"Jeez, man," the blond guy said, staring at his buddy. "More than three words strung together…what's up with you?"

Black hair glinting blue in the dimness, Wick flipped his friend the bird.

"Oookkay…back to normal on the no-talking front." The blond grinned. "I'm relieved."

Silence met the pronouncement. A pause followed, like everyone was readjusting, and as the quiet pounded through the loft, the vibe shifted. Mac went on high alert and got ready. For anything, because whoever had linked *peace* with *quiet* had been out of their minds.

"Looky-looky, Wick." Decked out in leather, the blond guy slowed his roll beside the kitchen island, red eyes narrowed on him. "Blockhead's up."

The name-calling flipped a switch in Mac's brain. Oh yeah…Dickhead (aka Venom). The one he didn't like. Mac growled as Dickhead planted his hands on the countertop, jackknifed into a turn, and ass-planted himself on the island top. Shitkickers dangling in midair, the guy grinned at him, baring his teeth in blatant challenge. Mac snarled back, wishing for a fist instead of claws so he could pop the SOB again.

"Venom," Bastian said, planting a hand on Mac's chest. He pushed against his scales, sending a clear message that said, *Stay where you are, buddy, or else.* "Back off. We don't need that shit right now."

"What…like I need to worry?" He swung his legs, boots flashing black in the gloom. Funny thing, though? Now that the dots had cleared, Mac saw everything with perfect clarity: the individual threads of the bastard's bootlaces, each stitch sewn into the leather, the smirk on Venom's face as he looked him over. "Hell, I could eat the pissant fledgling for lunch in human form and not need a toothpick."

Bastian growled, the sound one of warning.

Mac bared his fancy new fangs, his mind supplying more links in his memory chain. Each one rattled his cage, filling his brain like water pouring into a jar. Something about a woman. The bastard had tried to touch the one that belonged to him.

Rage flexed its muscles and, as Venom laughed, Mac lost control and hissed. Something nasty shot from his throat. As he choked on the bad taste, Dickhead cursed, ducking as slimy liquid sprayed the wall behind him. Brick exploded. Small chunks went airborne, flying up and out with a sizzling pop. Mac blinked. Holy shit. Despite the disgusting aftertaste, that was cool. The slime was eating through the masonry and burning holes in the wooden floorboards.

"Awesome. Did you see that, B?" Venom sat up and glanced over his shoulder. "Wick, come look at this shit."

A look of delight on his face, Wick jogged over as the crackle-n-pop of whatever had come out of Mac's throat got louder. A little horrified, but mostly intrigued, Mac craned his neck to get a better view of his handiwork.

Sliding to a stop, Wick inspected the damage. "Cool. Water-acid."

"Wicked lethal."

Leaning in, Wick smelled the slime. "I think it's flammable, too."

"Gonna have to test that theory." Hopping off the counter, Venom nudged a chunk of brick with the toe of his boot. "Take the new boy out for a spin—"

"Or two," Wick said, finishing his buddy's sentence. With one last whiff, Wick glanced at Mac with golden eyes full of speculation. "That's gonna be fun. Big damage."

"Huge." Venom retracted his foot before the slime—water-acid…whatever—ate through the sole of his boot.

Mac's brows collided as instincts hopped on his it'll-be-a-cold-day-in-hell bandwagon. No way he wanted to go anywhere with those two. Venom couldn't wait to kill him. And Wick? Jesus, the guy's eyes told the story. Flat. Cold. Hard. He possessed all the warmth of a frickin' psychopath.

He glanced at Bastian. "What the fuck?"

"You'll get used to them," he said, thumping Mac's chest with a closed fist. "For now…ignore them. We've got a lot of work to do before sunset."

Mac frowned, alarm bells clanging inside his head.

Bastian grinned. "You need to learn a few things."

"Like what?"

"How to shift form…from dragon to human and back again."

"I can do that?" His breath caught. The first glimmer of excitement ghosted down his spine. Shifting forms sounded cool. At least then he'd feel normal…more like himself, less like a monster.

"We all can," Venom said, ass connecting with the countertop again. "Just wait until the flying lessons begin. Big fun, then."

"Huge," Wick murmured, eyes fixed on Mac as he headed across the loft. Pivoting into an about-face, he planted his shoulders flat on the wall between two high windows.

Torn between wanting to know more and mistrust, Mac's gaze ping-ponged, moving from Venom to Wick, then back again. Were they serious? He rolled his shoulders, glanced at the wings attached to his new body. He flapped them without unfolding the suckers. Not enough room in the loft for—

Wow. Okay…now *that* was cool.

The webbing stretched, giving him a sense of his wingspan, and…bam. It hit him. The things worked. Totally nuts, but weirder than that was the realization he might actually be able to fly.

His heart rebounded inside his chest. All right, then. Guess they weren't kidding, but that didn't mean he would give the SOBs the "fun" they so obviously anticipated.

Holding Venom's gaze, he tossed the challenge back in his face. "Game on, dickhead."

"We'll see, fledgling," Venom said, ruby-red eyes gleaming.

Yes, they would.

Mac eyed Bastian. "Show me."

Let the games—er…lessons—begin.

Chapter Thirteen

Curled on her side in the center of the bed, Angela watched the second hand tick. Fifteen minutes. A whole nine hundred seconds spent awake and unmoving, feeling the steady rise and fall of Rikar's chest against her back. And as the wall clock completed its quarter turn, and she listened to him breathe, Angela decided she was an idiot. In total mental patient territory for clinging to Rikar in the dark. A guy she barely knew. Didn't trust. All while staring at the opposite wall, watching the stupid clock face glow above glossy white cabinets.

Tick-tock. Tick-tock. Time's a-wasting. And still, she couldn't make herself move.

It was sad, really. How much she needed him in the moment…in the quiet stillness that made her think too hard and feel too much. And as she nestled in, taking everything he unknowingly gave her while he slept, she didn't recognize herself. Wondered when she'd disappeared and a stranger had taken her place.

Needy.

She'd never been that before. Never once thought she needed anyone, but as the second hand continued its ticking and Rikar his breathing, Angela recognized lost when she saw it. The MIA? Her. She was the POW this go-around and, for the first time in a long while, she missed her dad. Mourned his death. Felt like a little girl again, more frightened than ever. *Lost.* Yeah, she really was…adrift in a place she didn't want to be or know how to navigate.

Fighting tears, she closed her eyes. She'd been so clueless. All those victims. All the one-on-ones with them: taking their statements, telling them not to worry, that everything would be all right. What a load of crap. Total BS disguised by an empathetic wrapper. Nothing was *all right* and wouldn't be for a while. The hurt simply ran too deep.

She turned her face into Rikar's arm. Sprawled on his back, one hand relaxed in the center of his bare chest, Rikar didn't react to her movement. Man, he probably didn't even know she was in bed with him. She lay in the V, the sweet spot where his arm met his body, her back up against his side, her cheek against his biceps, hugging one of his arms to her chest, fingers curled around the Glock 19. The finger grooves on the grip felt good in her hand. Felt familiar and right, and as she opened her eyes and checked the clock's progress, she said a silent thank-you.

She was alive. Hurt, sure…damaged inside and out, but still breathing. No small thanks to Rikar, the man-dragon sleeping like the dead against her.

Angela sighed. The whole *nonhuman* thing gave her the shivers. She should get up. Get out. Beat feet before he woke up and started asking questions. No doubt he would, but…

She didn't want to. Comfort wanted her to stay close to him. Compulsion demanded it. Both made good arguments. After all, what could it hurt? Nothing came back at her. A big goose egg from the counter-argument department. Her brain was fried. All the intellectual reasons had flown. Her inner turncoat was alive and well, dressing up bad ideas to look like good ones.

Not good. Especially considering she wanted her life back, to feel like her normal strong, tough, and unafraid self. A tall order? Probably, considering the damage to her internal compass. The dial was bent, spinning out of control, sending her in stupid directions…each one leading right back to Rikar.

God, had she said *mental patient*?

Angela blew out a long breath. No doubt about it. She was officially a guest in Insanityville. But even as she realized her peril, something inside her whispered, asking for more time. Argued that staying curled against Rikar was a temporary side trip, just an off-ramp on her emotional highway. She was in the driver's seat, after all, and with one turn of the wheel could drive back onto the road, put the pedal down, and leave him behind. Nothing but a memory on the faded tarmac of her mind.

The thought made her want to do something she almost never did…cry.

Which was beyond dumb.

He was part dragon, her enemy if there ever was one. The need to stay with him was dangerous. Ridiculous. Totally unhinged. She knew it. Felt the truth of it in her bones, but like it or not, her need for him tied her up, tethering her so well she couldn't pull out of his orbit.

Rikar's arm flexed under her cheek as he grumbled in his sleep. Angela went stone-still, praying he stayed asleep. She wasn't ready to face him yet. Needed more time to figure things out and decide where to go from here.

Luck, however, wasn't on her side. The clock was headed into twenty-five minute territory. It was now or never. Time to get up, get out, and get gone.

Swallowing the lump in her throat, Angela tightened her grip on the gun. Metal pressed into her palm as she turned a little, dislodging her shoulder from beneath Rikar's arm. The IV tugged, tape pulling across the back of her free hand, but she kept going, untangling them inch by slow inch. As her body left his, cool air rushed beneath her plain white tee, along the backs of both legs, under her boxer shorts, attacking all the places she'd pressed against him.

Tragic. The loss of contact was something to mourn, but not right now. This moment was meant for escape. For the stillness of being alone in a private place. She needed her head screwed on straight. And tucked against Rikar? Yeah, not an environment where any solid thinking would get done.

With a shimmy, she slid toward the side of the bed. The IV's tube knocked against the metal pole, the ping sounding loud in silence, and she expected pain. A truckload of *ow-ow-ows* after all the scrapes she sustained on her trip down the mountainside. When she got nothing but a twinge, she frowned at the bandage wrapped around her thigh. She remembered getting hit, the striking agony as something sharp sliced her, but…

Her leg felt okay now. Better than all right, actually. Like she'd healed up tight while she slept.

Continuing the shuffle-and-slide, she slipped her legs over the mattress edge and stared at her feet. Nothing. No cuts. No bruises. Just a yellow patch of skin on the top of her right foot where a tree branch had thumped her. Okay, that was disconcerting. So weird that—

"Not really. I put you on the accelerated healing plan."

The voice slid through the dark, gloving her spine. Sensation exploded into a tingle, and with a gasp, Angela spun around on the mattress. The overhead lights came on, flaring bright, making her blink. He shifted. She jumped like a jackrabbit. A second before she fell off the bed, she caught her balance and raised the gun. Sleepy blue eyes met hers, dipped to the Glock, then rose to meet hers again. His mouth kicked up at the corners, and she wanted to shoot him. Right between the eyes.

"Don't laugh at me." The warning in her tone—the strength of her voice, the steadiness of her hand—surprised her. Made her feel more like a cop, less like a victim. Good thing, too. The wounded Angela couldn't deal with Rikar, but the homicide detective? No contest. She'd eat him for breakfast. "Or I swear to God—"

"It isn't loaded, angel," he murmured, his deep voice full of gravel.

With a hand bob, she tested the Glock's weight. "Thought it felt a little light."

Turning onto his side, he propped his head on his hand. "Couldn't chance you shooting me in my sleep, now could I?"

"Smart of you," she said, eyeing him, resenting him for being so relaxed when she felt like jumping out of her skin.

Not that she would show it.

But man, she had a feeling Rikar wasn't fooled. Didn't care that she wanted to be left alone. All he saw was the gaping wound inside her. How did she know? She could see it in his eyes. The concern. The respect. The careful way he moved…slowly, like he didn't want to startle her.

Crap. And well, just…crap.

Trust Rikar to throw a monkey wrench into the whole operation. His worry screwed her up. Made her second-guess her plan, the escape route…the whole flipping thing. He shouldn't be part of the equation. He should be nothing but an obstacle that needed removing. But as she stared at him, and he met her gaze, lying wasn't an option. For some awful reason, his presence chilled her out, soothing her until she almost forgot to be afraid.

Which scared her beyond reason. She couldn't go there with him. Couldn't imagine ever trusting someone that way after all she'd been through.

Scrambling to shore up the crack in her defenses, she drilled him a look. Tightening her grip on the Glock, she said, "Of course, that doesn't mean I won't brain you with it."

"You could try." Like snowflakes in the sun, his eyes sparkled a second before he got serious and sat up. She flinched. He kept his distance. Bending one leg, he propped his forearm on his raised knee. "I'm not laughing at you, love. I'm just…relieved you're okay, that's all."

God, not even close. *Okay* wasn't in the cards. But holy hell, she couldn't deny that she appreciated the sentiment.

And there she went again…taking a trip into Insanityville.

"I…" She cleared her throat, struggling to unknot the tangled mess inside her. The pressure pushed down, made her chest tight and her heart hurt. But now that he was awake, she refused to leave without having her say. Or giving what she owed. Holding onto her tears, she whispered, "Thank you."

His blond brows popped skyward.

"You didn't have to come after me, and I—"

"Yes, I did…I so fucking did."

"I don't understand." Hugging the Glock to her chest, she shook her head. "Why?"

"I couldn't…Christ, no way I could leave you there." His voice hitched, and he looked away, as though he didn't want her to see his pain. But she did anyway: heard it in his tone, tasted his agony as he said, "I imagined so many things, awful things and…God, Angela. I'm so sorry…so fucking sorry. That I couldn't find you…that I didn't get there fast enough…that he hurt you and…fuck." His hands curled into fists and, all of a sudden, the temperature in the room dropped. Each breath turned into a frosty cloud and goosebumps rose on her arms as he growled, "The second I find that bastard? He's dead. I'll rip his fucking head off."

Tears blurred her vision. Angela blinked them away, tried to ignore his anguish, but God help her, she couldn't. She hated that he suffered…for her.

"Rikar, look at me."

Staring at the quilt, he shook his head.

"Please?"

His brows drawn tight, he lifted his chin, and she saw all of it: his guilt and pain, the need to turn back time. But that wasn't possible. Not for her. Not for him. The past couldn't be changed, and it surprised her to realize she didn't want to fight with him. Or make him pay for something that wasn't his fault.

"Look…what happened to m-me?" As her voice wobbled, Angela suppressed a shiver as the ugly memory surfaced.

She didn't want to think about it—not now, not ever—but that was one wish that would never come true. Emotional baggage never went away. It just got lighter over time, and only if you unpacked it, folded it up nice and neat, then put it away. Angela knew it. Had convinced victim after victim to get help, seek counseling—whatever they needed to feel whole again. "It's not your fault. I want you to let it go and—"

"I can't. Not until—"

"—if you're going after him, I want in," she said, cutting him off, surprising herself.

As Rikar blinked, her words echoed, banging around the recovery room. She frowned. Okay. Change of plans. She hadn't meant to go all in and decide to stay, but as the idea sank deep, the cop in her nodded. Made sense. Felt right. She couldn't go after Lothair by herself. She needed a partner—a man-dragon to help her find and kill the rat-bastard.

Justice. On her terms. Lothair laid out on a slab.

"I want in." The words cemented her resolve, leveling her chin.

Rikar's gaze narrowed on her.

"He hurt me." She tapped the gun muzzle against her chest, right over her heart. "Me! Not you."

"Bullshit." His eyes the color of ice chips, a muscle jumped along his jaw. "What happens to you, happens to me. We're connected now, angel. I feel you with every breath I take."

"Then help me," she whispered, knowing what she asked wasn't fair. Strong men didn't give up control or react well to manipulation. She didn't care. He was her best chance. The only one she had to make the bastard pay. Holding his gaze, she pulled an ace out of her sleeve and begged,

"Please, Rikar...I can't do it by myself. I deserve justice. Please help me get him."

He growled, and Angela held her breath. *Please, Rikar.* The silent plea whispered through her mind. His hand flexed in the quilt, white-knuckling the patchwork fabric like it would keep him from exploding. And as she watched him she wondered...

Could he read her mind?

It seemed like a strange idea. But weirder than changing into a dragon? Not by much. Add that to the realization he'd messed with her that night at McGovern's, and...yeah. The whole mind-meld thing seemed less like fiction and more like fact.

Her eyes narrowed on him.

He leaned back, the movement so small she wouldn't have caught it had she not been watching closely. Jackpot. No doubt about it. His reaction to her went soul-deep, beyond the physical. She felt the connection, the drawing pull, a neediness just like her own. The knowledge made her heart ache for him. No good would come from wanting her...from the push-pull of craving what could never be.

She didn't belong in his world. He didn't belong in hers. But maybe for a little while they could work together toward a common goal. She wanted Lothair dead and knew, without a shadow of doubt, Rikar would lay the bastard out to please her. So instead of backing away like she should have, Angela opened her mind wide, determined to persuade him that she was right.

Sensation slid over his temples as Rikar stared at Angela. The tingle turned into a throb, tightening muscle over his bones as silence echoed between them. She used the quiet like a Brillo pad, rubbing him raw, pushing her agenda as she met his gaze: no shyness, no bullshit, one thing on her mind. She wanted access to his world, in on the action… with his blessing.

Tempting. It was oh so tempting to give in and help her.

Which was no doubt her plan. Diabolical to the next freaking level.

She was playing both ends against the middle, making him choose between keeping her safe and giving her what she wanted. Right. Wrong. Two polar opposites that didn't mean shit while seated across from a beautiful female determined to get her way. And as the fine line between *should* and *shouldn't* became blurred, Rikar shook his head.

Clever, clever female. Angela was undeniably brilliant. Zeroing in like a pit bull. Sniffing out his weakness for her. Using it against him…without conscience or mercy. So, yeah, he was pretty much screwed; stuck trying to make himself say "no."

Planting his palms, he went chin-to-chest, then rolled his shoulders to ease the tension. The muscles bracketing his spine stretched, stinging as he shifted to the center of the bed, putting more distance between them. He needed a minute to pull himself together. To forget for a moment how much he wanted to please her and instead formulate an argument. One that started and ended with *no fucking way*. Or *over my dead body*. Whatever. Either would work, just as long as she got the point and left the hunting up to him.

"Rikar?"

The hitch in her voice—the soft, yet undeniable plea—lit him up. He clenched his teeth as the bonded male in him came to attention. Uh-oh. Big trouble now. The territorial bastard that lived inside him was on board. With what and which plan—his?…Angela's?—Rikar couldn't tell, but whatever the agenda, having his baser instincts banging around couldn't be a good thing. At least not for him.

On her knees now, she leaned toward him, concern in her tone. "Are you all right?"

"Ah, just…give me a second, okay?"

She murmured something he didn't quite catch. Assent? Impatience? He didn't know, but the tingle hit him again, firing up neural pathways with a shitload of give-her-what-she-wants. Rubbing his hands over his skull-trim, he pressed down on the nape of his neck, fighting the need to reach out and touch her. God, what he wouldn't give to wrap his arms around her…hold her close while he told her everything would be all right. That she didn't need to be involved. That he would get the fucker and bring him home like a trophy.

Alive. Dead. A combination of the two. Any way she wanted.

But first? He had to grow a pair, draw a line in the sand, and bookend it with a big-ass *NO*. In Technicolor. Maybe present a slide show, too. With lots of noise and big, black letters.

Pansy-ass pathetic. Yup. That was his new title. Now all he needed was a plaque, one that read *World's Biggest SAP*, to stick on his bedroom door.

With a sigh, Rikar dropped his hands and raised his head. And nearly jumped out of his skin. Shit, she was close. Less than an arm's length away and…

God. She was so beautiful. All pleading hazel eyes and messed-up auburn hair.

His chest constricted, making him ache from the inside out. And only one thought prevailed…the softness of her skin. He knew how fine it was—how smooth it felt against his own—and he wanted to reach out and pull her in. Let his hands do the walking as he set his mouth to hers and tasted her for the first time.

Then again.

And again.

His gaze dipped to her lips. She shuffled back a little, as though she knew what he was thinking, and the IV clanged against the metal stand. The sound set him straight. Christ, he was deranged. She was barely healed, hardly out of danger, the IV still embedded in the back of her hand, and he was hard for her. Disgust curled his hands into fists. He took a deep breath to calm down and got a lungful of her.

Her scent more than anything brought him clarity. She wasn't ready for him. Not yet. Maybe not for a while. She smelled like vulnerability, like teardrops and evergreens and fresh snow. The combo pulled on his heartstrings. The last two were all Angela, her natural scent one he recognized, had dreamed of, loved more than anything he'd encountered before. The first? Sadness and hurt that skipped into hopelessness. The mix told him to back off, that she needed a champion, not a lover.

At least not today.

So yeah…it had to be no. And the line had to be drawn hard.

His world wasn't an easy one. And homicide detective or not, she didn't understand the ground rules. No matter what she said—how many skills she possessed or abundant the brains between her pretty ears—it was too dangerous. The Razorbacks weren't human criminals. They were Dragonkind. A Glock and a shitload of female determination didn't make the cut. And that was before he threw in the bonded male problem. His instincts were on overdrive, desperate to keep her safe. No way could he let her anywhere near the hunt or the bastard when he took him down.

But as the tingle came at him again, it morphed into words—*Rikar, please, help me get him.* As he flinched, his gaze flipped back to hers and…no fucking fair. Sheened by tears, hazel eyes begged him to give her what she needed, to toss his "no" out the nearest window, and temptation dragged him in the wrong direction.

What was the matter with him? His brain had gone AWOL, totally out of bounds. And, man, was he really hearing that? Or was the guilt getting to him, making him imagine the whisper.

He shook his head, dislodging her voice from between his temples. It came right back. *Please, Rikar.* Tilting her head, she settled onto her knees in front of him. The IV tube pinged off steel again. His breath came faster as she tipped her chin, urging him to—

His brows collided. Wait a second.

What the hell was she doing? Suspicion took a nasty turn and…

Holy fuck. She knew. Had figured out exactly how to play him. His lips twitched. Beautiful female. She was too smart by half.

"Angela…stop it," he murmured, tone full of warning, trying not to laugh.

Her eyes widened the tiniest bit. "What?"

"Figured a few things out, have you?"

She shrugged.

He shifted, conjuring a pair of army shorts as he shoved the sheet aside and sat Indian-style directly in front of her. The pose was comfortable, more suitable for sparring. The verbal kind or otherwise. 'Cause, yeah, he and his female were about to get down and dirty. Go toe-to-toe and will-to-will. He could tell by the determined look on her face. And even as he told himself to man up and stay strong, she got to him. Made him so damn proud he could hardly stand himself.

Simple. Straightforward. Her strategy was stone-cold brilliant. And as she leaned toward him, giving him loads of eye contact, she pushed all his buttons: the ones that made him want to give her all she wanted.

Fighting a smile, Rikar shook his head. "Angel…you're playing with fire here."

"Why? Because I'm using your secret weapon against you?"

"Secret weapon?"

"The mind thing." Pursing her lips, she fought to keep them from curving. She lost. He took it as a good sign as he grinned back. Even after her horrific experience, she could laugh with him. And at herself. Which just launched his respect for her into the stratosphere. "Turnabout is fair play, you know. And right now, I'm guessing you're tapped into what I'm thinking."

"Didn't mean to, but…yeah, you're bang-on." Watching her closely, he set his elbows on his widespread knees. "That doesn't freak you out?"

"A little, but…" She trailed off, adjusted her grip on the Glock, an adorable pucker between her brows. "I'm more interested in the endgame."

"Which is what?" He raised a brow. "Playing dirty?"

"No…convincing you," she said, not bothering to hide her intention. "Look, I know I'm out of my league here. That's why I need your help. I can't let it go so—"

"It's too dangerous, Angela."

"I need to be a part of this. I can't sit on my duff and do nothing. I'll go nuts."

Fucking hell. So much for his line in the sand. The thing had just gotten shoved a gazillion feet. In the wrong direction. "It's not that I don't want to let you, but…shit. I'm afraid for you."

"Rikar—"

"Just hear me out, okay?"

When she nodded, he frowned and flicked at the quilt. As he played with the corner edge, winding the patchwork between his fingers, he searched for the right words. The ones that would make her understand. In the end, he settled for, "Our world isn't like yours. Dragonkind…the males I fight don't play fair. We're at war…locked in a bitter feud without end. It's kill or be killed. No rules, no boundaries, no mercy. I want to protect you from that, not send you into the middle of it. Especially after—"

"Don't say his name!"

The outburst cracked him wide open, and he bled for her. For all the pain. For all the suffering and fear. And as she struggled for composure and he watched tears pool in her eyes, he cursed the daylight. He wanted to go right now: hunt that fucker down, rip his still-beating heart from his sadistic chest, and bring it back to her.

Moving carefully, he reached out and slid his hand into hers. She flinched but allowed the contact as he fused their palms and examined the IV punching her skin. So fragile.

So fine. So dangerous to let her win. He needed her to listen. To stay home. Stay safe. Stay out of trouble so he could do his job.

"Angela, love," he murmured, giving her a gentle squeeze. "Listen to me."

"No..." Blinking tears away, she shook her head. "You listen."

Her voice was sharp, stronger than he expected, and he wanted to say "attagirl." Give her a pat on the back and applaud her bravery. He stayed silent instead. What else could he do? Saying no wasn't working. Explaining the danger wasn't getting either of them anywhere. Seeing her tears didn't help, either. Her pain sent his will to resist into a nosedive, and just like that, he was floundering again.

Laying the Glock on the mattress beside her knee, she pressed the back of his hand into the mattress and took hers away. He mourned the loss of her touch, but not for long. She came right back. Her mouth curved as she traced the lines on his palm. "Do you believe in fate, Rikar? That all things happen for a reason?"

Another light stroke against his skin.

Rikar shifted, fighting a full-body tremor. "I don't know."

"I do. All the other cops make fun of me, but I believe it anyway." She shrugged, brushing away their derision, and Rikar had the sudden urge to visit the precinct and bash every one of their heads in. Her featherlight caress distracted him, kept him still as her eyelashes flicked up, and she met his gaze. "I'm stronger than I look, you know. I got out of that place...no help. No rescue on the horizon. One hundred percent alone. So don't tell me I can't manage in your world. I already have."

He wanted to say something—anything—to refute her, but…hell. His brain was on hiatus, giving him nothing but a load of blankety-blank-blank.

The sheets rustled as she moved closer. "Look, I know what you're trying to do, and I appreciate it. I really do, but it's a load of crap. I have skills. I have information. If I'm part of the team I can—"

He growled. Part of the *team*? No chance in hell.

"—learn anything you need me to," she said, talking so fast she tripped over each word. "Teach me how to fight in your world. I can help. If you let me, I can help…please."

She paused a beat, hope in her eyes.

Rikar sighed. Fuck. He might as well admit it. The battle wasn't just uphill, it was already lost. So, yup. New strategy, here he came.

Withdrawing his hand, he untangled from her touch—from the witchy, mind-altering contact…call it whatever you like because…yeah, her soft caresses were fucking him up. "Come here, female."

She hesitated, leery of him as she leaned away a little.

Rikar slid forward on the sheet. He heard her quick intake of breath, felt her pulse skyrocket, but didn't stop. As he settled alongside her, she shied, jumping like a scared rabbit, body language screaming *don't touch me.* He ignored the message. Trust wasn't something a male took. It was earned, and here—right now, in this moment—he needed to show her fear had no place between them…that she was safe with him.

"Easy, angel." Cupping her wrist gently, he stopped her retreat. "I will never hurt you. All right?"

She shivered, still apprehensive, but no longer moving away. "O-okay."

"Relax." Rikar kept his touch light as he rotated her hand and picked at the tape holding the IV in place. Peeling the strip all the way off, he held the needle still with the pad of his thumb and grabbed a cotton pad from the table beside the bed. "Take a deep breath."

She did.

He nodded his approval.

With a care born of patience, he slid the needle out and pressed the gauze over the small wound. As he applied pressure to stop the bleeding, silence gathered, sounding loud, echoing against nothing. She tugged her hand. He held firm, keeping her in place as he palmed a roll of tape.

He glanced at her sideways. "What information?"

Her brows collided.

"You said you have—"

"Oh, right," she said, following the change in topic like a pro. "The Razorbacks, ah…the place they took me to…I'm not sure where it is exactly. Somewhere north of where you found me, but I know there are other women being held there. The bastard talked about cellblock A and that I'd have company and…" Her face grew pale as she paused.

Her agitation lit him up, and he fought to keep his cool as she rubbed the bandage on her thigh. Even knowing the gash had healed didn't help. He hated that she'd been hurt at all. Detested her uncertainty and the strain in her voice. Christ, he didn't want her reliving the pain but needed every scrap of information she could give him. So he waited, giving her time as she struggled to tell him.

"They did tests on me…medical stuff. Needles in the stomach. Forced drugs down my throat," she said, the words so quiet he leaned in to catch each one. "I heard them talk about a…a…serum for a breeding program or something.

I didn't catch it all, but…God, Rikar. Those bastards have other hostages. We have to get them the hell out of there."

He sighed. Shit. The situation was beyond FUBARed. Ivar, the mad scientist, had finally lost it. Now he was unleashed and headed in bad directions. The fact that females were involved only made it worse. So, yeah. No question. They needed to get the imprisoned females out alive. And do it fast before the Razorbacks fucked them up permanently.

Which gave him an idea.

"Are you good with computers?" He ripped off a sticky strip from the roll.

Angela blinked, then nodded. "I can hold my own."

"Good with police databases?"

"Yeah."

Rikar couldn't believe what he was thinking. Or about to do. Talk about an idiot. He was a big one. Should be sticking with the "no" strategy, but he couldn't blame Angela for wanting to play a part. She deserved revenge…justice…whatever. And Sloan—their resident computer genius—was tapped out. Hell, the male was so busy monitoring the human world and filtering information that he hardly ever left the lair. And if Angela could help his buddy with the workload, it was win-win all the way around.

Plugging her into a computer would kill two birds with one stone: keep her at Black Diamond while he smoked Lothair out. But the bigger bonus? Access to Angela. Every hour of every day. Time enough to convince her of his worth. To make her want him, need him…crave him as much as he did her. All while keeping her safe.

Jackpot. The perfect solution wrapped up in a tidy package.

"All right, then." Tossing the roll, he ignored the thud as it landed on the tabletop and laid the tape across the back of Angela's hand. "If you want in, there are ground rules."

"Lay them out."

"When you're not with me, you stay in the lair. No running off half-cocked. No going it alone when something doesn't go your way. I let you in…you take the tasks assigned to you. I lead. You follow." Smoothing the tape across her skin with his thumbs, he turned his head, drilled her with a *don't fuck with me* look. "Got it?"

She frowned. "But—"

"My way or not at all, Angela," he said, debating how far to push, how much to tell her about Dragonkind and the feedings.

Her high-energy status might not freak her out, but the fact Lothair had taken a piece of her would. She didn't need to know that. Not yet. Frightening her was the last thing he wanted to do. But if push came to shove, he'd nail her feet to the floor—keep her safe inside the lair—by explaining the Razorback could track her now. The instant she stepped outside Black Diamond's energy shield, her signal would go live, transmit her location and…

Wham.

The SOB would come after her. No holds barred.

"That's the deal, love." Releasing her hand, he slid his legs over the side of the bed and stood. As the cold floor met his bare feet, he glanced over his shoulder at her. "In or out…what's it gonna be?"

She glared at him. "In."

His satisfaction swelled like tidal wave. Well, all right, then. Score one for the home team. Now all he needed to do was stay in the game. And one step ahead of Angela. Too smart for her own good, stubborn to the core, she wouldn't give him a straight-up victory. She'd play dirty…work him a bit at a time until he gave ground. And before he knew it? He'd be on his heels, scrambling to keep her out of trouble.

The thought gave him chills. Which, of course, he relished, the challenge cranking him into high gear. An easy win, after all, was never as sweet as one well-earned.

Chapter Fourteen

Lothair arrived at 28 Walton Street to a whole lot of nothing. No fanfare. No explosions. Nothing being thrown at him. Thank Jesus. He didn't need Ivar's temper right now. Or any more of Denzeil's trucker talk either.

"D…shut the fuck up, would ya?" Tossing his comrade a loaded look, Lothair grabbed the remote out of the center console of the Oldsmobile. On cue, the industrial-size garage door opened, old chains rattling as the sun crested the horizon. Just in time. Another five minutes and they would've pulled into a secluded spot, parked, and bunked in the trunk for the day. Could've been fun back there…a party of four, hold the champagne, fuck you very much.

"What are ya gonna tell Ivar?" Hands working out a beat, Denzeil drummed his fingers on the steering wheel, waiting for the door to rise enough to drive in.

Rat-ta-ta-tat. Rat-ta-ta-tat.

The sound was a nervous one, the action telling. His comrade was scared shitless. Not that Lothair blamed him. Only a male with suicidal tendencies messed with Ivar. Good thing he wasn't just any male and he had an ace up his sleeve. Ivar loved him like a brother. Would no sooner hurt him than cut off his own arm, and that was before his connections got thrown into the mix. Yes, sirree. Powerful friends in the Archguard made for one hell of an insurance policy.

Lothair glanced at D's hands, then raised a brow. The rat-ta-ta-tat stopped instantly, making his mouth curve. The fear factor—and the male's reaction—was one of his favorites.

"So, what's the plan?" Denzeil glanced at him.

Pinning him with a glare, Lothair raised a brow.

White-knuckling the wheel, his comrade swallowed, then shifted, ass walking all over the worn velour seat. "We need to get our stories straight, man. He's gonna be pissed we lost the she-cop and—"

"The truth, D," he said. "We don't hide this kind of shit from Ivar."

At least not if they wanted to stay alive. Ivar had a nasty streak, sure. But he was a reasonable male. Lothair frowned. Most of the time anyway. The science experiment, though, worried him a little. It had gone from the usual strange to downright hinky in recent days.

"Ten-four."

More with the trucker crap. Lothair sighed. "Just drive through. My eyes are stinging."

With a nod, D put his foot down and drove them into the shadowy recess of the old fire hall. As the garage door closed with a grinding clank behind the ass-end of the car, darkness fell, bringing relief from the breaking dawn, and so much more. The sunlight was a bitch, sure, but escaping the supernova wasn't what made him relax. Dipping his chin, he rolled his head left, then right, stretching out the knots, and thanked his lucky stars.

Home. After weeks of sleeping in that rat hole, he was finally home.

And who did he have to thank? A pack full of Nightfury assholes. Ironic, wasn't it? The males who tried to kill him every night had just done him a huge favor, liberating him from the old lair. No way Ivar would send him back now. He'd rage about his plan hitting the skids—that the new cell-block wasn't ready for habitation yet—but his commander wasn't stupid. Going back in for any reason now was too risky. It wouldn't take long for Tweedledee and Tweedledum to infiltrate and tear the place apart looking for clues.

Maybe the males had broken through the energy shield already. Derr`mo, he hoped so. The faster they worked, the better for him. Lothair snorted. Who would've thought the idiots would ever come in handy?

His mouth curved as he popped the latch and shoved the car door wide. Rusty hinges squawked, echoing through the dark. Jacking himself through the opening, his boots touched down on the smooth concrete. Poured just weeks ago, the floors qualified as a definite upgrade. No more pockmarks. No more oil stains. Just new on new. The condition of 28 Walton was light-years from the shitty accommodations when he and Ivar had bought the place. Each day brought changes, and with each small improvement, the lair became more livable. And that was without counting the network of underground tunnels that now sat beneath the old structure.

After years spent in subpar conditions—caves, run-down factories, basements, and old wine cellars...you name it, he'd been there—the facility was a revelation. Modern, high tech, the Razorback's new home was über comfortable. Something to be proud of, and for once, he was thankful.

So attached to the fire hall now, he would fight to defend rather than abandon his home at the first sign of trouble.

Lothair shook his head. The sentiment was stupid, but no matter how hard he tried to quash it, the feeling wouldn't go away. Acceptance. The sense of belonging. Both were powerful things, forces that shaped a male. He'd never been truly welcome anywhere: not with his family or by his former pack, not by anyone other than Ivar.

Slamming the car door behind him, Lothair glanced over his shoulder. He met D's gaze over the roof of the car. "Deal with the females. I'll handle Ivar."

The male nodded, relief shining in his dark eyes.

"Get them something to eat after you lock 'em down." Heading for the stairs at the far end of the ten-car garage, he skirted Ivar's ride. Kitted out vintage style, the 1963 'Vette owned sweet curves, a set of wicked rims, and an engine that purred like a female in heat. He should know. He'd picked a coed up in it last week. Let the engine rumble as he banged her in the front seat: pulling her into his lap, spreading her thighs, thrusting deep as she begged for more and he fed.

Not his favorite memory. The willing ones were never as much fun.

He paused at the base of the steps, the smell of new cement making his nose twitch. "Make sure they get enough, D. We lose those two, and the Ivar'll go postal on our asses."

Pace even, footfalls silent, Lothair took the stairs two at a time. Taking a tight turn, he continued up, double-timing another set of concrete treads. Thirty seconds later, he stood on the third-story landing. He scanned the shadows, the bank of cracked windows yet to be replaced, hardly noticing the devastation that years of neglect had wrought. Built in the 1950s, the fire hall had sat empty for years. Decay liked it that way, but things were about to change. Right now the underground lair had priority, but soon Ivar's worker bees would turn their attention to the brick structure sitting on terra firma.

Lothair could hardly wait.

The underground lair—while comfortable with its bedroom suites, modern kitchen, computer center, and Ivar's lab—didn't have a game room. Cards. Pool. Foosball. Ping-Pong. Video games. Whatever. The game didn't matter as long as he got to play. And kicking his comrade's asses? Hmm…yeah. He liked that best of all.

Skirting a jagged hole in the wooden floor, he headed for the elevator. Hidden behind a wall of paneling, the modern wonder waited, the hum of powerful magnets barely audible above the street noise. He reached out with his mind. The lock disengaged with a snick, and the hum got louder. Floor-to-ceiling wainscoting pushed into the room, then slid sideways, steel glinting behind polished mahogany in the dimness.

The double sliders retreated, opening into the Otis. His mouth curved into a satisfied smile. Beautiful. Excellence in a steel box.

Lothair stepped inside and pressed the solitary button. Closing his eyes, he leaned against the back wall, arms crossed over his chest, reengaging the security system with his mind as the elevator descended. The soft beep told him the wainscoting had closed, sealing the entrance to the underground lair tight.

An unnecessary precaution? Probably.

Denzeil and the females were no doubt right on his ass, but…well, a male could never be too careful. Not with a new home to protect.

The Nightfuries were a clever bunch: well organized, skilled warriors, tenacious with a shitload of vicious sprinkled on top. A lethal combination, one he didn't want anywhere near Ivar. The male had taken a hit at the shipyard. Was still recovering from Rikar's ice daggers and—

Fuck, he hated that prick. More than Bastian or any of the others. Tonight's dance on the beach only cemented the feeling. The pale-eyed, white-scaled male had taken his prize, and because of it, he was headed into an unpleasant conversation. One that would end with him making concessions.

Lothair growled. He'd rather chew his own arm off than admit failure…or give up an ounce of power. But Ivar would take his pound of flesh. No sense putting it off.

The double doors slid open, dumping him into a high-ceilinged, double-wide corridor. The smell of wet plaster and fresh paint hung in the air as he strode toward the lab. Ivar spent most of his time there, at the farthest recesses of the lair. With project supervirus in full swing, the male practically slept in the antechamber.

Not good on any level.

He turned the last corner and punched through a set of swinging doors. White from floor to ceiling, the lab's antechamber was Ivar's domain. The space suited the male, showcasing his preference for all things neat and tidy. Lothair almost snorted. *Neat and tidy?* Jesus, it was more than that. Call it OCD on steroids, but whatever you labeled it, normal wasn't one of the choices. Neither was colorful. The only things with an ounce of flash were the computer screens running down the left-hand side of the room and the fruit basket sitting on the table beside his commander.

One shoulder propped against the wall, one arm supported by a sling, Ivar glanced away from the one-way window into another chamber.

Lothair tipped his chin. "How's it going in there?"

"They're not dying fast enough." Black wraparounds in place, Ivar shook his head. The sunglasses slipped, sliding down the bridge of his nose, exposing pink irises and a visual load of pissed off. "Two aren't even sick yet, and it's been five days."

Moving away from the entrance, Lothair crossed the room. "So superbug number one is a bust?"

"A total fucking failure."

"Then gas 'em." Slowing his roll, Lothair stopped beside his friend. He looked through the glass into the hermetically-sealed chamber/apartment. Decked out with the best, the suite boasted everything a human could want: high-tech kitchen, comfortable bedrooms with en suite bathrooms, a kitted-out living room with modern furniture, and a sixty-inch plasma TV complete with every video game console known to mankind. Why Ivar bothered with the luxury when the humans inside were nothing but guinea pigs, he didn't know. A quirk of character, maybe. "Clean up the mess and start over with a new batch."

"I like this bug." Ivar sighed, dark red brows furrowed behind the Oakleys. "I'll give it a few more days."

Lothair wanted to shake his head. He didn't dare. His friend would kick his ass if he thought for one second he wasn't 100 percent on board. Not that he wasn't. He hated humankind as much as, if not more than, Ivar, but…

All the science stuff was above his pay grade. He didn't understand it—wasn't sure he wanted to—but Ivar loved the shit: playing with viruses that would scare the piss out of human doctors, never mind the best biochemical experts in the business.

To what end?

The extermination of the human race.

Stupid insects. The assholes were killing the planet with their greed and neglectful attitude. Global warming. Entire rain forests laid to waste. The oil spills, nuclear power plant leaks, companies spilling toxic chemicals into lakes and rivers…into the fucking sky. Where he flew every night. If they didn't wipe the humans out soon, there would be nothing left to save.

"I'll get another batch of humans together. Strong ones with healthy immune systems."

Ivar scowled at him.

"Just in case," Lothair murmured, not pushing his luck. His commander was touchy enough already. Ivar liked fast results and positive outcomes when his babies (aka superviruses) were involved. "I'll get some low-energy females to throw into the mix too."

"Good idea." Pushing away from the wall, cradling his injured arm, Ivar limped over to the bank of computer monitors. A couple of quick keystrokes and the screens went active, scientific data, spreadsheets as well as the video feed from the chamber, coming online. "Vary the ethnic backgrounds as well…Latino, Caucasian, Asian. You name it, toss it in there. I want to test exactly what kind of RO ratio we'll get for both male and female."

Lothair frowned.

"RO ratio?" Ivar raised a brow, enjoying the science lesson. "Rate of infection."

"The faster, the better."

"Not necessarily." Fingers flying, his friend tapped a command into the keyboard. A spreadsheet complete with a pie graph morphed on the screen. "We need an infected human to stay alive long enough to spread the contagion to at least five or six other people. We want a global, systemic epidemic. An untreatable one."

"Deadly with a extra dose of kick-ass."

"Exactly." Ivar's mouth tipped up at the corners.

Lothair grinned back, then turned his attention to the humans caged inside the chamber. Some were coughing. One was passed out on the La-Z-Boy recliner. Two were playing Xbox, a version of Halo. He loved that game. Would probably play some himself before he hit the sheets for the day. But first? Eats. He was as hungry as hell.

Filching an apple from the basket, he bit into the red, juicy, and delicious. As the sweet taste hit his tongue, he glanced sideways at his friend. Jesus, even with his injuries half-healed, Ivar was in rough shape. He took another bite and murmured around the mouthful, "Two high-energy females are in the house, Ivar. You should feed."

His friend nodded. "You're coming with me."

Without a doubt. No way would he let Ivar go alone. His commander liked killing females too much. Would drain one of the coeds dry if Lothair wasn't in on the action. His balls fisted up tight as he swelled behind his fly. He could do with some action right now. Particularly after the goat-fuck his night had turned out to be.

He tipped his head toward the door. "Let's go now."

"Tell me about our other project first." Turning away from the computer, Ivar ass-planted himself on the lip of the desk.

Ah, hell. Here it came. His confession and talk of the breeding program.

So not what he needed right now. He'd hoped to Zen Ivar out with an energy feed first. No such luck. The male was too savvy. Was reading his level of pissed off and making the right conclusion. The one that had shot-to-hell written all over it.

Lothair sighed. "We ran into a snag tonight."

"Shit."

No kidding. Losing another high-energy female didn't bode well. Not for him. Not for the breeding program Ivar wanted operational, oh, say…yesterday.

Designed with one purpose in mind, the program was simple. At least in principle. Dragonkind males didn't produce female offspring. Why? Something about a vengeful goddess and a curse, but…whatever. Lothair didn't believe in old wives' tales. As long as Ivar knew how to manipulate the DNA and map the genomes to allow a Dragonkind male to produce a girl-child, it was all good. He'd hunt down however many females his commander wanted. Impregnate as many as needed when the Meridian realigned.

He was happy to do it. For results. For a daughter of his own.

A Dragonkind female with the ability to feed males of her own kind. Hmm, what a concept. Something worth striving for if it eliminated his dependence on humankind once and for all.

For the program to be successful, however, they needed six females to start: all healthy, high-energy, and of breeding age. Anyone under eighteen need not apply. Which meant he needed to track, trap, and imprison six twenty-something candidates.

No easy task.

High-energy females were the rarest of the rare. Smart. Tenacious. Skilled in their chosen fields, there was nothing run-of-the-mill about them. Which meant he was in FUBAR territory before he even stepped outside the lair each night. The theme song from *Mission: Impossible* thrummed through his head. Forget Tom Cruise. Hands down, he had the actor beat in the crazy mission situation.

Ivar's gaze zinged him from behind the dark lenses. "What happened?"

Fuck. Truth time. All of a sudden, Lothair wished he could choose *dare.* But whatever…truth, it was. "Lost the third tonight."

"The she-cop?"

"She ambushed me before I could get her in a cage," he said, angling his face, showing off his cheek. "Got out through the ventilation system."

"Smart," his friend said, pushing away from the computer console. The sound of his boots thudded as he came at Lothair from across the room. The approach was slow and measured. Dangerous by any standards. Lothair tensed, waiting for the blow, refusing to fight back, knowing he deserved the beatdown. But as his friend stopped in front of him, he didn't lash out. He reached out instead and with a gentle touch grasped Lothair's chin. Leaning in, Ivar got up close and personal with the butterfly bandages. "Nasty cut. You okay?"

The question wasn't about physical injury. It was about headspace and intention. Ivar wasn't stupid. He knew exactly what kind of male he'd chosen as his XO.

"*Nyet,*" he growled, shaking free of Ivar's hold. "I'm not fucking *okay.*"

"You looking for some payback?"

"A shitload."

"So retrieve her come nightfall and..." Ivar trailed off as Lothair cursed. Reading him right, his eyes glowed pink behind the Oakleys. "Goddamn it, Lothair. Tell me Bastian didn't—"

"His evil twin...Rikar."

As the name rolled out, a sour taste filled his mouth. Unpleasant in more ways than one. Not only must he admit the bastard had gotten the better of him but also that he'd come home empty-handed. With a snarl, Lothair swallowed the name like a mouthful of mothballs. Unable to stay still, he rolled his shoulders to work out the frustration. When that didn't work, he put his boots in gear and paced the length of the antechamber.

He strode back in the opposite direction, his footfalls echoing off the glossy walls. Coming within inches of Ivar, he passed his commander, then stopped, dead-ending at the computer console. Asleep from disuse, the touch screen that controlled the "apartment" was black. He stared at his reflection a moment, seeing himself, but not really. "I hate that asshole."

"Fucking ice princess," his friend hissed, dissing Rikar with his usual slur. "So we've only got two in the tank."

Yup. Two high-energy females. Four short of what Ivar wanted—needed—before the Meridian realigned in the spring. The electrostatic current's realignment happened twice a year, and it was the only time a Dragonkind male was fertile. Just his luck. His genetics were a natural frickin' disaster, working against him with the force of a hurricane.

Uncurling his fists, Lothair cracked his knuckles. "I'll get you the others."

"And the she-cop?"

"She's out of the program." With a big *REJECTED* stamped on her forehead.

"Lothair." Ivar's tone was full of warning. "She's high-energy. She's prepped with the serum. We can't afford—"

"To what...waste her?" His boot soles squeaked as he spun and glared at the male he loved like a brother. Any other time, he would've backed down, but not today. Or tomorrow. Or the day after that. He wanted Angela Keen to suffer: pure, simple, no negotiation required. "Bullshit. I don't care how rare a female she is...or how high her energy. When I find her, I'll fuck her hard while I drain her dry."

"Jesus Christ, man." Ivar popped the wraparounds off the bridge of his nose. As he rubbed the corners of his eyes, he shook his head and sighed. "Okay, look...I've got no problem with you laying her out, but if you want her dead, you pay the price."

"Name it."

"Seven," he said. "I want seven females instead of six in the next two months so they can be prepped and ready to go before the Meridian realigns."

Diabolical. And difficult. Lothair didn't care. Killing the she-cop was more important. If he needed to bust his ass, serve up five females in eight weeks, so be it. He loved a good challenge. "Done."

Ivar huffed. "Just like that?"

"I'm working on something," he said, holding his friend's gaze, mind churning over the facts. High-energy females might be elusive, but he'd noticed something while hunting them over the last month. HEs often stuck together...find one, find more. "A new hypothesis."

"Feel like sharing?"

"Not yet," he said. "When I know, you'll know."

Wasn't that always the way? Ivar planned. Lothair put the plan in motion and made it happen. The how, where, and why held little consequence. So…

No problem. Seven high-energy females, coming up.

Chapter Fifteen

Stream rose like a curtain, fogging up the glass as Angela planted her hands against the shower wall. Cool marble pressed along each palm as she leaned in, bowed her head, warm water streaming down her spine. The contrast was classic. Hot versus cold. Fight versus flight. The will to resist battling the urge to give in. And there she had it…her relationship with Rikar in a nutshell.

Angela snorted. *Relationship.* Wow. Now there was stretch. Not a very comfortable one, either. Especially since she'd woken up the second time around tonight A-L-O-N-E.

Why that upset her, she didn't know.

Happy to be alone had always been her MO. Not today, though. All by her lonesome meant peace and quiet, the last thing she needed. The silence gave her too much time to think. To feel. To relive all the bad stuff and none of the good.

God, how could Rikar leave her like this? Skip out on her without leaving a note…without so much as a *Hey, angel, don't worry, I'll be back at X o'clock* on a scrap piece of paper. Was that too much to ask?

Goddamn it, no. It wasn't.

He could've shaken her awake after his trip through the shower. Could've rubbed her back, rustled her hair, murmured to her as—

Angela touched her forehead to the shower wall. Good God. *Rub her back.* How stupid was that? Very. Beyond idiotic.

She barely knew the guy. Shouldn't trust him. Need him. Want him. But the truth was a bitter pill to swallow. Especially since she craved those things from him.

Leaning into the spray, she fought the sudden tightness in her chest, tried to breathe through it, around it, refusing to shut down. Or show any fear. Rikar. No Rikar. It didn't matter. She couldn't afford to freak out. The moment she broke down, he would cut her out of the investigation: say it was too dangerous, try to shove her somewhere called the *Safest-Place-on-Earth.* The certainty of the assertion gave her perspective. Made her want to prove him wrong even as she soaked up the concern she saw in his eyes.

And, okay. There she went again, driving straight into Crazytown.

She couldn't be weak and strong at the same time. Not with Rikar. He was too demanding, too watchful…too afraid for her. Which meant keeping it together long enough to earn the right to stand shoulder-to-shoulder with him. Easier said than done. At least she understood the parameters and inherent challenges. Had climbed over all kinds of gender bias when she'd been transferred to Homicide from Vice. All the old-timers had balked, hating the idea of a woman detective on their squad. She'd shown them, given the boys' club the finger, and then left them in the dust.

And she could do it again.

But first? She needed to man up and hold the encroaching panic at bay. And find Mac. Which meant locating Rikar.

She wouldn't get far in a lair full of man-dragons without him.

With a shove, Angela pushed away from the wall. Water rolled over her shoulders, then headed south, cascading between her breasts as Rikar's voice whispered through her mind. *Angel.* She sighed, enjoying the endearment way too much. She shouldn't like the pet name at all. It was just a word, nothing special to him. He no doubt called all his—

Ah…strike that thought. No sense going there. It didn't matter what he called other women. Rikar's personal life was just that…*personal.* In other words? None of her flipping business. But even as she cemented the "he's not mine" in her mind, the hair on the nape of her neck stood straight up, like a she-lion's might when another lioness encroaches on her territory.

Raking a hand through her wet hair, Angela took refuge behind her no-chance-in-hell attitude. She wasn't at Black Diamond to hook up. All right, so Rikar was gorgeous. So he was gentle, caring, and willing to give her space. None of that mattered. She had a job to do, one that entailed killing a certain Razorback, so, yeah, the whole attraction problem could take a backseat. In another country. Or universe. Wherever…just as long as it stayed the hell away from her.

Angela nodded. Excellent plan. On to the next issue. Rikar and his disappearing act.

Freaking guy. She could just picture him, tiptoeing past her and out of the room.

She'd made it easy for him. Curling up in his spot on the bed while he showered behind a closed door. Using his pillow, burrowing so deep his scent rose from the sheets, enveloping her in a masculine richness that was all Rikar.

Allowing the splashing sound of water and the warm quilt to cocoon her until…

Yeah. Classic rookie mistake.

She'd taken her eyes off the target. Literally. Allowed them to close instead of keeping them glued to the damned door. Now—courtesy of her additional four hours in la-la land—he was gone. No explanation. No first assignment. No clue about how, when, or where. Just a neatly folded pile of clothes at the end of the bed and an empty room.

Which she appreciated. Really, she did, even though she wanted to stay pissed off. But as far as gestures went, the tank top, track pants, and Lululemon hoodie was a thoughtful one, particularly since naked wasn't something she needed to be in a lair full of man-dragons. Add that to the fact the hoodie was her favorite color—a green so dark it reminded her of a forest full of evergreens—and well… Rikar had scored a few points. Enough maybe to get off with a verbal thrashing instead of a smack upside the head with her shiny new Glock.

Reaching out, Angela turned the shower off. Time to get out. Time for some reconnaissance. Time to help Mac.

She cranked the door open, stepped out of the shower, and onto the bath mat. Her mind raced as she flipped a towel off the heated wall rack, sorting through the possibilities. Which emergency room had he been taken to…the Seattle General hospital? Swedish Medical? She frowned. Probably the latter. Most cops ended up there when injured in the line of duty or—

Nope. Not going there. Her partner wasn't dead. No way. Not Mac.

Fear for her partner rose fast as she toweled off. The new clothes went on in record time. Finger-combing her hair, she zipped up the hoodie, slipped her feet into a pair of girly-girl flip-flops, and grabbed her Glock. As she headed for the exit, she slid the gun into her waistband, cranked down on the handle and, swinging the door wide—

Got an earful of baby sounds: soft gurgles of happy cooing.

Angela frowned as she pivoted toward the bed.

"Hey, you're finally out," a soft voice said. "I thought you'd melted in there."

Habit made her slip her hand around the Glock secured against the small of her back a second before she spotted the owner of the voice. Blonde hair pulled into a ponytail, Myst Munroc sat cross-legged in the center of the king-size monstrosity. Serious blue eyes met hers, concern and more in their depths, and Angela cringed. She couldn't stand the pity or the certain knowledge she saw in Myst's gaze. Both made it hard to hide: to throw her shoulders back, put on a brave front, and pretend that she was all right.

She tried anyway, deflecting Myst's concern. "Hey…are you okay?"

"That should be my line." Myst worried her bottom lip as though she had something important to say but couldn't decide how to say it.

Angela swallowed. Oh, so not good. She didn't want to talk about the shipyard. About their capture, attempted escape, or…what had happened to her afterward. The topic wasn't up for discussion. Not that Myst cared. Her expression said it all. Talk was exactly what she wanted to do.

"Look, I know you probably don't want to see me right now, but…" Tears filled Myst's eyes, making the irises appear more violet than blue. "It has to be said and—"

"Don't," she whispered.

Myst didn't listen. "I'm sorry…so very sorry. It's my fault. Had I listened to Bastian and not run away." Her breath hitched, breaking up the fast-paced spill of guilt. "God…the explosion at the precinct, the shipyard…the whole damned thing wouldn't have happened, and you…y-you would be all right. W-would never have been h-hurt."

Angela closed her eyes. She couldn't handle this, not now. Work. She needed to work, to distract herself with something she excelled at. Something that made her feel strong. An activity like, oh, say…outsmarting and catching bad guys. But Myst and her Dr. Phil moment were mucking up the plan, making her remember when she wanted to forget.

Please, God. Someone just shoot her now.

"It wasn't your fault. You couldn't have known and…" Angela paused to collect her thoughts, to find her brain before she broke down. If she started to cry, Myst would cry and then…hell. They'd both be knee-deep in a blubberfest with no way out. "I'm all right. Myst, really…I'm good. Rikar's helped a lot."

Okay, she hadn't meant to admit that last part. But, well…crap. Just crap. It was true. Rikar had helped. Was still helping: making her feel safe, supporting her without demanding anything in return, giving her a shot at justice. And boy oh boy, she really needed to get a grip. Otherwise she'd fall out of *anger* with him.

"I'm glad," Myst said, her voice soft. "But if you ever want to talk—"

"I won't…not for a while. Maybe never."

"I get it, but…" Myst cleared her throat. "The offer stands…anytime, okay?"

Angela nodded and glanced away, silence stretching until she felt like an elastic band. Ready to snap any second: to run, hide, and never come out.

The small bundle of blue blanket next to Myst caught her attention. Thank goodness. A distraction. She needed one. Much more of the trip down memory lane and she'd lose it for sure. But the baby was a ray of sunshine. A gift in the face of tragedy.

Unable to stay away, she walked toward the bed. As she got her first glimpse of him, her mouth curved. Little cherub. Sweet angel. He was so beautiful. Dark Mohawk of hair running down the center of his head, the little guy cooed and grabbed hold as Myst gave him her finger. Angela huffed, the sound more amazed than amused. Man, he was small and...happy. So perfect he made her ache with a sudden gladness that almost overwhelmed her. And in that moment, as she stared down at him—memorizing his features, seeing his happiness, and knowing he was safe—the pain pinching her chest eased just a little bit.

Reaching out, she touched the dark hair gracing the top of his head. With a suddenness that startled her, the baby turned his head and...

Angela blinked. Wow. He was extra alert for a little guy. Maybe too alert. "He's Dragonkind?"

Liberating her finger, Myst rubbed his belly and nodded.

"Is he Bastian's? The guy you—"

"No. He belongs to the male chained in the basement."

Oh, of course. Chained in the...what? "Excuse me?"

"It's a bit of a story," she said, adjusting the blanket, tucking the baby's arms in as she swaddled him. "And speaking of which, we'd better get moving."

Okay, now they were *going* somewhere? Jeez. Talk about a switch-up. The conversation had gone from bad to bizarre in a heartbeat. "Ah, you want to fill me in? Who's chained in the basement?"

"Forge. Gregor-Mayhem's father." Scooping up the baby, Myst tucked him against her shoulder and slid toward the edge of the bed. "I think you need to meet him."

"Why?"

"He's spent time with the Razorbacks. He might know something that might help you catch the assholes."

Bingo. Myst had her attention. The only problem? Mac. Her partner was the priority, not the guy imprisoned in the dungeon. "I need to talk to Rikar first."

"Not a good idea," she said. "At least not until after we visit Forge."

Well, wasn't that cryptic? "What about a cell phone?"

Patting Gregor-Mayhem's bottom—man, the kid needed a shorter handle…like G.M. or something—Myst turned toward the door. "There aren't any phones in the lair."

"A computer, then?"

"What do you need?"

"My partner, Mac, is in trouble and—"

"Not anymore." Blue eyes fixed on her, Myst stroked the back of G.M.'s head. "Rikar left an hour ago…at nightfall… to go get him."

Closing her eyes, Angela said a silent thank-you. Mac was safe, but even as relief sent her sideways, she wondered whether Rikar going after her partner was a good idea. Probably not. Especially considering Rikar's track record. She'd gone into McGovern's in great shape, for pity's sake, looking for a glass of Cran-Raz, and come out one memory light of a full load.

"Rikar won't hurt him, will he?" He'd better not. Otherwise she'd find some 9 mms to go in her Glock's empty magazine clip.

"Nah, I don't know what happened exactly, but the plan is to bring Mac back here. Which means…we really need to get moving before my mate and the boys get home."

Angela blinked. "Mate?"

"Bastian. I'm mated to him." After tossing her a grin, Myst headed for the door on the opposite side of the room. "Sounds crazy, I know, but I love him, so staying with him is a no-brainer…the best decision I've ever made." Pausing at the exit, her expression went from lighthearted to serious as she glanced over her shoulder at Angela. "The only thing that bothers me is leaving Tania. I miss her so much it hurts."

Angela nodded, remembering Tania from when she'd hauled her into the precinct for questioning. "She misses you, too."

"You talked to her?"

"We interviewed her when we couldn't find you."

"Is she all right?"

"Yeah," she said. "Pretty determined to find you, though."

"Crap." A pained look on her face, Myst shook her head, battling the sudden threat of tears. "I'm dying to call her, but it'll only make things worse. A catch twenty-two, you know? If I contact her, she'll try harder to find me. It wouldn't be fair to pull her into this world, so it's better if I disappear. But it's killing me that I can't let her know I'm all right."

"I hear ya," she murmured, understanding Myst's dilemma. Damned if she did, damned if she didn't…such a nasty place to be. Which meant it was time to change the subject before Myst got weepy-eyed again.

Angela cleared her throat. "So…you live here now?"

"New home. New life. But here's the real kicker." Cupping the baby's bottom with one hand, Myst patted her stomach with the other. "New baby on the way, too. How's that for a trifecta of holy crap?"

"Game. Set. Match," Angela said. "The win goes to Ms. Munroe."

She laughed. "Pretty much."

"What else should I know?"

"Rikar's important around here. Well, actually…all of the guys are, but your male is Bastian's best friend and first-in-command of the Nightfuries."

Your male. Just two words, but wow. They packed a punch. One that left Angela breathless for all the wrong reasons. Fighting the backward slide into the Kingdom of Stupidosity, she concentrated instead on the last bit of intel. Bastian's go-to guy. Nothing like being informed of that by the man-dragon himself. Jeez. Rikar didn't have a collaborative bone in his body. Or any idea what *partner* meant, for that matter. Angela pursed her lips. Just wait until she got a hold of him. He wouldn't have a clue what hit him.

"Can you grab the container on the bedside table?" Halfway across the room, Myst pointed to a blue-and-white metal tin. When Angela raised a brow, her new friend explained, "Cookies for Forge."

Skirting the end of the bed, she grabbed the container and hightailed it after Myst. "And we need cookies because…?"

"To bribe our new inmate." Shifting the baby, Myst cradled him in one arm and opened the door with the other. Hinges hissed. Metal clicked and…bingo. They were out of the hospital room and into the wide corridor on the other side. "You should know he's a hard-ass."

"Terrific," she said, thinking of Rikar…the poster boy for *hard-ass.* "Just what I need. Another one."

Ignoring her sarcasm, Myst turned left, footwear flip-flip-flopping against the linoleum floor, sound bouncing off white walls. Spotlighted by twin rows of halogens, the hallway was wide, the ceiling high, not a picture in sight. Plain. Utilitarian. Function over form, just like a hospital.

"So that's your plan? Ply him with cookies and hope he cracks?" Strangest interrogation technique she'd ever heard of, but all right. It was worth a shot.

"Forge has a sweet tooth," Myst said, eyes twinkling, expression impish. "He'll take one whiff of the shortbread and cave."

A Scottish treat, one of Mac's faves. "Is he from Scotland or something?"

"The Highlands." Upping her pace, her new friend made a beeline toward the end of the corridor. And a set of double doors. "Just wait until you get a load of his accent."

"Gerard Butler good?"

"Better. Think Sean Connery on steroids."

Oh, boy. Angela loved that actor. And couldn't wait to meet Forge. No, scratch that. Make it *hear* the guy talk.

"But…" Myst paused to crank open one of the doors. "We need to get to him before the boys come home because the second they do, Daimler will squeal on us."

"Don't tell me." Right on Myst's heels, she jogged into a clinic of some sort. Neat and tidy, the setup was high-tech with stainless-steel countertops, a crapload of medical machines, and supplies. The smell of antiseptic hand wash hung in the air as she skirted the examination table on the way to a sliding glass door. "Daimler is Black Diamond's eyes and ears."

"Yeah…the nosy butler." Turning into another corridor outside the clinic, the combined flip-flip-flop of their footwear ricocheted off ancient stone walls. Medieval looking, the granite blocks bore grooved tool marks—probably made by equally old chisels. "Love him to death, but he's got a big mouth. And what Bastian says goes."

Angela raised a brow. "But not for you."

"Not always. I know how to get around my mate." Myst tossed a grin over her shoulder as they passed a bank of elevators. The hallway dead-ended soon after, and she stopped in front of a reinforced steel door. With a flip, she opened the electronic keypad and punched in an access code. The locks clicked. The door swung inward. "Stick around long enough and you'll figure out the best way to handle Rikar too."

One could only hope.

But *sticking around* wasn't part of the plan. Do the job. Get even, and then get out. Ding-ding-ding. That had a much nicer ring to it than settling into domestic bliss with a man-dragon. So yeah, no matter how appealing, Rikar was a means to an end. Nothing more. Nothing less. Now all she needed to do was remember that important fact. Maybe writing it on a Post-it would help. Maybe if she taped it to her bathroom mirror and recited it each morning, she'd learn to cope. Maybe with enough practice, she'd kill the disease.

The one called Rikaritis.

But as Angela followed her new partner in crime over the threshold, something warned her there wasn't a cure for that.

Ahead of the pack and on point, Mac took the last flight of stairs two at a time, the echo of three sets of boots on the metal treads behind him. It was his lucky day. Venom and Wick had joined the parade, bringing up the rear behind Bastian. Man, like he needed an audience for this shit?

Fly or die.

Venom's words, not his.

Mac felt them all the same as he reached the landing and punched the metal handle barring the security door. The wind took over, grabbing the steel and slamming it back against the skyscraper's facade. He stepped out onto the rooftop, onto gravel and rock dust, aware of nothing but the building edge thirty feet away. Goddamn, it was a long way down. How did he know? He climbed the whole way up, pounded the flights between floors like a gym rat on a stair-climber.

Nine hundred and sixty-three feet above Cherry Street. Seventy-six floors of I-wanna-see-Mac-go-splat.

Or maybe that was just Venom. Bastian didn't seem to want him dead. The guy had coached him the whole way over in the Denali, going over it again, making sure he understood. Still, he couldn't help thinking…

Where the fuck is Rikar?

He needed the guy. An ally. Before he hit the point of no return. Before he fell seventy-six floors and got messy on the asphalt in front of McCormick's Fish House and Bar.

Lovely thought, wasn't it?

But it wasn't as though he had much of a choice. Unless, of course, he wanted to look like a pansy. Normally, the crack to his tough-guy reputation wouldn't bother him.

That's what his middle finger was for…to say fuck off to anyone who gave him grief. Tonight, though, he was off his game. The whole dragon thing still freaked him out.

Mac ran his hand through his hair. His leather jacket stretched across his shoulders, reminding him he'd learned to conjure the thing less than an hour ago.

Conjure.

Mother of God, that sounded weird. Like something a voodoo high priestess said during ritualized killings or something. Okay, so the skill was useful. He'd cop to that. No one wanted to see him bare-assed in the moonlight, but man, the ability to whip up leather gear with nothing but a thought fit nicely into the little bag of horrors he'd been carrying around all day.

Which, naturally, pissed him off.

He'd never been the kind of guy who got rattled. Uh-huh. Cool under fire, that was him. But tonight, standing on top of the Columbia Center in downtown Seattle, Mac wondered if that was about to change.

Blowing out a breath, he glanced at the night sky as gravel crunched under his boots. The real estate above him was cloudless and clear, a strange occurrence for Seattle, especially for the time of year. Fall brought rain and cold, damp weather. Bitter wind aside, though, tonight was picture perfect. A wash of midnight blue with pinpoint stars that winked at him from their beds beyond the earth.

Another gust pushed against his back, spinning into mini tornados around his boots. Rolling his shoulders, Mac headed for the raised edge of the roof.

Venom passed him on the left-hand side, brushing shoulders with him.

"Dickhead," he said, trying out his fancy new mode of communication.

Ruby-red eyes flashed, then narrowed as Venom mind-spoke, *"Pansy-ass fledgling."*

Mac clenched his teeth, holding on to his grin. Ah, the sweet stab of predictability. The touchy SOB had been rising to his bait all day. Made for an easy target and even more fun. And hey…wonder of wonders, he'd graduated sometime in the last two hours, moving from *blockhead* to *pansy-ass fledgling.*

Pretty soon the guy would call him *brother,* instead of slinging insults. Mac would make sure of it. Make Dickhead eat his words before the night was done. Yeah, he might be new, but he wasn't a lightweight. He belonged with the Nightfuries. Felt it in his bones. Knew it with more certainty than he had anything in his life.

He was one of them. No fucking doubt. Now all he needed to do was prove it.

The toes of his shitkickers touched the skyscraper's metal lip. Mac peered over the edge. His stomach pitched then rebounded, leaving a bad taste in his mouth. From seventy-six stories up, everything looked miniature, like the detailed mock-ups architects constructed for their clients. Small green trees, tops swaying in the breeze. Tiny people rushing to get somewhere: home, the market, maybe even a restaurant to meet their spouses. And the cars looked like colorful Hot Wheels instead of life-size versions.

Mac frowned at the ground. "You're out of your fucking mind."

"Myst's building isn't tall enough." Shoulder-to-shoulder with him, Bastian glanced at him sideways. "You need lots of height for the first go-round. Columbia Center is the tallest building in Seattle…the best bet to get you airborne."

And what? There wasn't a happy medium between five stories and…shit. *This?*

Bastian raised a brow. "You used to jump out of airplanes for a living."

"With a parachute."

"You've got better than that now," Bastian said. "You've got wings."

Did he ever. And yeah, those fuckers were cool, but only if they opened. Only if he figured out how to work them. And what did that depend on?

Wait for it…

Shifting into dragon form while free-falling from a thousand feet up. Not something he was all that confident he could do. Sure, he'd spent the day practicing, but if there was one thing he'd learned in the SEAL teams, it was that stress screwed with performance. Practice made perfect. That's why they'd drilled so hard, running through training ops until everyone had it down cold. But what Bastian wanted him to do wasn't about practice. It was trial by fire… do it right the first time or go splat.

"All right." Rolling his shoulders, Mac worked out the kinks. He went through the usual checklist, the way a pilot would his preflight routine. Body ready? Check. Mind focused? Double check. New magical abilities? Okay, so the jury was still out on that one, but what the hell. It was now or never. He wanted to become a member of the Nightfury pack. If he acted like the blockhead Venom liked to call him, he'd never earn their respect. "Tell me again."

"Venom's on point. You follow him." With a flick of his hand, Bastian pointed to the building across from them.

Moonlight reflected off the glass, throwing black scales into stark relief. Hanging upside down like a bat, talons curled around the steel structure, Wick tipped his chin, acknowledging him without speaking. "Wick'll help you with trajectory, flank your right wing while I keep you cloaked and stay on your left."

Cloaked. Another new trick. "When will I be able to do that?"

"One thing at a time. Tonight's for flying. Once you're back at the lair, we'll teach you the other stuff."

Good enough. One thing at a time sounded like an excellent strategy and about all he could handle at the moment. Putting himself in reverse, Mac counted out each step as he backed away from the edge of the roof. Take a running leap while yelling *Geronimo!* the whole way down. His kind of plan.

Seven feet from the ledge, he settled into a runner stance. "Who's got my six?"

"I do." Like a wraith in the dark, the voice came out of nowhere.

"Jesus Christ!" Mac spun, dropping into a fighting stance.

His fists raised, he searched the shadows and saw…nothing. A heartbeat later, a white dragon uncloaked, becoming visible in the darkness. Rikar. Mac knew it without asking. He recognized the vintage, 100 percent lethal. Horned head cocked to one side, pale eyes narrowed, Rikar looked him over as he tucked his wings. Jesus, he was a sight to behold, blinding against the night sky, so beautiful in dragon form he took Mac's breath away and…

Goddamn it. After the hellish day. After wishing Rikar hadn't split—that the male had been around to show him the ropes instead of off saving the world—he was so happy to see the bastard, he said, "Well, aren't you pretty."

Rikar snorted, tendrils of frost rising from his nostrils.

Venom grinned, amusement slaying his perpetually pissed-off attitude. And Wick? Per usual, the Nightfury didn't make a sound.

Bastian laughed. "Yeah, the prettiest form of lethal. That's our boy."

And just like that? Crisis averted. Pansy-ass status revoked. He was back on solid ground, a Dragonkind male with the chops to hold his own with the others.

Meeting Rikar's gaze, Mac tipped his chin. The question was a silent one and…thank fuck. His new XO was quick on the uptake.

"She's safe. Was sleeping when I left the lair."

"Good," he murmured, relief riding him hard. Ange was his best friend—a great detective, his little sister by choice, but man, she had a knack for finding trouble. She'd been his responsibility the last two years. Now he had help—thank you, God—and knowing she was safe did wonders for his confidence. Nodding once at Rikar, he turned back to face the ledge. "Heads up, boys."

Venom shifted, skin morphing into green scales, wings spread wide as he left his perch on the rooftop. Arms and legs pumping, Mac hauled ass toward the edge. Rikar took flight as Bastian transformed, midnight-blue scales flashing in Mac's periphery. No turning back now.

No second chances. It was now or never.

With a curse, he planted his boot on the raised lip and leapt, launching himself into the open sky. Stretching his arms wide, he swan-dived into a freefall, clearing his mind, waiting for enough wing space to transform. One

Mississippi. *Please, God.* Two Mississippi. *I'll do anything.* Three Mississippi. *If you'll...just...let...me...clear the...*

Presto chango.

Hands and feet turned to claws. Skin morphed into blue-gray scales, and his spine lengthened under a razor-sharp blade as he unfolded his wings.

Rikar hoorahed.

The rest echoed the sentiment.

Mac growled and, fangs bared, took a tight turn, banking around the sharp edge of another skyscraper as he flew toward the ocean. Bastian cursed. Mac didn't care. He needed to swim, and it had to be now.

Chapter Sixteen

Bastian dropped another f-bomb. Rikar growled, seconding the motion, becoming chairman of the committee to kick Mac's ass. The male had gone AWOL, flying off half-cocked, losing his mind in downtown Seattle. All without the ability to cloak himself in dragon form. And with Venom and Wick out of the picture—peeling off from the pack to investigate Lothair's disappearing Houdini act from the night before—that left him and B scrambling to pick up the slack. And leapfrogging over the cityscape to cover the new guy's flank? Not on his list of favorite things to do on a Saturday night.

Especially with Angela at home waiting for him.

Freaking male. Mac was fucking up his plans.

Rikar snarled, baring his fangs. Just wait until he got his claws on their new boy. The cop was in for a smackdown of epic proportions. But first things first. He needed to catch the crazy SOB.

Easier said than done.

Mac flew incredibly well. Had gone kamikaze with a capital K.

"Mac!" he said through mind-speak, trying to drag the male back to reality.

No answer.

Rikar yelled at the cop again.

Nothing.

Banking hard, Rikar rocketed around the Space Needle, hoping to intercept Mac on the other side. A no-go. Christ, the male was fast. And not even close to normal.

Most fledglings flopped around like baby birds before they learned to use their wings and maneuver with any speed. But oh, no. Not Mac. The cop cornered like a pro. Had the weave and dodge down cold, maneuvering between low-lying buildings and high-rises with equal efficiency. Headed for where exactly?

The fucking ocean. Rikar's least favorite place in the world.

Not that he blamed Mac. His reaction wasn't uncommon and…joy, oh, joy. The carnival ride called crazy he and Bastian were on was Rikar's fault. He should've known the flash-and-fly would happen once Mac got out into the open. Despite his inexperience, the male was a warrior. His aggressive nature and history with the military—not to mention his record with the SPD—proved it. So it stood to reason the male would react the same way he and the other Nightfury warriors had after the change.

Rikar knew all his comrades' war stories. Had listened to each one recall the experience at one time or another. Usually while sitting around the dining room table playing poker. Texas Hold 'Em, at Wick's insistence.

They'd all gone a little nuts after transition. Bastian, he knew, had gotten up close and personal with a lightning strike once or…ah, make that seven times. A fire dragon, Wick had burrowed deep into the earth, cozying up to lava flow. And Venom? Shit, that male had spent an entire week in the ozone, breathing in poisonous fumes. His own transition hadn't been much better. He'd flown into a glacier crevice, enveloping himself with nothing but ice and subzero temperatures, and hadn't come out for three weeks.

So, yeah. He understood the instinct driving Mac. As a water dragon, he wanted to be deep in the ocean, surrounded by nothing but SeaWorld.

Which was a major frickin' problem.

Downtown Seattle was prime hunting ground. For Nightfury and Razorback alike. If he didn't rein Mac in soon, the enemy would detect the energy Mac threw out like a beacon and—

"Shit," Bastian growled, banking hard around another skyscraper. *"Heads up, man."*

Ah, hell. That didn't sound good. *"Whatcha got?"*

"Incoming. Five strong."

A tail length behind Mac, Rikar mirrored his commander, rocketing around the other side of the building. As he came around the corner, he flew up and over the spikes on B's back. *"Talk to me."*

"Razorbacks…three miles out and closing fast."

Translation? ETA a minute and a half. Not good on any level. Except…

Maybe that wasn't true. Maybe he'd just been given a gift. Maybe he could end it here and give Angela the justice she wanted and the closure she needed. All without allowing his female into the mix or putting her in danger. Rikar's heart thumped a little harder. Please, God, let the asshole rogue XO be with the pack headed their way.

Wings spread wide, almost directly over the cop now, Rikar growled, *"Is Lothair with them?"*

"No."

"Fuck."

"Rikar, man...we'll get him. Just not tonight."

"Take one alive." The plan? Beat the snot out of the asshole. Question the rogue until he gave up the goods, the longs and lats of the Razorback lair. Angela wanted the other female captives rescued. And what his female asked for, she got. Shit, he'd do anything—gift wrap and lay them at her feet—just to see her smile. *"Cull the weakest from the pack. I'll ice him up. You bring him to ground."*

"Fucking A," B said, Nightfury speak for "oh, goody."

His gaze still locked on Mac, Rikar's sonar pinged. Sensation curled around his horns. Close. The fuckers were so close. Another minute and the rogues would engage. *"Lay it out, B."*

Pulling his gift for reading a male's strengths and weaknesses out of his bag of tricks, his best friend said, *"Four breathe fire. The fifth...toxic fumes."*

Well, all right. A poison breather. Nothing like mixing it up a bit.

Within takedown distance now, Bastian flew in on the cop's right wing tip. *"What about our new boy?"*

"Let him go." Taking another tight turn, Rikar slowed his roll, letting the distance between him and Mac lengthen. *"We'll pull him out of the water after we're through."*

The strategy was a good one. Even outnumbered almost three to one, Rikar didn't want the cop anywhere near the battle. An untrained dragon was more hindrance than help. Combat required tactical coaching, and aerial maneuverability—the ability to fight with claws, fangs, and tail instead of hands, feet, and AK-47s—took time to develop. So, yeah, he needed Mac in the water and out of the line of fire ASAP.

Almost there. Thirty seconds and Mac would be—

The cop's head snapped to the side. His shimmering aquamarine eyes narrowed and—

Fuck. The male was more than AWOL. He'd crossed into clusterfuck country. Wings angled, Mac wheeled away from the waterfront, turning into the rogue's flight path. Rikar raced to intercept him.

Too late.

Mac was already in the mix and on enemy radar. In fighting formation, the Razorbacks came in like vipers: fast, hard, without hesitation or mercy.

Bastian growled.

Rikar cursed.

Mac hissed. And water-acid flew, shooting between the cop's fangs. Right on target, the slime hit the lead Razorback dead-on, spraying into his eyes and over the top of his horns. The rogue screamed and, clawing at his face, fell out of the sky like a lodestone.

Flying in fast, Rikar engaged a red dragon to protect Mac's flank. Grabbing the male's head, he snapped the rogue's neck while B exhaled. His best friend's electrostatic pulse flashed across the night sky. The lightning bolt hammered another rogue in the chest as, claws deployed, Mac attacked a yellow dragon.

Fantastic.

Trust the cop to snap out of his water fixation and fuck up a perfectly good plan. Christ, he was in neck-deep in Holy-Shitsville. 'Cause…yeah. Angela would find some 9 mms, load the Glock he'd given her, and use Rikar for target practice if he didn't get Mac to Black Diamond in one piece.

Stupid fledgling. Idiot male.

Intercepting a Razorback on a collision course with Mac, Rikar sideswiped the enemy dragon with his claws. Blood arced in a violent splash, painting Rikar's white scales red. Mac snarled, tucked his wings, and swung around, lashing out with his bladed tail. Rikar ducked to avoid the backlash. The rogue wasn't as lucky. His eyes went wide a second before a thin line appeared at his throat and the male's head left his body. As the enemy dragon ashed, the remains of the dead blew into Rikar's face. And for a split second, he thought maybe…just maybe…the cop would make it out alive.

Man, he hoped so because after the firefight he was going to beat the shit out of Mac for insubordination.

Mac reeled as the rogue landed another uppercut. His head snapped back. The yellow dragon came at him again, ramming his skull into his rib cage. Pain ripped through him as his body torqued and his senses exploded. A second ball-busting sideswipe. More sharp claws digging into his scales. Another gut-wrenching head butt and he was spinning, lost in the cloud of agony and whirl of night sky. His vision dimmed, blurring at the edges as city lights streaked into long-tailed comets.

Sucking wind, Mac lost sight of the enemy as blood washed over his fangs. The metallic taste burned, slid down the back of his throat and—

Goddamn, he was fucked. In an endless freefall. Tumbling so fast he was in for the mother of all face-plants if he didn't pull his head out of his ass. And his body out of the nosedive.

He thrust his wings out, using the webbing like a parachute. Air caught and held. Rushing into an updraft, he flipped in midair and made a tight turn. Thank God. He was airborne again, able to maneuver, gain speed, avoid the enemy.

Bleeding like a sieve from innumerable places, he searched the sky and—

Motherfuck. The yellow-scaled pissant was persistent. And as the Razorback came at him again, Mac dodged, avoiding another body shot as he flew around the curve of a water tower. Another rogue met him on the other side. Brown with a horn in the center of his forehead, the rogue swiped at him. Mac twisted, trying to compensate, his newfound dragon instincts screaming in warning.

Too late.

The Razorbacks were smart, working in tandem, tag-teaming him—one herding him from behind, one coming at him head-on—using his inexperience and their skill to hem him in.

Dark eyes aglow, the brown dragon exhaled. A thick, green cloud shot from his mouth. Noxious fumes rolled out in front of him. The cityscape faded behind the toxic fog. The yellow Razorback banked hard, dodging behind Mac, splitting wide right, and…

Bam.

The toxin hit Mac full in the face. He gagged. His throat closed as his lungs seized. Pain squeezed around his rib cage, made his eyes water and…oh, man. The stuff smelled nasty and tasted worse, a bad mix of dead fish, Pepto-Bismol, and paint thinner.

Racked by a fit of coughing, Mac wing-flapped, desperate to gain altitude. The rogue inhaled again. Mac flew harder, chest heaving, struggling to get out of the way. Goddamn. This wasn't good. He had a bull's-eye on his forehead, and he'd lost momentum. He might as well pin a frickin' sign to his chest. One that said, "Hit me here. Kill me dead."

A second before the rogue hammered him again, movement flashed in his periphery. A white streak, more blur than actual substance, rocketed passed him. Frost rolled in its wake, blanketing the air, icing up building facades, killing the poisonous gas. The brown-scaled rogue shrieked, trying to change course.

But Rikar was faster. With a nifty flip, his XO grabbed hold and torqued the rogue into a full-body twist. The tilt-a-whirl took both males up and over before Rikar let go, hurling the asshole like a shot-putter and—

Clang!

The sound warped the air as the enemy dragon collided with the water tower skull-first. The rogue's neck whiplashed, but the hard-headed asshole didn't fall. He bounced, rebounding off the steel. Shaking off the should've-been concussion, the male growled and came back for more.

"Mac! Go!" Rikar shouted. *"Get out of here!"*

Mac snarled. No way. Not in this lifetime.

He refused to leave Rikar. So he was inexperienced. Didn't know what he was doing. Could hardly tell his claws from his tail. Big deal. There were too many Razorbacks. B and Rikar needed him. So fuck it. Whether his XO liked it or not, Mac was sticking around. If nothing else, he was an excellent distraction. With Jackass and Fuck-Face chasing him around, the bastards wouldn't be able to blindside his friends.

Stupid, crazy-ass idea? Maybe. A serious case of ego? Absolutely.

But no retreat meant *no retreat.* And Mac had something to prove. Even without dragon combat training, he belonged here. Among the Nightfuries in the heat of battle. He felt it keenly, knew it deep down where truth lived and honor made a home.

"Rikar," he said, firing up mind-speak. *"Split wide right."*

Rikar growled a warning.

Mac didn't care. All he wanted was—

Rikar banked right.

The second his XO cleared the line of fire, Mac exhaled. Water-acid streamed between his fangs. The yellow dragon dove, heading for a rooftop. Shit. He'd missed. Snapping his head around, Mac spotted Fuck-Face. He tucked into a spiral and breathed out again. The Razorback drew up short.

The bastard wasn't fast enough.

Mac slimed him, coating his left side. As the deadly splatter went to work eating a hole in the Razorback's wing, the male screamed and plummeted toward the ground. Mac rocketed between two high-rises. Windowpanes rattled as he zeroed in, timed it just right, sliced his enemy on a flyby. The sharp blade of his tail sank deep, cutting through hard scales to reach the beating heart beneath soft flesh. With a sudden implosion, the rogue ashed, turning to dust in the midnight breeze.

"Good boy," Rikar said.

"Fuck off." Frickin' guy…he could stick his praise up his ass. And rotate.

His XO laughed and, white scales flashing, attacked another Razorback.

Mac swung around and searched the skyline. One down. One to go. His eyes narrowed, but…nothing. No flash of yellow scales. No fireball hurtling through the air. Scanning the alleys between buildings, Mac sped over rooftops, flying fast, looking for the enemy dragon.

"Come on, Jackass," he murmured. "Come out and play."

Seconds ticked by, slipping into more. Something flashed in his periphery, and Mac spotted him. Stupid Razorback. Jackass was the same color inside and out. Yellow. The coward was in full retreat, flitting between buildings, using the rooftops for cover as he slunk away from the firefight.

Mac growled. Uh-uh. No way. He refused to let the rogue escape. Not after taking hit after hit from the bastard. The Razorback would pay for each bruise, every cut, all the stitches Mac would need once the fighting was over.

Wings spread wide, Mac streaked over an apartment complex, hoping all the balconies were empty. The last thing he needed was to come face-to-fang with a stargazer. If he did, the guy would get a load of something he really didn't want to see, but without Rikar, he was hopeless in the cloaking department. Didn't know how to go dark and silent like the other Nightfury warriors.

Man, he really needed to read that handbook. The one entitled *Fangs and Claws: A Rudimentary Guide to All Things Dragon.*

But oh, no. Not him. He didn't do anything the easy way. Ass-backward was more his style. So when it came to the Razorback up ahead, he planned to do it the hard way. The strategy went something like…

Hit hard. Hit fast. And hope for the best.

Cranking his kill-o-meter all the way to lethal, Mac rolled in hot. Thirty feet out, the yellow dragon's head snapped around as though the male sensed his approach. Jackass hissed and changed course, wheeling toward him instead of away. Ah, wasn't that sweet? The rogue wanted to play, and Mac knew the perfect game to teach him. One called kick ass.

As he came within range, Mac lashed out, aiming for the Razorback's throat. The rogue pulled a roll-and-dive. Fuck. He missed by an inch, catching nothing but air. Not wasting a second, Mac flipped up and over. He struck again. Jackass tucked his wings, but not fast enough. Muscles pulled along Mac's side as his claws raked yellow scales. Blood sprayed, splashing up his forearm. The rogue shrieked. Mac twisted in midair and hammered the back of Jackass's skull. His talon cracked against bone. The brutal sound pinged off the steel and glass, reverberated between buildings.

Winging out, the echo reached the ocean.

Mac blinked. Jesus. The ocean.

The perfect plan. A midnight swim *and* a dead rogue. Oh, goody. Two for the price of one.

The Razorback flipped into a tight turn. His speed supersonic, the dragon came at him like a shark, attacking from below. Mac banked hard. Wind whistled in his ears. The smell of saltwater infused him as he flew toward the water.

Thirty seconds away, the bay sparkled beneath the clear sky, choppy waves illuminated by city lights and the full moon. White streaks streamed from Mac's wing tips, then curled behind him in the cold air. Right on his tail, the wisps blew into the rogue's face. He caught a flash of fangs from his periphery as Jackass snapped at him.

Mac changed trajectory. Flew hard for Seattle's shoreline, leading the Razorback where he wanted him to go.

Come on, you little shit. Come on.

Wings vertical, Mac flew between two warehouses. Industrial cranes soared up ahead, dark sticklike silhouettes jutting skyward from a concrete pier. He flew between them. Over stacked shipping containers and a bobbing ocean freighter and…

Eureka. Elliott Bay, dead ahead.

Straightening out, Mac increased his wing speed and glanced over his shoulder. The rogue was still there. Beautiful. Jackass had taken the bait, was staying right on his tail.

Dipping low, Mac came in like a viper over the bay. Fine mist washed over his scales. He breathed deep, loving the scent of ocean brine. With a quick shift, Mac wheeled toward the rogue. Jackass wing-flapped, surprise flaring in his shimmering eyes. Trying to compensate, the Razorback sucked in a breath. An orange ball of flame gathered at the back of his throat. Before he could release it, Mac struck, hitting the rogue head-on.

Timed to perfection, he grabbed the rogue's tail. Sharp spikes ripping at his talon, Mac yanked hard. The Razorback squawked, clawing at thin air as he got dragged down and—

Splash!

Saltwater rushed over Mac's scales, filled his nose, his mouth, his lungs, and…

Oh, yeah. That was wicked good. Nothing better than deep blue waves, a whole lot of cold, dark, and wet. Not that the rogue appreciated it. The male was too busy squawking, splashing, flailing around. And as the rogue struggled to lift himself clear of the water, Mac took over.

Baring his fangs, he grabbed the SOB by the scruff of the neck and pushed his head under. A second later, he allowed him to surface. Watched his enemy sputter and heave, beg in the moonlight for his life. But mercy wasn't part of the plan.

Dunk. Hold under. Let the bastard surface. Listen to him beg.

Mac repeated the roll over and over. When Jackass went limp and begged for death instead of life, he took pity and dove, dragging the rogue deep under the surface of the water.

Jackass had wanted to play. It wasn't Mac's fault that he was now in over his head.

The last rogue turned tail and ran, streaking across the night sky like a long-tailed comet. Rikar watched the Razorback bug out, wanting to go after him. Hunt the enemy down. Make 'em pay. That was his motto. But not tonight, apparently. He had bigger fish to fry.

One that Bastian kept insisting was his responsibility—lucky him—but the addition to his to-do list was the least of his problems at the moment.

He couldn't see Mac anywhere. Had lost sight of the male in the cityscape while slashing the turquoise dragon's throat. Hmm, such a *nice* memory. Too bad the here-and-now wasn't as pleasant. Where the hell had their new boy gone?

Rikar scanned the dark horizon where land met water. Worry twisted his gut up tight. It didn't make any sense. He should be able to track the cop. Feel him from anywhere.

He'd connected to Mac's core energy while getting him through the change. Now he recognized the guy's vibe as well as he did his Nightfury brothers'. Unique to the individual, each male possessed a signature, a signal they sent into the world like radio waves. Once a male linked to another, he could track a fellow dragon for hundreds, sometimes thousands of miles.

Made it hard to disappear. Get good and ghost if a male close to you didn't like the endgame. Shit. He should know. B had come after him a time or two. Of course, the opposite was also true.

So, yeah. Getting a lock on Mac should've been easy. But *easy* wasn't in the mix. The male's signal was muffled by something, a thick barrier that distorted the beacon. But at least Rikar could feel him now, and that meant their boy wasn't dead. Yet.

That might change, though, when he got his hands on him.

The male had disobeyed a direct order. Refusing to retreat when he told him to. Rikar frowned. Freaking cop. Mac had balls made of steel. And although he respected him for it, an equal and opposite reaction had him by the throat. One that wanted him to rearrange Mac's face for scaring the hell out of him.

Rikar shook his head and kept searching, mining Mac's energy vibe. God, he'd almost lost the male tonight. One false move and Mac would've been nothing but ash. Another urn on a shelf. Another name carved into the wall inside Black Diamond's Hall of Memories.

Reveling in the night chill, Rikar exhaled long and smooth. Frost rolled between his fangs. The icy mist washed out in front of him, then blew back to coat his scales as he increased his wing speed. Wood smoke and the smell of furnace oil drifted on the autumn air, held high by the north wind drifting in over the city. In another month winter would come, settling over Seattle like a frosty blanket of mmm, mmm good.

Man, he could hardly wait.

As he circled over apartment buildings, Rikar scanned the alleys below. His night vision sharp, he cast a wide visual net, sonar pinging, sending out calls he hoped Mac would answer. But maybe the male was down. Or hurt. Unable to link in through mind-speak.

Bastian flew by, thumping him with the side of his tail.

The love tap brushed one of his bruised ribs. Rikar flinched. *"Ow! Shit, B…that hurt."*

"Suck it up. There are worse things."

"Like what?"

"The fact you're about to get wet."

Rikar blew out a long breath. The exhale started off smooth but ended on a growl. He should've guessed. The water. No way could Mac resist its allure for long. *"Elliott Bay?"*

"Smack dab in the middle of it."

"Fuck." Dawn was only three hours away. If he couldn't talk Mac into coming out by then, he'd be forced to go in and pull a grab-and-go. With Mac fighting him every step of the way. *"I hate my job."*

Bastian laughed. *"You got him through the change, my man. He's one hundred percent yours."*

Fantastic. Most males got a fire dragon as a sidekick. But oh, no. Not him. He landed a water dragon. Just his freaking luck.

He only hoped Mac went the reasonable route. Otherwise Elliott Bay would end up as one big ice bath. Not something the human authorities would understand. Or get over quickly.

"He's got a rogue down there with him."

He threw Bastian an incredulous look. *"You're shitting me."*

"Nope," B said. *"The yellow fucker...the male that kept attacking him."*

Rikar's heart picked up a beat, thumping hard. A Razorback. Mac had gotten a hold of a rogue, one that might have valuable intel. Holy shit. Maybe the night didn't have *screwed up* plastered all over it. Maybe he could salvage something from the snafu. Bring Angela home the information she wanted and—

He needed to reach his boy...fast.

Putting his wings to good use, Rikar streaked over the Port of Seattle. Still a mess from their showdown with Ivar, the shipyard lay in shambles. Busted-up steel containers, cracked concrete, a beat-to-shit industrial crane, and an ocean freighter with a huge dent in its hull were only part of the tally. Nothing but dark dots on shadowed pavement, the humans scurried around. In clean-up mode, men drove forklifts and front-end loaders in the hopes of returning everything to the status quo.

Rikar snorted. Good luck with that. The second Wick—the brother that liked to toss heavy machinery around for kicks and giggles—flew by, the place would only get fucked up again.

Reaching the middle of the bay, Rikar circled once, searching the water beneath the spray of four-foot waves. A pinpoint glow caught his attention just below the waterline.

Bingo. He had a lock on Mac. Aquamarine eyes aglow, the male surfaced with the yellow dragon. Bladed tail swishing, webbed claws out in full force, Mac controlled the Razorback completely, playing with him, letting him take a breath before dragging him back under.

Rikar's mouth curved. He couldn't help it. Mac was vicious, beyond the pale of good behavior. And shit, that just made him proud. Too bad he didn't have time to let the cop explore the good, the bad, or the ugly side of his nature. He needed the enemy male alive. Conscious enough to spill his secrets.

"Mac."

The male growled in answer.

"Bring the Razorback up."

"No." Holding the rogue's head under, the nine-inch-high blade running down the center of Mac's spine broke the surface of the water. Rikar stared at it for a second, watching it knife through the choppy spray. Christ, a shark's fin didn't have a thing on the male. The sight freaked Rikar out a little. It would be next to impossible to haul Mac out of the ocean if the cop didn't want to come. Mac was in his natural habitat. Even a frost dragon couldn't compete with that. *"He's mine."*

"Come on, man. I need him." White scales flashing in the moonlight, Rikar made another pass, watching the distorted shadows beneath the waves. *"Stop fucking around."*

Mac hissed.

Rikar snarled in return, the sound aggressive and sure. All about being an XO, not a buddy.

Air bubbles popped like blisters, breaking the surface of the water. Afraid the rogue was already dead, Rikar snapped, *"Mac! Get your ass up here! Or I swear to fucking God, I'm gonna turn you into an ice cube."*

"Miiine."

Terrific. Threatening the idiot wouldn't get Rikar what he wanted. Mac was too far gone. It was a case of instinct over intellect. For a fledgling, it was normal. For a warrior, it could prove deadly.

Rikar changed tack, using the one thing he knew Mac would respond to...even with the mind-fuck the male had going on. *"Angela needs him, Mac. He's got intel that your partner needs. Without it, I can't keep her safe."*

"Fuck." A pause then, *"Your word. I get to kill him after... my way."*

Circling in behind him, Bastian joined the party. *"Deal."*

In an instant, Elliott Bay's choppy surf went smooth. No waves. No ripples. Absolute stillness, like a pane of blue-white glass. Freaky. And really fucking cool. Especially when the water shifted, began to turn and dip, getting sucked toward the bottom of the harbor. As a whirlpool opened beneath Rikar, the wind came up, howling as it whipped the smell of brine into the air.

"Incoming," Mac said. *"Catch."*

Yellow scales flashed in the swirling depths of the funnel. A second later, Mac launched the rogue out of the water and into midair, turning the enemy dragon into a torpedo.

Chapter Seventeen

In his usual spot, flat on his back in the middle of the concrete floor, Forge cracked an eye open as steel clicked against steel. It sounded like a gun being cocked at close range. But nay, it was just the door to his prison getting put to good use. The soft hiss of hinges slithered through the silence. Quiet footfalls followed, ping-ponging off the walls and down the wide open space in front of the cellblock to reach him. The whispers came next. Held high by the rush of air from the ventilation system, the murmurs drifted, sounding as loud as a shout to his sharply keen senses.

Forge hummed. Visitors. How nice.

Even better? They came with a plan and clear purpose. Came to play a deadly game of mental chess. One he excelled at, too bad for them.

Allowing his eyes to drift closed again, he listened to the voices. Studied the tone and nuance of each. Picked up the tenor. Read the determination that hinted of desperation. He added a dab of well-meaning manipulation to the pot, and…boom! He had a recipe for disaster in the making.

With a sigh, he folded his arms behind his head, waiting for…ah, and there it was. Right on time. Her scent reached him. Myst was back. And she'd brought a friend. Another female along with his son.

Forge's mouth curved. God love her. Aye, she might be planning an ambush, one with him as the main meal, but at least she wasn't cruel. And as he listened to his bairn's happy coo echo down the corridor, he thanked his lucky stars. A male would've used his lad as leverage. Taunted him with the promise of seeing him if Forge traded information, but not Myst. She believed a father had a right to his son. And that a son needed his father.

A shortcoming on the strategy front?

Maybe. But Forge didn't think so. He was more inclined to talk to her—help and give her what she wanted because of her kindness.

Which made him a first-class fool.

He should be using her soft heart against her. Not admiring her for it. But it was what it *was*. No changing that. So he went with it instead, ears attuned to their every move, picking up the faint noises like a stray dog did table scraps.

It was sad, really. How much he wanted to see Myst and her guest, to hear their voices up close and talk to them in return. He'd been alone for a while with nothing but silence and his own thoughts to keep him company. Well, that, and the sound of his own heartbeat. He took the fact it was still thumping as a good sign. Especially with Frosty beating a death drum with his name on it.

So, aye. The females were welcome. Even though he knew it wasn't a courtesy call.

Myst was too single-minded for that. She needed information. Intel she believed he possessed, so coming to him was a logical choice. Too bad he couldn't give her what she wanted. Not yet. Not until Bastian caved.

Such a shame. He really didn't want to hurt her.

His ears tuned, he listened to his visitors' approach. Flip-flip-flop. Flip-flip-flop. Bloody hell, he loved that sound. It was such a feminine one, so lovely and familiar he smiled. Which was a bad idea. Especially if he didn't wipe it off his puss before Myst saw it. No sense handing her that kind of tactical advantage. The second she thought he was glad to see her, she'd use it against him.

Oh so unwise.

Forge wanted her to believe he was a brute, capable of anything, unworthy of her concern and attention. Maybe then she'd realize he was a lost cause. Stop trying to save him. Win him over. Make him believe second chances existed for a male like him.

Dangerous. The game she played was so bloody dangerous.

And one he'd bet his eyeteeth Bastian didn't know about yet. He snorted. Jesus, the male would lose it when he found out. But for now, Forge would enjoy her visits. And hope for more.

Without opening his eyes, he knew the exact moment she cleared the corner of his cell. "My lady Munroe…to what do I owe the pleasure?"

"Oh, shut up and get over here," she said, tone tart. "Your son wants to see you. And I want to introduce you to someone."

Forge grinned. He couldn't help it. It was hard not to like Bastian's female. "Let me guess…one of SPD's finest."

He tried to sound casual, but fuck him, relief came through as his throat went tight. Rikar had gotten her out, rescued her from Razorback hell. And no matter his beef with the Nightfuries, he couldn't help but be grateful for their cunning efficiency. No female deserved to be treated that way. Left to linger in pain and despair.

"It's Angela…or Ange," she said, voice soft yet somehow strong. "Take your pick."

Unfolding his arms from behind his head, he planted a hand on the cold concrete and popped to his feet. As he turned toward the front of his cell, he got a load of the newcomer. Halle Berry short, her red hair shone in the low light and…shite. She was pretty with her intelligent hazel eyes and a whole lot of edge. No surprise there. Plugged into the Meridian, she was high-energy, power personified, her aura flaming bright and true. But unlike Myst's gentle warmth, Angela's was jewel-like: hard, cold, rooted in icy resolve and a never-say-quit attitude.

No wonder Rikar wanted her so badly. Her chilly energy was exactly what Frosty would crave and…hmm. Had he mentioned she smelled lovely too? Like ice and evergreens, fresh as a cold winter morning. A beautiful combination that reminded Forge of his Highland home. He tipped his chin, his acknowledgement of her a silent one.

Playing shuffleboard with the container she held, she shuttled it from one hand to the other. After a second, she mimicked his movement, greeting him without words.

"Crap," Myst said.

With a frown, his focus snapped to Bastian's female, concerned something was…

Nay. Nothing wrong. No threat but the scowl on her face as she noticed the new decor. À la Japan, large square cushions sat on the floor. Set up a safe distance from his cell's invisible barrier, smaller pillows flanked the whole, acting as backrests, inviting the females to sit down and get comfortable. But the best part? The minibar. Pushed against the end wall, it contained all sorts of fun stuff: fancy fruit juice, milk, bottled water, Perrier in pretty green bottles, chocolate treats wrapped in colorful packages. And he should know. He'd watched as it was stocked. Sat with his back propped against his cell wall while the whole deal went down.

His lips twitched. "The Numbai was here."

"Obviously." Cradling his son in her arms, Myst stared at the thick floor cushions and grimaced. "Oh, man, we're totally screwed."

Ah, just as he suspected. "Bastian still doesnae know?"

Chewing on her bottom lip, she shook her head. "He's going to flip out the second he sees this. Freaking Daimler. Talk about a dead giveaway."

"Thought the butler loved you," Angela said.

"He probably does," Forge murmured, watching the two together. He got the sense they'd just met, but…aye. They were a solid match personality-wise and would become fast friends before long. "But he cannae stand the thought of Myst being uncomfortable."

Angela threw him a questioning look.

In an answering frame of mind, he said, "The Numbai are the serving class, lass…the caretakers of Dragonkind. Daimler's sole purpose in life is tae see tae his master's comfort."

"And by 'master'…" Lifting her free hand, Myst scrunched her middle and index fingers, making quotation marks. "He means everyone under Black Diamond's roof."

"A bit archaic," Angela said.

"I thought so, too, at first." Stepping over the large, square cushion, his son cradled in her arms, Myst sat, folding her legs Indian-style. "Until I realized he runs this place.

Because at Black Diamond? Daimler's the boss. He's valued for his service and loves every minute of it."

Angela mouthed "oookay."

And Forge understood. She hadn't been with the Nightfuries long. All the differences—the idiosyncrasies—of his race were new to her. Would seem strange when looked at from human experience. That would change soon enough. Rikar's scent was all over the female. The Nightfuries' first-in-command had fed her, and now whether Angela knew it or not, they were connected through energy-fuse. No way the male would let her go.

Which explained why these two were ganging up on him.

Not that he minded. He liked their company. Craved conversation the way a child did affection, and the females were just what the doctor ordered.

Following her friend's lead, Angela sat down on a neighboring cushion. As she got comfortable, nestling into the makeshift seat cross-legged, she set the container down in front of her and slipped her hand behind her back. She came away with a gun. One glance at him and she set the piece down gently, muzzle pointing in his direction on the concrete floor.

"You gonnae shoot me?"

She shrugged. "Only if I feel like it."

Forge laughed. He couldn't help it. He liked Angela Keen. He really did. She was strong, direct, with a whole lot of moxie. Rikar had chosen his female well.

"I'll be careful, then," he murmured, zeroing in on the blue tin Angela set down next to the gun. Covered in small snowflakes, the container piqued his interest. Made his eyes narrow and his heart thud a little faster.

What the hell was in it? A bomb? No, wait. Poisonous gas that would pour into his face the second he flipped the thing open. Nah, not really Myst's style. Not Angela's, either. Shite, that female would rather shoot him than poison him, so...

Something sweet, maybe? Oh, man, he hoped so. After watching Daimler stock the minibar, he could use a sugar infuse.

Curiosity killing him, he asked, "Whatcha got there, female?"

She glanced at Myst, a question in her eyes.

Myst tilted her head, like she was debating the state of the union or something.

"Ah, come on," he said, enjoying the game even as his stomach rumbled. "Share."

Angela flipped her hands, palms up, and raised a brow.

Her lips pursed, Myst hesitated a heartbeat, then nodded.

The round container got shoved in his direction. The blood-red top flashed, and the energy shield hummed, crackling as the metal slid through the barrier. Forge grabbed his gift, popped the top and—

Oh, hell, yeah. Shortbread cookies. His absolute favorite.

Inhaling hard, Forge drew in a lungful, the smell of sugary perfection as close to heaven as he was likely to get any time soon. God, the beautiful sweetness reminded him of home, of the Highlands and holly at Christmas when his mam—

With a swift kick, Forge booted the memory out of his mind. He didn't need to remember. Not now. Never again.

Without looking at his visitors, he held onto the tin like a greedy five-year-old and sat down where he stood in the middle of his prison cell. Hunger out of control, he bit into the shortbread and moaned. Bloody hell, that tasted good. Melt-in-your-mouth perfection. The second mouthful was even better than the first. And the third? Divine.

"Diabolical…" Forge paused to stuff another cookie into his mouth. A male would never have thought of the strategy. Toss a female into the mix, however, and tactics changed, veering way off course. "Using my sweet tooth against me."

Angela snorted.

Myst grinned at him. "We have a few questions."

"I know." And he did. More than they knew or would like him to.

For instance? Aye, the females might be here under a united front, but they wanted different things. Putting his talent to good use, he mined their intentions. The ability to read another's aim was a rare one. And the gift he'd been born with was strong—grew more potent with every year he lived—and he used it to effect.

Actions. Thoughts. Words. Important, sure, but on a lesser scale. But the intention behind each one? Well, now, that's where the magic lived. Anyone, after all, could fake a thought, tell a lie, or live one. But true intent was ground zero, the jumping-off point for all else. And as he stared at the two females sitting across from him, he read each like an open book.

Dusting off his hands, he zeroed in on Rikar's female. The detective with the wounded soul. Aye, she tried to hide it, but Forge saw through the act. Holding her gaze, he tipped his chin in her direction.

"You wish to know about…" he trailed off as she tensed, as though preparing for a physical blow. He should've guessed. Angela didn't want him to say the bastard's name.

Forge switched tacks, using the nickname he picked up on her frontal lobe. "The rat-bastard."

She released the pent-up breath, relaxing a little, but not enough. Unable to meet his gaze, she glanced away and nodded.

"Look at me, Angela." She shook her head. Forge held his ground. He wanted her to understand something. Aye, he might be a stranger, but she needed to accept what he was about to tell her. "If you want tae know…look at me."

A muscle twitched in her jaw, but she obeyed.

The second her gaze met his, he said, "It's not your fault. He was bigger than you. He was stronger than you. Any male worth his salt would've protected you…not hurt you. Accept that you did your best, Angela. That you're alive because you did, and move on."

"What are you? Sigmund freaking Freud?"

"I know a thing or two about being hurt." God, what was he doing? Revealing way too much, that's what, but… screw it. In for a penny, in for a pound. He couldn't stand all the pain he sensed deep inside her. "About having another's will forced upon me."

Angela blinked, battling to stay even. "What do you know about…him?"

"Not much. I dinnae spend too much time with the Razorbacks." Disappointment crossed her face. And something else, too. Real dismay. Forge folded, just caved beneath the onslaught. He frowned, searching his memory banks to come up with some small detail for her. "He likes games of all kinds. And coeds. He hunts for young females. Ones that have just come into their energy."

"Seattle U?" Myst asked.

"Yeah." Angela's eyes narrowed. Palming the Glock, she fiddled with the safety, flicking it on and off. Click-click-snick. Click-click-snick. "Dead college girls have been showing up around there lately."

"Ivar's doing, no doubt," Forge said with a curse. Fucking bastard. Like Lothair, the Razorback commander liked the young ones. Enjoyed draining them dry while he fed.

"Thank you. You didn't have to…" As Angela's gaze settled on him again, she laid the gun down in her lap. "But that's good intel. It gives me a starting point."

Uncomfortable with the gratitude, Forge shifted, rolled his shoulders, stretched out his neck, got busy examining the grainy pattern of the concrete floor. When that didn't work, he started on his hands, cracking each one of his knuckles. The sharp snap-snap-snap nipped at the silence, but after a full minute of nothing but quiet, it became too much. He'd had enough silence in the last twenty-four hours. Didn't want to waste the precious minutes he spent with the Nightfury females lost in thought.

"And you," he murmured, his gaze flicking over Myst. "You wish tae know about energy-fuse."

Angela threw a load of WTF at the female next to her. "Energy *what*?"

"It's a special bond between mates…a form of energy sharing," Forge said. "When a male feeds, he connects to the Meridian through his female, staving off hunger, which keeps him healthy. A female needs her mate's energy tae thrive and heal. The connection is very rare for a Dragonkind pairing. Myst and Bastian share it, and so do…"

He almost said *you,* but Forge stopped himself, wondering how much to reveal. If Rikar hadn't explained, then his female didn't know the bond already existed between them.

Forge could smell it on her, sensed the combined energy like a hound scented a fox.

"And so do…?" Angela leaned forward, the barrel of her formidable intellect pointed in his direction.

Forge frowned, hesitating. As much as he wanted to sabotage Frosty, it wasn't his place to tell Angela. *That* conversation belonged between mates—was a special moment for a male, a commitment he made with his chosen female.

And something that precious must be respected.

Besides, Rikar already wanted his head on a pike. Maybe tweaking the bastard's tail wasn't the best idea. Yet.

So he backpedaled and said, "Other males of my kind."

"But it isn't enough to protect me, is it?" The movement gentle, Myst rocked his son. Back and forth. Back and forth. Caroline was on her mind. He knew it like he was sitting in a cell, the memory of his female lingering in his own thoughts. Desperate for a distraction, Forge glanced at his bairn. His mouth curved. He was almost asleep, his eyes already closed, sucking on his wee thumb to soothe himself. "Something else has to happen, right?"

Good instincts. Which was a problem. Bastian's female was too smart for her own good.

He dragged his gaze from his son's face. Worried eyes met his, and Forge's heart sank. He hated to deny Myst the information. Her life, after all, depended on it, but…

Shite.

No way he could tell her about the ceremony, the ritual that completed the magical loop, fusing a bonded male's energy to his female's for life…keeping his mate young and healthy until he died. Forge knew of energy-fuse through his parents. The firsthand knowledge coupled with the ancient book his sire had made him memorize gave him the edge. He'd read the detailed account again and again, hoping one day to perform it with a female of his own.

But that hadn't happened. No matter how much his human half had wanted her, the dragon in him—the magic that forged the connection—hadn't bonded with Caroline, refusing to accept her as his mate. His mistake—one he would pay for every day for the rest of his life. But as he'd told Angela, the past was over and done. He couldn't change it, so he must move on.

What did that entail? Screwing Myst over.

Bloody hell. What a stupid set of circumstances. He wanted two things: his son *and* Bastian's female to live. But in order to secure the first, he must hurt the second. The information he held about the ritual was his last bargaining chip. The only way to force Bastian's hand and regain his bairn. The fact Myst was stuck in the middle was a terrible burden to bear. But Forge was banking on one thing. Bastian would never allow his female to suffer needlessly. Would do anything to keep her safe, healthy, and whole.

So like it or not, he must hold the line.

If his theory held true, by this time next month he'd be out of his cage. Free to fly away from Black Diamond with his son in tow. To leave the Nightfuries and their females behind.

Which, strangely enough, made his heart ache so hard he actually felt a pang.

Rikar ducked, avoiding the backlash of Mac's tail as the male crash-landed on the LZ. Shit. Forget the crash part. Make that *spinning* into an uncontrolled death skid. Man, the new boy needed a *crash course* in the art of landing. One that pointed out the benefits of not taking his comrades out like a matched set of bowling pins.

Another full revolution. Rikar ducked again.

Holy Christ. The male was out of control, paws scrambling, scales flashing, body torquing all over the freaking place. Which, yeah, he and B should've expected. Mac's fledgling status didn't come with built-in landing gear. Or brakes, apparently. Too bad. Rikar really didn't want to get whacked by Mac's wicked sharp tail.

Leaping backward, Rikar vaulted over the Honda. As he landed on the other side, Mac whipped into another 360-degree spin. Blue-gray scales rippled in the low light as Mac bore down to stop the tilt-a-whirl. His claws ripped grooves in the granite, and stone dust flew. Musty air rushed, making the light globes bob against the cavern's ceiling even as they disappeared behind the haze of gray cloud.

Mac's tail came around again. The bladed edge sliced the hatchback, cutting through steel. Metal screeched. Glass exploded. The car got decapitated, and the roof went flying, flipping end over end in midair.

"Fuck." Dark-blue scales flashing, Bastian dove for cover behind a row of stalagmites.

Rikar dropped an f-bomb of his own and shifted into human form, making himself a smaller target, and put himself in reverse. The metal panel pinwheeled, somersaulting over the LZ's edge, falling to the aquifer below. The horrendous sound of claws on stone stopped as Mac slammed into the wall at the back of the cavern.

"Motherfuck," Mac groaned, collapsing into a heap on the floor.

Bastian popped his horned head up from behind a boulder. *"Is it safe to come out yet?"*

"Go for it," Rikar said, beating feet toward Mac.

The thud of his footfalls echoed, bouncing in the vastness as he skirted the roofless wonder's front bumper. The second he got a load of Mac, concern hit Rikar chest-level. The male was in bad shape. One big bruise punctuated by shallow cuts and deeper gashes. The worst ran along the curve of Mac's shoulder. A clean slice, but it was bleeding like crazy now.

Their new boy needed a stitch-up job…fast.

Angry at himself, Rikar shook his head. He should've left Mac in the water a little while longer. Allowed him to play with his prey for another hour before he hauled him out and headed for Black Diamond. The saltwater had done the male a world of good: soothing bruises, helping to close the nicks and cuts, sealing up the less serious wounds. But the flight home hadn't done the male any favors, undoing what the ocean had started.

Rikar slowed his roll, approaching Mac with caution. Not that he thought the male would hurt him. At least not on purpose. But a dragon was a dragon. And underestimating one in pain while he approached in human form wasn't a good idea.

Holding his hands up, he murmured, "Mac."

The male flinched. A second later he snorted, steam rising in twin tendrils from his nostrils.

"I need you to shift, big guy." The movement slow, Rikar reached out and put his hand on Mac's shoulder. He kept his touch gentle, not wanting to startle the male. The dark-blue tattoo Mac sported on his scaled torso shimmered beneath

Rikar's hand. When he didn't move, the pattern settled into flat, dark ink once more. "We need to get you inside."

Mac blinked, his eyes drifting closed, then opening again. He tried to raise his head. "I wanna go back in the water."

Bastian jogged over. "There's a salt bath inside, my man. Let's get you inside the clinic and into it."

Planting his paw, Mac pushed up, muscles trembling, groaning low as he transformed. Rikar winced. The cop looked even worse in human form. Poor bastard. The first night out and he'd caught real action.

Not the least bit fair. Or wise.

Fledglings were fragile in the beginning. Exhausted from the change. Overwhelmed by their new bodies and baffled by how to use them. So, yeah. A new Dragonkind male was always protected, kept away from the world and other dragons that weren't family until he learned how to handle himself.

But oh, no. Not Mac. The male had dove right in. No hesitation. No fear. No freaking common sense. Which, Rikar suspected, would be their new boy's MO from now on. Not a bad way to go, but…man. He was going to be hell to protect until he was up to speed and combat ready.

Rikar slung the cop's arm around his shoulder. Mac cursed. He murmured "sorry," but didn't stop. B had called in their ETA on the fly. Sloan expected them, so…

No time like the present.

Muscling Mac across the LZ, Rikar pinged his buddy. *"Sloan. You ready?"*

"All set." Plastic crinkled, the sound coming through mind-speak as the male said, *"Triage is good to go. How's our boy?"*

"Shitty," Mac growled through clenched teeth.

"Run the salt bath," Bastian said, bringing up the rear. *"And get Myst. He needs stitches."*

"Ah...about that," Sloan said, tone hesitant.

Which cranked Rikar's shit in the wrong direction. Oh, Christ. What the hell was that about? His buddy rarely, if ever, hesitated.

"Where's my female?" B asked.

"I'll let Daimler explain."

Mac's arm slung around his shoulder, Rikar threw his best friend an alarmed look.

B returned it, then muttered, *"Shit on a stick. Freaking female."*

Shitkickers pounding granite, B hauled ass ahead of them. Rikar picked up the pace. Yup, no doubt about it. Myst was up to a whole lot of *nothing good*. Which meant Angela was in the thick of it. Shit, she'd probably instigated the entire mess.

Fantastic. *Freaking female* was right. Just wait until he got his hands on her. He'd either wring her pretty neck or kiss the hell out of her.

His body jumped at the idea. His mind seconded the motion, making him ache from the inside out. And no wonder. After feeding Angela and all the fighting, he needed an energy-infuse like an addict needed a fix. Hunger gnawed at him, turning his gut into a bottomless pit. Rikar swallowed to combat the burn and clamped down on his need. Hungry or not, his female was nowhere near ready to feed him. If he touched her now, she'd run scared... hate him before he ever got the chance to prove his worth.

No way could he let that happen.

He wanted her to want him, not fear him. So only one way to go. Keep his hands to himself and his dragon side under control. He'd gone hungry before, weeks if necessary, and he could do it again. He was a warrior; self-mastery was his middle name. So yeah, even if it killed him, he would respect Angela's timeframe.

But as he muscled Mac into Black Diamond, doubt slithered deep, and he prayed he could keep his word. Not to mention his distance.

Chapter Eighteen

Sitting cross-legged on a cushion, Angela studied the guy behind the invisible barrier. Even with the steel collar clamped around his throat, Forge reminded her of someone. It was the little things. The way he gestured with his hands. The tilt of his head when he smiled. The way his eyes narrowed when he paused to think about something and...

Weird, but even his features seemed familiar. Had she met him somewhere before? Passed him on the street or something?

Her gaze narrowed on his face. She would've remembered a guy like Forge. He was too big to miss, and as she listened to him talk, her eyes trained on his face, Angela gave it another shot. Nada. No spark of recognition.

With a frown, she closed the door on her memory vault, forcing herself to pay attention. As she refocused—picking up his body cues, measuring the pauses in his speech pattern—Myst hammered him with questions, trying to bust through the impenetrable force that was Forge. Her lips twitched. He was a tough nut to crack. Hedging each question. Skirting the real issues. Feeding Myst tidbits of information without telling her anything. And all with that smooth-as-silk voice, rolling Rs interspaced by smooth As and long Os.

Pure magic on the vocal front.

He skirted another tough question. Angela bit down on a smile. Bullshit on top of bullshit. Freaking guy. He would've made a good cop. Hell, he was the verbal equivalent of a tap dancer. A nice-sounding one, but a big fat liar just the same.

Which, naturally, reminded her of Rikar. Because really? Everything did today.

Angela rubbed the bridge of her nose. God, she really needed to get a handle on that. She was far too interested in Rikar. And he was way too accessible. Yup. No fight from that quarter. He wanted her. Angela saw it in his eyes, knew it like her butt was planted on a Japanese cushion. That meant resisting the attraction would be up to her.

Not a problem under normal circumstances. Her willpower was solid, but her reaction to Rikar crossed boundaries. Was anything but *normal.*

Raking her fingers through her hair, Angela massaged the nape of her neck. Muscles stretched and discomfort streaked down her spine. The pain didn't slow her roll or the curiosity propelling it. But then, she was an idiot. One with a bad idea and a huge problem. And what was that?

One word. Energy-fuse.

Man, what a concept. One guy. One girl. And boom! Instant attraction. Mutual need. A match made in heaven.

Angela sighed, trying to deny her interest. No. Strike that. Her *fascination* with the idea Rikar might need her in that way. Something powerful existed between them…no question. She felt it even when he wasn't with her. The zing of connection—the powerful pull of sensation that spilled into passion. Deep down—even though she didn't want to admit it—she hoped he felt it too and that he came to her to get what he needed.

A little batty, she knew...to want to feed him. Particularly after everything she'd been through. But no matter how hard she tried, she couldn't deny the compulsion. The urge to be *the one* for him.

The one and only.

And holy crap, there she went again. Tumbling into the rabbit hole head-flipping-first. 'Cause, honestly, did she really want to be Rikar's next meal?

Swallowing hard, Angela stifled a shiver. Had she fed him that night at McGovern's? Seemed like a good guess. Too bad it was still fuzzy. She remembered certain things—like the way he touched her—with perfect recall. But other details were gone. Which was beyond strange. Her photographic memory never missed a beat. Great for a homicide cop. Not so good for a girl who wanted to forget the rat-bastard had—

She flinched, shying away from the memory, slamming the lid on the mental box so fast the bang echoed inside her mind. She hung onto the pleasure instead...to the feel of Rikar and the deep connection she felt when he came near her.

Palming the Glock, she played with the safety. Click-click-snick...on. Click-click-snick...off. Click-click—

"Yo, Ange. You still with us?"

Angela glanced up. Forge raised a brow. She set the Glock down in her lap, wondering if she should ask him. Myst had certainly run him through the gauntlet, so...

She hesitated a second, weighing the pros and cons. Screw it. Why not? Rikar wasn't here to ask, and she wanted to know. "Hey, Forge?"

His amethyst eyes steady on her, he murmured, "Aye?"

"Got a question for you."

"Hit me."

"What does it feel like?" Unable to hold his gaze, she dropped her own. It landed on the gun that brought her comfort, even though it shouldn't. A Glock for a security blanket. Talk about bizarre. And damaged. She was undeniably damaged, absolutely beyond repair. "I mean…when a male feeds? Does it hurt or…?"

"It shouldn't." A furrow between his brows, he turned a piece of shortbread over in his hand. "Should feel good. A lotta pleasure for the female if she is willing."

"And if she isn't?"

He studied her for a second, expression serious. Angela resisted the urge to squirm. If she fidgeted, he'd know. Hell. He'd probably already guessed, but no way would she admit to being…hurt…by the rat-bastard. It was bad enough that *she* knew it. Felt it. Had to live with the failure and guilt. Saying it out loud would bury her alive.

"It's not…" He paused as he set the cookie back in the container. "I would imagine it is very painful for a female if the connection is forced."

"Oh. Well…" Uncurling her hands, she wiped her sweaty palms on her thighs. "Asked and answered, I guess."

Silence met her inept attempt at deflection, stretching out like infinity in front of her. Goddamn it. She sounded so small. Vulnerable. Not what she'd been going for in any way, shape, or form. But holy hell, she'd needed to know and—

"I like feeding Bastian," Myst said, jumping into the void, tilting the conversation away from Crazytown and back into Evensville. "A lot."

Angela blinked. "Really?"

"Yeah. Especially when we're, ah…in bed." Making a face, she glanced at Forge. "TMI?"

"Wicked TMI," he said, sounding disgruntled even though his eyes twinkled. "Look, Ange, nothing about this is easy. Not assimilating into our world or leaving your own. Not dealing with the shit that happened tae you. If you let him, Rikar will help. Feeding him will take some of the anxiety away. Bring peace while you become accustomed tae him…" he paused, throwing Myst an amused glance, "ah… in bed."

Her new friend grinned, enjoying his play on her words.

Angela rolled her eyes, wanting to hit them both. "A temporary fix?"

"Better than enduring the pain alone, aye?"

"Maybe," she murmured, willing to concede the point. "But how am I supposed to—"

The door banged open, smashing into the steel wall behind it. A moment later a deep growl rolled into the corridor.

"Ah, crap," Myst muttered.

Angela palmed her gun and popped to her feet. Stance set, she focused on the entrance. Which also served as the only exit. *Way to go, Ange. Brilliant detective work.* Nice to only notice that bit of info now, with the doorway blocked by a huge guy dressed in leather. The Harley Davidson attire matched the PO'd look on his puss…kick-ass with a whole lot of hardcore.

Green eyes aglow, his gaze flicked over her, then narrowed on Myst. Angela swallowed, resisting the urge to take a giant step backward. And take Myst along for the ride.

She chanced a quick glance at Myst and whispered, "Bastian?"

"Ding-ding-ding." G.M. snug in her arms, Myst rolled to her feet. Her scowl every bit as fierce as her mate's, she said, "Don't go postal, Bastian. I can explain."

"I hope so, *bellmia*," he said, more growl than actual words. "Especially since I *asked* you not to come down here."

Ooh-oh. *Asked.* Not ordered. Interesting word choice and one that put Myst neck-deep in trouble. A girl could ignore an *order* from her man. This wasn't the twelfth century, after all. A request, however? Angela grimaced. That wasn't so cut and dried. And judging by her guilty expression, she guessed Myst knew it. Knew she didn't have a leg to stand on as Bastian rolled in like a human thunderstorm.

"I'm not one of your warriors," Myst said, her words sharp, her gaze narrowed on the man she claimed to love. As far as strategies went, it was a good one. Attack instead of retreat. "You wanna talk to me? Change your tone."

Bastian growled again.

"Don't blame her."

Angela blinked. Good God. Why the hell had she said that? Well, whatever the reason, it was a bad one. Especially since Bastian was now focused on her, his green gaze hitting her like twin spotlights. Okay. No sense panicking. She'd gotten herself into trouble. She could get herself out.

Clearing her throat, intent on backpedaling, Angela opened her mouth and…made the mistake of glancing at Myst. Ah, hell. She couldn't do it. No way could she leave her friend twisting in the wind like that.

"Please don't blame Myst," she said. "It was my idea."

He glared at her.

Angela gave ground, backing up a step.

"It's all right, Ange." A muscle twitched in her jaw as Myst glared right back, slamming Bastian with a loaded look. "Bastian would sooner put your gun to his head than hurt me."

"True," the guy said without slowing his roll. Long legs carried him forward, the thud of his heavy boots sounding loud in the quiet. "Doesn't mean I won't turn you over my knee, now does it, *bellmia*?"

While Myst sputtered, choking on the threat, Angela regrouped. Okay, so the guy wouldn't hurt her friend. Good to know. Didn't mean he wouldn't make good on his threat, though and…really. No one needed to get spanked today. Unless, of course, they wanted to, and neither she nor Myst was volunteering for that one.

"Look, Bastian." Holding her hands palm up, she tried to placate him. "It really is my fault."

"Fucking hell. I knew it," a deep voice growled. "Always neck-deep in trouble, aren't you, angel?"

Angela's head whipped toward the open door. Oh, crap. Rikar. He had the worst timing. Or the best, depending on which way you looked at it. At least Bastian wouldn't get the chance to throttle her with her man-dragon in the room. But man oh man, that didn't mean Rikar wouldn't take a shot.

Lie or not, she'd just shot herself in the foot.

An unhappy look on his face, he stood between the jambs, a wide-shouldered, long-limbed, too-gorgeous-for-words man. Angela swallowed, trying not to eat him with her eyes, but…mmm, it was hard. She liked looking at him.

Liked the way his pale eyes glowed and the way he moved toward her, lethal grace in each stride, muscles coiled with a controlled strength she knew he could unleash without warning. Or mercy.

But not on her.

She could see the truth of it in his eyes. In the pale shimmer of ice-blue irises. In the way his gaze roamed, looking her over to make sure she was unhurt. All right. He was pissed off at her—might even growl and yell—but he wouldn't touch her with anger. No need for heavy-duty explanations. No need for proof. Angela knew it instinctively.

The second he stopped in front of her, Angela whispered, "I have a good reason to be here. Let me explain."

"Too late for that, angel."

His gaze flicked over her again, repeating his examination at close range. Angela stifled a shiver. Holy hell, it wasn't fair. The way he looked at her was, well…God. It made her feel powerful, desirable, and something else, too…brave. Strong enough to stand her ground. Willing enough to take a chance. To trust him a little further.

Which had crazy written all over it.

She should be backing up a step. Or ten. Giving him a wide berth while she skedaddled out the door. But oh no, not her. What was she doing? Getting courageous at the wrong moment. Wondering about the damn connection they shared. Wanting to get up close and personal to see if she got zapped. Zinged. Carried away by the same mindless pleasure she'd felt in McGovern's the night he'd touched her.

Rikar stepped in close, crowding her. Raising her chin, Angela planted her feet, refusing to succumb to intimidation. Too bad he was good at it.

Using his body to block her, he met her gaze head-on, tethering her with eye contact as he herded her away from the cell. Planted between her and Forge, he threw her a warning look. Angela chewed on her bottom lip. Message received. He wanted her to stay put. Wanted her behind him where Forge couldn't see her.

"Frosty," Forge said, the hum of challenge in his voice. "So nice of you to visit. I've been chatting with Angela… thinking about giving you a bit of competition on the suitor front."

Rikar's pale eyes went icy, then sparked, making his irises glow.

Angela swallowed. Oh, so not good. Rikar in a snit was one thing, but in full-on lethal mode? That was something she didn't want to see.

"Isn't that right, lass?" Giving the tin of shortbread a shove, Forge sent his snack spinning toward the back of cell. The container bumped against the wall, and he pushed to his feet, taking a step toward them. As the invisible barrier snapped, the collar around his neck beeped in warning. "We've been planning your future."

Frost gathered, coating Rikar's temples, blowing arctic air into her face as he spun to face Forge.

"Knock it off, Forge," she said, trying to dial down the frost factor. Seeing more of Rikar's back now than the prisoner, she peeked around his shoulder. He widened his stance, trying to block her. Angela gave in to the childish urge and rolled her eyes. Uh-huh, right. As if she needed protection from a guy locked behind a force field with a dog collar around his throat. "You're being an idiot…not helpful."

"Never said I'd help, Ange," Forge said, purring her nickname like a lover.

Angela winced. Well, crap…just crap. The jerk was obviously angling for the Stupidest Move in History Award, because winding Rikar up to watch him go wasn't the best move. Unless, of course, the guy wanted to get his head ripped off.

A distinct possibility, considering—

Rikar snarled, cranking his fists tight.

Ah, hell. "Rikar…don't. He's just trying to get a rise out of you."

"Oh, come on, *angel*," Forge said, borrowing Rikar's endearment for her. A wicked gleam in his eyes, he rolled his shoulders, getting ready for the fight he was trying to start. "Admit it. I'm the better male. You'll be happier with me."

Angela's mouth dropped open.

"B?" Rigid with fury, Rikar cracked his knuckles. The sound ricocheted, sending shivers down her spine. "I'm gonna mess him up a bit. You can still talk to a quadriplegic."

"I'm good with that," Bastian said, tone soft yet somehow lethal.

"Ah, Bastian?" Myst said. "I don't think that's—"

"Time to go, *bellmia*."

The soft scrape of boots on concrete drifted from behind Angela. Movement flashed in her periphery, and Myst gasped. Wonderful. Bastian was on the move, scooping his mate up and headed toward the door. Next stop? Angela. She read his intention without any effort. He planned to grab her on the fly and haul both her and Myst out of the cellblock. Which…yup. Would leave Rikar to beat the snot out of Forge in private.

One eye on Bastian, Angela kicked out of her footwear. She needed traction, and bare feet worked better on concrete than smooth-soled flip-flops. Timing it just right, Angela slid beneath Rikar's arm, avoiding Bastian's hand as he reached for her. A quick one-two sidestep and...

Bam!

She planted herself in front of Rikar. "Back off, man. It isn't gonna happen."

Ice-blue eyes met hers. She held up her hands. Rikar growled, warning her without words. Angela stifled a shiver but stood her ground. No way could she allow him anywhere near Forge. She needed the guy. He'd provided valuable intel. Would no doubt give her more. So, yeah. Rearranging the prisoner's face wasn't on Rikar's menu. Not today. Maybe not ever.

"I'm touched, Ange," Forge said, playing it up for his audience. "I didnae know you cared so—"

"Shut up," she said, snapping at him. "Stop being such a jackass."

"Move, angel."

"No."

A muscle jumped along Rikar's jaw. He dodged right. She slapped her hands against his chest, keeping him in front of her.

Electricity leapt, arcing from her palms. She sucked in a quick breath. Rikar cursed as the current grabbed hold, swirling up her arms to flow unrestricted to her heart. It paused midbeat as pleasure spun through her, making her skin tingle as sensation lit her up and heat settled woman-low.

She gasped. Holy moly. Heat lightning. Orgasm in a bottle. Full-on pleasure. How fascinating. The big bang without the sex.

"Fuck me," Rikar groaned, retreating as she pushed him toward the back wall. "Angela...let go. You gotta...oh, God."

Let go? No chance in hell. He felt too good. She didn't want to back away and…

God, he smelled fantastic, like chilly winter mornings and fresh arctic air. Combine that with the current throbbing through her veins, and oh, man…she needed more.

"Rikar? Can you…just…" Her breath caught as she closed the distance, brushing her body against his. Moving closer, she pressed her cheek to his chest. Right over his heart, and gasped, "Gimme more."

"Good Christ." His back collided with the wall as he encircled her wrists. Pressing his thumbs to her pulse points, he drew her closer while simultaneously trying to push her away. "Baby, you're…holy shit."

Forge laughed. "A wee bit peckish, arenae you, Frosty?"

Ignoring the jerk in the cage, she said, "Please, Rikar."

"God, angel. Whatever you want." Threading his hand through her hair, he cupped her nape while his other arm came around her. She moaned. He hummed and picked her up, pivoting into a 180-degree turn. Cold steel settled against her back as he whispered, "My beautiful angel, I know you're not ready for me, but I'm so hungry, love. So fucking hungry."

Hungry.

Panic swirled for a second. Fear followed suit, but Angela refused to listen. This was her chance. Maybe the only one she would get to experience the relief Forge had promised her firsthand. So, yeah. All her uncertainty could go hang itself. She wanted Rikar. Needed to touch him and be touched in return. To feel peace instead of the pain. To forget for just a little while and pretend she was the same as she'd always been. Untainted. Unchanged. Unashamed by what had happened to her.

"Relax for me, love. Let me in." Flicking at her hoodie, Rikar slipped his hand beneath the hem, seeking her skin. As his hand settled, fingers splayed wide on her lower back, he murmured to her. Sweet words filled with praise and reassurance: promises to be gentle, to go slowly, giving her ultimate control. His breath warm against her temple, he pressed his knee between hers, spreading her thighs to make room for his own. "Please, Angela. I need you."

His *please* did her in. Made her blink back the hot burn of tears. The rat-bastard hadn't asked. He'd taken: forced and hurt and brutalized. But Rikar wasn't like him. His hands were gentle, and his voice pleading. Asking her permission. Giving her the choice to draw him in or push him away.

Myst's voice came back to her...*I like feeding Bastian. A lot.*

And just like that, the last of the fear vanished. Rikar needed her. She would provide for him. End of story.

With a welcoming murmur, Angela pressed her cheek to his. He burrowed into her embrace, nestling in as he set his mouth against her temple. Bliss swirled, reaching deep, rising hard, flowing fast in the face of desire. She slid her hands over his shoulders, exploring his strength before cupping the nape of his neck. God, his hair was soft. Short, yes, but unbelievably thick. And as she marveled at the feel of him, allowing her fingers to play, his teeth grazed the pulse pounding beneath her skin, making her gasp as she did as he asked and invited him in.

His breath hitched.

She pulled him closer. "It's all right, Rikar. Take what you need."

"My beautiful female." He kissed her softly, an ache in his voice as he whispered, "Forgive me for my greed."

But as he hugged her close and drank deep, Angela knew there was nothing to forgive. He was what he *was.* She possessed what he needed. No changing that fact. No going back, either.

A delicious scent all around him, Rikar woke up riding a wave of glory-glory-hallelujah. With a hum, he opened his eyes and blinked, getting nothing but blur. He let his lids drift closed again. Shit, he was groggy, deep in the layer between sleep and wakefulness where dreams lived and reality stood on the fringes. And wow. For the first time in a long while, he was full. Completely satisfied. Without the sharp edge of hunger that always gnawed on him from the inside out.

Rubbing the grit from his eyes, he cracked his lids, giving his vision another try. Steel glinted overhead, refracted arcs of light spilling like colorless rainbows across the ceiling. Rikar frowned. What the fuck? A sleepy murmur sounded as a soft body snuggled against him and…

Angela.

Sucking in a quick breath, he glanced down and…oh, yeah. There she was, fast asleep, her back to his chest, her behind nestled against his groin. Memory flooded him, providing the details.

With a curse, Rikar laid his head back down. He was an idiot. One who'd screwed the pooch and wound up in the middle of clusterfuck territory. God help him. He shouldn't be here with her. Should be in his own bed, holding her close while she slept not…*here.* The instant she touched him, he should've picked her up and carried her to his room. What he'd done instead was lose his mind and back her into one of the prison cells. Now they shared real estate. Were horizontal without the possibility of getting vertical anytime soon.

On a fucking prison cot.

Christ. Had he said idiot? Well, he'd meant asshole.

Even knowing he should do right by her—scoop her up and carry her out of the cellblock—Rikar couldn't move. He wanted to stay right where he was, curled around his female, listening to her deep, even breaths, enjoying the full-body contact. It didn't matter that they were both still dressed. Being with her wasn't about sex. At least not this time around. Eventually, it would be, and he'd claim her. But today all he wanted to do was hold her. Protect her. Win her trust by showing her that he could be patient. That being close to her would be enough until she was ready to take things further.

Shifting backward on the twin mattress, he nudged her onto her back. Her brow puckered, and she muttered, not liking the change in position. He murmured to her, using his voice to soothe her. With a sleepy hum, she turned toward him, giving him her profile as she nestled her face into the curve of his biceps. Unable to help himself, he traced her bottom lip, wanting to taste her so badly his mouth watered.

He brushed a kiss to her temple instead, then turned north, burying his nose in the soft strands of her hair. Hmm, she smelled like evergreens and ice…and him. Oh, yeah. His scent was all over her, and he loved it. So did the territorial bastard deep inside him. Now any male that came near her would know she belonged to him.

Or more accurately, that he belonged to her.

His gaze roaming, he studied the contours of her face. The adorable up-turned tip of her nose. The high cheekbones above the gentle curve of her oft-times obstinate chin. The ripe fullness of her mouth. God, his female was beautiful—so lush she took his breath away.

Raising his hand, he followed the curve of her eyebrow with his fingertip, marveling at the softness. She sighed as he caressed her, eyes still closed, body relaxed, not awake but not quite asleep either.

Post-feeding was like that for a female…bone-melting peaceful in the aftermath of intense pleasure. Well, if done right, anyway.

His mouth curved. Yeah, the location sucked, but at least he'd done right by her while he fed. Thank fuck. The last thing he wanted to do was hurt her. His hunger had been terrible. Voracious. But he'd managed to temper it, taking only as much as she could afford to give. She'd tasted just like he remembered, like ice and snow. As decadent as chilled vodka straight out of the freezer.

Dipping his head, he kissed the corner of her mouth, the touch soft, a barely-there caress. He wanted to thank her for what she'd given him. She'd fed him so well…filled him so full his body hummed and his mind pulsed with renewed energy. And magic. The power lit him up from the inside out, rushing in his veins, making his fingertips tingle.

God, had he ever felt this good before?

Nah. Not even close.

Rikar kissed her again, nuzzled her before he backed off and shook his head. He couldn't help but be amazed by her. But mostly, he was surprised at himself. His attitude was such an about-face. A total 180-degree turn from the independent SOB he'd been less than a month ago. Angela, though, was special. A rare female who gave without thought to herself. But then, that was his job now. To think of her, provide for her, give her all she needed to thrive at Black Diamond.

All excellent intentions. With a huge freaking caveat that hinged on one thing. Would she accept him as her male? Let him care and provide for her?

Rikar hoped so, but convincing her would take some work. He knew that. Wasn't naive enough to believe she'd give up her life—throw away all she'd worked so hard to achieve in the human world to become part of his. One feeding, no matter how willing she'd been, did not a relationship make. He wanted one with her, though. A long-term arrangement that started now and ended at forever.

Rikar snorted. It was official. He'd lost the battle and his heart to a hazel-eyed beauty with attitude. Fallen prey to Angela just as his best friend had with Myst. He shook his head. What a pair they made. Jacked up over a couple of females. Had someone told him such a thing was possible a month ago, he would've punched the dummy first and asked questions later.

Angela's eyelashes flickered. She shifted a little, bumping his chest with her shoulder. "What are you laughing at?"

The question came out slow, words slurred. Rikar's lips twitched as he caressed her cheek. "Not you."

"Smart."

"I'm all about self-preservation."

"I'll bet."

Her mouth tipped up at the corners, blooming into a slow, sassy smile. A second later, he got a load of sleepy hazel eyes. Green, gold, even a little dark gray swam in the depths, a complicated combination, just like his female. Holding her gaze, unable to resist, he dipped his head, coming in slow, giving her lots of time to turn away. When she didn't, Rikar brushed his lips against hers: a tender touch, gentle desire in a soft kiss.

"Good morning, angel," he murmured, backing off a bit. He hovered a breath away, gauging her reaction. Not wanting to frighten her.

Angela sighed, and he got bolder, flicking the corner of her mouth with his tongue. He pulled back again. She tipped her chin up, prolonging the contact, lips parting as though she wanted more. He gave it to her, but kept it light, one gentle stroke at a time. Careful not to crowd her, he slipped inside her mouth, introducing her to his taste, getting a contact high from hers.

Fuck, she was unbelievably good. So soft and sweet, and he was a bastard for taking advantage. She was still so relaxed—deep in post-feeding euphoria. It wasn't fair to kiss her when she wasn't firing on all cylinders, but he couldn't make himself stop. She tasted so damned good, and he was addicted. But more than anything, the kiss was for her. He needed to show her that the instant she said no, he'd back off and give her space.

All right. So it would kill him if she did.

No wasn't a word he liked to hear. At least not very often. And especially not now when he finally had Angela in his arms and wanted to be deep inside her. Wanted it so badly his heart pounded and his balls ached. But that didn't mean he would cross the line. He wasn't like the rogue who'd hurt her. Rikar needed her to know that he could touch her without the heat of expectation. That he would wait until she was ready.

That the lesson came with added benefits—namely tangling his tongue with hers, tasting her deep while her hands drifted through his hair? Oh, man, he loved her heat, the softness of her mouth, her taste, and God, the sounds she made. Each sigh, every soft moan, cranked him tighter until the bastard behind his button fly begged for release.

Time to stop.

With a groan, Rikar nipped her bottom lip, then retreated. She murmured in protest. Unable to stop himself, he returned, kissed her gently, but in the end pulled away again. He wanted to continue. Could go on kissing her forever, but that would defeat the purpose. And the lesson. He was only a male, after all. With faults and weaknesses. And a libido that was now in overdrive. Much more of her taste and…fuck him, he'd be trying to undress her.

So instead of unzipping her hoodie like he was dying to do, he distracted himself by asking, "You okay, love?"

"Um-hmm." Her eyelashes flickered again. On a soft exhale, she rubbed her eyes, and Rikar felt her mind sharpen. "I was scared at first, but then…I wasn't."

He bit down on a grin. Okay, maybe "sharpen" wasn't quite the right word. She was still fuzzy around the edges, coming back a little at a time. "Good."

"You didn't hurt me."

She sounded surprised. Rikar didn't blame her. Would've been just as surprised had he been brutalized by—

Christ. No way.

His enemy didn't belong anywhere near her. Or this bed. Not in thought. Nor in deed. Lothair would get what was coming to him—his fucking head ripped off. Here and now was for Angela. For him. For them and the new start he wanted to make.

Leaning in, he nestled his cheek against hers. "The last thing I want to do, angel, is hurt you."

"I know," she whispered, breaking down the doors to his heart one thump at a time.

Her trust floored him. Her courage, too. And as he came unhinged, Rikar hugged her close, his throat so tight he could hardly breathe, never mind talk. He managed to anyway and rasped, "You are the most extraordinary female I've ever met."

"Met a lot of us, have you?" She rubbed her cheek against his, the movement playful. "What's the tally?"

Rikar blinked. Was she actually asking him how many females he'd been with? Man, he hoped not, 'cause…hell. He'd lost count years ago.

Propping himself on his elbow, he pulled back, needing to see her face. A teasing glint in her eyes, she grinned at him. But he saw it for what it was…a deflection. She wanted to change the subject. To move out of uncomfortable territory—his feelings for her—and onto safer ground. He held her gaze, trying to decide whether to let her sidestep him. In the end, he gave in and retreated. Pushing her too far, too fast wouldn't do him any favors. He'd take what he could get. And with her still snuggled against him, the getting was pretty damn good.

He raised a brow and teased her back. "Should I be asking you the same question?"

Angela snorted. "I'm not the one with the number crisis."

Number crisis. Freaking female. She knew exactly where to hit him. Right below the belt.

Faking an offended look, he sputtered, making a show of it for her. She laughed, and his heart lightened at the sound. He wanted to hear more of it, and so often her smile became the status quo when he was around. He shook his head, acting his ass off, praying she laughed again. She didn't disappoint. Hiding her grin behind her hand, her eyes sparkled as she gazed up at him. He gave her a stern look. More laughter. Shit, he deserved one of those shiny Oscars.

"All right, angel," he murmured, tapping the end of her nose. "You've had your fun, so...you gonna tell me now?"

"What's that?"

"Why you came down here? With fucking cookies, no less and—"

"Shortbread...there's a difference, you know."

"—what you found out from the asshole down the hall," he said, ignoring her interruption.

"So, what...*now* you're interested in my intel?"

"Was always interested, love."

"Tit for tat then. You go first. Tell me what you found out tonight."

Bingo. His homicide detective was back on board. Watch out, world.

"Not much to tell." Rikar frowned, pissed off at his lack of progress tonight. Even after bribing Mac and getting the rogue out of the water, he knew dick-all about the new Razorback lair. "The Razorback we cornered didn't know shit. He didn't tell us anything we don't already know."

"For instance?"

"Ivar's building a new lair, but most of his warriors don't know where it is."

"Is that normal?" she asked. "I thought you guys lived in packs."

"We do." Caressing her shoulder, he ran his hand down the back of her arm. When she stayed relaxed, Rikar pushed it a little further, trailing his hand lower, watching her reaction. Prepared to back away if she shied. She didn't, and his heart picked up a beat as his hand settled on the curve of her hip. "But the Razorback ranks outnumber us at least ten to one. If not more. So it makes sense to have more than one lair."

"So he's…what? Keeping the new one for his inner circle?"

"Yeah, I think so," he said, flexing his fingers on her hip, wanting to slide around front and lay his hand flat on her belly. "Ivar's smart. A real psycho, but smart. If he keeps his base of operations a secret…only allows those closest to him to know where it is, none of the bastards we interrogate will out him."

"So, those girls. The ones imprisoned—"

"I'm sorry. Unless we nail Lo—"

"The rat-bastard, you mean."

"Right," he murmured, seeing the hurt in her eyes.

She tried so hard to hide it behind an *I'm tough…don't worry about me* attitude. But Rikar saw the act for what it was and hated every second of her pain. Despised knowing he couldn't take the memory away. Mind-scrubbing her wasn't the answer. He'd do more harm than good. Sure, he could take the memory but not the emotion behind it…or the context that made what she felt make sense. To heal she needed to remember why she was hurting. It sucked, but there it was. Healing required hard work. And hard work functioned best within a clear set of parameters.

Rikar cleared his throat. "So, unless we take down Ivar's XO or another close to him, we won't locate his new lair."

"Crap."

No kidding. He didn't like it any better than she did. He never liked dead ends. Or outcomes that rested on big fat "ifs."

Lost in thought, Angela chewed on her lower lip. Rikar stared at her straight white teeth and swallowed. When that didn't work, he shifted, suddenly uncomfortable in his own skin. Christ, the stuff felt five sizes too small, and man, forget her bottom lip. He wanted to be the one getting nibbled on.

"Your turn."

She blinked and refocused on him. "Oh, right. According to Forge, the rat-bastard likes coeds and games. So forget downtown. If we wanna find him, we need to look on campus and all the bars close to it."

"Student pubs and hangouts."

"Exactly."

Made sense. He'd never seen Lothair in any of the downtown clubs the Razorback warriors always favored. Where he and his brothers always found them. Well, all right. They were off and running.

With Forge's intel.

Fucking male. What the hell was Forge up to? He didn't act like any rogue Rikar had ever met. Or rather, had the pleasure to kill. Something was wonky. Way off with the guy. It was worth investigating. But not with Angela hanging around.

He needed to stash her somewhere while he teed up the cellblock's surveillance video. Thank God for Gage and his foresight. He'd installed the system just before he'd taken off for Prague and the Archguard's festival. Now Rikar would be able to see and hear exactly what Forge had said to Angela. Word for word. Read between the lines by watching the male's expression. Each nuance. Each hesitation. All the little stuff that spoke volumes.

But first? A distraction for his female.

And Rikar had the perfect one. Mac. No way would she be able to resist checking in on her partner. The male might be neck-deep in a salt bath, but she'd want to sit with him. Be there when Mac woke up. Which meant Rikar would know exactly where she was…at all times.

Simple. Perfect. Brilliant. Just the way he liked things.

Leaning in, he took a chance and kissed her again. She hummed softly, parting her lips, inviting him in. With a groan, Rikar accepted, sliding his hand into her hair as he got busy blissing her out. And pleasing himself. Gentle desire slid into need, becoming greedy as she turned toward him. Cupping his nape, she played with his hair, tangled her legs with his, putting them breast to chest.

And bing-bang, just like that he wanted her hoodie gone. The cotton was too goddamn thick. He couldn't feel a thing through it and—

Shit. What was he doing? The plan was to distract her. Not give himself a massive case of blue balls.

"Ah, Angela?" Breathing hard, he nipped her as he drew away.

"Hmm?"

"Got something for you."

"What?"

"It's a surprise."

Suspicion glinting in her gaze, she murmured, "Uh-huh."

Christ love her. She was smart. But then, he was too.

With a quick shift, he slid out of her arms before the urge to spread her beneath him took over. One more session like that and…hell. Hoodie, no hoodie, he'd peel her out of those yoga pants and be deep inside her in under a minute flat. But that was a big no-can-do. At least today. Tomorrow? Who knew, but for the moment the plan didn't include making love to her. It was all about the string-along. Keep her guessing, and his female would follow him.

No questions asked.

Okay. Maybe not *no questions.*

Angela was built to interrogate. She'd pepper him with questions the whole way, but she'd be walking while she did it. And that was the point.

Swinging his legs over the side of the mattress, Rikar stood and glanced at Angela over his shoulder. Raising a brow, he held out his hand. "You coming?"

Her eyes narrowed. "You're fighting dirty."

"Did you expect anything else?"

Her lips pursed, she glared at him. Rikar fought a grin, waiting her out and…jackpot. Curiosity grabbed hold, making her eyes sparkle as she accepted his offering. As her hand slid into his, he pulled her to her feet, but held tight, lacing their fingers together. She murmured a protest, tried to shake free. He held firm, and she gave in. Hallelujah. A small victory, but hell, he'd take it.

Grinning like an idiot, he tugged her toward the door. All the while thinking…*Fucking A.* Holding her hand felt good. Right. Everything it should be and more.

Now all he needed to do was persuade Angela to stay. To become a permanent part of his life after he took Lothair down.

Chapter Nineteen

White-knuckling the steering wheel with both hands, Tania drove into the SPD's parking lot. And straight into a war zone. Yellow police tape crisscrossed the far end. Bits of glass and steel littered the asphalt. A telephone pole, snapped midshaft with tangled wires, lay in the middle of a super-duty truck that had seen better days. And wow, the uniforms were everywhere: cops, firefighters, and tow-truck drivers, all working to clear the debris and damaged cars. Some were beyond repair, lined up in a haphazard row with smashed-in roofs, blown windshields, and flat tires. Others had escaped the pileup with little more than a scratch or two.

Jeez, Baghdad had nothing on this place.

And that was before she saw the huge hole in the side of the building. Holy crap. It looked like the precinct had been bombed.

Taking her eyes off SPD's little shop of horrors, Tania wheeled her '64 Mini Cooper into a tiny spot between two big all-terrain vehicles. The huge four-by-fours obviously belonged to wannabes. Every woman knew the type. Guys with inferiority complexes, more concerned about what they looked like than how they acted. Yup. Men like that always went for the "monster" rides.

Compensating for what they lacked behind their button flies, maybe?

Tania snorted. Probably. Today, though, she was happy to take advantage of the testosterone-induced stupidity. She'd just had her Mini repainted—cherry red with white racing stripes…sweetness personified. No sense risking her girl getting dinged by the load of muscle getting flexed at the other end of the parking lot.

Taking a deep breath, she stared out through the windshield at the chain-link fence, doubting the viability of her plan. Detective MacCord wasn't a pushover. The guy was like cyanide. Painful. Persistent. Annoying as heck. Infecting her like slow poison.

God, why couldn't she get him out of her head? She'd tried everything. Had even eaten a boatload of chocolate—before ten a.m.! Gone for a run at lunchtime. Left work early, complaining of a headache, to take another swim at the Y, pushing herself so hard she could barely lift her arms by the end. But oh, no. Nothing worked. MacCord stuck like gum to the bottom of a shoe. And no amount of mental shuffling scraped him off.

Leaning forward, Tania rested her forehead against the steering wheel. The urge to thump herself—just crank her head back and take her anxiety out on her frontal lobe—warred with self-preservation for a second. But giving herself a goose egg wouldn't help. She'd just end up looking like a bad version of Frankenstein when she saw MacCord. 'Cause…yup. She was going in there. To hammer him over the head with the fact she'd been doing his job. Had dug up some new information about her missing best friend.

The case MacCord was supposed to be working on solving. Flipping jerk. *He* was supposed to be keeping *her* in the loop, not the other way around.

With a sigh, she pushed away from her perch, took the keys from the ignition, and reached for her handbag. The Coach purse came when called, settling in her lap while she dug inside for her iPhone.

"Please, please, please," she murmured as she scrolled through her missed calls.

Nothing from Angela Keen, partner extraordinaire to the jerk. Crap. She'd left…what? Seven messages? Yet Detective Keen hadn't called her back. Which seemed strange since Tania got the feeling the cop never missed a beat. And especially since she'd laid out the new lead in the voice mail.

Myst was alive. Still MIA, but *alive.*

Tania knew because she'd discovered the damp towels. Okay. So that just sounded crazy, but someone had used her best friend's shower. Left shampoo bottles in disarray. Makeup strewn all over the bathroom countertop. Ransacked Myst's dresser drawer—the one where she kept her hospital scrubs—and left a pile of terry cloth behind. Proof positive. Myst had been in her loft sometime in the last twenty-four hours.

She knew it like she was sitting in her Mini, her handbag clutched in her lap. Why her friend hadn't called she didn't know. Maybe the kidnappers had a tight leash on her.

Tania shook her head. She didn't want to think about it or any more awful scenarios. It was now or never. Time to oust the detectives from their roost.

Popping the latch, she swung the door wide, careful not to hit the truck parked beside her, and stepped out onto cracked pavement. The click of her three-inch heels disappeared beneath the high whine of a buzz saw, getting swallowed up by men's shouts as firefighters cut through steel. Tania watched the sparks fly, arcing into the air as she crossed the lot. Slipping between cars, she bypassed the downed telephone pole and headed straight for the front doors: shoulders back, head held high, acting as though she belonged. The last thing she needed was for someone to stop her, turn her away…tell her to come back when the SPD was done cleaning up the mess.

Not gonna happen. Not today. Myst needed her.

Her pace even, she reached the front entrance. Cold metal settled in her hand, chilling her palm as Tania swung the door wide and stepped inside the lobby. The smell of sulfur and floor cleaner made her nose twitch. Ignoring the toxic mix, she nodded to the janitor, skirting his mop and the yellow *Caution! Wet Floors* sign, and hightailed toward the front desk.

A bleached-out blonde already occupied the real estate, updo teased within an inch of its life. The closer Tania got, the more details jumped out at her. Yikes. The woman looked like a racing stripe. Red lacquered lips tipped up, she leaned against the high countertop and flirted with the cop on desk duty. Black skirt painted on tight. A severely cut leather jacket over a frilly, barely-there top that left nothing to the imagination. And the shoes? A pair of leopard print Louboutins. Hmm…very *nice* footwear. And about the only classy thing about Ms. Man-Eater.

"Look, Ms. Newton, I'd love to—"

"Clarissa," the woman murmured as she leaned in to straighten the officer's tie, giving him what amounted to a free peep show. "We're on a first name basis now, aren't we, Clark?"

And jackpot.

Clark's eyes dipped, diving straight into Ms. Man-Eater's cleavage. He swallowed. Tania's lips twitched. Sexual manipulation at its best. The woman knew what she was doing.

Fiddling with his tie pin, Clarissa glanced at him from beneath her lashes, acting demure. "Now, Clarkie-baby… what can you tell me about what happened here?"

Tania almost rolled her eyes. She stopped herself at the last second, curiosity getting the better of her. She settled in behind Ms. Man-Eater at the countertop instead. She wanted to know what had happened, too. And if riding on Clarissa's coattails got her the information without her having to lift a finger, so much the better.

"Look, Clarissa." The cop glanced around, shifting as though his bottom half had just woken behind the desk. "Captain Hobbs'll have my ass if he sees you here. We're not supposed to be talking to reporters and—"

"No harm, no foul," Clarissa murmured. "Meet me after work? At Deuce's across town?"

Oh, boy. Match. Set. And Game. *Clarkie-baby* was toast. Deuce's was a hotspot known for dark, cozy corners, under-the-table antics, and a lot of backroom dealing. Tania had never been, but…wow. The rumors abounded. Especially since membership into the club came with a hefty price tag.

The cop nodded and glanced around again.

"Good." Clarissa smiled, smoothing her hand down the front of his shirt before letting him go. "See you there, baby."

As the blonde turned, she arched her back a little, posing for the guy before she put the beautiful Louboutins in gear and, with a finger wave, headed for the exit. Tania shook her head and watched her go. Jeez. Man-Eater was right. A real student of the game. And the cop's dumbstruck expression? Testament to the woman's skill. Clark had bought the act, was 100 percent on board.

"Excuse me?" Tania said, hoping to snap the cop out of his blonde bombshell fixation.

"What?" His eyes narrowed on her.

Oh, snap. What was the load of pissed off and nasty all about? "Ah, I'm here to see Detective Keen and—"

"No one's coming in or out today, miss."

"But—"

"The precinct's closed to visitors. Only essential personnel allowed."

Frig. He sounded like he was reciting a direct order or something. Not good. On any level. "I have some important information about a case they're working on and—"

"So call 'em. Leave a message."

"I did that already." Cupping the lip of the counter with both hands, she leaned in, using her big, brown eyes to effect. "If you'll just let me go up for a minute, I won't take—"

"N. O." He gave her a stern look.

Tania blinked. Nuts. For the first time in her life, she wished she was blonde. Things obviously got done when a woman possessed the right hair color. "Please, Officer Clark? Detective Keen told me to come see her *anytime.* All I need is five minutes."

"Off you go, miss." With one last head shake, he waved his hand, dismissing her as he picked up a stack of paperwork. "Come back when there isn't a hole in the side of our building."

Tania sighed, disappointment hitting her chest-level. No way was she getting in today. Not with a couple of cops flanking the elevators and watching the stairs. Turning toward the exit, Tania wrenched her handbag from the crook of her elbow. As she slung it higher, the leather dragged at her shoulder and…God. She'd been carrying the thing around forever, but today was the first time it felt heavy.

Crossing the lobby, she pushed one of the doors open and stepped out. The air smelled fresher outside, without the taint of lemon and sulfur in the crisp autumn air. She stared at the tips of her Manolo Blahniks, racking her brain for a new plan.

So…what next? Follow Detective Keen home like a lost puppy? Corner her in an underground parking lot? Tania snorted. Yeah, like she wanted to sneak up on a woman with a loaded gun on her hip. That kind of stupidity would only get her shot.

A lighter snicked nearby. Cigarette smoke drifted, perfuming the air a second before a husky voice said, "You in trouble, gorgeous?"

Tania glanced toward the shadows to the right of the front doors. Oh, lovely. The Man-Eater, sucking on a cancer stick, lying in wait for her next victim.

But…wait. Maybe that was a good thing. The cops wouldn't listen. Didn't seem to care that her friend was still out there. All alone. Or that Tania had information that could save her life. Myst might be alive now, but for how much longer? Whoever had kidnapped her wanted something. And as soon as they got it, her best friend would be found with a bullet in her skull.

Her grip tightened on her handbag. Over her dead body. No way would she let that happen.

Tipping her chin at Ms. Man-Eater, she asked, "Are you an investigative reporter?"

"For KING-Five TV."

Hmm. Seattle's biggest local broadcaster.

"Got a story to tell about missing women and police incompetence," Tania said, laying it on thick. Normally, she didn't like lying, but with Myst's life at stake, she considered it just another bump in the road. Holding the reporter's gaze, she raised a brow. "Are you interested?"

"Interested is my middle name," Clarissa murmured, coming out from her natural habitat—the shadows.

Tania smiled. Excellent. Ms. Man-Eater had bitten. Hook. Line. And sinker. Plan B was officially deployed and on track. If the cops wouldn't listen to her story, greater Seattle would…on the six o'clock evening news.

Chapter Twenty

His head half buried under a pillow, Mac woke up so fast he flinched. Blinking to clear his vision, he wondered where the hell he'd landed. Big bed. White sheets. Nope, definitely not his.

Oh, hell.

He didn't like waking up in strange places anymore. A decade of one-night stands had been quite enough, thank you very much. He'd lost interest in that kind of arrangement a while ago. Now he had his favorites. His go-to girls: the type who liked to have fun without any strings attached. Worked for him. Worked for them. No harm, no foul.

All part of the game.

At the moment, though, the red flags were flying. He couldn't see anything through the pillow pile, but his hearing worked just fine. Better than *fine*, actually. He could hear everything. The hum of the dimmed-out halogens overhead, water rushing in the pipes behind the walls…the faint sound of someone breathing. And something else too. A flipping sound, almost as though paper rasped against paper.

Keeping the movement smooth, he reached for the other side of the bed. Nada. No warm body. Not an ounce of soft skin anywhere. Mac thanked God, then paused to wonder what the hell was wrong with him. He'd never been relieved to wake up alone before and...

Goddamn. He was losing it.

He scrubbed his hand over the rat's nest on top of his head. Man, he needed a haircut. And a fucking clue.

Frowning so hard the space between his eyebrows stung, Mac thought back and—

Ta-da. The memory surfaced on cue. Mac blew out the breath he'd been holding. The last thing he remembered was the salt bath. And Sloan sewing him up.

Fifty-seven stitches.

He knew because he'd counted, trying not to whine like a little girl while the needle got pulled through again and again. Frickin' Sloan. Someone needed to haul the guy out of the dark ages. Inform him topical anesthesia and painkillers existed. Spare the next guy in line the one-way trip into Ouchville.

He didn't feel bad now, though. In fact, he felt pretty damn good, considering the Razorbacks had used him as a pincushion less than...

Mac pushed the corner of a pillow out of his line of sight. He squinted at the wide-faced wall clock hanging above glossy white cabinets across the room. Shit. He'd been whacked less than six hours ago. That was wild. A few hours of sleep and he'd healed up good and tight. All right. Maybe he was exaggerating a little. His right shoulder still ached, after all, telling him that although the sliced muscle was on the mend, he wasn't quite 100 percent. At least not yet. Give him some more Zs, though, and he'd be good as new.

Fingering the bandage, he turned onto his side and—

"Jesus Christ!"

"Rise and shine, partner."

Dark green hoodie zipped all the way up, half a deck of cards in her hand, others spread out on the quilt in front of her, Angela sat cross-legged at the end of the bed. Solitaire. Fuck. Wasn't that just like her…to sit with him, patiently playing a game while she waited for him to wake up. While she waited to see if he was all right. His throat went tight as he spied the concern on her face.

Biting her bottom lip, she shuffled the cards in her hand. "How we doing this morning?"

"Jesus, Ange," he said, voice cracking as his gaze met hers. Her eyes filled with tears. His followed suit, stinging at the corners. God, he was so frickin' glad to see her. "You trying to give me a heart attack?"

Without warning, she launched herself at him. Cards went flying. Mac sat up in a hurry, catching her in midflight, wrapping her in a big bear hug. The kind a brother gave his sister after not seeing her for a while.

Hanging on tight, she gave him a squeeze. "I'm so happy to see you."

The viselike pressure banding his chest backed off a notch, allowing him to take a full breath. Thank God for Ange. She had that effect on him. Always calmed him down. Made him think before he acted, which was why he'd lasted on the force for so long. A quirk of fate had paired them up just over two years ago, and he was so grateful for that. He'd gained more than a kick-ass partner that day. He'd found his family.

But now, he had a new one. Dragonkind.

Mac swallowed, suddenly nervous. Would Angela understand his new circumstances? Would she accept what he was and would become with the Nightfuries' help? Or would his dragon side freak her out and send her running?

He hoped not. The last thing he wanted to do was lose her.

Taking a fortifying breath, he backed out of the embrace. She gave him one last squeeze, then released him, shuffling backward on the mattress, putting a comfortable distance between them. And yeah, that was about right. He and Angela might love each other, but it was purely platonic. Exactly the way both of them liked it. So hugging didn't happen often, and when it did, the embrace was heartfelt, but brief.

Wiping beneath her eyes, she ran her gaze over him, cataloging the almost-healed scrapes and fading bruises. "Are you all right?"

"Yeah. You?"

"Right as rain."

He raised a brow. "Liar, liar, pants on fire."

With a huff, Angela settled on her knees, bum to heels, and flicked the edge of his bandage. "Like you're one to talk?"

He shrugged, ignoring the twinge of pain, trying to figure out how to tell her. Where should he start? At the beginning? Near the end? Mac didn't know, but somehow blurting out *Surprise, I'm half-dragon, just like the bastards that kidnapped and tortured you* didn't seem the right tack to take.

Yeah. Like that would win him any brownie points.

"I didn't know you were inked." Reaching out, she touched one of the tattooed lines on his forearm.

"I wasn't…until yesterday," he murmured, staring at the design—the swirling navy-blue lines he'd never consented to getting.

Rikar thought magic was at the root of the tattoo. Something to do with being a water dragon. Mac frowned at it, flexing his arm, watching the pattern shift with his muscle. Maybe his XO was right. The tat, after all, had come with his transition. Along with his claws and the sharp blade running along his spine in dragon form. But unlike the horns on his head, the ink stayed in place, shifting from scales to skin, marring one half of his torso before moving over his left shoulder, down and around his biceps to his forearm. Human. Dragon. It didn't matter what form he took, the pattern never changed.

Which meant he was stuck with the thing. Whether he liked it or not.

"Wow, look at that." Her gaze on his tattoo, Angela leaned closer and watched the ink morph on his skin. The marking shimmered, moved from dark to light blue where she touched his arm. "Cool."

Cool? He blinked. Okay, he bought that. Most chicks liked ink, but right now that wasn't his primary concern. He needed to man up, grow a pair, and tell her things had changed. That *he* had changed.

Mac cleared his throat, searching for the right words. None came, so he copped out, and said, "You think?"

Angela snorted. "You're a pansy, you know that?"

Mac frowned and glanced up. Angela met his gaze head-on. His breath hitched as he saw the understanding in her eyes. "Holy shit. You know."

She nodded. "Rikar filled me in."

Mac closed his eyes, relief hitting him chest-level. His partner knew, and yet she was still sitting with him. Wasn't running in the opposite direction. Still wanted to be his friend…his family. Jesus. Her strength floored him, renewed his faith in all things good. And had the situation been reversed, he probably would've been out the door.

"I always knew you were different," she said, smiling a little, breaking his heart. "I just didn't know how different. So I guess dragon DNA explains it."

"God, Ange," he said, so proud of her his heart ached. "I didn't think you'd—"

"I saw him, you know," she said, tone soft with wonder. "Rikar…in dragon form…when he came to get me. I have to admit, it was pretty spectacular. Could've been the blood loss and delirium talking, though, so don't get your hopes up. I might freak out yet and shoot you."

"Right…" Grabbing her hand, he gave it a gentle squeeze. "I'll get ready for the psychotic break."

She huffed.

Mac grinned at her. He couldn't help it. Trust Angela to accept easily what would scare the pants off of most people. She'd always been like that. Insatiably curious. Way too smart for her own good. Which begged the question. One that revolved around his new XO. Mac's eyes narrowed. He took a deep breath. Huh. He could smell Rikar all over her—the scent screaming *Stay away, or get your ass kicked.*

Interesting. And dangerous.

Two of his favorite words. Especially since he'd be the one doing the ass kicking if Angela got hurt along the way. First-in-command or not, Rikar would treat her right or answer to him.

Holding her gaze, he tipped his chin. "You hooking up with him, Ange?"

"Who?"

"Don't play dumb."

She threw him a hardcore it's-none-of-your-freaking-business look.

"Bullshit." No way would he let her con him. He wasn't buying it or about to let her off the hook. He wanted answers. Needed to know what he was dealing with because…shit. He might not understand a lot about Dragonkind yet, but Mac knew it was serious business. And her welfare was too important to shrug it off. "Anything to do with you…here." Releasing her hand, he raised his own, circled his index finger in the air, the gesture all-encompassing. "In this world. At Black Diamond. You're my business. So get over it and dish."

Chewing on her bottom lip, she sighed and looked away. Not a good sign. It reeked of uncertainty. He could practically smell her vulnerability. And that was before she started picking at the quilt, worrying a loose thread with her fingernail. Mac's stomach twisted into a giant knot.

Motherfuck, he didn't like her reaction. Angela was the only constant in his life. No matter how screwed-up things became, he could always count on her to kick his butt when he needed it. But now she was the one hurting. So, yeah. He would be the steady one…for a frickin' change.

"Tell me what's going on."

"I don't know," she said, sounding way too young. Way too confused. Way too vulnerable. "I'm drawn to him. It's like we share a weird connection or something. The more time I spend with him, the closer I want to get and…crap. I know it sounds crazy, but…" Plucking a seven of spades off the bed, she turned the card over in her hand. "I like him, Mac…a lot. But I'm afraid, too."

Like was good. Scared was not. "Has he hurt you?"

She rocked backward on her knees, shock flaring in her eyes. "No. He would never do anything to hurt me."

"Then you're good to go."

Her brows collided, and Mac knew exactly what she was thinking. The unspoken *you're nuts, bro* didn't need saying to be heard.

Hell, maybe he was. He didn't know Rikar all that well. All right, so he respected the guy, liked him even. It was easy to do. But that didn't change the facts. The Nightfury first-in-command was a warrior with loads of aggression to spare. A good thing on a battlefield. You wanted that kind of male covering your six in a dogfight. But with a woman, it wasn't the best combination.

Then again, what did he know?

He was just as deadly as Rikar—always had been—and he'd never hurt a woman. Not once. Would rather blow his own head off with a matched set of Sigs then abuse a female. So the question then became: Why would Rikar feel any differently? The short answer? He wouldn't. The male was straight-up solid. No way would Rikar ever hurt Angela.

Mac blew out a long breath. All right, then. Crisis averted. Which meant he could play the hell out of Cupid. There were definite advantages to the whole Angela/Rikar hookup. He wouldn't be forced to give up his baby sister. Selfish much? Without a doubt. Mac didn't care. The upside of keeping her around was too tempting to pass up.

"You're cool with the fact he's half-dragon?"

"Duh. I'm okay with the fact *you're* Dragonkind, so…"

"Okay, chill. Just checking," he said, settling back into their normal routine, loving the fact nothing had changed between them even though everything else had gone to hell around them. "So you'll give Rikar a shot?"

Angela shrugged. "The whole thing still freaks me out, but…yeah, I guess."

"Take it slow. Give yourself time, Ange, but don't let fear shut you down. Rikar's a patient guy. He'll wait for you to figure it out."

She flicked the card at him, nailing him in the center of the forehead. As he cursed, she said, "So what now…you go half-dragon on me and suddenly you're channeling Dr. Phil?"

He rubbed his forehead. Shit, like he didn't have enough bruises, already? "Smart-ass."

"You know it." She laughed, giving him a big grin. Oh, how he'd missed her. "Now, are you gonna stick around here or…?"

Mac raised a brow, waiting for the punch line. Angela loved alternatives. And he enjoyed it when she came up with them. The fact her options nearly always landed them in trouble—and closer to the truth—just threw more fun into the pot. Kind of like the bonus round on a game show.

"Are you coming?" She scooted to the edge of the bed.

He followed, conjuring a pair of Lucky Sevens as he went. As the denim settled at his waist and against his thighs, he asked, "Where we going?"

"To ambush Rikar," she said, tone nonchalant as though she'd just suggested they go for a couple of lattes or something. Not tweak a dragon's tail. "He's hiding something from me. I wanna know what it is."

His lips twitched. "You know where he's at?"

"No clue."

"Hmm…a scavenger hunt."

"X marks the spot." Angela hopped to the floor. Slipping her feet into a pair of flip-flops, she headed for the door.

Not bothering with boots, Mac hotfooted after her in his bare feet. Oh, goody. Angela scented blood in the water, and he couldn't wait for the show. Rikar was so frickin' dead when she caught up to him. And lucky him. He'd have a front row seat while it all went down.

Mac smiled. God love her. It was just like old times.

Standing in Sloan's computer lab, Rikar faced off with the bank of wall monitors, wondering where the hell to start. The com-center was class-A complicated—freaking NASA on steroids. Nothing but big screens and hard drives, soup-to-nuts Techie Town. A place he didn't belong.

Didn't want to, either.

The IT stuff had never interested him. Chasing info around cyberspace took patience. The kind he didn't have. Good thing Sloan possessed it in spades, trolling the underbelly of human networks, digging up intel, keeping an eye on enemy activity. Wicked good stuff. His buddy was truly talented in the realm of IT. Too bad the aptitude didn't extend into the world of interior design.

Rikar glanced at the beat-to-hell desk stretching wall-to-wall below the wall-mounted screens and grimaced. Man, what a travesty. The thing had to be at least a bazillion years old. All right. So it was massive and solid-looking, which under normal circumstances would've passed muster…had it been the only visual impediment in the room.

But something far worse sat in front of it, rounding out the nasty factor.

One ugly-ass chair.

With its tall curved back, cracked leather, worn seat, and fraying seams, it looked like something that needed to visit the inside of a Dumpster. And quick because…shit. The thing was purple—as in Barney, here we come.

He shook his head. Sloan needed an upgrade…another place to sit his ass every night while he tried to keep up with the flow of information. But then, their resident computer genius was funny that way. Sentimental to the point of stupidity, the male never threw anything away.

Especially his favorites.

Skirting the purple monstrosity, Rikar planted one hand on the desktop, leaned in, and palmed the mouse. The system woke up, the swirling pattern on the screen flaring blue a second before—

"Fuck," he muttered. "Password protected."

He should've guessed. Sloan was intense when it came to firewalls, hackers, and privacy. No way would he leave his system unattended and vulnerable. Or open for any of his Nightfury brothers to saunter by and screw up. It had been known to happen. Christ, Wick and Venom had crashed the entire system one afternoon playing online video games.

So needless to say, the expression "no fucking way" got used vehemently whenever one of them wanted to take a turn on one of Sloan's computers.

With a growl, Rikar flipped the wireless mouse, sending it skittering across the desktop. Fantastic. So much for sneaking in on the sly and making a fast getaway. Not that he didn't want his buddy knowing what he was up to, but he didn't know what was on that video. Had Angela told Forge what had happened to her? Revealed personal things?

Rikar cursed. He hoped not.

Not that he didn't want her talking about it. She needed the healing that talking would bring. It was just...well, *he* wanted to be the one she came to for comfort. The one she confided in, not some stranger.

And certainly not Forge. Asshole male. Meddling idiot.

Jealous much? Without a doubt. But even with the little green monster sitting on his shoulder, Rikar's head was screwed on straight. At least when it came to Forge. Which was a total switch-up. He'd gone from wanting to rip the male's head off to his instincts ding-ding-dinging. Nothing about the situation made sense. Not the male's easy capture. Not the interest he showed in his son. Or the way he treated Angela and Myst.

All of it was very un-Razorbacklike.

He scowled at the door, then turned to glare at the empty chair. Where the hell was Sloan? Just his freaking luck. His buddy practically slept in the com-center—probably in his uglier-than-shit chair. But the second Rikar needed something like a video cued up, zip-bang, gone. The male was nowhere around.

"Sloan, man," he said, reaching out through mind-speak. *"Where you at?"*

"Right here, my brother."

His head snapped toward the door. Mocha skin looking darker in the dimness, his buddy crossed the threshold. Tipping his chin in greeting, Rikar's gaze dropped to the file box in the male's hands. "Whatcha got?"

"Missing persons reports for your female. I went back eight months." With a shrug, Sloan veered right toward the large table near the back wall of his domain. Set up like a conference room, black leather chairs—looking decidedly normal…thank fuck…easier on the eyes than ugly-ass purple—crowded around the solid wood top. Setting the box down on polished cedar, he said, "All young females, late teens to late twenties. No idea whether they're high-energy or not, but maybe Angela will find a connection. Something we can tie to the Razorbacks."

"Hunting habits and prey drive." Rikar nodded, liking the idea.

If Angela could put names and faces to the female captives with the MP reports, it would help identify the variables: age, background, race, and habits. Males tended to like one type of female, and if Lothair was the one doing the cherry-picking, there might be a pattern of behavior. A method to his madness, so to speak. Locations. Dates. Times.

But even better, analyzing the data—nailing the victimology—would take time. Would keep Angela busy and safe inside the lair. And while she shuffled paperwork, he'd be out killing the bastard who'd hurt her.

Perfect.

Now all he needed to do was convince her the plan was a good one. And get a freaking move on. Rikar didn't trust her to stay put. Not after she'd given him the hairy eyeball as he left her planted in a chair beside a still-sleeping Mac. Smart and suspicious were her middle names, after all, and she'd guessed right. He *was* up to something. Planned to watch the video and still have time to beat the snot out of Forge if the male had so much as looked at her the wrong way.

"So…" Dark eyes full of speculation, Sloan raised a brow. "Whatcha need?"

"Video feed from the cellblock."

Pushing the box into the middle of the table, his buddy strode over to his expensive toys. One flick of the mouse. A few command keys tapped and…voilà. The giant screen came alive, showcasing a frozen image, complete with throw cushions and females.

"Christ." Rikar leaned in to get a better look. Shit. Sloan was *da bomb.* He grinned at his buddy. "You cued it up already."

"Figured you'd want to see it. What with your female and Myst playing *Spy Game* down there."

Rikar snorted. *Spy Game.* He liked that movie. No surprise there. Espionage was his thing, after all. Well, except for now. He didn't like the game Angela played. Or the fact she'd been anywhere near Forge. The male was not what he seemed. Which made him incredibly dangerous.

"So, what are we thinking here?" Sloan asked. "Something off with the Razorback?"

"Yeah…way, way off." Snagging a chair from the conference table, Rikar dragged it over and dropped into the leather seat. He glanced at Sloan, wanting to see his buddy's reaction as he said, "I don't think he's a Razorback. Or ever was one."

Sloan's brows popped, reaching his forehead. "Helluva risk to us if you're wrong."

"I know." His eyes on the screen, he leaned forward, planted his elbows on his knees, and settled in for the show. "Just roll it, will ya?"

Palming the back of his ugly-ass chair, his buddy unloaded his weight on the thing. Metal groaned while stitching popped, standing out in stark contrast against the hideous purple leather. A crease between his brows, fingers flying over the keyboard, Sloan worked his magic and…

Roll film.

Rikar held it together until the ten-minute mark. After that, everything went downhill. Jesus fucking Christ. Forge and his big mouth…his solid heart, too. The male's concern for Angela—his kindness and advice—floored Rikar, and as his throat went tight, the male nailed him again by saying…

"It's not your fault, Angela. Let it go."

"Fuck me," Rikar murmured, his eyes stinging as he watched his female struggle.

God, she was so strong. Made him so proud. She bore the hurt like a warrior: keeping it together, not crying, digging deep even though she didn't have to. And Forge…goddamn, the male was straight-up honest. Giving Angela the truth instead of polluting her with fear. Pushing her toward Rikar instead of urging her to back away.

The SOB could've ruined Rikar's chances with her. Instead, he'd done the legwork, belying her fears while he piqued her curiosity. Rikar frowned. No wonder she'd let him touch her. She'd wanted to know…to experience feeding him firsthand. But stranger than that was the fact Forge was now his ally on the win-Angela-over front.

And that posed a huge problem.

He had an innocent male chained in the basement. How screwed up was that? Very. A freaking brain twister. One that needed to be solved. Pronto.

"Holy shit." Sloan hit the pause button, a frown on his face as he rocked back in his seat. "He doesn't act like a rogue…I'll give you that. What the hell are we gonna do with him?"

"The only thing we can." The answer came to Rikar in a flash of inspiration. "Flip him."

"Are you frigging insane?"

"He's a strong male, Sloan. A warrior." His eyes narrowed in thought, Rikar plucked a pencil off the marble desktop. Staring at the lead tip, he twirled it between his fingertips. "We can use him, man. Ivar doesn't care who fights for him or why, so he replenishes his numbers faster than we do. We get Forge on-side, and he'll be a powerful Nightfury asset."

"Bastian's not gonna like it."

"B's already thinking it, buddy...guaranteed."

Leaning back in his chair, Rikar stared at the frozen computer screen. His gaze riveted on his mate, he studied Angela's face while his mind churned, sorting through and then discarding one plan after another. Flipping Forge would take some work. Real ingenuity and team effort...100 percent acceptance from the entire Nightfury pack.

Easier said than done.

His pack was a closed group. Untrusting. Suspicious of outsiders. And protective of one another. Inviting a male as strong as Forge into the mix would threaten that balance if Rikar didn't do it right. Control the variables. Manipulate the outcome. Rikar's eyes narrowed as an idea sparked, then took form. Pairing him with Mac might work. Would give Forge someone to teach and protect while he assimilated into the group.

So...a two-pronged attack. Get Forge to agree to join them, and then give him a job.

Could work. Might be the answer. Only time would tell. But first things first, he needed everyone on board and in on the action.

He glanced at Sloan. "Meeting in fifteen?"

With a sigh, his buddy pushed to his feet. "I'll round up Venom and Wick. You get B."

"Shit," Rikar muttered.

Hauling his best friend out of bed and away from his female would be tantamount to walking into a fist face-first. Hello, Concussionland. Then again, Sloan's job wasn't any easier. Digging Venom and Wick out of video game central would be like pulling teeth…with a spoon. While flying backward.

Rikar grimaced. Fantastic. The day had officially tanked and hit the shitter. And Christ, Angela hadn't even caught up with him yet.

Chapter Twenty-one

The flip-flop of her footwear echoing in the quiet corridor, Angela zipped her hoodie all the way to her chin. Not that she was ever cold. Her internal thermometer always read north of normal. Which was why she kept the temperature in her condo so low. She appreciated a good chill, so the need to button up now was all about confidence.

Or rather, lack of it.

Holy hell. Feeling this exposed wasn't normal. Was it?

Angela didn't know. Couldn't figure out why she felt as though she was about to jump out of her own skin. Her reaction didn't make any sense. Especially since Mac trailed her, watching her back as she paused at an intersection in the double-wide corridor. Maybe it was the absolute silence. The eerie echo of, well…nothing. No movement. No other voices. Just the thump of her heart and the soft pitter-patter of Mac's bare feet behind her.

Which freaked her out the most. Her partner never made a sound. Ever. He was silence personified when he moved. So the fact she could actually hear him didn't qualify as a good sign. Where the hell was everybody?

Okay, so it wasn't *everybody* she wanted to find. Rikar was the target. Too bad he'd decided to play the part of the invisible man. Freaking guy. Everywhere she looked—the clinic, the computer room, the gym…which, holy crap, had a section with equipment for sharpening dragon claws—she'd come up empty.

"We gonna walk around all day?" Mac asked. "Or do you have a destination in mind?"

She glanced over her shoulder and met Mac's gaze. Inquiring minds wanted to know. So did she, but she'd lost his energy signal thirty seconds ago. "Give me a sec. I need to recalibrate my Rikar radar."

"Rikar radar? Jesus," he murmured, looking intrigued and alarmed at the same time. "You can actually *feel* him?"

"Yeah, it's more of a vibration, though…like I'm tuned into his radio frequency or something."

Mac huffed. "He might as well have a GPS chip embedded in his ass."

Too bad he didn't. She was accustomed to technology-based stuff. Enjoyed high-tech computer systems and wiretaps. And using satellites to track phones, cars, and people? Awesome with a capital A. But the sudden appearance of a built-in supernatural homing device inside her head would take a little getting used to.

Along with a crapload of practice.

Controlling it wasn't easy and concentration was key. Mining the signal—connecting to him—took effort. Maybe with time it would get easier, but for now, she needed to stay focused and in tracking mode.

Taking a deep breath, Angela turned inward, sank into her center, the place where stillness lived and chaos took a backseat. The connection flared, linking her to Rikar like an electrical appliance plugged into a wall socket. The muscles bracketing her spine coiled. Sensation swirled across the nape of her neck, then ghosted down, releasing the tension thread by thread.

She glanced at the ceiling. "Got him. We need to go up."

"Gotta be stairs somewhere," Mac said, brushing her shoulder as he strode past her.

Angela put her feet in gear, following his lead.

Embedded in the concrete floor, twin tracks of light acted like a runway, drawing her eyes forward while illuminating the walls with splashing V patterns that didn't quite reach the twelve-foot ceilings. The place was impressive. Big. Modern. Clean as hell. Jeez, whoever cleaned Black Diamond had a serious case of OCD. Well, either that or was a total germophobe.

Mac slowed his roll as he came to another intersection. Two options. Continue straight along the main corridor. Or turn left down a narrower one.

He glanced at her. "Which way?"

"Straight." Yup. Definitely. She knew exactly where she was now from her foray into the lair with Myst. "There are elevators farther up."

"Goddamn, this built-in GPS shit is wicked good."

Angela snorted. "You won't think so when some woman nails you with it, Mr. Commitment-Phobe."

"Am not." He tossed her a dirty look and lengthened his stride. No doubt in a hurry to leave the conversation behind.

Too bad. No way would she let that one lie. Mac was delusional if he thought for one second she didn't see right through him. Besides, like any self-respecting sister, she couldn't pass up teasing him. Poking at him was way too much fun.

"Oh, please." Keeping pace with his cut-and-run routine, Angela jogged alongside him. "The thought of settling down scares the crap out of you."

"Does not."

"Does too," she threw back, sliding to a stop in front of twin Otises.

He hammered the up button with the side of his fist. "God, you're a pain in the ass."

"Missed me, didn't ya?" He rolled his eyes. She grinned at him. Man, settling into routine with him felt so good. Normal. Comfortable. Just like old times. Unable to resist, she stuck it to him again. "How many different women do you sleep with in a week? Five…ten? How do you keep them all straight? Assign each chick a night? You know… Candy the stripper is on Mondays. Fluffy the airhead takes Tuesdays and—"

"Oh, shut up." He tossed her a disgruntled look. "A guy's got needs, you know?"

Oh, boy, did she ever. Kissing Rikar had reminded her of that. Reminded her of something else, too…that she was a woman with needs of her own. Umm, his mouth. He tasted like icicles and snow cones at midnight. Decadent. Delicious. Rich with male spice and pure pleasure. That she could crave his touch after all she'd been through surprised her. Most victims didn't want anything to do with a guy after the attack. But she was headed in the opposite direction.

Well, at least she was consistent. Running toward trouble instead of away had always been her MO. And, yup, curiosity always played a huge part. Incurably intrigued. Her cross to bear. A problem, particularly since it landed her in…

Angela bit her bottom lip. Oh, man. Was she really thinking about hopping into bed with Rikar?

Frowning, she ran through the list of pros and cons in her head. On one hand, it might be too soon for physical intimacy—might freak her out and send her into a tailspin. On the other, she'd really enjoyed feeding him; ran hot when she got that close to him; craved his touch; went nuts for his taste; responded to his gentleness and the desire she saw in his eyes whenever he looked at her. Add in the curiosity factor—about him, his magic, and the connection they shared—and the con column ran more than a touch thin. It was practically anorexic.

So the count was…what now? Seven reasons pro-Rikar and one big fat con.

"You gonna roll him when you see him?"

Angela glanced sideways at her partner. Mac raised a brow, a knowing glint in his eyes. She pursed her lips, considered lying for a second, but well…hell. What good would that do? Mac had always been way too perceptive, and a boatload of dragon DNA hadn't changed that.

With a shrug, she admitted, "I'm thinking about it."

The elevator pinged and the shiny double doors slid open.

"Think fast." Grabbing her arm, Mac hauled her into the elevator behind him. "And play fair, Ange. No teasing allowed. Lay him out or don't. But know which way you're gonna jump before you step off the elevator. Rikar deserves better than a ball-busting letdown."

Crap. So much for "all's fair in love and war." But she knew Mac was right. Getting Rikar jazzed only to run away if she got scared wasn't fair. She needed to go all out…or not at all.

Angela sighed. Just her luck. She had less than a minute to decide which way to jump.

Seated on a stool at the end of the kitchen island, Rikar looked at the males gathered around him. Wick and Venom sat to his left, shoulder-to-shoulder in their regular spots. Sloan bookended the pair at the other end while Bastian leaned against the cabinets across the way, arms crossed, an unhappy look on his face.

And no wonder.

Rikar would've been pissed too, had someone pulled him out of bed and away from his female for a round-table discussion. Meeting his commander's gaze, Rikar raised a brow, wanting B to get the powwow underway. Angela was on the move. He could feel her, icy sensation ghosting down his spine as he tracked her progress in the underground lair below the main house. Christ, she was close to the elevators now, zeroing in on him like a heat-seeking missile.

Just his freaking luck.

The last thing he needed was his female in on the convo. Especially since the second she realized what was up she'd want in on the action. Which…yeah, pretty much jacked his reaction into no-chance-in-hell territory.

Bastian scowled at him, then tipped his chin. Rikar's mouth curved. Well, all right. Looked like he had the floor.

His focus returned to the males around him. He looked at each one in turn, remembering past battles, their strengths, and how well they all worked together. Cohesive. Tight-knit. Committed to one another, bonded by lineage, experience, and shared purpose. The Nightfuries were a strong pack. And as Rikar glanced around the huge island now dwarfed by the warriors around it, he was proud to call each one his brother.

Even Wick.

Big surprise there. Rikar hadn't held out much hope for the golden-eyed male when he'd first arrived. Wick had been shut down in more ways than one, but the tough SOB had come a long way. Earning Wick's trust was part of it. Complete acceptance from the pack was another. Time and effort were good teachers, and eventually he and the other Nightfuries had broken through Wick's ultrathick guard. Now he was a solid member of their pack.

Thank fuck for that. Lethal, after all, was always welcome.

"So we're all agreed?" Rikar asked.

As his gaze shifted to Venom, the male said, "You sure it wouldn't be better if I just bashed his head in?"

Rikar grinned. Trust Venom to pick the path of least resistance.

Bastian snorted. "Come on, Ven. If we flip Forge, we gain another strong warrior. Better for us."

"If?" Venom perked up. "You mean there's still a chance I'll get to—"

"Shut the fuck up, Venom," Wick said, planting his forearms on the countertop, golden eyes shimmering as he stared unblinking at his friend. "I was worse than Forge when you pulled me out. After that BS..." Wick shrugged, broke eye contact, and murmured, "Flipping Forge'll be a piece of cake."

Silence ballooned like an air pocket in the wake of the male's words, filling the space. Rikar blinked. Holy Christ.

Three complete sentences. A huge first for Wick. One Rikar didn't know what to do with.

It was like watching an infant take his first step. A necessary thing, but painful to endure without reaching out to offer help. And as Venom laid his hand on the back of Wick's neck and squeezed, Rikar asked the same question he always did when faced with their friendship. What the hell had happened to them? He knew something serious had gone down. Had pieced together some of it—like the fact Venom had pulled Wick out of a nasty shithole before his change. But beyond that, no one knew much. None of them had ever asked, and the two warriors sitting shoulder-to-shoulder never volunteered the information.

"So..." Sloan cleared his throat, breaking through the uncomfortable silence. "You want us to go at him as a unit?"

"Solidarity," Wick murmured, shrugging out of Venom's hold. "Pack mentality."

"Yeah," B said. "All hands on deck with this one, boys."

"So what? We gonna have a love-in or something?" A sour look on his puss, Venom leaned back in his chair. Wood groaned, protesting the sudden shift of muscle. "Sing 'Kumbaya' with the meathead?"

Rikar laughed. He couldn't help it. The mental image cracked him up. The look on Venom's face made it worse. Shit, he loved the male and his wicked sense of humor. "He needs to know the entire pack will accept him, Ven. No tricks. No possibility of ambush."

"And that'll make him cave?"

"It's worth a shot," he said, pushing the half-eaten pastry away, watching it ooze jelly until it blobbed on the white plate. Rikar grimaced. He should probably eat the damned thing. Daimler would be disappointed if he didn't. After all, the Numbai worked hard to keep them in good eats. Too bad he wasn't hungry...for food. Hot, sweaty sex with Angela, however, was something he could devour with ease. "I think Forge is looking for a home. For a pack to pull him in."

"Or maybe he's just got a death wish," Venom said, unwilling to let go of the dream in which he ripped Forge's head off. Rikar didn't blame him. Normally, he would've hopped on that bandwagon. Trusting an outsider wasn't something any of them could afford. Not when the wrong discussion—pulling an enemy spy into their inner circle—could mean death for one of their own. "He just lost a female."

"All the more reason to hit him now." Chasing an itch, Bastian shifted sideways, rubbing his shoulder blades on a corner cabinet. "He's vulnerable. In need of support and a strong pack to give him direction. Besides, he wants his son."

Sloan's eyes narrowed. "Leverage."

"Yeah," B murmured. "Let's crank the shit out of it."

Venom opened his mouth, no doubt to protest again. Wick elbowed him in the rib cage. "Ow! Easy, Wick...jeez."

"Shut up," Wick said, getting back on the two-word train.

Glaring at his friend, Venom rubbed his side and grumbled, "All right. I'm on board. But I'm available anytime you want to switch to option two, B."

"I'll keep it in mind, my man."

"So...Rikar." Rolling his shoulders, Venom stretched. Rikar went on high alert. He knew that tone, and nothing good ever followed it. "I got a solution for you."

"Oh, Christ." While the others laughed, Rikar eyeballed his friend. "Didn't realize I needed one."

Venom rolled his eyes. "Buddy, you got all kinds of trouble."

Rikar raised a brow.

"Sooner or later, man, you're gonna have to pull your head out of your ass. You can't keep her locked up forever."

Her. Translation? Angela. Freaking male. Venom was butting in where he didn't belong. No one meddled better than Venom, and the fact the warrior was thinking about Angela—for any reason—made Rikar want to kick his ass.

"She's my problem. Not yours," he said, voice soft with lethal undertones. The male needed to get a clue…right now. Before Rikar felt the need to rearrange his face.

"I know that," Venom said. "But Lothair can track her energy. Why not use that and her to our advantage?"

"No fucking way." Rikar curled his hands into fists, prepared to back up the statement with a beatdown. "Not happening."

"Come on, man. She could—"

"Leave it alone, Ven." Bastian pushed away from the cabinets, ready to intervene if shit went critical. A good guess considering Rikar's launch code had been punched in, and he was about to go nuclear. "Don't go there."

"Why not? It's a good plan, B. She's a cop, for God's sake…with a skill set that's cranked to kick ass. Using her as bait to lure the bastard out into the open makes perfect sense." Leaning in, Venom planted his elbows on the countertop. Ruby-red eyes earnest, he said, "Rikar, man, it'll work. We'll protect her while you KO the asshole. Angela will get closure. Where's the downside?"

"Oh, my God." Whisper-thin, the voice came from the archway behind him.

Rikar bowed his head. Angela. She'd snuck up on him in frickin' flip-flops. Talk about inattention. But then, Venom and his stupid plan had distracted him completely. Now he would be forced to deal with the aftermath and Angela's fear.

Swinging around on the stool, he turned to face her and...goddamn, the look on her face broke his heart. Terror—abject and terrible—was on display in her wide hazel eyes. His breath stalled in his throat, making his chest ache as he put himself in gear. He couldn't leave her standing there alone, itching to run as panic grabbed hold. Okay, so technically she wasn't alone. Mac stood just behind her, his eyes so stormy the color churned, moving from aquamarine to turbulent blue-gray.

"Motherfuck." His load of pissed off pinned on Rikar, Mac asked, "Is that true? Can he track her?"

Rikar didn't answer. He was more interested in reaching Angela than answering Mac's question. Stopping in front of her, he slid his hand into hers. A tremor rolled through her into him. He laced their fingers, hoping his touch, the closeness of his body, the reassurance in his gaze calmed her. Helped her realize he would never allow anyone—or anything—to hurt her.

Never again. Not while he lived.

"Angela," he murmured, moving in tight, wanting her in his arms so badly his palms itched.

But forcing an embrace wouldn't work. Not with Angela. She was warrior-strong, able to fight her own battles and decide whom she wanted by her side. The juvenile part of him jumped up and down, yelling, "Pick me, pick me!" Rikar held the line and waited, hoping she took what he offered, the comfort of his touch. Seconds ticked by as she held his gaze, a question in her own, then—

It happened. She folded, closed the distance between them—fisted her hand in the back of his shirt, pressed her cheek to his chest, asking without words to be held. His heart thumped, shattering into shards as he drew her in. Wrapping her up tight, he absorbed her shivers, nestled his cheek against the top of her head, soothing her the only way he knew how…with his body and touch and understanding. "Sweet angel. It's all right."

"S-sorry," she whispered back, apologizing for some imagined weakness.

"No need. You have every right to be afraid. Only a fool wouldn't be, love." Nuzzling her, he kissed the sweet spot behind her ear. "But you're safe. Black Diamond is secure. He can't get to you here."

"And if I leave?"

"He'll find you."

Her hand flexed, bunching his shirt against his spine. He gave her a gentle squeeze as she lifted her face from his chest. She looked up at him. Her eyes clung to his before she took a deep breath, glanced away from him and then around the kitchen, meeting each pair of eyes head-on. His warriors nodded in turn, greeting her with silence and a whole lot of respect. Rikar's throat went tight. Thank God for his brothers. Their show of strength—of solidarity and commitment—was just what his female needed.

"It's my energy, isn't it?" she asked, returning her attention to him. "He's got a lock on it now?"

"Yeah."

"Fucking hell," Mac growled, staring at Venom, his gaze shimmering so fiercely it lit the male up with blue light.

"Forget the bait plan, dickhead. No way you're putting my partner in the line of fire."

Rikar huffed. Well, shit. At least he had one ally in the group. Everyone else looked far too interested in Venom's suggestion.

Use her as bait? No freaking way.

"Wait a second." Angela's eyes narrowed, and alarm bells went off inside Rikar's head. He didn't like that look or the fact the cop in her was coming back online, pushing fear and a healthy dose of caution out of the way. "Let's not discount Venom's idea. You get me the right firepower…a long-range rifle, maybe? Three or four clips full of armor-piercing ammo?" She tilted her head, wheels turning behind her eyes. "Yeah, I should be able to—"

"No." Rikar shook his head to reinforce his denial. Armor-piercing bullets, his ass. He couldn't decide who was more insane: his female or Venom.

Angela frowned at him, no doubt formulating an annoyingly well thought out argument. He reiterated the "no." She leaned away, releasing her death grip on his shirt. He cupped her nape, using gentle hands to keep her against him when she tried to pull away.

She sighed. The soft sound all about exasperation. "Listen, Rikar—"

"It's too dangerous, angel."

"Not if you energy-regress her," Sloan said.

Good Christ. Rikar glared at his buddy. *Energy-regress* her. Was the male out of his fucking mind?

Seemed like a good guess because…shit. Energy-regression took a helluva lot of trust, never mind all kinds of commitment. On his part. On his female's part, too. The only way a male could alter a female's energy signature was to make love to her. Repeatedly. Bliss her out so well—and so often—a link opened to the Meridian, allowing a male access to the unique frequency woven into a female's life force. It was like mainlining energy, druglike, addictive, wild as hell. Or so he'd been told.

Rikar swallowed. Just the thought of spending a week with Angela that way made him go hard. Aroused to the point of pain. God help him. He wanted her that way. Would die to lay her out and use the connection they shared to ensure her safety. The question was…could he do it without hurting her?

He honestly didn't know.

He didn't know the first thing about energy-regression. All right. So he knew how it worked in theory. Had read about it in the annals handed down by Dragonkind ancestors. Had heard other males talk about it, too—how they'd used the magic to keep others of their kind from finding a female again. Cool idea, sure, but with potentially devastating consequences.

Angela wasn't ready to make love with him yet. Not after all she'd suffered, so…yeah. It was a bad, bad, *bad* plan. Tack on the fact if he changed her energy beacon, she'd not only be safe from Lothair but able to leave Black Diamond. And him. Forever.

Fuck.

Just what he didn't need. An ethical dilemma. One that would make him choose between his need for her as a bonded male. And Angela's desire for freedom and independence.

"Rikar?" Smoothing her hand over his shoulder, she stared up at him, confusion and more in her eyes. "What's—"

"I'll explain, but...not here." No way would he explain energy-regression in front of his warriors. They'd never let him hear the end of it. He glanced at Bastian, looking for encouragement.

Per usual, B was Johnny-on-the-spot. "Take your time. The other shit can wait a while."

"Come with me, angel." Tightening his grip on Angela's hand, Rikar tugged her toward the exit. And the corridor that led to his room.

He needed privacy. Loads of it. If she let him lay her down and love her like he yearned to, he wanted a bed and soft-as-silk sheets to do it in. Maybe then he'd find a way to show her how much she meant to him. How much he loved her. And if he did it right—got really, really lucky—maybe... just maybe...she'd fall head-over-heels in love with him, too. Become his mate in every way and...

Stay with him forever.

Chapter Twenty-two

After walking in on the Killers R Us convention doubling as Black Diamond's kitchen, Rikar's bedroom was as quiet as a crypt. As chilly as one, too. But the cold suited Angela just fine. The cool air calmed her down, made her less edgy, allowing her to handle the situation without freaking out.

A shiver rolled through Angela as fear flung her into uncharted territory. The rat-bastard could track her. Find her. Hurt her again. The thought pushed her up against psychological boundaries not meant to be approached and... goddamn it. There she went again, imagining the worst.

She banished the memories, refusing to act like a sissy. No sense repeating her performance in the kitchen. God, talk about needy. But she'd been unable to help herself. Had needed Rikar's arms around her like she needed legs to stand on. Too bad his friends had witnessed the whole mess, watching while she clung to Rikar and soaked up his reassurance.

Lovely. Nothing like acting like an idiot to start the day.

The Nightfury crew probably thought she was a lightweight now. One who cried at the drop of a hat. Angela rubbed her hand over her heart, combating the ache, trying to shore up her confidence. Not an easy feat considering the mother of all surprises she was about to drop in Rikar's lap.

Or try to anyway.

But even after making the decision, the follow-through tripped her up. She kept swinging back to the memory. To the sights. And sounds. And the pain.

Stupid black-eyed son of a bitch.

He'd taken more than her body; he'd killed her confidence. Slashed at her self-esteem. Decimated her courage along with her know-how. But with Rikar, she wanted to believe she could get it all back. That recovery was possible. That bravery and self-belief hinged on the fact he desired her. Even knowing another had hurt her, he wanted her all the same. And his acceptance made all the difference.

The door clicked closed behind her.

Her hand still laced with Rikar's, she glanced over her shoulder. The man meant to be hers gazed back, serious, patient...beautiful. She smiled at him. Not a lot, just a subtle curve of her lips, but her message was clear. Alone at last. And though she was happy to have him that way, the irony of their situation wasn't lost on her.

All the way up in the elevator she'd fantasized about it. About dragging him into some dark corner, imagining what she would do to him. How she would turn him on, *roll him* as Mac had so ineloquently put it. But now that they were alone, all she wanted to do was cry. Twist the knob on her internal pressure cooker and let loose. Mourn the loss of her old life and get on with the new one because...yeah. She could never go back.

The realization should've freaked her out even more.

Somehow, though, it didn't. Rikar made the idea of staying in his world—of joining the team—appealing. And even as the brain cells staked out at her intellectual base camp said, "whoa, Nelly," her heart accepted the truth. Angela didn't want to go back. She wanted to be with Rikar. For as long as he allowed her to stay.

Forget the freaky magic. Forget the dragon part of the equation. Forget the Meridian and her connection to it. Rikar was all that mattered. So screw it. She was going for it...and him. Case closed. File it under done.

"Angela," he murmured.

Her eyes drifted closed. Hmm, his voice. She loved the way he said her name. Smooth. Deep. Rich with promise and hidden delight that said *mine*. And as she felt his presence, his strong body at her back, she prayed that's what he meant. That she was his. That he was hers. That they belonged together.

With a sigh, she leaned back against him. He hummed, accepting her weight, enveloping her in the richness of his scent as he wrapped his arms around her from behind. Pulling her in tight, he settled her back to his front. His chin brushed her hair a second before he pressed a kiss to the top of her head.

So sweet. So gentle. So flipping hot.

Even in the midst of uncertainty, she craved the comfort of his body against hers. Murmuring his name, she wrapped her arms over his, ignored the gun digging into the base of her spine, and hugged him back.

"Thank you," she said.

"For what?"

"Holding me together back there." Shifting in his arms, she glanced over her shoulder, forcing him to lift his head. As Rikar met her gaze, she asked, "Lothair wants to kill me now, doesn't he?"

"I won't let him."

"I know."

And she did…*know.* Rikar would protect her with his life. Which scared her more than she liked. Having her in the mix would put him at risk. She understood the game. Knew what she faced. Dragonkind didn't play by a set of rules or check their weapons at the door. Theirs was a world at war, with death the ultimate sacrifice, and she was way out of her league. And yet, she couldn't leave it alone. Couldn't sit this one out and let Rikar handle it, even though Angela recognized that she should.

She wanted Lothair dead. Bullet to the brain dead.

And she needed to be the one to pull the trigger. To put the rat-bastard down before he hurt any more women. There would be more. Count on it. Sadists like Lothair got off on that kind of thing…on torturing those weaker than him.

She shivered, mourning what she'd lost at his hands. Less than twelve hours. God. She'd been imprisoned less than a day and…goddamn son of a bitch, look at what the psycho had done to her! In less than a half hour, he'd taken her pride and given her shame in return. Left her uncertain of her own abilities. Made her afraid of taking things to the next level with Rikar.

But oh, how she wanted to. Wanted to lay him out flat. Explore every inch of him. Love him so well he wouldn't remember his own name in the aftermath. Only hers.

Giving Rikar another squeeze, she pushed out of his arms. He murmured in protest, but let her go, allowing her to move away from him. She walked farther into the room, picking up details she hadn't noticed standing by the door. As she scanned the space—skimming the cream-colored walls and dark hardwood floors, the peaked timber-beam ceiling and the colorful Hudson's Bay wool blanket thrown over the foot of the four-poster bed—she got a better sense of the man who lived in it.

Like her, he enjoyed simple things. Cozy, unfussy, streamlined. Rustic charm à la wood cabin. No nonsense, yet undeniably striking, just like Rikar.

Kicking out of her flip-flops beside a pair of old-school rocking chairs, she stepped onto the oriental rug and glanced his way. His focus locked on her, he stood motionless, hands shoved into the front pockets of his jeans, shoulder blades flat against the bedroom door. Her stomach did a quadruple somersault. Then vaulted into a backflip. Beautiful man and 100 percent hers. She could see the truth in his eyes. In the way he looked at her. Pure magic… desire-filled, I-need-you-five-minutes-ago magic.

One small problem, though. She was as nervous as hell.

Angela rubbed her upper arms, feeling like she was fifteen years old again, contemplating sleeping with a guy for the first time. Silly, she knew, but it felt as though she'd never been with anyone before. Somehow the slate had been wiped clean, and she'd slid backward twelve years, landing in an enormous pile of teenage angst.

"Do you know…" she said, trailing off as she paused at the end of the king-size bed, working up the nerve to broach the subject of sex. Yeah, Rikar wanted to talk about it, but she wasn't ready yet. So she skirted the issue, working up the courage while she held his gaze. "That winter is my favorite season?"

Glacial eyes locked on her, he shook his head.

Reaching out, she traced the footboard with her fingertips, stroking over the smooth wood, imagining what he would feel like beneath her hands, every hard-muscled, long-limbed, gorgeous inch of him. "I used to skate, you know."

"Figure skate?"

She nodded. "I haven't been on the ice in almost a year, but I love the chill. The colder it is in the arena…or out on the pond…the better I like it." Palming her Glock, she pulled it from her waistband and set it on the end of the bed, right on the navy-blue wool stripe, before she turned to face him. "Do you think that's why I like you so much?"

His brows collided. "*Like*?"

"Hoping for something stronger?"

"Try a lot."

She tilted her head, raised a brow. All right. Screw it. She was jumping in. With both feet. "How about…want. Need. Crave. Those words suit you any better?"

"Christ, yeah, but…" His eyes shimmered, the glow full of heat that tumbled into a kaleidoscope of desire.

"But?"

Rikar scrubbed a hand over the back of his head. "We should talk, angel. About what Sloan said…about the energy-regression. There are things you should know… agree to, and—"

"Tell me later." She unzipped her hoodie.

His mouth parted. Loving his reaction, Angela almost smiled. She held it in, shrugged her shoulders instead, letting the Lululemon fall to the floor, exposing her thin cotton tee. His hands curled into fists. Angela bit the inside of her lip, watching him want her.

His reaction was gratifying. Made her feel powerful. Desirable and needed. All that and she wasn't even naked. Yet. Wasn't busty, curvy, full of sexpot appeal like some women. Sure, her B cups held their own. Were high, taut, full enough for most men to appreciate. And currently braless. Which left little to the imagination. Especially when the chill in the room hit and her nipples furled tight beneath the cotton.

Rikar's chest rose and fell, each breath coming harder… faster. "Unfair, angel."

"Did you expect anything less?" she asked, playing the tease, throwing the words he'd used in the cellblock back at him. "Why don't you come over here?"

"I'm…holy shit…I think maybe…" His throat bobbed as he swallowed.

Angela watched his fingers curl and uncurl, the action telling. He couldn't wait to touch her. Was imagining what her nipples tasted like. Her mouth curved. He was easy to read. A classic case of tug-of-war…right versus wrong. Option one: forget *right* and make love to her. Option two: reject *wrong* and talk. She nibbled on her bottom lip, watched his focus shift to her lips. She lost the battle and smiled.

Time to put option one into play. Tempt fate a little. Or rather, help it along.

Her eyes on his face, Angela grabbed the hem of her T-shirt. She heard Rikar's breath hitch. But mercy wasn't in the cards. With one controlled movement, the cotton rolled up and over the top of her head. He choked. She hummed. Just the response she was looking for. The guy was toast and knew it. His *talk* had just gone out the window. No way would he be able to resist touching her now. Not while she stood bare-breasted in the lamplight, cotton dangling from her fingertips, chin raised in challenge.

Breathing hard, he stared at her, dark desire in his gaze. And oh, boy. No shoes. No shirt, but his expression said it all. She was about to get excellent service…Rikar style.

"Sweet Christ," he rasped, pushing away from the door. "You're so fucking beautiful, Angela."

She murmured a thanks, but stayed perfectly still, letting him look, tempted to roll the yoga pants off her hips, down her thighs, and give him a real show. Hell, she'd do a pirouette for him. Perform a freaking ballet just as long as he crossed the room and touched her.

Right now.

His approach, though, was slow—predatory, animalistic—driving her crazy with anticipation.

One hand gripping the footboard, she turned up the heat and said, "You waiting for a formal invitation?"

Pale eyes aglow, he dragged his focus away from her breasts. As his gaze met hers, he asked, "What do you want, Angela?"

She swallowed. "You."

"Be sure, love."

She hesitated less than a heartbeat. "I am."

"Then ask me." His boots scraped against the wood floor as he moved toward her, more prowl than actual walk. "Spell it out. I need to hear you say it."

"I want you to…" Angela chewed on the inside of her lip. Watched him approach. Working up the courage to say the words. "Make love to me."

"You want me inside you?"

"Yes."

"Any way I please?"

A tremor rolled through her, dragging a memory with it. She wanted Rikar, no question. But not the way the rat-bastard had—

Angela clenched her teeth. No way. Not here. Not now. She refused to allow shame to taint what she had with Rikar. It wasn't her fault. But as tempting as it was, she couldn't bury the pain. Hiding from him—lying to him—wouldn't do either of them any good. He needed to know. She needed to tell him. Honesty was part of the package.

"Not from..." She cleared her throat and whispered, "Not from behind. He hurt me that way. I can't handle that...not yet."

"I won't love you that way...not until you're ready." His voice was soft, full of compassion, but not pity. He understood, accepted her without reservation or judgment. And wow. Didn't that just made her want to cry all over again. As she blinked back tears, Rikar stopped in front of her. "But I'll take you every other way...long and hard, soft and sweet. No holds barred. You ready to give me that?"

She nodded.

"Yes or no, angel?"

Angela whispered another "Yes."

"Fair warning then, love." With slow deliberation, he reached out. His fingers slid across her skin, stroking her lightly before he cupped her cheek.

She turned in to the caress, reveling in his scent, the softness of his touch, the pure pleasure of connection. Tilting her chin up, he leaned in, making her heart pound and her lips part. Oh, man, she needed the taste of him on her tongue and in her mouth, the satisfaction of having him deep inside her. The warmth of his breath touched her first, his mouth second. She hummed, invited him in. He kept it light. A gentle nip. Another kiss. A featherlight caress on her skin.

He lingered, drawing her deep, prolonging the pleasure, delivering his taste in easy sips instead of long swallows. When she moaned, he drew away, holding her prisoner with his gaze. "If I make love to you now...give you the release you crave...I won't let you go. Not in five minutes. Not in five years. Not ever, Angela."

Thank you, God. Just what she needed to hear. He'd claimed her...word before deed. Honorable, in the way of the warrior. In a way she could accept and respect.

Tipping her chin up, she asked for another kiss, watching him beneath her lashes. He gave it to her, flicking the corner of her mouth with his tongue. Angela hummed, enjoying the gentle play as she slid her hands up his arms and around his neck. The tips of her breasts brushed his chest. Her breath caught, sensation spiraling in a bliss-filled wave.

She kissed him again, softly, sweetly—in warning. "I won't ask you to let me go, but it works both ways, Rikar. If I accept you, you're mine. No going back. No other women. Just me."

"An easy enough bargain to make, love." With a groan, he parted her lips and delved deep, tangling their tongues, making her moan as his arms came around her. His hands roamed, exploring her back, pulling her into the curve of his body. God. He felt so good...tasted even better, like dark pleasure and erotic spice, urgent need and blistering desire. Exactly as a man should. Growling low in his throat, he caressed her bottom, nipped her once, then lifted his head. "There has never been, nor will there ever be another female for me. I knew it the moment I met you."

Angela drew in a quick breath. Her heart dipped, cracking wide open as he slipped inside and found a home. Oh, what a man: supportive, passionate…unafraid in the face of commitment.

Okay, so it wasn't candy-coated. Or sugary the way *I love you…stay with me forever* would've been, but it was close. So almost there Angela's throat went tight. And as her fingers played in his hair, she kissed the corner of his mouth and whispered his name.

Close was *close,* after all. And yeah, it would do.

For now.

As Angela settled in his arms, Rikar's heart went jackrabbit, thumping hard against his breastbone. She whispered his name, making him ache with need as she deepened the kiss. Mmm, mmm good. She was unbelievable. Delicious. Lush. Rich. And so fucking hot he didn't know what to do first. Lay her out and love her hard. Or get down on his knees, spread her legs, and taste her deep.

Christ, yeah. That was his first choice.

He wanted at the red curls between her thighs. Needed her cream on his tongue. Deep in his mouth. Down the back of his throat. He wanted to feel her come while he licked into her slick folds. The image alone held the power to slay him. And as his erection thumped behind his button fly, he groaned, splayed his hands against her back, reveling in the smoothness of her skin, the beauty of her scent, the unbelievable taste of her mouth. He stroked deeper with his tongue. Hummed as she opened wider, inviting his possession.

Shit. *Possession.* Not even close. *Possessed* was more like it.

Beautiful female…his mate, his match in every way.

He was bewitched. Completely ruined by her willing abandon. The absolute trust she placed in him. She was so soft. So needy. Spectacular in her passion and the way she accepted him. A dream come true?

No kidding.

He'd dreamed of her, just…like…this. Had spent an inordinate amount of time imagining her in every sexual position known to Dragonkind. Christ. Forget the *Kama Sutra.* That shit had nothing on him. And yet, no amount of imagining had prepared him. Nothing approached the reality of having her in his arms.

One hand buried in her hair, Rikar slid the other down, exploring her curves, heading for her bottom. He loved her body. Smooth skin poured over lithe, athletic curves: strong, sexy, undeniably female. And all his.

His. Every glorious inch of her.

Withdrawing from the kiss, he nipped her lip, playing, teasing, flirting with pleasure as he fingered the waistband of her yoga pants. "These need to go, angel."

"You first." She smiled against his mouth, stroked her hands over his shoulders, tugging at his T-shirt. "God, Rikar. You're so strong. I love the way you feel." Her soft hum of appreciation drew him taut, and muscles across his abdomen tightened, pulling at his hipbones. Her teeth plucked at her bottom lip, driving him crazy, making him want to taste her again as her hands traveled, sliding south, caressing his chest through the cotton. "Off. Take it off. I want to see all of you."

Rikar shivered as desire flicked him with sharp claws. Each nick drew him closer to the edge…to desperation and the urge to forget what she needed—a long, gentle loving—and take what he wanted. Bury himself to the hilt inside her. Ride her hard while he made her come over and over, again and again.

But even if she agreed, he couldn't love her that way. Not the first time. Later would be soon enough. He'd take her the way he yearned to after he'd pleased her so well she couldn't remember her own name. Just his.

Nuzzling the underside of his chin, Angela slipped her hands beneath the hem of his shirt. He cursed as she caressed him, clever fingers brushing his nipples as she planted a kiss in the center of his chest.

Christ help him. What was he supposed to be doing again?

Rikar frowned, tipping his head back to give her more access. Oh, right. Getting naked for her. Fan-fucking-tastic. He was so on board with that plan.

Unleashing his magic, Rikar ditched his clothes, tossing his jeans, shirt, and shitkickers into his mental vault.

"Oh!" Startled by the fast-n-fly, she jumped a little in his arms. "Holy hell…you're…oh, man."

"One of my many talents."

"I like that one," she said, hazel eyes dark with need.

He tried to be patient, to let her explore and look her fill, but…fuck. She had busy hands—talented frickin' hands—and as she caressed him, heading south, his chest pumped and his balls fisted up tight. He needed to stop her now, before she went any lower. If she wrapped her fingers around him, he'd lose it. Come so hard and fast she wouldn't get what she wanted. Or what he was dying to give her.

She raked her nails in a light pass over his abdomen. "*Nice.*"

"Glad you like it," he said, sounding like a weak-ass, totally besotted pansy. Which he was. He still hadn't grabbed her hands. Was letting her drift south even though he knew it was a bad, bad, *bad* idea. "Angela…baby, I can't… if you palm me, I'm gonna…oh, fuck!"

Rikar groaned as her small hands encircled him, one curling around his length while the other dipped lower. Unable to say no, he muttered a curse when she cupped him from underneath, massaging gently as she stroked him base to tip. His hips rolled into her rhythm, curling on the base of his spine. Holy shit, that felt un-freaking-believable. The way she handled him…goddamn. Angela knew what she was doing. Each stroke and release brought him to the edge of rapture, but never quite threw him over.

"Rikar?"

"Sweet angel…you're killing me."

"Then get ready to die happy, gorgeous. I'm going down."

"No…don't," he rasped, making a grab for her bare shoulders.

Too late. She was already on her knees between his legs, her hot mouth on his shaft. Without mercy, she lollipopped him from root to tip. A wet flick. A soft swirling suck and—

"Holy fuck…Jesus Christ!"

She swallowed him whole. Took him deep. Tortured him. Enslaved him with each devastating stroke of her tongue. And Rikar surrendered, becoming slave to her master.

Which was all, well, not wrong exactly. Maybe strange was the right word.

Usually, he controlled the play, dominated, and gave while the female submitted and took. But not with Angela. She was different, an incredible sight to behold in her power. He wore the chains with pride, curled his fingers in her hair, groaned as she took him on a ride of unmitigated delight.

Pressure built at the base of his spine. Rikar gritted his teeth—cursed, egged her on—while she showed no mercy. He pulsed against her tongue. Angela pressed her thumb to the base of his shaft, stalling his orgasm, calming him down only to go at him again. She kept him like that: on the edge, throbbing hard, a breath away from coming until he pleaded for release.

The second he said "please" she lifted her head. Hazel eyes full of mischief, she peeked up at him. "Is it my turn yet?"

Little vixen. Gorgeous tease. She was so going to pay for that.

Baring his teeth, he growled at her. She grinned. Rikar retaliated. Hauling her off her knees, he picked her up and tossed her into the middle of the bed. She bounced once, laughing as she settled on the mattress. Not wasting a second, he leapt after her, surrounding her with his body, pinning her underneath him. Shifting above her, he grabbed her waistband and peeled her out of her pants. She lifted her hips, arching her back to help him, the tips of her breasts rising and falling in wanton display.

"Beautiful fucking female." Feasting on her, Rikar's gaze roamed as he tossed the yoga gear over the side of the bed. Pink nipples. Red curls. Pale, smooth skin. Yum…lucky him. "I'm going to eat you alive."

Her tongue peeked out to lick her bottom lip. "Where you gonna start?"

Holding her gaze, he palmed her knees and pushed them wide. As his hips settled between her thighs, she hummed his name. The needy sound made him greedy, and he dipped his head, flicking her nipple with the tip of his tongue. A soft touch. A little tease. Payback in its purest form.

"Mmm, yeah. More of that," she said, trying to order him around.

He smiled against her skin, then got to work blissing her out. With a breathy moan, she tipped her head back, arched her spine, asking for more. He gave it to her, engulfing her with his mouth, suckling until she became desperate, undulating beneath him. Her hips pressed up. He held her down and moved to her other breast.

As he bathed her in heat, she gasped, "Rikar, come on. I need—"

"And you'll get it, love, but not yet."

Shifting up her body, he kissed her deep, letting her feel his desire. Tongues tangled, he hitched her knee around his hip, then left her mouth, tipping her chin up to expose her throat. Tasting her skin, he felt her energy swirl, reveled in her excitement and the heat of her response.

Man, it wouldn't take long. She was primed, on the verge of orgasm already, and as Rikar stroked over her pulse point, he took a sip, feeding himself, delighting her. She moaned his name. He sucked gently, measuring each beat of her heart as his own pounded.

"After I have my taste, I'll let you come."

Spread beneath him, her breath hitched on a sob. She rolled her hips into his, bathing him in slick heat…tempting him, trying to control the tempo. "No way. I want it now. Give it to me now."

"You gonna beg me?"

She growled at him, impatient and pissed off. "Screw you."

"We'll get there, angel," he said, loving the control and her. "Now spread your legs, love. I need my taste."

With a growl, he slid down her body, laved her belly button, drawing out his pleasure, making her writhe. Pushing her thighs wide, Rikar settled between, holding her still, getting a contact high from her scent. She was beautiful here, too. Pink and slick. Hot and creamy. So aroused she took his breath away. But only for a second. And in the next? He spread her curls, dipped his chin, and without mercy, licked into her folds.

His eyes rolled back in his head. Oh, fuck, she was good: hot, wet, and delicious. A feast for a starving male. Drinking his fill, Rikar worked her. Listened to her keen as he sucked the bud of her sex and slid one finger inside her.

"Oh, God…yes. Like that…" Grabbing fistfuls of his hair, Angela tilted her hips, rolling on a wave of delight. "Just like that…Rikar!"

He sent a second finger deep, stretching her, sucking hard. She arched, twisted beneath him, lips parting on a moan. He nipped her gently. Angela screamed, coming in a pulsing wave around him, blasting him with mind-numbing energy. Pleasure rocked him, then grabbed hold, hurling him sideways into oblivion. Unhinged. Enthralled. Addicted to Angela, needing inside, he surged between the spread of her thighs and thrust deep, burying himself to the hilt.

She convulsed again. Wrapped her legs around his hips and begged him for more.

Surround by her tight heat, his breath hitched as she clung to him, moved with him, using her body to milk his.

Perfect. Powerful. Unprecedented. And for him, right as hell.

No one compared to her. She was the sun and moon. His bright and shining star. And as he invaded her mouth—kissed her deep and felt her throb around him—Rikar lost control, losing all of himself to her as she took him home.

Chapter Twenty-three

Shoving the last bite of pasta primavera into his mouth, Mac umm-yeahed and got busy chewing. Goddamn, that was good. A culinary masterpiece. One that fired up all the right taste buds while simultaneously filling the bottomless pit that had become his stomach. Which…yup, was a total understatement. No matter how much he ate, he couldn't get full. Was always one step away from feeling half-starved.

Normal, he guessed. A side effect of going through the change, one he would suffer for a while. At least that's what his new friends told him. But man, he'd never been this hungry before, and constantly hitting Daimler up in the eats department was getting embarrassing.

Not that the Numbai minded. The guy's eyes lit up every time he saw Mac coming. Could hardly wait to feed him the next meal. Snack. Or shit…snack between snacks.

Mac shook his head. Jesus. He might as well just camp out beside the fridge. Drag his bed right into the kitchen and set up shop. It would make the free-for-all a whole helluva lot more efficient.

With a satisfied sigh, he leaned back on the stool, away from the kitchen island, and put his fork down. Silver clinked against fine china. Mac's mouth curved up at the corners. The highfalutin utensils were a marked difference from what he was used to: a sign his life had changed for the better. Usually, he ate off a paper plate or out of a Chinese takeout container. But not here. Black Diamond wasn't anything like the tight quarters on his boat, and Daimler had never been at his service.

The Numbai said that more than was healthy. *At your service, master. Of course, master. Anything else I can get you, master?* Daimler was a one-man Martha Stewart with elfish pointy ears and built-in bling thanks to his gold front tooth. And as he watched the Nightfuries' resident go-to guy move around the kitchen—stirring the contents of bubbling pots, checking the timer on the stove—Mac thanked his lucky stars.

Black Diamond was his home now. The Nightfury warriors and Daimler, his family. Hallelujah. About fucking time. He'd found the one place he truly belonged.

Nudging his plate away, Mac pushed the stool back and stood. After a full-body stretch, he snagged the long, black case sitting beside his chair off the floor. "Hey, Daimler?"

Planted in front of the six-burner stove, the Numbai glanced over his shoulder. A hopeful glint in his eyes, he asked, "Another serving, master?"

He shook his head.

"A piece of chocolate cake?"

Mac laughed. The guy never said quit. The elf lived to serve, and he could get used to the star treatment. "Not right now. I've gotta get going, but thanks, man."

A wooden spoon poised in midair, Daimler's face fell.

The disappointed look backed Mac up a step. Or five. The last thing he wanted to do was hurt the guy's feelings. "Toss it in the fridge for me, will you? I'll come back for it."

Daimler perked up, happiness lighting him up as he opened a drawer and took out a big serving knife. Mac shook his head, heaved the heavy case, and turned toward the exit while the Numbai went at the cake, whacking an enormous slice from the whole. Mac hummed. No doubt about it. He'd be back for that puppy. And another just like it. Chocolate was his favorite, after all, but…

Later. Right now he had work to do. Rikar had hit him up with mind-speak an hour ago, requesting a special delivery. Thank God.

Two days. Forty-eight frickin' hours of waiting. Of wondering. Of worrying about Angela. And finally his XO was coming up for air.

Not that Mac blamed the male.

Angela was beautiful, smart…sexy as hell. At least every guy Mac knew thought so. And he should know. He'd warned enough of them away from her. Had even beat the snot out of a few when they'd gotten too persistent. Not that Angela knew about it. Which was how he wanted to keep it. Mac grimaced, imagining her reaction. Jesus. You'd think he had a death wish or something, messing with her love life, and if she ever found out, she'd kick his ass from one end of Seattle to the other.

Not advisable. Not much fun, either.

The rifle case bumping against his thigh, Mac walked along the artsy-fartsy gauntlet that doubled as Black Diamond's main corridor. His combat boots brushed over hardwood floors, barely making a sound, while white walls gleamed under halogens, spotlighting paintings with names like Picasso and Jackson Pollock, van Gogh and Renoir scrawled across the bottom corners of the canvases.

Large and small. Colorful. Monochromatic. Etchings or charcoal line drawings.

Hell, the place had it all. Was serious art gallery material—the Louvre on steroids.

Not that Mac knew much about art. But from what he saw in the corridor, a boatload of cash had been dropped to dress up the walls. Not that he cared at the moment. He was too busy counting doors. The ones that marched down the hallway, interrupting the colorful art show with honey-colored wood.

Nine. Ten. Eleven...jackpot. Rikar's bedroom door.

Mac faced off with it for a second. The thing looked innocent enough. Just a collection of antique planks put together to form a barrier between here and there. Well, at least until you considered what had been going on behind the thing for the last two days. Mac clenched his teeth. Frickin' guy. He didn't know what to do first. Congratulate Rikar for keeping Angela in bed for forty-eight hours straight. Or knock the SOB's teeth down his throat for sleeping with his baby sister.

It was a toss-up, really.

He wanted to do both. Play Cupid and the protective big brother all at the same time.

Blowing out a breath, he rolled his shoulders, stretching out tense muscle. He needed to get himself under control before he knocked on the door. Hammering his XO wouldn't win him any brownie points with Angela. She wanted Rikar—might even need the guy for more than just the physical pleasure he gave her.

Exhibit A? No one had forced her into Rikar's bedroom. No one was forcing her to stay there, either. So treading carefully was a good plan. Especially if he wanted to keep his balls where they belonged.

Raising his hand, Mac rapped on the wood with his knuckle. Supersonic dragon hearing up and running, he heard sheets rustle, a sleepy murmur, then quiet footsteps approach the door. Within seconds, the knob turned and the door swung wide. Arctic air blew into his face, the kind that rivaled an Alaskan winter. He blinked, adjusting to the climate change, distracted as hell before—

Jesus fucking Christ.

His grip on the case's handle tightened as his gaze met Rikar's. Mac swallowed a growl. The male looked way too satisfied: pale eyes shimmering, body relaxed, so well fed he oozed nothing but mmm, mmm good. A vibe that bordered on obscene.

Lucky bastard. Freaking jerk.

Mac's free hand curled into a fist. "How is she?"

"Sleeping, but good." Blocking the view into the room with his body, Rikar raised a brow. "You wanna hit me?"

"Fucking right I do."

"I would kick your ass if you didn't," he said, his eyes full of understanding. "I get your need to protect her. I feel it, too, but…she's my mate, Mac. The one I've been waiting for. I need her."

Need wasn't good enough. Not for his baby sister. "Do you love her?"

"Yes."

A quick affirmative. Good for Rikar. Less great for him. Looked like he wouldn't be knocking any of his XO's teeth down his throat. At least not today.

"All right, then," he said, exhaling a pent-up breath. His muscles uncoiled, following the natural flow, and the tension drained, washing down his spine and out through the bottoms of his shitkickers. "But you hurt her…so much as one hair on her head? I'll open up your skull and rip out your brain. We clear?"

"I hear ya." Rikar's lips twitched as he stepped toward him. Slapping his hand to Mac's shoulder, the male squeezed, then nodded at the rifle case he carried. "Is that it?"

"Yeah."

Rikar frowned. "You sure about this?"

"She's a better shot than I am." Which was saying something. Mac was an excellent marksman, his reputation in the SEAL teams garnering him some serious high-five action back in the day. But Angela's skill with a long-range rifle outdid even him. She could hit a target—just KO the frickin' thing—from nine hundred yards out. Incredible by any standards, but in sniper circles and among Seattle SWAT, she was revered for her steady hand and lethal accuracy. "Set her up a thousand yards out, and she'll shred the target every time."

"What about a moving one?"

"How much time we got to practice?"

"A week or so."

Translation? The energy-regression was still on-the-go. Sloan had explained the process—the how and why a male altered a female's energy beacon, keeping her safe from other Dragonkind. Pretty cool stuff, and man, Mac hoped it worked. No way he wanted to get out in the field and discover that Lothair could still track his partner. Having her there would be bad enough. No one needed the op to go south right out of the gate. Just the thought made his blood pressure rise, launching him into no-fucking-way territory.

"I'll get her up to speed on the shooting range," Mac said, eyeing his new buddy. "You gotta do something for me, though."

"What's that?"

"Let her out of frickin' bed."

Rikar raised a brow. "You think it's my fault we're still here?"

"Motherfuck," Mac muttered, shaking his head, trying not to laugh. The guy was begging for an ass kicking… Angela style. "I'm telling her you said that."

"Better not." Rikar reached for the gun case. As Mac relinquished the load, he murmured, "Unless, of course, you want your balls handed to you on the end of a blade."

"Jesus." Wincing, Mac cupped his package with both hands. "Bad visual."

"Even worse outcome," Rikar said, grinning.

Heaving the case, he turned into the room, and Mac got his first sneak peek. Laid out belly down—covers up around her shoulders, head half-buried under a pillow in the center of the king-size bed—Angela was fast asleep but 100 percent okay.

Relief hit Mac chest-level, making his throat go tight.

Good for her. She'd followed through on her promise. Hadn't copped out or run away even though she'd been afraid to let Rikar make love to her, giving her relief from the pain. Mac swallowed. He was so proud of her. And so thankful he didn't know what to do.

Rikar distracted him—thank fuck—flipping the case up and setting the kit on the mattress beside her. The handle rapped against hard plastic, echoing in the quiet as his XO glanced at Angela. After a second, Rikar leaned in, planted his hands on either side of her, and pressed a kiss to her temple. She murmured in her sleep, more sigh than hum as her mate lingered, resting his cheek against her hair as though he couldn't get enough. Or be that close to her without touching her one more time.

Mac's heart throbbed a crazy beat as he watched the pair, wondering what the hell he was doing. He shouldn't be in the room. Shouldn't be witnessing a precious moment between mates. Should have the decency to back up, but his feet were nailed to the floor. He couldn't look away. Was forced to play the voyeur while Rikar stroked his hand along his partner's back. To witness another tender kiss. To hear the soft murmur and see his XO's expression.

Awe. Gratitude. Devotion. All took a turn on the male's face.

The entire situation suited Mac just fine. Case closed. Slap a sticker on that bad boy and bury the file six feet under. Fait accompli. No way would Rikar ever let Angela go. Not now. So, ycah. His little sister was at Black Diamond to stay.

Turning away from her, Rikar conjured a length of ribbon. Slippery satin sliding in his hand, he tied it around one end of the narrow case, finishing it off with double loops. Ah, how cute. A present complete with a shiny red bow.

Mac bit down on a grin. What a total pansy-ass thing to do. One Angela would no doubt appreciate when she woke up. Most women wanted jewelry—something expensive and pretty—from their men. But not Angela. Rikar had it right. His partner liked weapons. Which made the M25 sniper rifle the perfect gift.

After scribbling a note, the besotted SOB left it next to the bow, then slid the bedside table drawer open. Metal rattled against cardboard as Rikar set a box of 9 mm ammo for her Glock next to the slip of paper. His eyes on her face, he paused, stood poised above her for a heartbeat, then kissed her one last time and turned toward the door.

Mac raised a brow, letting his XO see his amusement.

"Go to hell," he growled, coming at him like a human steamroller. Unwilling to get flattened, Mac backpedaled into the corridor. Pale eyes narrowed on him, Rikar crossed the threshold. As the door clicked closed behind him, he turned right down the hallway. "Let's go, water rat. The others are waiting."

"We headed to the cellblock?"

"Collision inevitable."

"About time." And it was. He'd been waiting for days to meet Forge. "What's the play?"

"Bastian and I will handle it," Rikar said, heading for the elevators. "You and the boys are on standby…there for support."

In other words? Be seen, not heard. "Why do I suddenly feel like a three-year-old?"

"Eyes and ears open, all right?" An intense expression on his face, Rikar glanced over his shoulder at him. "Put all of the cop shit to good use. Feed me cues…body language, expression, anything else you notice. If you see something that'll help crack him, connect through mind-speak and give me a heads-up. Got it?"

Mac nodded. Good plan. One he and Angela had often employed. One interrogated. The other listened, concentrating on speech pattern, body language, and emotional cues. No matter how small, a suspect always gave something vital away. Information that sometimes helped break a case wide open. The fact the Nightfuries were about to deal with

Forge the same way—and wanted his help—jazzed him. It made him feel included, like a valued member of the pack.

"Hey, Rikar?" Mac stopped as the corridor dead-ended at the elevators. Reaching out, he hit the down button with the side of his fist, then stepped back to stand shoulder-to-shoulder with his XO. "Got a question for you."

"Shoot."

"The whole energy-regression thing?"

"What about it?"

"Once Ange's energy signal is altered and Lothair can't track her anymore…" Mac trailed off, struggling to tie all the threads together: the how, what, and whys of Dragonkind. "How the hell are we gonna set the ambush?"

"Easy."

The elevator pinged as the doors slid open.

Rikar glanced at him before stepping inside. "I'm tapped into her life force now. That connection gives me access…the ability to manipulate her unique energy frequency and mimic it. Old. New. Doesn't matter. Once we're set…when Angela's in place and ready to go…I'll send out her original beacon. Lothair will pick up on the signal, think it's her and—"

"The fucker'll come running." Setting up shop at the back of the Otis, Mac planted his shoulder blades against the stainless-steel wall and crossed his arms over his chest. "Go after her and get us instead."

"Bingo."

The perfect plan. Except for one thing. "I don't want her anywhere near the front line."

"She won't be," Rikar said, icy gaze glittering. "An M-twenty-five rifle and a thousand yards out with you watching her six, remember?"

As if he could forget. He'd gone over the plan again and again, running every scenario, looking for holes, weaknesses…a better fucking strategy. Any reason at all that would keep Angela at home instead of putting her in the middle of the firefight.

But that wouldn't happen.

The second he and Rikar tried to sideline her, she'd go it alone and end up hurt. So it didn't matter that the odds made him jumpy. The situation wasn't SOP (standard operating procedure). Was opposite of normal with a pack of freaking dragons in the mix. Anything could go wrong and—if things went true to form—usually did. Which scared the hell out of him. He would never forgive himself if Angela got caught in the crossfire.

Or worse. Ended up recaptured by the sadistic SOB who'd hurt her.

Rolling his shoulders, Forge craned his neck to one side. The collar dug in, scraping the underside of his jaw. Shite, the thing was driving him around-the-bend crazy. Chafing his skin. Tightening around his throat with each movement, cranking his internal pressure cooker into KABOOM territory.

Volcanic. Nuclear. Whatever.

The description didn't matter. And Forge didn't care. He wanted the collar off. Zip, bang, gone…nothing but history. Not that it would happen any time soon. Bastian had made that abundantly clear.

Cranking his fist tight, Forge paced the perimeter of his cell, feeling like a caged lion. Back and forth. Around and around. The cycle was nonstop. Bare feet silent on the concrete, the noise inside his head catastrophic, he tried to come up with an action plan. A strategy to use the next time Bastian visited.

Bloody hell. Two days of blah, blah, blahing. Of doing the verbal dance with the Nightfury commander, and still, Forge didn't have a clue what the male wanted. All the yakkety-yak-yak made him nervous.

Which, come to think of it, was a good thing.

Despite the lockdown, his reaction told him his instincts were still bang-on accurate. Bastian didn't do random. He visited for a reason. Was the male setting him up for something? Testing the waters?

Forge shook his head. He didn't know. A huge problem, if there ever was one.

Usually, his skill at picking up another's intention was rock solid. But the Nightfury commander was powerful. He gave nothing away. No matter how many times Forge tried, he couldn't penetrate the bastard's thick skull and eavesdrop on his thoughts.

A pity to be sure, but if he had to guess, he'd bet on Myst. The violet-eyed beauty was job one for Bastian.

So, aye. It made sense that the male would butter him up to get the information he needed to keep his mate safe. By establishing trust, Bastian no doubt hoped he would relent and share his knowledge of the ancient ceremony. The one that would complete the energy-fuse and protect his female. It was a good plan. One that—despite everything—was starting to work. Stupid as it seemed, he liked the male. Respected the hell out of him. The Nightfury was a strong leader, a fair one, something Forge hadn't encountered in a while and—

Bloody hell. He was losing it, unraveling at the speed of light. No way should he be thinking about coughing up the info. Not with stakes this high, but Forge couldn't deny he toyed with the idea. Playing fast and loose with his son's life, not to mention his own. But maybe showing some good will—walking Bastian through the ceremony, telling him all he knew—would get him farther, faster. Maybe if he gave a little, he'd get a lot in return.

Maybe. Maybe. Maybe.

It was one helluva word.

"Shite," he muttered, his voice sounding loud in the silence.

Forge stopped in front of his cot. Grabbing fistfuls of his hair, he stared unseeing at the thin mattress, trying to decide. What was the best course of action? Give the Nightfury what he needed to keep Myst safe. Or hold out and hoped she persuaded her mate to hand over his son and let him go.

Uncurling his hands, he laced his fingers across the back of his neck and pressed down. Muscles stretched, and pain screamed down his spine. But it wasn't enough. He needed a distraction. Something to release the pressure building inside his head and bring him some small measure of peace.

Food would've done it, but Daimler hadn't visited in a while. Well, all right. That was an exaggeration. The Numbai had brought a plate of pasta an hour ago, but he was still hungry. And with all the shortbread cookies gone, he had nothing to munch on. No distraction at all.

With a growl, Forge dropped to the concrete floor. His hands planted shoulder-width apart, legs straight out behind him, he launched into a brutal set of push-ups. No sense mourning what wasn't coming. The hunger was just a symptom of a larger problem.

He needed a female.

Not for sex. Caroline's death had pretty much KO'd that need. He couldn't even imagine making love to another female right now. So, aye. The nameless, faceless fuck in a dark corner of some club with a stranger would have to wait for a while. That didn't, however, change the facts. He was a Dragonkind male. He must feed from time to time. Take his fill of female energy or die.

And right now, he was headed down a slippery slope. One that pushed him closer to energy-greed—a condition all males feared—and into mindless need with each passing hour.

Thrusting his arms, Forge popped to his feet. Sweat rolled down his spine as he landed, splattering the floor. He launched into a series of boxing exercises. His fists flew, striking thin air as he pivoted on the balls of his feet, picturing an imaginary opponent.

He snorted. Right. *Imaginary*, his foot. The face belonged to a Nightfury warrior. The one with glacial eyes and a frosty outlook.

His muscles screamed as he worked out. Quick jab. Left cross. Duck, bob, weave. Right hook into an ascending uppercut. Rage built with each punch, narrowing his focus to...just...one...thing.

Freedom. He needed to get the hell out of his cage.

Spinning right, he brought his feet into the fight, balancing on one leg to kick high. At head level. Right where Rikar's face would've—

"Nice form."

Forge stilled, held his leg at the height of the kick. Well, fuck him. The crafty SOB had snuck up on him. Huge surprise there. Especially since it had never happened before.

"Frosty," he said, reversing course without looking at the male. Keeping each movement controlled, he set his foot back on the floor, lowered his fists, and pivoted toward the front of his cell. "What a lovely surprise and…oh goody, you brought company. How nice for me."

Or not. Shite, he was in trouble. The whole fucking pack had come to play.

"Stow the bullshit, Forge." Pinning him with a glare, Bastian broke from the pack. As he strode through the energy field guarding his prison, the barrier snapped, and the Nightfury commander cursed. Rolling his shoulders, the male shrugged off the electrical zap and entered his cell. "We didn't come to fight."

"Speak for yourself." Red eyes glowing, Venom set up shop against the back wall of the corridor and cracked his knuckles. "I could use the exercise."

A dark-haired male thumped Venom on the chest, then pivoted and ass-planted himself beside his buddy. "Zip it, Ven."

Three syllables loaded with lethal. Forge's lips twitched. He might not know the golden-eyed male, but he liked the Nightfury's style already. Especially if he could keep Venom in line.

Rikar came through the force field, cursing, muscles twitching as he left the other Nightfury warriors to join his commander inside his cell. Forge scanned the faces of the four standing in the corridor. Venom and Sloan he'd seen before. The other two he didn't recognize but knew just by looking both were fighters. Although Venom's buddy was seasoned, the other male was not. A fledgling maybe. Powerful, but as of yet unaccustomed to his new body and the magic he could wield.

"I hate that fucking thing," Rikar said, shaking off the aftereffects of the force field.

Forge tugged on the collar. "You should try it from my end."

"I'll pass."

"Figures." Sweat rolled over one of his eyebrows. Forge swiped at it, wiping the droplet away before it dripped into his eye. "Fucking pussy."

Rikar laughed, throwing off the insult like air. Which was beyond strange. And a wee bit alarming. So much for getting a rise out of the male. "What's up, lads? We in for a communal beatdown?"

"Nah," Bastian said. "Just a chat."

Forge's eyes narrowed on the Nightfury commander. He watched Bastian lean, back flat, against the far wall, one ankle crossed over the other. The position said relaxed. The body language screamed alert.

Forge frowned. "You gonnae clue me in, then?"

"Sure," Rikar said, stopping a few feet away. Close enough to provoke. Far enough away to avoid getting coldcocked. A distinct possibility, considering Forge was surrounded on all sides. "Something you should know first, though."

"What's that?"

"This place?" Pale eyes riveted on him, Rikar twirled his finger in the air. "Wired for sound, my man."

"Bloody hell." Forge sighed, the exhale all about exhaustion. He glanced up at the ceiling, looking for hidden microphones while remembering what he'd said to the females. "You heard."

"Everything," Rikar said. "Watched it, too."

"Video?"

Frosty nodded.

"I should've guessed."

But he hadn't. Which embarrassed the hell out of him.

Curling his hands into fists, Forge shook his head. Jesus. He was slipping in a major way, letting imprisonment, all the smoke and mirrors, get to him. The Nightfuries were clever. Beyond smart. Hooked into the human world, and that meant they were masters of modern technology, using it to manipulate and monitor channels, picking up all kinds of useful intel. All of which he would've picked up…had he done his flippin' job and paid attention.

"Look, Forge. You don't trust me, I get that, but…" Rikar cleared his throat, looking uncomfortable in his own skin. "My female needed to hear what you said. You helped her. Made her trust instead of fear me. I owe you for that."

"The fuck you do," Forge said through clenched teeth. The Nightfury XO could go fry himself. No way would he accept the gratitude. "I did it for her, asshole, not you."

"I know. Still…"

"Christ, Frosty. Whatcha want from me? A love-in or some shite?" Forge growled, heart aching for the proud SOB who was thanking him. For the male whose female had been brutalized by the Razorbacks. Had Caroline been hurt like that he would've—

Fuck. Torn the city apart to find the sadistic bastard. Ripped the rogue's spinal cord out with one vicious yank.

He glared at Rikar, wanting to hit the male for making him sympathize. For making him feel anything at all. "Wannae give me a hug and call it even?"

Venom snorted, the amused sound carrying through the barrier.

Bastian's mouth curved. "Hugging isn't really Rikar's MO."

"Mine, either."

"Good to know," Rikar said, his eyes glinting with humor. "I got something that is, though. Wanna hear it?"

"Depends."

"On what?"

Forge cracked his knuckles. "Whether or not it involves me beating the shite out of you."

Rikar grinned. "I'll give you a shot…after you agree."

He raised a brow, asking without words.

"To become part of our pack," Bastian said, his tone casual, the words heavy-duty.

The offer hit Forge like a body shot, knocking the wind out of him. He blinked, trying to breathe. It was a no-go. His lungs were on lockdown. His brain? The thing was in WTF mode, sending his body the wrong signals, and as his hands started to shake, Forge knew he'd misheard. No way the Nightfuries wanted him as one of their own.

"You're shitting me," he rasped, sounding like an idiot. But it was the best he could do under the circumstances. Just the thought…of…of…Jesus save him from assholes. If the males aimed to hurt him, they'd hit the bull's-eye dead center. He yearned for a home. A place to belong again. A chance to raise his son, make a difference, and kill some rogues while he put a dent in Ivar's operation and avenged Caroline. "What kind of game are you playing, Nightfury?"

"No games," Bastian said. "Just straight-up logic."

Forge frowned so hard the space between his brows stung. His gaze ping-ponged, moving from Rikar to Bastian, then back again. Holy shite. They were serious. No kidding. No pulling any punches. Just hardcore, all-in commitment.

He shook his head, viselike pressure snaking around his chest. He glanced at the other Nightfuries, meeting each of their gazes through the invisible force field. No one laughed. No one shouted, *Surprise, asshole…you've been punked!* The entire pack was tight, down with the idea of him staying at Black Diamond.

His eyes started to water. Tears? The fuck-you of surprise? He didn't know. Didn't care much either as he asked Bastian, "Your idea?"

"Mine, actually," Rikar said, surprising him. Of all the males to push for his induction into the pack, he never would've picked Frosty. "You need a home. We need another warrior. It's a win-win, my man."

"Decision time, Forge." Bastian pushed away against the wall. "Yes or no?"

Forge opened his mouth. Nothing came out. He closed it again. Fuck him, he needed to get a grip, but surprise had him by the balls, stealing his voice, pushing mental acuity into a holding pattern. Only one thought resonated. Acceptance. A real, honest-to-God pack to call his own. He scrubbed his hand over the back of his head. It was a no-brainer. Better than he'd expected. More than he deserved.

Swallowing the burn of unshed tears, he murmured, "Aye."

Rikar's mouth curved. "Good. I'd rather have you for my brother then KO your ass."

"You tried that once already, remember? Didnae go well for you," Forge said, getting his brainpower back, enjoying Rikar's snort of amusement as he held his soon-to-be commander's gaze. "There's a ceremony, one that will complete the energy-fuse with Myst…tae join your life force with hers. It must be performed before the birth tae keep her safe."

"*Mervaiz, zi kamir,*" Bastian said, speaking to him in Dragonese. *Many thanks, my brother.* "And we'll get to that, but first, I want your blood oath."

To be expected.

The ritual was a time-honored tradition among warriors. As a male being offered membership into a new pack, blood must be spilled to honor the bond and cement his status. Still, as Forge lowered himself to one knee and bowed his head, a pang of uncertainty hit him.

What if the Nightfury didn't mean it? What if it was all a nasty joke? One designed to lower his defenses so Rikar could deliver the death blow?

Acceptance in one hand, death in the other. It was a helluva gamble.

Forge released a long, slow breath, trying to stay calm as Bastian approached from across the cell. All of his senses amplified, firing up instinct and the need to protect himself. He stayed the course, remained unmoving, picking up trace like a garbage man picked up litter.

Shifting through sounds and scent, he heard the soft scrape of Bastian's footfalls on the floor and the creak of leather. Scented the male along with a hint of Myst's fragrance still on his skin. Listened as the other males murmured in the quiet. But mostly, he heard his own heartbeat, the rush of blood in his ears along with the thump-thump-thump. And as the Nightfury commander came within striking distance, Forge murmured a silent prayer, banking on acceptance instead of trickery.

He yearned to hold his son. Wanted a new life. Needed a second chance.

But if he was wrong, and the male struck, death, at least, would come quickly.

Chapter Twenty-four

Backing Bastian's play, Rikar crossed the prison cell. As the soles of his shitkickers rasped against concrete, he heard the other Nightfury males shift behind him. Uh-oh. Not a good idea. No way he wanted them anywhere near Forge. Not right now. The male's dial was already cranked to nuclear. Add any more muscle to the inside of the cell, and things would go from manageable to messy in a heartbeat.

Slowing his pace, Rikar glanced over his shoulder. He met Venom's gaze and shook his head. His warrior nodded, receiving the message loud and clear, and took a step back, resuming his previous position—shoulder blades flat against the back wall, arms folded over his chest, one boot planted on the floor, the other against the wall. With a quiet shuffle, the other Nightfuries followed the big male's lead, staying on the other side of the invisible barrier, settling in for the show.

Rikar swallowed a snort. *Show.* Right. Like he needed any more freaking entertainment this week? With Mac's transition, Angela's rescue, and all the energy-fuse hoopla, he'd met his quota three days ago.

Rolling his shoulders to work out the tension, he glanced at Bastian. His commander tipped his chin. Rikar nodded in return and moved forward, closing in from one side while B came at Forge from the other. His gaze locked on the male, Rikar kept his approach slow and even, giving Forge time to adjust, accept…trust. But man, the closer he got, the more tense Forge became, his unease rising like smoke curls, perfuming the air around him.

Rikar's throat went tight. Unbelievable. The male was straight-up courageous. And as he watched the male bow his head and wait for Bastian to reach him, Rikar's heart went AWOL, cramping inside his chest, messing with his head, firing up his *thank you, God* reaction.

He really hadn't wanted to KO the trash-talking idiot.

Which was a big surprise. Not to mention a dumb-ass reaction. Especially since he'd never been averse to killing anything, no matter the circumstances. But with Forge, he'd been dreading the endgame. Hadn't wanted to repay the male's kindness to his female with brutality or face Angela with Forge's blood on his hands. On the way down to the cellblock, he'd dared hope for something more, a meeting of the minds, so to speak. And now that he had it, relief grabbed him by the balls.

Forge would soon become one of them, a Nightfury bound by duty, honor, and purpose. Another strong addition to their pack. Good for him. Better for them. So, yeah. No time like the present.

Rikar wanted the induction ceremony underway and the blood oath done sooner rather than later. Angela would wake up soon. He needed to be there to see her reaction to his gifts. Wanted to see her eyes light up, her smile of pleasure, and to benefit from her gratitude.

Self-serving of him? No doubt, but he couldn't wait to touch her again. To feel her soft skin against his and have her taste on his tongue. Just the thought—the bold, beautiful promise of her—did unspeakable things to him. Two days with her hadn't been enough. Hell, he'd never get enough, and if that made him a full-fledged sap, he'd wear the title with pride. He'd claimed his female. She accepted him wholeheartedly. All was right in his world.

He stopped next to Forge, taking up space at the male's shoulder. The warrior tensed, the taut flex of muscle rolling beneath his T-shirt. Which told Rikar all he needed to know. The male was packing some serious edge. Yeah, he might be on bended knee, but he wasn't certain about it. He was on lockdown, waiting for the situation to go sideways. Maybe even for death to come.

Rikar didn't blame him.

What they asked of him wasn't fair. Total trust without proof. Complete submission without substance. Soul-baring vulnerability without the chance of self-protection. Mindfuck material. The fact Forge stayed the course—possessed the strength to endure—pushed Rikar past respect right into pride. He shook his head, calling himself fifty different kinds of crazy. Being proud of a warrior he barely knew, one as powerful as Forge, was a touch north of normal.

Not that it mattered. It was what it *was*. No sense arguing with it.

Wanting to reassure him, Rikar laid his hand on their new boy's shoulder. Forge flinched. He gave him a squeeze. "Easy. It's all good. Keep it tight."

Forge nodded but adhered to tradition—respected the ritual—and kept his head down.

B stopped opposite him, flanking Forge's other shoulder. His movements slow, his best friend reached out and laid his hand on the back of the warrior's head, just above the collar. Time stilled and silence reigned, throbbing through the cellblock as he and B stood over Forge, their message clear. *Trust us. You're safe with us. We've got your back.*

Seconds ticked past, falling into more. Forge trembled as he uncurled his fists. As his tension drained, his body unwound thread by taut thread and muscle uncoiled, relaxing beneath their hands.

"All right, then," B murmured, acknowledging the trust, praising the effort.

Rikar tipped his chin in B's direction. "The collar?"

"Yeah." Shifting behind the big male, Bastian planted his feet on either side of Forge and grasped the collar with both hands. The pads of his thumbs pressed against the locking mechanism just below the base of Forge's skull as his fingers spanned the steel, wrapping around his throat from behind. "Hold still while I get this fucker off, okay?"

"Off would be good." His chin pressed to his chest, Forge quivered, a body twitch full of impatience.

No kidding. Rikar was twitchy just looking at the thing, and had the steel band been clamped around his throat, he would have lost it by now.

Inhaling smooth and deep, Bastian closed his eyes. Rikar kept a steadying hand on the male's shoulder. He didn't want Forge to move at the wrong time. Packed with C4, loaded with magic, the collar was volatile, a bomb just waiting to go off. The band took a shitload of concentration to put on, but even more to take off. B needed the time and space to unlock, shift, and toss the thing into the magical landscape inside his mind. A place he could implode steel and explosive, keeping them all safe. Intact. Unvaporized, so to speak.

One Mississippi. Two Mississippi. Three Mississippi... four. Chickety-chick-click. The lock snicked open, and steel rattled, sliding from around Forge's throat.

Forge shuddered, instinct urging him to move.

A death grip on the male, Rikar said, "Not yet."

As the warrior listened and settled, Bastian bared his teeth on a growl. His best friend's grip tightened on Forge as he bore down, using the male to lean on. An instant later the collar disappeared. B threw it into his mental junk drawer and—

Pop. Pop. BOOM!

Bastian flinched. The explosion rippled, the sound faint, barely audible at all. A blast of air gusted through the cellblock, clawing at Rikar's clothes, blowing Forge's longer hair back. The energy field snapped, powerful bands flickering, fading little by little before vanishing completely, leaving the mouth of the prison cell unguarded.

Breathing hard, Bastian opened his eyes. "Good to go."

Conjuring the ceremonial dagger, Rikar handed it hilt first to his best friend. B palmed the blade and stepped around to face Forge. As was custom, his commander knelt, hitting one knee in front of the male. His boot even with the instep of Forge's bare foot, he settled in place, aligning their legs, inside knee to inside knee.

The blade in one hand, B raised his other. "Give me your right hand."

His head still bowed, Forge raised his arm. Muscles flexed in his forearm as Bastian cupped the back of the male's hand. The knife came up, steel flashing in the low light as B drew the razor-sharp blade across Forge's palm.

Blood welled, flowing unchecked toward his elbow. Not wasting a second, Bastian turned the dagger on himself, slicing an identical cut on his own hand. As Rikar took the weapon, his commander locked palms with Forge, pressing the wounds together.

As their blood mixed, red droplets fell, splattering the floor between them. With a howl, magic rose, twisting into a funnel cloud around them. Invisible yet majestic to behold, powerful and potent, the Meridian surged. The energy grabbed hold, linking the two males locked knee to knee, palm to palm, and now…heart to heart.

"Blood of my blood," Bastian murmured, reciting the ancient words of the blood oath. "Of one mind. Brothers in battle and for all time."

Lifting his chin, Forge repeated the incantation. As his gaze met B's, the connection flared, snapping into place, binding them together in the way of their kind…the time-honored tradition of the warrior. Bastian nodded once, then released his grip on Forge to step aside. Rikar sliced his own hand and took his commander's place. Locked together by touch and magic, he completed the ritual, recited the words, heart hammering as he tied himself to Forge. The blood bond rippled between them as he accepted the male and was accepted in return.

The other Nightfuries crossed the threshold into the cell. Each male took his turn kneeling with Forge. First Venom and then Wick. Sloan. And finally Mac.

When the last word had been spoken and the last blood droplet spilled, Bastian stepped forward. Standing in front of a still-kneeling Forge, he held out his hand. The warrior took the offering, allowing B to pull him to his feet.

"Welcome, my brother," Bastian murmured.

Forge blinked, combating the sheen of moisture in his eyes. "*Mervaiz*, commander."

"Well done, *zi kamir*." Fiercely proud of the male, Rikar palmed the side of Forge's neck. The newest member of the Nightfury pack met his gaze and nodded, thanking him without words. Rikar jostled him in answer, then let go, stepped back, and tipped his head toward the corridor. "Now go…meet your son."

Forge's focus snapped toward the front of the cell. Rikar's mouth curved. Thank fuck for Daimler. Per usual, the male was right on time, standing just outside the cell beside a mound of floor cushions. A wide smile on his elfin face, a precious bundle in his arms, the Numbai murmured a greeting, then offered Gregor-Mayhem to his sire.

Tears pooled in Forge's eyes. Rikar looked away, his own eyes burning, his chest gone tight as the newest member of the Nightfury pack walked toward Daimler to hold his son for the first time.

Messy piles of papers spread out on the kitchen table. Lothair tapped the tip of his pen against the bottom of his new list. The latest one. Number one hundred and forty-fucking-whatever.

With a sigh, Lothair tossed the BIC on the table and leaned back in his chair. Seemed about right, and he was starting to hate lists. And family trees, but…derr`mo. He couldn't argue with results. Or that three days spent compiling—checking and rechecking—had finally paid off. He'd hit the jackpot last night.

Twins. Friends of the two females already locked in cellblock A. Blonde. Beautiful. High-energy. The pair were Ivar's favorite kind of female. Needless to say he'd made the boss very, *very* happy last night.

Himself, too.

The pleasure of securing the pair in cellblock A, however, took a backseat at the moment. With the afternoon light waning, he needed a new target. Several new ones. He was still three females short of the seven Ivar needed to round out the breeding program. Which meant he didn't have time to waste, never mind celebrate the fact he'd proven his theory.

There remained little doubt. High-energy females were drawn to each other. Were either born into the same family or became the best of friends. They lived together. Worked together. Hung out together. Recognized something in each other. A likeness, maybe. A shared energy vibe as the Meridian reached out, touched, and connected them.

His eyes narrowed on the list of potential candidates, Lothair shrugged. Whatever. He didn't give a shit about the whys and wherefores. All he cared about was pinpointing another female to go after when night fell.

Find one…find more. That was his stupid motto now, and would be for the foreseeable future. Until he had all seven in the kitty for Ivar to play with.

Four down. Three to go. A small victory, but a hollow one.

The she-cop was still on the loose.

Growling low in his throat, Lothair flipped his laptop open. As the MacBook fired up, he slid a sheet of paper from beneath a messy stack. He couldn't stand it. The fact Angela Keen was still out there drove him insane. He couldn't sleep during the day. Kept dreaming of her…of what he would do when he finally got his hands on her. He needed to hurt her. Shame her. Wrap his fingers around her neck and squeeze the life out of her.

"Hey, Lothair."

Unclenching his teeth, Lothair glanced toward the door. He tipped his chin, greeting Ivar as the male strode into the kitchen. "Fun afternoon?"

Well fed, his friend's eyes glimmered behind his wraparounds. Skirting a row of cabinetry, Ivar strode behind the huge island on his way to the fridge. His mouth curved, he tossed Lothair an appreciative glance. "Jesus, man…love the twins."

"They're prime."

"Got any more surprises for me?"

Lothair planted his forearms on the table and looked at his paper trail. "I'm working on it."

"Any word on Myst Munroe?" Ivar asked, cracking the fridge door, tone casual.

But Lothair knew better. There was nothing *casual* about Ivar's interest in Bastian's female. The boss man wanted her. Had from the moment he'd seen her picture. The fact she belonged to his enemy just deepened the obsession. Imagine, stealing a female your rival loved…craved, needed to survive? The ultimate conquest, and a victory that proved one male's supremacy over another.

"Nothing yet. Bastian's keeping her locked up tight," he said. "How's project superbug? Any progress?"

"Fuck, no. I've KO'd the first batch. I'll lock down the other humans and fire up the second viral load tonight." With a silent curse, Ivar pulled the milk out of the fridge. Popping the top, he drank right out of the carton, then plunked the container down on the granite countertop. "You hungry?"

"I could eat."

"Roast beef sandwich?" Ivar tossed a loaf of bread onto the kitchen island.

Plastic crinkled as the Wonder Bread slid across the flecked surface. Lothair nodded, watching his friend closely, an idea sparking. Ivar wanted the Nightfury's female, and Lothair hadn't checked in a while. He'd check her phone records again. Who knew? Maybe she'd been out sometime in the last few days. Maybe she'd used her cell phone. Maybe he could get his commander what he needed with a couple clicks of a mouse.

Turning the laptop toward him, he tapped in his password. Denzeil's program came up on screen. Inputting the female's number, he scrolled through phone records and…

Derr'mo. How the hell had he missed *that*?

Bastian's female had called one number more than any of the others. Lothair's heart started to pound as he brought up a fresh screen and typed in the number. The computer hummed, the whirl of the fan loud in the silence as it searched the new set of parameters. A second or two passed before a home phone, address, and name complete with picture popped onto the screen.

Lothair's mouth curved. "Hello, Tania."

Hmm, she was a beauty. Dark hair. Brown eyes. A mouth made for sucking.

A couple of key clicks opened a new browser window. His eyes narrowed on the screen, Lothair sifted through the World Wide Web, picking up more intel on the female, searching for the best way to nail her down. In less than ten minutes, he had his in…and her superintendent's name.

With a satisfied hum, he reached across a stack of paperwork and grabbed his new cell phone—the one he'd bought for just such a purpose three days ago. As his hand closed around the BlackBerry, he shuddered. He hated the thing... and the inferior race who'd invented it. He much preferred mind-speak with his fellow warriors to the humankind's preferred mode of communication. But necessary was just that...*necessary*.

Flying all over Seattle in search of a female wasn't a timesaver. So he always called ahead. Made sure she was home. And if she wasn't—he fired up his MacBook and the special program Denzeil had designed. Got her real-time location via the GPS chip in her cell phone. He didn't, after all, have time to fuck around.

Pressing on the black button, Lothair waited for the cell phone's dark screen to go blue, and then he dialed the number.

Time to see if Ms. Solares was home.

Standing on the threshold of her walk-in closet, Tania grimaced. Ugh. What a catastrophe. A den of iniquity full of pirates would've been easier to navigate than the travesty that had become her wardrobe. Stuffed to the ceiling, her clothes overflowed the large rectangular room. Dresses. Jeans. Skirts. Tops. Oh, and she didn't even want to think about the number of shoes and boots hiding in dark corners. Or underneath the pile of handbags that had grown monstrously large over the past year.

She chewed on her bottom lip. The abundance was kind of embarrassing, actually.

Stepping inside the war zone, she grabbed a wooden hanger and, wrestling with over-crowding, pushed her leather jacket aside. God. She really needed to jump on the Salvation Army's bandwagon and do some serious giving.

Well, either that, or stop shopping. An impossible endeavor if there ever was one. At least for her. Retail therapy was her specialty. Her drug of choice. While some people were heroin addicts, she was hopelessly in love with her American Express card and all the goodies it could buy.

A failing? No doubt. But nothing made her feel better than a pair of new shoes. A gorgeous handbag. Or hmm, boy, take her away…a beautiful piece of jewelry. And oh, how the list went on. Call her crazy.

Myst did. With unerring frequency.

Her throat went tight. Tania bowed her head, ignoring the organized chaos around her, and rubbed the bridge of her nose. She was so tired of crying, but God, she missed her best friend. Was so worried she didn't know what to do. The cops still hadn't gotten back to her. Three days and nada. Not one call. Nary a single text or e-mail. Something was really wrong. Tania huffed. Duh. What was her first clue? A very dead Caroline Van Owen. A missing baby. A still alive, but hiding, Myst. And two homicide detectives gone underground.

With a sigh, Tania tucked back into her closet, pushing more hanging clothes aside. She needed to find her—

"Ah, there you are," she said, spotting her travel bag on the floor near the back in the black hole where handbags went to die. Though what her favorite duffle was doing way back there, she didn't know. "Come to Mama, gorgeous."

Grabbing the leather straps, she hauled the Louis Vuitton out, then headed to the bedroom. A quick toss and it landed on the bed's silk duvet beside her neatly folded clothes. A weekend excursion was in order. Actually, it was a bimonthly event, one in which Tania visited her sister. At the Washington State Correctional Institution for Women.

Another failure. She'd missed all the signs. Had been so worried about putting food in their mouths—and decent shoes on J.J.'s feet—she'd failed to realize her sister had fallen in with the wrong crowd until it was too late. Now she made the drive every second week, bribing the guards with cookies to get a few extra minutes with her sibling.

This week it was chocolate chip.

Her heart aching, she made quick work of packing, laying two days' worth of comfy clothes in the bottom of her bag. Ballet flats went in next. She didn't plan on coming home tonight. Was in for a little more retail therapy after she got kicked out of the prison and left J.J. locked up behind bars.

"Buck up, Solares." She wiped beneath both of her eyes. Damn it all. Not again. "No one likes a crybaby."

With a quick zip, she closed the bag, then rounded the end of the bed and checked the answering machine on her night table. Nothing. No messages. None from Detectives MacCord or Keen. Zero info from the stupid reporter.

Crap on a crumpet.

She should never have talked to Clarissa Newton. But she'd been so flipping angry, and tweaking the police's noses had seemed like a good idea yesterday. Now she regretted sitting down with the reporter. Too bad the interview was already in the can. They'd done it *60 Minutes*–style, sitting at the back of a café in a couple of armchairs while the camera rolled tape. The station had agreed to run her interview as part of an exposé on police corruption in Seattle.

Tania stared at the buttons on the phone and shook her head. Part of her hoped MacCord would have a cow when he saw the interview. Come banging on her door, demanding to know what the hell she thought she was doing. At which point she'd have to admit she didn't have a flipping clue and kiss the heck out of him. For payback. And maybe just the tiniest bit of pleasure.

He deserved the tease. And let's face it, she needed the delight. Especially after the dreams she'd been having about him. And well…wow. Just wow. Talk about hot. Add in some steamy. Toss it all with oh-my-God-I-want-you-right-now salad spoons, and the dish came out somewhere south of holy crap.

She rolled her eyes. Stupid fixation. It wasn't healthy, particularly since—

The phone rang in her hand.

Tania gasped, fumbling with the thing before she found the talk button. "Hello."

"Ms. Solares?" Filled with gravel, the deep voice rubbed her the wrong way.

Tania tensed, reacting to the undertone. "Yes?"

"Are you home for a while?"

"Excuse me?" A whisper—ultra fine, barely there at all—ghosted through her mind. A warning, maybe? She couldn't tell.

"Oh, sorry, miss. Didn't mean to alarm you," the man said, no doubt reacting to her frosty tone. "It's Nick…Mr. Cannon's assistant?"

Oh, right. The superintendent's assistant. Tania relaxed. Mr. Cannon was a gem. A potbellied, tacky-mustache-wearing, all-around good guy. Although the fact he had an assistant surprised her. Then again, her building was older. A real charmer with its 1920s throwback vibe, but one that needed the kind of upkeep that ran the super ragged most of the time. So, good for Mr. Cannon for getting help.

"What can I do for you, Nick?"

"The tenant two floors below you just reported a leak," Nick said. "We need to check your apartment to see where the water is coming from. We've turned off the water, and the plumber is on his way. Can you let him in when he gets there?"

Ah, crap. She didn't want to wait around for some repair guy. "Yeah, sure. When will he be here?"

"Shortly."

"All right," she said. "I'll be here."

Hanging up, Tania grabbed the latest *Cosmo* off her bedside table and plopped belly down on the silk coverlet. Looked like she had some time to kill.

Chapter Twenty-five

Lying belly down in the damp dirt, Angela adjusted her grip on the M25. The butt of the rifle nestled against her shoulder fit just right as she sighted her target through the scope. The smell of fall swirled on a rising breeze, tousling the tops of huge oaks above her head, sending colorful leaves pirouetting toward the ground. It was a slow dance. Colorful. Grace-filled. A yearly event in which the trees got a haircut and lost their abundant foliage.

She measured the distance to her target. Checking her windage, she zeroed in on the yellow flag that waved from a steel pole planted at the edge of Black Diamond's compound.

Nope. Not good enough. Time for a readjust.

Without lifting her head—or losing sight of the pumpkin sitting on the stone wall—Angela uncurled her finger from the trigger and fine-tuned her long-range optic scope with a click. Seven hundred and fifty feet sat between her and the target. Two and a half football fields. Big, big distance without any room for error. She needed to be bang-on accurate. The slightest miscalculation and the bullet wouldn't reach its intended target.

Another click and…

Jackpot. Oh, so much better.

Resighting her mark, she listened to the treetops rustle as a north wind blustered, bringing a glorious chill with it. She loved it when fall turned cold, dipping closer to winter, moving into the beginning of her favorite season. The days got shorter. The nights grew longer. Soon, she'd enjoy the nip of frosty air while skating outside.

There wasn't much better.

Although some things topped a triple salchow jump. And one came to mind right away. Rikar. A close second to her man was the rifle in her hands. She tested its weight, loving the M25's smooth contours and elegant lines.

God, what a gift.

She appreciated it even more than the 9 mm armor-piercing ammo, and considering how much she loved the Glock strapped to her thigh, that was saying something. So yeah, as much as she enjoyed skating, the activity came in a distant fourth on her *best of* list, 'cause…duh. Gourmet coffee always landed in the top three. No matter what.

Addicted to Rikar. Addicted to guns. Addicted to caffeine.

In that order.

Her mouth tipped up at the corners. She was really going for addict of the year here. Not that she cared. Rikar made her happy. She laughed with him. Loved with him. Missed him when he was away from her. Wanted to be with him the second he came home, and despite the unfamiliar tether of dependence, felt more like herself than she had in years.

Gag…just shoot her now, *please.*

With a snort, Angela shook her head even as she accepted the inevitable. She was good and caught. Too far down the rabbit hole to ever get out.

Not that she wanted to. No way. She was locked and loaded, sights set on him. So screw the hardcore independence. Rikar was worth the adjustment. Her job. The few friends she possessed and the life she knew. She was all in, 100 percent AWOL…out of the human world and now a part of his.

Not that it was perfect. Oh, no, nothing quite so humdrum.

Perfection had its perks, she supposed, but she didn't want it. Not with Rikar. She wanted what they'd had this afternoon. A wicked good argument that ended in a spectacular round of lovemaking. Angela hummed, remembering his touch, reliving his taste, wanting another romp with him oh, say…five minutes ago.

Giving her head a shake, she gave herself a mental jolt. Freaking guy. He'd turned her into a nymphomaniac. Not a bad thing if only he were around to take care of the problem.

"Concentrate, you idiot," she said, hoping the sound of her voice would KO her sex fixation. No such luck. Rikar stayed with her, but at least she managed to see straight enough to sight the target. "One more bull's-eye, then it's homeward bound."

Or rather, kitchen bound.

Daimler was cooking up a storm, trying to keep Mac's stomach full. Angela grinned against the M25's stock. She'd never seen her partner eat that much. Then again, he'd been through a huge change, so she guessed they were in for a new normal. Fine by her. She didn't mind. Although the whole sun allergy Dragonkind had going on bothered her. Especially since she was outside shooting alone.

She didn't like it. Not because it frightened her. She was okay flying solo for a few hours and safe inside Black Diamond's energy shield. Angela just missed his company... and her spotter. Mac always came with her to the gun range. Always coached her through each shot, gauging the windage, the distance to target, giving her pointers on grip and trigger-finger speed.

Thank God tonight would be different.

She wouldn't be laid out on the ridge waiting for Lothair to show all by herself. Mac and Forge would be with her every step of the way while Rikar and the other Nightfuries drew the rat-bastard into the trap. They'd been over the plan a million times. Or at least it seemed like it. Every time Rikar got anywhere near her, he drilled her, making her repeat each detail until her head ached and she wanted to hit him.

Or shag him again.

Both strategies worked really, *really* well. But the second option was her favorite and usually the go-to plan. He never said no to making love to her. Which always made him forget about the plan and shut his yap.

Hallelujah. She needed the peace and quiet from time to time.

Which was the reason she'd come out to the shooting range and was currently KOing members of the squash family. Setting the scope's crosshairs on the fruit, Angela drew in a steady breath, exhaled slow, and squeezed the trigger. One potato. Two pota—

Splat!

Bingo. Mission accomplished. Pumpkin annihilated.

Angela pushed the bolt up, then forward, and emptied the rifle's chamber. The casing ejected, the chick-chick sounding brutal amid nature's charm, the creak of tree branches, and the soft twitter of birdcalls above her head.

Policing her brass, she picked up the 308 shell casing and, rolling to her feet, slipped it into her side pocket of her army pants. Angela's lips twitched. The BDUs (aka battle dress uniform) were another gift. One Rikar insisted she wear when she stepped outside the lair. She didn't need to be camouflaged while on Black Diamond grounds. No way the Razorbacks could find her here, but…

Whatever.

If wearing the camo gear made Rikar feel better, she'd do it without hesitation or complaint. She understood the concern—his need to shelter and protect her—because she worried just as much about him. Maybe more.

She wasn't the one going out night after night to fight the rogue idiots mucking up the planet. Rikar was, and although Angela knew he was more than capable of taking care of himself, she worried anyway. Had paced around the lair, drunk way too much coffee, praying he returned home safely at dawn for the past week.

And that wouldn't change any time soon. At least not if she stayed at Black Diamond. But who knew, right? Circumstances changed. Relationships tanked all the time. Particularly when things went unsaid between couples.

Cradling the gun, Angela headed for the lair, trying not to worry about that too. She didn't want to doubt Rikar, but uncertainty was circling. Not on her end. She wanted him, but other than saying he wouldn't let her go—and making love to her every chance he got—he'd gone silent on the commitment front. Hadn't told her he loved her. Hadn't asked her to marry him. Hadn't mentioned the future at all. Well, except to plan how to take down the rat-bastard, and well…crap. That just wasn't good enough.

She needed him to love her as much as she did him. Craved the words. Needed the ceremony. The whole kit and caboodle.

Calling herself an idiot, Angela trotted up a set of flagstone steps. As her boots met the patio, a gust of wind came up, rattling the windowpanes of the French doors. The dining room lay on the other side of the glass—her office for the last week. She'd started out in the computer lab, but Sloan liked his privacy, and Angela understood. The high-tech com-center was the guy's baby, and even though he tried to hide it Sloan didn't want anyone else in there.

So she'd packed up the boxes—all the missing persons reports—and moved upstairs. Which, of course, delighted Mac. It put him a hop, skip, and a jump away from the kitchen and his new best friend…Daimler, the culinary wizard.

With a snort, she closed the distance to the house. A soft click. A hard yank. The door swung wide and she stepped inside, out from beneath the setting sun. Night wasn't far off. An hour, maybe two, and the Nightfuries would be itching to set the trap and line up a bunch of Razorbacks to kill.

Angela couldn't wait. She needed to feel powerful again. To sight down the barrel of her M25 and put a hole in the rat-bastard's forehead.

Her gaze on the neat stacks of folders piled on the glossy tabletop, she kicked the door closed behind her and approached the table. Two new files sat in the center of her work space, yellow Post-it notes with Sloan's messy scrawl front and center on the cover of each one. Crap. More missing women. Angela swallowed past the sudden lump in her throat.

There were so many. Young girls. Teenagers. But it was the ones in their late teens to midtwenties she concentrated on.

According to Rikar, a female didn't come into her energy until then, so no use wasting time on those the Razorbacks wouldn't go after. Or try to enslave. Angela grimaced. Nasty rogue bastards. They'd imprisoned two she knew about and tried to do the same to her. How many more had they kidnapped in the last week and a half?

Lifting the M25, she set the rifle down on the end of the tabletop—gently...Daimler would kick her ass if she scratched the glossy surface—and reached for the twin folders. Just as her hand closed around them, movement flashed in her periphery.

She glanced toward the archway into the kitchen. Daimler came roaring into the dining room, a plate piled high with cookies, eyes sparkling, a big grin on his face. Mac was right on his heels, trying to reach over the Numbai's shoulder. The butler dodged the attempt, holding the plate out of reach.

"Hey, man...come on," her partner said, the whine in his voice unmistakable. "Gimme some of those."

"These are for my lady," Daimler said, thwarting another of Mac's sneak attack attempts. Angela bit down on a smile as she watched the pair, trying to wrap her brain around the *my lady*. Jeez, talk about prim and proper. The Numbai needed to move into the twenty-first century. "You may have some after she has taken her fill."

Mac looked at her over the butler's head, and she got hit with big puppy-dog eyes, the please-please-please unmistakable. She huffed, amusement spreading like a disease. Torture by way of cookie. How fun.

"Thanks, Daimler," she said, denying him her treat.

Mac grumbled, giving her a dirty look.

She grinned at her partner. "You help me with the MP reports, and I'll give you some of my cookies."

"Extortionist."

"You know it."

"My lady!" Daimler's high squeak brought her head around. Oh, crap. He'd noticed the M25. Pursing his lips, he gave her a stern look. "No guns on the dining room table."

"Sorry." Ditching the folders on the table, Angela scrambled for her rifle. She heard Mac chuckle as she scooped it off the tabletop. She glared at her partner, then turned apologetic eyes on Daimler. "Won't happen again."

His brows raised, the Numbai gave her a pointed look.

She crossed her heart. "Promise."

The butler stared a second longer, then nodded, and set the plate down next to her stack of reports. His eyes back to twinkling, he tipped his head in Mac's direction. "Don't let him eat them all, my lady. They're your favorite, after all."

Yes, they were. Peanut butter chocolate chip, heavy on the chocolate. And oh, boy, did they smell good—like Saturday afternoons and snacks at the skating rink.

With a murmured "okay," Angela set her gun in the black case beside the door and returned to the table. She grabbed a cookie, dug in, and...oh, wow. That was unbelievable. So good she hummed and took another bite. The second mouthful was even better than the first. She moaned in delight, playing it up for Mac.

He growled.

Her lips twitched, and mouth full, asked, "Anything new?"

"Other than the torture factor in here?" Almost drooling, he watched her chew. "Nothing's come up yet."

Angela waved her hand at the plate. Mac jumped at the invitation, swiping three PB and chocolates off the plate. As he shoved them into his piehole, her attention strayed back to the folders Sloan had brought her. Brushing the crumbs off her fingers, she flipped the first one open and scanned the contents. Name. Personal info—height, weight, eye and hair color. Address. Phone number and—

Angela frowned. Wait a second. Back up a step. She recognized that address. She'd seen it in another file.

"Hey, Mac?"

"Whatcha got?"

She shook her head and reached for the stack filed under *possibles.* "Don't know...I'm just..."

Bingo. The one she was looking for. Tagged with a red sticker, the folder contained two MP reports. Roommates at Seattle U, the pair of twenty-year-olds had gone missing the same night. She flipped the report open and—

"Holy shit." Her gaze bounced back and forth, confirming what she already knew.

"Tell me."

"These two girls went missing sixteen days ago." Holding up the two-week-old report, she bounced it in her hand. The newer file grasped in the other, she said, "This one? Two days ago. All three are roommates...they lived together. And they fit the profile...same victimology."

"Jesus. It isn't random."

"Not even a little." Open on the folds, she set the two folders aside and cracked the other one Sloan had brought. "Bingo. Proof positive."

Mac glanced over her shoulder. "Motherfuck…twins."

"The rat-bastard's cherry-picking," she said. "Hunting females that are related or are good friends."

"Not a coincidence."

"Nope. Are high-energy females attracted to one another?"

Mac raised a brow, his expression full of speculated interest. The kind that had nothing to do with being a cop and everything to do with being a guy.

She whacked him with the folder. "Not that kind of attracted, you big dope."

"A guy can dream."

"Oh, shut up," she said. "I need to talk to Rikar. See what he knows about this."

Mac might have murmured, but Angela didn't hear him. Folders tucked under one arm, she was already moving, her focus absolute. Rikar. She needed to see him. If what she suspected was true—that the Meridian drew high-energy females together—the investigation into the missing women had just gone from shaky to rock-solid. With that information, Angela knew she could track them. Make connections. Find other women that might be targeted by the Razorbacks and thrown into their awful breeding center.

Wicked good intel. The kind that cracked a case wide open.

Although, to be honest, the break in the investigation wasn't the only reason she pointed her boots toward the underground lair. Angela wanted to share more with Rikar than just information. Tonight was a muck-hole in the making. A potential mess that had death written all over it, and Angela refused to waste a second. She needed to make love to him again before night fell. Before the Nightfuries weaponed up and headed out to set the trap. It might be her last chance to hold him.

Angela picked up the pace. The work of minutes, and she stepped inside the Otis. She suppressed a full-body shiver. Elevators weren't her favorite things anymore, not after taking a trip in one at the Razorback lair.

She hit the down button anyway. The doors closed, and she was on her way, headed into the depths of Black Diamond. Huge with a network of interconnected tunnels beneath the main house, the underground lair was pretty darned cool, fascinating in every way but one. The sucker was difficult to navigate. Especially when you didn't know the layout. Not a problem for her, though. With her Rikar radar up and running, she knew exactly where to find him.

The gym.

Impatient to reach him, she shuffled her feet, scuffing the elevator floor with her boots, waiting for the stupid thing to open. Thirty seconds later, and instant freedom as doors slid to the side, dumping her onto the corridor. To the right lay the clinic. To the left? Her man. She could hear him now, his voice bouncing down the hallway as he yakked it up with another guy.

She jogged the last few feet, making a beeline for the gym. She crossed the threshold, getting an eyeful of high-tech cardio equipment, weight machines, and—

Holy crap.

Dragons.

Three of them. Horned heads nearly touching the high ceiling.

Angela stopped short, felt her eyes go wide as she got a load of the kick-ass trifecta. Rikar, she recognized. Almost pure white with gold-and-blue-tipped scales, his razor-sharp talons were curled around a vertical post in the shape of a cross. With a steady stroke, he drew one claw across the horizontal part of the contraption—a sharpening blade maybe? A horrendous sound echoed, like nails on a chalkboard.

She wanted to cringe, press her hands over her ears, and shriek along with the awful noise. And she would've if she'd been able to look away. No chance of that. She was too busy staring, being completely mesmerized.

Most women would've been scared brainless. Not her. Fear wasn't her usual MO. Curiosity had always been her poison pill, sending her into investigation mode. As she compared each dragon, cataloging their differences, she took note of their mannerisms, enjoying the show, and… man, oh man. Rikar was beautiful in dragon form.

She remembered seeing him on the beach the night he'd come after her, but nothing came close to watching him now, when she wasn't in pain and filled with terror. Gorgeous. No other word matched up to that one…or him.

No sloppy seconds, his companions were equally as eye-catching.

A midnight-blue dragon sat beside a second post. One paw raised, green eyes narrowed on his talons, he inspected each digit as though checking his handiwork, making sure his claws were sharp enough. The third was jet-black with amber-tipped scales and a golden gaze. Wick. It had to be. None of the other guys had eyes that color.

The first to notice her standing on the threshold, Wick snorted at her, smoke rings rising from his nostrils. As far as greetings went, it lacked a certain…umm, something. Angela didn't care. She choose to spin it her way, took it as a hello and said, "Hey, Wick. Got 'em sharp enough yet?"

Wick's lip curled off his fangs. A smile? Kind of, so she grinned back. He shook his head and thumped Rikar with the side of his tail.

Rikar looked up from his sharpening operation. The second he saw her, he purred long and low. "Angela."

The deep-throated hum made her tingle all over. Oh, the anticipation. She L-O-V-E-D that tone, enjoyed the erotic pitch and rumble. Why? Every time he used it she ended up on her back. Not necessarily in his bed, either. So, yeah. The gym was fair game in the lovemaking department.

First things first, though. Privacy. She needed to get rid of the other Nightfuries.

Except Bastian and Wick handled that all by themselves. Shifting into human form, leather fighting gear in place, the pair strode toward the door. And her. Angela high-tailed it out of their way, taking refuge beside a rack of free weights. Wick passed first, and naturally, snarled at her. She growled back. He blinked and tossed a load of WTF over his shoulder at Bastian. The Nightfury commander shrugged and, lips twitching, paused on the threshold.

He tipped his chin in his XO's direction. "Meeting's in an hour."

Rikar nodded, iridescent scales shimmering in the low light.

Glancing away from his friend, Bastian nailed her with a no-nonsense glare. He held up his index finger, shook it at her. "One hour, Angela. You keep him beyond that? I'm coming down here to drag your ass up to the kitchen, and believe me when I say you wouldn't like it."

Rikar snorted, his amusement barely contained.

Her eyes narrowed on Bastian as she met his gaze head-on. Flipping guys…blaming her for the nympho circus over the last week as though she'd been the one doing the *keeping*. Jeez, Rikar had been insatiable. Way out of control in the do-me-now sex arena. Thank God.

Bastian's eyes twinkled as he scowled at her. "Got it?"

"Got it," she repeated, wanting him gone a minute ago.

The second Bastian turned his back and skedaddled, boot heels ringing in the quiet, Rikar wrapped his arms around her from behind. The folders hit the floor mats in a messy sprawl. Angela ignored them. The paperwork could wait. There would be time to tell him about her high-energy theory later. When she wasn't enveloped by his scent, cocooned in his strength, and surrounded by an oh-my-God gorgeous male. 'Cause…oh, yeah. He'd pulled her favorite trick. The naked one in which he came to her wearing nothing but skin.

With a hum, Angela glanced over her shoulder and met his gaze. "Kiss me."

"Bossy female." Desire made his eyes glow as he dipped his head and did as he was told.

She sighed, accepting his taste as he delved in, mating their tongues. No preamble. No messing around. Nothing polite or nice about it. Just deep, intense, and fast…exactly how she liked it: him all over her. Deep in her mouth, he went to work, unbuttoning her BDUs, splitting the fly wide to slide beneath the waistband. His callused palm caressed her belly, then headed south, brushing over hypersensitive skin.

"Hmm, yeah…just like that," she gasped against his mouth. Locked in her embrace, he raised his head, his gaze on her face as he sank into her curls and stroked deep. Pleasure rushed through her, streaming into her veins like a drug. "Rikar…"

"Christ, love…so wet already." Showing no mercy, he amped her up, pushing the pants down her thighs while his fingers circled, the rhythm diabolical. And just like that, she rode the edge of orgasm, panting, gasping, begging for him without words. "Want me, do you?"

"Yes."

"My way this time."

Angela's breath hitched. *His way*. God, he'd been trying to take her like that all week. She'd shied every time: afraid, not ready, beyond freaked out by the idea.

"Let me, angel," he murmured, his breath hot against her ear. His hands stilled as he nuzzled the side of her throat. "Trust me, love. Let me love you that way."

From behind. He wanted to—

A tremor rolled through her. "Rikar, I—"

"Please?"

Unzipping her jacket, he slipped his hand beneath her T-shirt, stroking gently as he drifted over her rib cage. The cotton snagged on his forearm, and cool air washed over her. Angela quivered. He growled and cupped her breast, burrowing beneath her bra to hold her in his palm. As she arched, he pressed in, molding his chest to her back, thumbed her nipple, and then plucked with delicious deliberation. Surrounded by him, his hands on her skin, his body hard against her, Angela shifted in his arms, uncertainty battling desperate need.

"It won't hurt." He kissed the side of her neck, sucked gently as he rotated his fingers against the top of her sex. As the stroke and withdrawal started up again, Angela moaned and pressed back, trying to get closer. He rolled his hips against her, the curl and release keeping time with his fingers. “Let me show you, Angela. You’ll like it with me. I’ll make it good for you.”

She knew what he wanted, and it had little to do with sex. What he craved reached beyond physical intimacy into trust. He needed her to trust him completely. To throw caution aside and have faith—in him and herself. Enough to let go of the fear and give him everything. No misgivings. No holding back. Just straight-up, in-your-face vulnerability.

It was psychology 101: face what you most fear.

His fingers continued to play, winding her tight, coaxing her with pleasure. Her breath hitched as he kissed her and waited for an answer. For the green light and…

Screw it. She was going to let him. Rikar deserved better than that from her. He yearned for her trust, so she would hand him the power to give while taking and trust him to catch her when she fell.

Holding his gaze, she dipped her chin. A simple nod. A barely-there shift in movement, but it was all he needed and everything he asked. Murmuring her name, he nipped her once, then kissed her deep, walking them forward toward the padded lip of a weight machine. Within seconds, he stripped her bare and wrapped her up, holding her close while he—

“Oooh, God.” What clever, clever fingers he had. Smoothing his hand over her belly, he nipped her shoulder, kissed her nape, and then bent her forward. Her hipbones pressed into the padded edge of a weight machine, he settled behind her, his hips against her bottom. “Rikar?”

“Easy angel,” he whispered. “And hang on tight. I’m gonna take you on a ride.”

Her hands found purchase, grasping onto the metal bars in front of her.

Spreading her legs wider, he stepped between while his hands caressed her from shoulders to lower back, playing in delicate hollows and sensitive valleys. He took it slow, brushing kisses along her spine. One hand settled on her hip, the other traveled, slipping between her thighs. He stroked deep, making her moan, the pace so beautifully erotic she forgot what he wanted to do and moved with him. Simply existed, riding the pleasure he gave her.

A breath away from coming, he withdrew from her core. She moaned her disappointment. He answered, coming back to please her, entering her from behind. Angela gasped, arching beneath the press of his hands, fighting to accommodate him as he buried himself to the hilt inside her.

God, he was deep…so very deep.

"Fucking hell." His big hands bracketing her hips, he withdrew and came back, circling his hips, touching… just…the right…spot. "Sweet Christ, I…oh, yeah. That's it, Angela…move with me. Move, love."

Pinned beneath him, heart hammering, body throbbing, she used what little leverage she possessed to please him. To please herself. He cursed, the sound half pleasure, half pain, each thrust a slow, devastating glide. The coil and release of his body brought her closer, took her higher, made her ache and plead and need him more.

How. Amazing.

He was devastation in motion. Perfection personified. Made just for her. And as bliss swelled on a wave of delight, she moaned his name. He praised her in return, upping the rhythm, riding her so well she begged him for release.

"Come on, angel," he growled, working himself deep, his hips slapping against her bottom. "I want it. Give it to me."

With a gasp, she let herself go, lost herself in driving heat and greedy pleasure with the words *I love you* tangled on the tip of her tongue. Angela wanted to tell him. To lay herself bare and give him all but couldn't make herself say the words. Couldn't be that vulnerable. Not yet. Not until she was assured of his love in return.

So she showed him instead, took him to the hilt, trusting him completely, giving him her heart with deed instead of word. And as she exploded around him, Angela dragged him with her. Into the light. Into oblivion where bliss lived, and love, she hoped, had already found a home in the deepest reaches of his heart.

Chapter Twenty-six

His wings spread in flight, Lothair flew over the apartment complex. Eighth and Columbia Street. Perfect. He'd made it in under ten minutes. Then again, the female's home had only been a quick glide away. He could've reached her on foot if he'd wanted to, but hell, flying in was a better bet.

Safer, too.

He didn't want any Nightfuries mucking up the plan. The assholes had been everywhere lately.

Lothair's night vision sparked, picked up trace as he circled overhead. The full moon helped, glowing in a cloudless sky, washing Seattle in blue-gray light. He made another pass and scanned the terrain. Tidy brick pathways led to and from buildings below. Pushed by a chilly autumn breeze, colorful treetops swayed in the common. A grassy knoll swelled beneath the great beeches in front of the complex, providing a comfortable root base, rolling to the edge of a paved lot packed tight with cars.

All of it pulsed with energy. Animate. Inanimate. It didn't matter. Everything—big, small…alive or not—carried a signature. No female energy, though, came through the Meridian's midnight blanket. Nothing but a single male pushing through the front door. Destination unknown.

Not him, though. Lothair knew exactly where he was going and what he would do when he got there. Tania Solares awaited. Jesus, he hoped the female was high-energy. She was the second-to-last one: number six for cellblock A. Now all he needed to do was drop in and grab her.

Fifth window in. Eleven floors up.

The lights were on. Tania had taken the bait, and now she waited, his for the taking. And he would…take her. Probably in her own bed. Maybe several times before he carried her off to the Razorback lair and secured her in her cell. The instant that happened, he'd be one step closer to his real goal—killing the she-cop.

Angling his wings, Lothair set down without a sound on the female's balcony. He shifted without thought, scales turning to skin, claws and talons to feet and hands. As his boots settled on his feet, her name slithered through his mind. Angela Keen. He rubbed the side of his face, fingertips grazing the spot where she'd nailed him with the box cutter. Completely healed now, he didn't feel a thing. No scar or imperfection marred his cheek. But the gash had gone more than skin deep. It had cut him wide open inside. Now the wound festered, revving up his need to get even.

Rolling his shoulders, he mind-spoke to his warriors circling overhead. *"Wait for me. I'll be half an hour."*

He got a bunch of "roger thats" from the males flying with him.

"Need some help?" Denzeil asked, sounding hopeful.

"Stay outside."

"Have fun," D said, the grumble in his voice undeniable.

Lothair's mouth curved as he watched his friend fly overhead, looking for a place to roost. Unlocking the patio door with his mind, he slid it open and strode over the threshold. He took a deep breath, drawing the female's scent into his lungs, and scanned the shadows. As he swept the scene, he picked up details. No one in the living room or kitchen, but a cell phone sat on the granite countertop. Plugged into its charger, the light blinked on and off, sending a piercing green light through the dimness.

He took it as a good sign. Humans never went anywhere without their cell phones. It was an unwritten rule or something. Either that or an addiction. If they didn't have the stupid things plastered to their ears, their fingers were busy clicking on keyboards. The whole race was a step away from a catastrophic bout of brain tumors.

Which would be good. If the assholes all died of cancer, Ivar could get out of his lab. Concentrate less on his superbugs and more on hunting.

Lothair pivoted and went right. Double doors lead into the bedroom where he wanted to be, but still, no Tania. Just a magazine on the silk coverlet. He checked the bathroom and frowned. No sign of her.

He rolled through the apartment again, opening cupboard doors, checking closets, wondering if she was hiding. He picked up her iPhone and scrolled through the history but found no clues. She was gone.

Lothair's temper surged and magic swirled, exploding in a wave as rage took hold. Grabbing the edge of a cabinet door, he tore the wood panel off its hinges and hurled it across the kitchen, then repeated the process. Leaving nothing but kindling in his wake, he leapt over the island. He landed in the living room and attacked the couch, ripping holes in leather cushions. Stuffing flew like confetti, spilling all over the place while his heart hammered and his fists flew. After he was done, he ransacked her bedroom, tearing her mattress in two, bending the metal bed frame in half. And the rampage went on and on. The bathroom sink exploded with a knuckle-bruising punch. Vases smashed against walls, glass shards flying like shrapnel. Tables got upended. Mirrors shattered. All while he cursed the female who'd ruined his plan.

First the she-cop. Now Tania.

His chest pumping with exertion, Lothair stared at the shattered bathroom mirror. His reflection splintered like a sunburst, heading in multiple directions. His eyes narrowed as fury receded and mind sharpened, laying out a plan like playing cards on a table.

After a minute, he snarled, *"D."*

"Yeah, boss?"

"Go home." Uncurling his hands, Lothair raised one and examined his bruised knuckles. *"Fire up your fucking system and find Tania Solares. Track her recent credit card receipts, the GPS in her car...whatever. Get me a trail to follow."*

Hearing the pissed off in his voice, Denzeil didn't argue. The sound of wings flapping came through mind-speak as the male took flight. *"Ten-four. I'll hit you up when I find something."*

Of course the male would...if he knew what was good for him. The warrior's self-preservation instinct had always been bang-on accurate. Too bad Denzeil couldn't find Rikar for him. He would rip the Nightfury's head off as soon as—

Lothair jolted as a tingle slid over the nape of his neck. He stopped breathing, trying to get a handle on the signal, and...oh, happy day. He recognized the energy beacon. The she-cop. Angela Keen was out from beneath the Nightfuries' thumb and on the move.

Closing his eyes, he turned a slow circle. Wood splinters and ceramic tile crunched beneath his boots as he mined her energy, tracking the source. North…northwest. Near the coastline. Yes, that was definitely her.

Lothair's hum of satisfaction turned into a growl. It looked like the night hadn't been a total waste after all. The female was out on her own.

Time to unleash hell. And a shitload of payback.

Throwing Angela's old energy beacon out with supernova intensity, Rikar set down on the lip of a steep rock face. His claws scraped stone as he scanned the horizon and the flat plateau running out below him. A thousand yards of wide-open space, jagged cliffs falling off the edge into the ocean on one side, thick forest rising on the other, a swath of flat terrain interspacing the two.

The perfect place for an ambush.

He'd hunted all week for the location. Had done nothing but flybys, working his way up the Washington State coastline, searching for just…one…thing. Multiple points of cover. But above all, safety and a back door for Angela if things went wrong.

Rikar snorted, frost rising like smoke rings from his nostrils. Tonight didn't feel right. Nothing about having Angela in the mix did, but even as the thick rush of unease intensified, he broadcast the signal, wanting to get it over with even as he dreaded the outcome. But the setup was the best he could do. With the humans cleared out of the century-old farmhouse and Angela's Jeep parked beside it, the Razorbacks would come to the conclusion Rikar wanted them to—that Angela had come to the secluded spot to hide.

Not a bad trap.

Rikar still didn't like it. Wound tight, muscle flickered along his flank, rattling the spikes along his spine. The sound smacked of nervousness, forcing him to reevaluate. He'd never thought much about battle. Fighting was simply a part of his life, something he did to protect the race, and by extension, humankind. Nothing to wax poetic about, but tonight, everything hinged on Angela getting a clean shot. At a moving target. Within a very limited window of time.

Shifting into human form, he mind-spoke, *"B, heads up. Signal's gone live. Tell the boys to get ready."*

"You in position?"

"No," he said, aware he was about to catch hell. *"Making a pit stop first."*

"Jesus, man." When he remained silent, Bastian sighed, knowing a losing battle when he found one. *"Do it fast, then get your ass cliff-side. We're all good to go."*

"Two minutes tops, and I'm airborne again."

His best friend cursed.

Rikar ignored the warning and hopped over the top of a huge boulder. He caught air, free-falling ten feet to the ledge below. His shitkickers connected to the granite with a crunch. He swallowed another bout of unease as he got a load of the setup—of Angela, the M25 he'd given her, and the spot she'd chosen to shoot from.

Fucking hell. What had he been thinking?

Nothing good, that was for sure. But as he watched her stand shoulder-to-shoulder with Forge and Mac—listened to her give last-minute instructions to his warriors—he couldn't help himself. She made him so damned proud. His mate was unbelievably beautiful. So brave. So savvy. So…100 percent his. And God, he needed to protect her. Craved her safety more than he wanted to live, and as he stared, she turned, ignoring Mac's gum-flapping and Forge's response to smile at him. His heart flip-flopped, thumping the inside of his chest.

Giving the males a pat, she left the pair and approached him. "Hey."

The greeting was more than just a how-the-hell-are-ya. It was a question, one filled with concern. Throat gone tight, Rikar tipped his chin, returning the hello the only way he could…with action. Shit on a stick. She shouldn't be worried about him. He knew how to take care of himself. Angela needed to concentrate on herself, but…goddamn it. He couldn't stop his reaction. It felt so good to be cared about—to have her want him home safely each dawn.

Stepping in close, she smoothed her hands over his shoulders. Rikar couldn't resist. He wrapped his arms around her. As he buried his face in her hair, he breathed her in, saturating himself in her scent. He wanted to remember everything about her. The way she felt against him. How she smelled. The sound of her voice.

Everything. Just in case the worst happened and he lost her forever.

Cupping his nape, she kissed the side of his neck. "You okay?"

"No," he murmured, being honest with her. "I don't like this…you being here."

"Rikar, I'm—"

"I know you're kick-ass capable, angel." Spreading his fingers, he ran his hands down her back, touching as much of her as he could with one caress. "This isn't about how good you are at your job and your ability with a gun. I just… I can't stand the thought of you getting hurt. I almost lost you once. I can't do that again."

"Mac and Forge will be with me the whole time."

"I know."

"Forge will keep us cloaked and hidden, so worry about yourself, not me." Her grip on him tightened as she whispered, "Please, Rikar. I want you one hundred percent focused out there. If you're distracted by me, you won't look after yourself or be able to protect the other Nightfuries."

Good advice. Too bad he couldn't follow it. Not that he wouldn't try, but he was a bonded male now. He could no more ignore Angela's presence than his own fingers and toes. She was in his blood and a breath away from danger. His dragon would never allow him to forget about her, no matter how intense the fighting became.

Pulling back a little, she met his gaze. Her hands moved over him, caressing the tops of his shoulders and down his spine, bringing him comfort as she said, "I'm sorry. I know you're worried, but I can't let it go. I need—"

"Closure." He sighed, relaxing beneath the pleasure of her touch.

"Exactly." Fisting her hands in his jacket, she shook him a little. "So let me do what I'm good at. Trust me to do my job, okay?"

Rikar nodded, giving her what she wanted as he shifted focus. His gaze landed on the males standing less than six feet away. Shitkickers planted in the stone dust, not even trying to pretend disinterest, the newest members of the Nightfury pack stared at him.

Nosy fuckers. He needed a private moment with his female, and what was he getting? A curious pair of idiots with personal boundary issues.

Mac raised a brow, amusement all over his puss. Forge wasn't as easy to read. The warrior was stoic, without expression, but Rikar caught the wicked glint in his eyes. His gaze narrowed on them, Rikar mind-spoke to the pair, *"You leave her side for even a second, I'll rip your hearts out and feed them to you."*

"Well, now..." Forge's mouth curved up at the corners. *"That's more like it."*

"I'll say." Smirking, Mac jostled Forge with his elbow. *"Thought we were losing him there for a second."*

"Fuck off," Rikar said, trying not to laugh. But Christ, it was hard. In less than a week, the males had wormed their way into his heart. *"And be careful. They spot you—"*

"We'll move to the secondary location." Forge cracked his knuckles, looking as lethal as a coiled cobra.

"Don't sweat it, man," Mac said. *"We'll keep her hidden."*

Rikar nodded, trusting the males to do their jobs. No easy feat. Leaving his female in their care was tantamount to gutting himself with a dull blade. And just as painful. The sense of foreboding wouldn't let go. Was digging a hole at the back of his brain, stirring up a load of mental debris—the kind he always listened to before a firefight.

But with her asking for his trust—sounding so sensible and strong—Rikar ignored instinct and let it go, giving her a gentle squeeze as he kissed her. Raised on her tiptoes, Angela gave as good as she got, returning the hard press of his mouth.

Uncurling her fingers from his leather jacket, she stepped back, widening the distance between them, her gaze clinging to his. "Be safe."

Unable to look away, he walked backward toward the cliff edge.

"Go," she said, a slight hitch in her voice. "See you on the other side."

"Aim true, angel," he murmured, memorizing the contours of her face, praying he'd see it again before he dove over the ledge and into thin air.

Angela checked the M25 for the third time in less than a minute. She didn't want it to jam. Rikar was counting on her. All right, so she wasn't the only one on point. The Nightfury warriors were staked out too, poised to explode out of cover the instant Rikar came around the bend in the coastline and the enemy came into range.

Still, she couldn't bear the thought of not being ready.

Yes, her mate was a warrior: strong, lethal, and smart. But that didn't mean he couldn't be hurt, or worse.

Lying belly down on the lip of the ridge, Angela clenched her hand around the cloth ball full of chalk dust. Her palms were sweaty. Not a good sign. Especially since nerves had never been a part of the equation before. She'd always been rock-steady behind a scope. Tonight, though, was different. There was too much at stake, and as she checked her weapon again, she wondered what the hell she was doing. No matter how much she'd argued with Rikar to the contrary, she knew she shouldn't be in the Nightfury mix.

Her presence made them all uneasy. She could see it in their eyes. In the way they'd planned the mission, the bait and switch that would lead the Razorbacks into the ambush. Angela squeezed the chalk ball harder, feeling sick as one word registered above all the others. *Bait.*

Dear God, there was something wrong with her. Something twisted and sick about the whole situation.

The realization hit her like a epiphany. Shame followed. Angela squeezed her eyes closed, the consequences of her insistence to be included looming in her mind. She'd allowed Rikar to become bait, agreed to let him play mouse to the rat-bastard's cat. For what, exactly…revenge? Her throat went tight. It seemed so stupid. So petty when she considered the man she loved was risking his life to give her what she wanted.

Why she hadn't realized it sooner, Angela didn't know. Maybe she'd been caught up in the planning. Maybe she'd been too focused on herself. Whatever the case, she couldn't ignore her selfishness now. Or her love. Rikar's safety trumped vengeance any day of the week. So as much as it killed her to let go, maybe it was time to bow out and let dragons deal with dragons.

Adjusting her grip on the M25, Angela lifted away from the optic scope's eyepiece. She glanced to her right. Belly down in the dirt beside her, Mac looked through his own scope, one designed for a sniper's spotter.

"Hey, Mac? Maybe it's time I—"

"Incoming," Forge growled from behind them.

Crap. So much for backing out. Goddamn it. "How many?"

"Eleven strong." Perched like a gargoyle on the ledge above them, Forge held the line, cloaking them with his magic.

"Break it down for her," Mac said.

"All fire dragons but three," Forge said. "Two are rocking poisonous gas. The last asshole…acid."

Angela narrowed the crosshairs, zeroing in on the coastline a thousand meters away. "How far out are they?"

"A minute and a half." Mac turned the dial on his scope; the slow click cranked her tight with each rotation. "Southbound. We're good to go from here."

Angela nodded, struggling to stay steady, rechecking her position, the scope, her gun. The last-minute run-through didn't help. She flexed her fingers, then released the twin fists, willing her hands to quit shaking.

Shale rattled down the cliff face as Forge shifted his foothold. "Look for—"

"I know what he looks like," Angela said, tone tight.

Black scales. Black eyes. Black, soulless heart beating in the center of his chest. *Come on, Angela…get it together.* As her own voice whispered through her mind, she adjusted her grip, clearing the mental minefield inside her head, forcing herself into the zone. She sank deep, away from emotion and into the moment.

"Windage?"

Mac fed her the intel, working his scope like a pro. "Breathe, Ange."

"Screw off."

"She's ready." Her partner eyed Forge over the top of her head.

Angela caught the Scottish devil's grin out of the corner of her eye. "You too, Forge."

"Nae doubt about it," Forge murmured. "Wicked ready."

"Shut up," she said without heat, thankful for both of them. She understood what they were doing—diverting her into relaxation. The trash-talking was an old-time tactic, one used by cops in high-octane situations to power down before crap went critical. The calm-before-the-storm strategy worked wonders, cranking her dial to 100 percent focused. "Can't you see I'm working here?"

"Attagirl," Mac said without looking at her. "Get ready. Here we go."

Deep breath in. Smooth breath out. Trigger finger at the ready. Clear mind. Steadier hand and…

Holy crap. Here he came.

White scales gleaming in the moon-glow, Rikar rocketed around the last bend. Wisps of air curled from his wing tips, swirling behind him like jet fuel. The tendrils blew into the Razorback's face. The black-scaled bastard bared his fangs and snapped at Rikar's tail. Lock. Set. Match. The enemy dragon had taken the bait. Now he flew toward the kill zone…and Angela's crosshairs.

"Come on…come on," she murmured, timing it just right, waiting for the precise moment. The perfect opening in the shooting lane. "Turn, Rikar…bank left…hard left, baby."

Forge murmured, relaying the message.

Rikar split wide, heading for the coastline. Angela pulled the trigger. The rifle recoiled in her hands, thumping hard against her shoulder. Gunfire cracked. The sound ricocheted, echoing across in the starlit sky to reach the ocean waves. Time slowed, riding the tail end of revenge. Still sighting through the scope, Angela followed the bullet's path, praying it flew straight and true.

The black dragon's head kicked back.

Blood flew, the dark splash washing the moonlight with red. The rat-bastard's wings folded. Her heart thumped, the sound reverberating in her ears as she watched him fall. She needed to remember, to memorize the kill, recall every last detail and—

The Razorback blinked, one last reflexive response before death came to claim him. Angela sucked in quick breath. Oh, God…no. Blue eyes, not dark brown. It wasn't Lothair.

Her hands tightened on the M25. Son of a bitch. She'd shot the wrong dragon. Now Rikar had a bull's-eye painted on his back with multiple Razorbacks converging on him.

All because of her.

She'd made him turn the wrong way, left instead of right, away from the other Nightfury warriors. And even as she watched Bastian take flight, pushing skyward from their ambush position in the forest, Angela knew *screwed* when she saw it. The entire plateau stretched between him and Rikar. A minute of no-man's-land between the Nightfuries and her mate.

Terror closed her throat. "Forge, go. You're the closest—"

"I cannae leave you," he said, grim realization in his tone. "Angela, if I—"

"I don't give a shit…go!"

He hesitated, meeting Mac's gaze over the top of her head.

"Goddamn it, go!" Her scream echoed, bouncing off the rock face.

Mac nodded.

And Forge went. Arms and legs pumping, he charged toward the edge. He transformed as he leapt skyward, dark purple scales flashing in the moonlight as he rocketed to where Rikar fought for his life. The invisibility cloak dropped, leaving them vulnerable on the lip of the ledge.

Angela didn't care. She hunkered down behind the M25 and snarled at Mac, "Windage. Distance to target."

His eye on his scope, Mac fed her the information. Angela took aim and pulled the trigger, covering Forge, protecting her mate. A hundred dragons could fly over. She didn't give a damn. No way would she leave Rikar in the lurch.

Sharp claws raked Rikar's side, tearing through his scales to reach bone. Blood welled on his rib cage. He gritted his teeth and swung right, avoiding enemy talons as he hammered a Razorback on the flyby. The bright blue dragon recoiled, somersaulting into a backflip, smashing into one of his buddies. As their wings got tangled, Rikar heard the pair curse, but didn't pause to admire his handiwork. More rogues were coming, converging like a pack of raptors, all their focus on him.

The FUBAR factor should've fazed him. But he didn't give a shit. As long as the bastards stayed away from the cliff edge and Angela, he'd hold the line. Put a bull's-eye on his skull to keep her safe.

The next thirty seconds were all about time. About the dash and dive. About distracting the enemy pack long enough so B and the others could reach him. The instant they did, he'd fly for the ridgeline and his mate. He needed to get her the hell out of range. The aerial dogfight was too intense, the sky filled with dragons drifting closer to her position by the second.

Rotating into a side-flip, he avoided another set of enemy claws. The up-and-over did the job, positioning him above one of the bastards' spiked spine. Still upside down, half-way through the spin, he reached for the rogue's head. His talons curled around enemy horns. A quick grab. A faster twist and…

Crack!

Rikar snapped the male's neck. Quick. Effective. Deadly. Hoorah, one down. Nine to go. And it couldn't happen fast enough.

He couldn't see Lothair anymore. The male had slunk away, made for the beaches along the coastline, another dragon in tow. Fuck, the Razorback XO was smart: hanging back, using a look-alike and the other rogues as cover. Rikar snarled, knowing exactly what the asshole was after. Angela. The rat-bastard wouldn't pass up a chance to recapture her.

Fear lit him up at as he slashed a red dragon, snapping the enemy's forepaw. As the rogue howled, Rikar thanked God for Forge. The male would keep her cloaked and Lothair from finding her.

His wings stretched to capacity, Rikar banked into a tight turn. Four Razorbacks followed, coming at him from different angles. Rikar dodged, but not fast enough. Enemy claws struck, scoring his scales before sinking into his shoulder. With a curse, he twisted, shaking off the blow as he rocketed into a tight spiral.

The sharp report of rifle rang out, a harsh crack beneath a starry sky.

The yellow dragon chasing him jerked, head whiplashing, blood arcing from his temple. As the rogue ashed out, the night wind blew the gray flakes into Rikar's face. He growled. What was Angela doing…trying to put a target on her freaking back? Another round of fear rolled through him. She needed to move, right now. The report of the rifle was too loud, and if she didn't stop shooting, every rogue would turn in her direction.

A second shot echoed. Another rogue fell.

Rikar cursed even as he tried to be thankful for her help, but…shit. Just wait until he got a hold of her. He'd turn her over his knee. After he kissed the hell out of her, because man, she was good. Wicked accurate, picking dragons out of the sky like heat-seeking missiles took out fighter jets. Good thing Forge was—

"Rikar…hard left." A purple streak roared in on his flank.

Rikar shifted, tucking his wings as his comrade exhaled. Fire-acid flew from Forge's throat, setting a rogue on fire. The Razorback shrieked, falling out of the sky, the smell of burning flesh washing through the night chill.

Rikar hammered another Razorback and snarled through mind-speak, *"I'm gonna kill you."*

"Later," Forge said, breathing hard from his rocketlike flight from the cliff…where he'd left Angela alone and uncloaked. *"And she's safe."*

"You asshole." Whipping around, Rikar slashed a brown dragon with his tail.

Forge came up over his spine. Rikar ducked his head, giving the male the space he needed to maneuver. His new warrior came in hot, elbowing a rogue in the head. A crack sounded as he knocked the bastard's teeth down his throat. Rounding on another, Rikar's claws caught scales. He gutted the enemy, protecting Forge's flank with a shitload of down and dirty.

"Get back over there." Rikar slashed another rogue to keep the bastard at bay. *"I can't find Lothair and—"*

"Mac'll move her if shit gets critical."

"Son of a..." Rikar trailed off as he grabbed a Razorback by the tail. Pulling a spin and toss, he hurled the enemy toward the farmhouse below him. The red dragon hit the ground with a crunch and slid, cutting a swath through the paddock, mounding the earth before he smashed into the barn. Wood siding exploded into kindling. *"...bitch."*

"Fuck off, Frosty." Forge breathed out. A stream of orange flame shot from his throat, flashing across the night sky. Bang-on accurate, he torched the pile of rubble beneath the rogue on the ground, lighting the entire mess on fire. *"Eye on the ball."*

Freaking Forge. He didn't care how effective the warrior was with his flamethrower-cum-mouth. He would skin the male alive when this was over.

But first things first. Where the hell was the cavalry? Yeah, he and Forge might be doing the job keeping the rogues at bay, but not by much. It was hard, after all, to KO the enemy while playing defense.

"B," Rikar growled. *"Where the fuck are—"*

"On your six," his commander said, coming in hot. A Razorback squawked, wing-flapping to get out of Bastian's way. *"Shove over."*

No problem.

Rikar flipped, tucking into a tight sideways spiral. Midnight-blue scales streaked in his periphery as his friend arrived, flying in with a shitload of kick-ass and the other Nightfury warriors on his tail. As the pack rolled in, the Razorbacks recoiled. The idiots. They were bold when they outnumbered him ten to one, but give them even odds, it was Retreatsville for the assholes.

Thank fuck. He didn't have a moment to waste.

Swooping in behind Venom and Wick, he mind-spoke, *"B…I'm going cliff-side."*

Bastian grunted, cracking a rogue's skull. *"Get her out of here."*

Amen to that.

As much as he hated to leave the fight, he couldn't stay. Not with Angela alone and vulnerable up on the ridgeline. Okay, so she wasn't alone, but Mac was little better than a cub—unsure of his magic, unused to his new body, unable to use his strength to maximum effect. Leaving her with a fledgling male who didn't have a clue how to cloak himself, never mind her, wasn't an option.

Especially with Lothair still MIA.

Chapter Twenty-seven

Retreating to the secondary location wasn't Angela's idea of fun. Then again, neither was Mac at the moment. Freaking guy and his strong-arm tactics. He'd hauled her off the ground, stealing her rifle before she could get another shot away. Now he dragged her away from the firefight and Rikar, pushing her ahead of him down the rough pathway toward the beachfront.

Crap. The beach wasn't a place she wanted to go. Bad memories lay in that direction. Especially after spotting Lothair not far from their primary position on the ledge. Angela clenched her teeth and kept her feet moving. She didn't want to think about the cabin, the river, or the beachfront where Rikar rescued her. Nothing good lay in rehashing it. But as she navigated the steep incline, boot heels sinking into rock shale, blood rushed in her ears and fear came calling.

Her stomach knotted. She swallowed the sudden surge of bile, struggling to keep her footing on unfriendly terrain. Her boots slid on loose stone. Fist-sized rocks rolled down the slope in front of her, kicking up dust, cracking the sides of boulders. Angela grabbed for a handhold, fighting for balance. Her palm slid on the sheer rock wall. A second before she fell, Mac grabbed the back of her army jacket and hauled her upright.

Angela sucked in a breath. "Mac—"

"Keeping moving." He glanced over his shoulder, scanning the sky.

"We're sitting ducks out here," she whispered, her voice an octave lower than usual. Sound carried for miles out here. They were already in Deep-Shitsville. No need to give away their position by being an idiot. "You can fly. Shift and let's go airborne."

He shook his head. "Too dangerous."

She opened her mouth to argue.

Mac drilled her with a look, aqua-blue eyes shimmering in the gloom. "I haven't trained enough. Shit, I can barely protect myself up there, never mind you. Staying hidden's our best bet until we get to the water. Once we're in, no one will be able to touch me, and I'll swim you to safety. Get you home."

"But Rikar—"

"Can handle himself."

True enough. A bird's-eye view of his lethal abilities from the ridge told her that much. She'd gotten up close and personal through her scope. Watched him hammer enemy dragons…seen him twist and turn, white scales flashing as he went supersonic in flight to dodge Razorback claws. And that was before the other Nightfuries arrived on the scene.

Still, leaving Rikar out there—without her to cover him—made her go cold inside. Not that she'd had much choice in the matter. Proof positive of that was hauling ass behind her. With her M25 slung over his shoulder, leaving her nothing but the twin Glocks holstered on the outsides of her thighs for protection.

The guys had teased her when she'd strapped on the double gun belt, calling her a Lara Croft wannabe. Bet they weren't laughing now. Mac certainly wasn't.

Freaking guy...rifle-stealing pain in her ass.

Grabbing her shoulder, Mac pushed her sideways into a low-lying boulder, military-speak for hold up and get down. As he crouched alongside her, he checked the clip in her rifle, chambered a round, and whispered, "Besides, he'll kick my ass if I go airborne with you."

"Better an ass-kicking than getting me killed on the ground," she said, talking smack to ease the tension. Both of them were wound too tight. Life-and-death situations tended to do that to a couple of cops in over their heads. "He'll nail your—"

"Shut up," he said even as his lips twitched. "And keep your head down. We're headed into a straight stretch."

She peeked over the top of the huge rock. "An open area?"

Mac nodded. "About a hundred yards worth."

"Crap."

"No kidding."

Wonderful. Angela unholstered one of her Glocks and flipped the safety off. Just what they didn't need, a clearing complete with sheer rock walls. The perfect spot for an ambush.

After double-checking her weapon, she glanced at Mac. "The plan?"

"Shit," he said. "We're supposed to have a plan?"

Angela rolled her eyes. Her partner grinned at her, but she could see the strain and knew what he was thinking because...you betcha. She was thinking the same thing. Mac was Dragonkind now, fast healing, hard to kill in a firefight. Crazy durable, unlike her. She was human, packing nothing but her smarts and a couple of Glocks to protect her mortal self while he owned a kick-ass set of claws, armored scales, and a nasty exhale. And that was before she got to the whole magic thing. So, yeah. If Mac got tag-teamed, she'd be forced to face a psychopath in dragon form.

All by her lonesome.

"Okay," she murmured, blowing out a calming breath. With a shimmy, she slid sideways, popped her head around the edge of the boulder, giving the terrain another sneak peek. "I'll stick close to the rock face. There's an overhang at the base of the rock wall on the right-hand side. I should be able to squeeze under it. If things go south, I'll hide there. Good?"

"Good," Mac repeated, falling into their usual prebattle routine. It almost felt normal, as though they were headed into a perp's house, not about to cross a clearing in dragon country. "Be safe."

"You know it," she said, then completed their trash talk ritual with, "Don't do anything stupid."

He snorted.

She went commando, staying low, double-fisting her gun as she skirted the edge of a boulder. Entering the plateau on the run, Angela hauled ass, legs pumping, moving with more speed than stealth. A low growl slithered through the quiet, bouncing between the sheer stone walls surrounding her. A grinding noise echoed, the snick of claws scraping stone as dragons took flight.

Her heart scrambled, going AWOL inside her chest. "Mac!"

"Get the fuck down!"

Two shadows flew in, hard scales glinting in the moonlight.

Angela leveled her Glock at the brown Razorback. Mac beat her to it. Transforming into dragon form, he streaked across the plateau, heading for the far end where a cliff tumbled off the edge toward the ocean. Still running, she got low and slid sideways on stone, ripping her pant leg open at the knee. She raised gun again, trying to get a shot off, watching transfixed as Mac went to work.

No training, her ass. Look at him go.

Blue-gray scales nothing but a blur in the gloom, her partner leapt skyward. The enemy dragon stopped short, trying to compensate, hanging in midair. Mac struck, grabbing the SOB's spike tail at the top of his jump. With a snarl, he yanked. The Razorback squawked as Mac dragged him out of the sky. As Mac's talons touched down with a thump, the rogue slammed into the ground. Rock dust flew, clouding the clearing as the brown dragon slid toward the cliff edge.

Mac leapt on top on him. Angela dove for cover, using jagged pieces of fallen rock to hide her movements. She needed to get to the other end of the open space. With her partner pummeling the bastard, she couldn't get a clear shot at the Razorback's head. A bullet to the temple would help Mac out, but only if she didn't hit him by mistake.

Adrenaline made her fast. Her mind made her lethal as she beat feet to the opposite end of the clearing. Her gaze narrowed on Mac, a plan took hold. She'd climb. Get to higher ground, protect her partner, and shoot the bastard from above. Even in the dark, she could see a stretch of rock she could scale.

Holstering her gun, she sprinted toward the steep wall, looking for hand and toeholds. She checked Mac's position, watched him push the Razorback toward the cliff edge, and yelled, "Mac, don't go over the—"

Ah, crap.

With a snarl, Mac screwed up her plan, launching himself and the Razorback over the ledge. Her heart stopped beating as she watched them fall. Within seconds, the pair disappeared, tumbling through thin air toward—

Splash!

—the ocean.

All went quiet.

Not trusting the stillness, Angela searched the sky. Pinpoint stars winked at her, belying the seriousness of her situation. Mac had a hold of one dragon, but the other still hid, waiting to strike. Her heart in her throat, she backed toward the overhang, the narrow crevice that would protect her from Razorback claws. Loose rock crunched beneath her boot treads, sounding loud in the silence. Holding the gun against her thigh, Angela curled her finger around the trigger and waited, forcing herself to breathe through the fear.

"Come on, Mac…hurry up," she murmured, trying to make herself believe her partner was seconds away from reemerging over the cliff face. "Come on, man."

Ten feet from her hidey-hole. Now eight. She was almost there, but unease kept her eyes on the sky. She refused to turn her back on the clearing. The instant she did, the rat-bastard would make his move. So she backed up slowly, desperate to anticipate, knowing the sadistic bastard was out there…watching her, enjoying her fear, wanting her to feel it to maximum effect.

"Here, kitty-kitty-kitty-kitty." The awful hiss came from right above her head.

Angela went stone-still, the voice affecting her like slow poison, shutting down her ability to think. Those words… oh, God, his words. He'd used the same ones the night he chased her through the woods toward the beachhead. The memory kicked at her. She eviscerated it, reaching for every ounce of courage she possessed.

The mental readjust snapped her into motion. Angela scrambled for the jagged opening of the crevice. The rat-bastard growled. A gust of air blasted her back, shoving her forward. She lost her footing and went down, but she wasn't out.

Spinning into a speed roll, she hurtled toward safety, twisting to avoid the huge talon as it swiped at her. The womp-womp of heavy wings sounded overhead. Angela increased her tilt-a-whirl, her arms tucked tight to her chest, chunks of shale biting through her BDUs as she rolled faster. Razor-sharp claws glinted in the moonlight, reaching for her. An instant before Lothair caught her, she zipped beneath the overhang and into the opening.

"Fucking she-cop." The sharp click of claws echoed just outside her hidey-hole.

Her lungs so tight she could hardly breathe, Angela shuffled back into the fissure. She wanted to go farther, but… goddamn it. It only went about twelve feet. Surrounded by dank, slimy rock, she wedged her shoulders in tight and grabbed a handful of silt. She rubbed it on her shirt, drying her sweat-slick palm, then shifted her gun to the other hand and repeated the procedure. She couldn't afford to have her weapon slip.

The rat-bastard snarled. "More trouble than you're worth."

Finished with the drying routine, she leveled her Glock at the crack, toward the thin strip of moonlight. "Go home then, why don't you?"

Taunting him probably wasn't the best strategy, but she didn't know what else to do. Other than blow his head off if he crouched down to look at her. Please God, let him be that stupid. 'Cause, yeah. He might have her cornered, but the second she saw the dark glint of his dragon eye or he shifted into human form and came after her, she'd put a bullet through his brain.

Mining his female's energy, Rikar tracked her through the rough terrain. His eyes narrowed on the craggy coastline, he rocketed around another bend. The ocean roared, waves frothing, smashing against the base of the cliffs, throwing up cold spray. Slick with mist, water wicked from his scales, turning to ice before blowing back behind him in a frosty swirl. He increased his wing speed, scanning, searching… his aggression factor set on apocalyptic.

He needed to find her. Close. He was so freaking close. Less than a minute away.

Which was way too long. He could feel her fear through energy-fuse, heard the hitch of her breath, the hammer of her heart as if it were his own.

Fucking hell. Something nasty was going down. Angela didn't scare that easily. Add that to the fact he couldn't raise Mac through mind-speak, and situation critical took on a whole new meaning.

Night vision pinpoint sharp, he picked up all kinds of trace and discarded most of it. She wasn't on the beach or anywhere near the secondary location. Which meant she was stuck on the trail, up in the cliffs above the churn and chop of water. Flying harder, wings stretched to capacity, Rikar banked hard, heading inland. He came in low, following a rough trail up from the beachhead. Almost there. Another rise. Another fall, and he crested a sheer rock face. He heard the growl and the sound of claws on stone a second before he spotted the rogue.

The bastard was digging, clawing at the ground beneath a narrow overhang. Good Christ. Angela was under there, avoiding Lothair's deadly talons as he swiped at her.

Baring his fangs, Rikar came in hot. Arctic air whistled from his throat and ice daggers flew. Reacting to the magic hurtling toward him, Lothair's head snapped in his direction. Rikar snarled. Too late. The fucker wouldn't get airborne before—

Wham!

The frozen knives struck the Razorback XO, piercing his scales. Blood splatter arced as Lothair snarled and spun to face him. His velocity supersonic, Rikar swooped in and hammered the rogue broadside. His claws found flesh and bone. With a roar, he clamped down, ramming the ice daggers deeper as he spun his enemy away from Angela. Lothair's head whiplashed, exposing his throat. Rikar ignored the pain as the SOB's talons ripped at his shoulders, and flipped the bastard. Jumping on his spiked spine, he grabbed the rogue's wings and cranked, popping them from their sockets.

Lothair shrieked in agony, thrashing beneath his hold.

Rikar showed no mercy. With a twist, he snapped the male's spine, severing his spinal cord. Paralyzed from the chest down, Lothair screamed. Rikar applied more pressure, giving his beast free rein, and growled, "She's mine. You dare to touch what's mine...you die."

And fuck, he wanted to do it. To finish Lothair—deliver the death blow and punish him for hurting Angela. For taking what by right should've been hers to give. But he couldn't steal that from her. His female deserved justice, needed closure to heal from the pain. And if pulling the trigger helped her recover, he'd forgo his own need for vengeance in order to give it to her.

His claws buried in enemy flesh, he called to her, "Angela."

"Rikar?"

"Are you all right, love?"

He heard her move in answer. The shuffle sounded loud even though it shouldn't. Other noises trumped that...the crashing churn of ocean waves, the labored breathing of the enemy male he pinned to the granite. But his focus was absolute, and all about her. His dragon senses picked up each miniscule shift of movement, tapping into her heart rate, mining her emotional state.

The biofeedback bounced back like a boomerang. Scared, but all right. Rikar exhaled in relief. She wasn't hurt. Thank Christ.

The Glock clutched in her hand, she scrambled around the edge of a boulder, then froze. Just stopped short, hazel gaze widening as they landed on him. Pressing his prey into the ground, he tipped his chin at her, knowing what kind of picture he made. Blood spattered. Deadly. Aggressive. A bonded male presenting a gift to his female.

Tears flooded her eyes. She breathed his name, a thank-you in each syllable.

"Come finish it, angel."

One tear fell, streaking through the dirt on her cheek. She moved forward, the gun bobbing against her thigh, her attention shifting to the bastard who'd hurt her. As she approached, Lothair whined, pawing the ground, trying to get away even though he had nowhere to go. Rikar wrapped one talon around the rogue's front paws, holding him immobile, protecting Angela, refusing to feel sorry for the bastard.

The execution might not be nice, but was deserved. Justice at its best.

Stopping less than three feet away, Angela raised the Glock. She met his gaze, hers full of pain, his full of understanding. He nodded. She pulled the trigger, ending Lothair's life and his reign of terror. Over her. Over them. Over the females yet to be freed.

As the Razorback ashed out, throwing gray flakes into the air, Angela's breath hitched into a heartbreaking sob. Christ help him. Here it came, the emotional breakdown. Her pain was raw, too deep…and so necessary.

She needed to cry. To release the helplessness and sorrow, every ounce of pressure that had been building steadily inside her. Now that she'd ended Lothair's life, she had closure and could let the injustice she'd suffered go.

Shifting into human form, Rikar pulled her into the shelter of his body. She accepted his embrace like the gift he meant it to be, leaning on him, wrapping her arms around his waist, and let the tears fall.

"That's it, love," he murmured against the top of her head. Picking her up, he walked them both away from the ash pile and the stink of death. "Let it go…let it all go."

He kept talking to her, using his voice to comfort her. She didn't cry long. But then, he didn't expect her to. His female was battle honed and warrior strong. And now that the storm had passed, she'd mourn her loss and move on. Exactly as he or any one of the Nightfury warriors would have done.

"My beautiful female," he murmured, stroking his hand along her back. "You make me so proud."

"Rikar…" She trailed off. And he waited, giving her the time she needed to collect her thoughts. She burrowed deeper against him, holding him tight. "I know this probably isn't the best time to tell you, but…I love you. Even if you don't love me back. Even if you don't want me—"

"Sweet Christ, angel," he muttered, surprise blindsiding him. "I love you too. So much it wrecks me."

"Oh." She sniffled then raised her head to look at him. "Why didn't you say anything? I've been going nuts, trying to read you. To figure out if you want me to stay."

Brushing a tear from her cheek, he marveled at the irony. "What a pair we make."

She frowned and met his gaze, a question in her own.

He answered it without hesitation. "I've been holding back, afraid if I told you how I feel…that I want a future with you…it would freak you out. You've been through so much, Angela, and I didn't want to be *that* male. The one making demands, pushing you into something you weren't ready to accept. Expecting something you might never be able to give."

"Rikar?"

"Yeah?"

"You should probably know something right up front," she whispered, wiping at the corners of her eyes, making her eyelashes tangle together. God, she was incredible. So damned beautiful she took his breath away. "I'm okay with you making demands. All kinds of them."

"Good to know." His mouth curved as he dipped his head and touched his lips to hers. The kiss was gentle, undemanding, nothing like he wanted, but all that she needed. "The energy-fuse…and feeding me…doesn't bother you?"

"Not even a little." Her mouth tipped up at the corners, she ran her hands over his shoulders. "Fate, remember? You're my mate. We are meant to be together."

"Bang-on, angel," he murmured, his heart so full of her he felt close to bursting. "So…on the demand front. I've got another for you."

She kissed him softly. "Go for it."

"There's a ceremony, one Forge says will cement the bond we share." Nerves got the better of him. His stomach twisted as he said, "Would you—"

"Yes," she said, agreement quick, tone sure. She smiled, then popped up on her tiptoes to plant a kiss on the underside of his jaw. "Yes to everything and then more after that."

He laughed. "You should probably hear me out, love. Get some details before you agree to anything."

"If it means staying with you? I'm in…all the way in."

"Forever sound good?"

"Hmm, yeah." Her fingers drifting through his hair, she pulled his head down for another kiss. "Really, really good."

"Fantastic." He grinned against her mouth, nipping her gently, taking easy sips before he raised his head. When she protested, he said, "One more question, though."

"Uh-hmm?"

"Where the hell is—"

"Motherfuck!" The curse came from just below the cliff edge. A huge blue-gray talon followed. Claws spread, the sharp points bit into the ground. The scraping sound cracked the quiet as the paw slid, ripping grooves into granite.

"—Mac."

Angela snorted. "Guess that answers that."

Mac cursed again. A second later his horned head popped up over the lip of the cliff. His aquamarine eyes aglow, he locked onto Angela.

"I'm all right. Just a few scratches," she said, reassuring her partner.

Relief relaxed the fierceness of his expression. A moment later he shifted focus, throwing a load of pissed off in Rikar's direction. "Good of you to show up, Ice Cube."

Rikar clenched his teeth to keep from laughing. Only B called him that—an affectionate nickname his commander liked to throw out every once in a while.

He raised a brow. "The rogue?"

"Dead." Razor-sharp claw still digging into rock, Mac hauled his bulk over the ledge, bladed spine glistening with saltwater as he growled, "Can we go home now?"

"Yes, please," Angela murmured, pressing her cheek to his chest. "Home."

Home. That had a nice ring to it. Even better for the fact he wouldn't be headed there alone. He had Angela now, and no matter the battles ahead, she was the only home he would ever need.

Excerpt from *Fury of Seduction*

Chapter One

Sleep always eluded him. Night. Day. It didn't matter. A solid eight hours of shut-eye never made it onto Mac's schedule. He'd tried everything: swapping his firm mattress for a softer one, kitting the thing out with silk sheets, and the best pillows money could buy. Stretching out in his La-Z-Boy recliner. Hardcore sex before bedtime. Nothing helped. No matter what he did, the most he ever got was three hours in a row.

Which explained a lot, actually.

Like why he stood by himself in the gymnasium he shared with the other Nightfury dragon warriors instead of tucked in his bed getting the recommended number of Zs. Seven stories below ground, Black Diamond boasted the best of everything: state-of-the-art workout equipment, a basketball court, and a room full of tools used to sharpen dragon claws. The fact he was alone in the underground lair said it all. None of his brothers in arms suffered from insomnia. All were no doubt deep in la-la land, laid out under feather down, getting hot and heavy with an imaginary dream girl. Which...

Uh-huh, you guessed it. Made Mac the sole patient in the sleep deprivation department Chez Nightfury.

Damned annoying. And even more of a problem today.

Combating a boatload of pissed off, Mac rolled his shoulders to work out the kinks. He couldn't afford to screw up. Or let his new family down. The other warriors were counting on him. Trusting that he'd learn to master the magic he commanded as a Dragonkind male to become a solid member of the Nightfury pack. Did it matter that he'd only just learned he was half-dragon? That the magic encoded in his DNA had jump-started the *change*—allowing him to shift from human to dragon form and back again—less than a week ago?

Not even a little.

Time didn't wait for anyone or give a shit about ability. And neither did Mac.

To fight alongside his brothers, he must prove he belonged with them. Which meant he needed to pull it together...right now.

Too bad the plan was goat-fucked six ways to Sunday.

His dragon half was AWOL, getting in his face, fucking up his flow, denying his will to control it. Cajoling didn't work. Neither did babying the bastard. And threatening it? Shit, he'd gotten zapped with nasty-ass energy shards each time he tried that approach. So what did that leave him?

Begging.

Mac blew out a long breath. Just the thought gave him a raging case of no-can-do—the obstinate SOB belonged to him, after all, not the other way around—but desperate times called for desperate measures. If he continued to screw the pooch he wouldn't get what he wanted. Hell...make that what he *craved*. He needed the Nightfury warriors' acceptance. Without it, he wouldn't get his warrior status rubber-stamped in the war against the Razorbacks, a rogue faction of Dragonkind whose endgame included the extermination of the human race.

He glared at the weight machine nearest him. Steel rattled, picking up the vibe he threw off, and shifted against the rivets that kept it bolted to the floor. As the calamity got going, clanking out a rhythm, industrial grade fluorescents flared above his head, crackling through the quiet. A second before the light bulbs exploded, Mac shut the energy overload down, more disgusted with himself than ever.

KOing gym equipment wouldn't get him anything but more attention. The kind he didn't need from the crew still asleep upstairs. He snorted. Now there was an understatement. Bastian, his new commander, would deep-fry his ass if he wrecked anything else this week. Especially since he was still on the hook for putting his fist through a wall.

Raising his arms, Mac cupped the back of his head and pressed down, pushing his chin toward his chest. Taut muscles pulled and pain screamed up his spine. As agony slammed into the back of his skull, he frowned at the real estate between his bare feet. The Velcro of the exercise mats lined up, connecting the whole, not even a millimeter off as each clung to its counterpart. Any other day he would've appreciated the precision. Enjoyed the tidy corners and neat edges. Today the sight just made him sick.

So together. So on the same page. So perfect in every way.

Unlike him. He was a total frickin' catastrophe. The only guy in Black Diamond who didn't have his shit together.

Mac's headache morphed into a full-blown throb, pounding between his temples. The whole thing was a total mind-fuck. The failure. Each defeat. The fact his magic defied him. And as uncertainty came calling, he shook his head. It shouldn't be this difficult. He'd always excelled at everything—school, sports, the military, and martial arts. Nothing had ever pushed him to the edge of what he could endure…until now.

Why was he having so much trouble? Was it the water angle? Most dragons hated water and spent their lives avoiding it. Not Mac. True to his water dragon roots, he preferred to be in the ocean. The deeper the better, but any body of water would do. Give him a lake, river, or Olympic-sized swimming pool and he was good to go. The difference between him and the other Nightfuries, though, didn't explain why his magic refused to obey him.

He frowned, turning the questions over in his mind, searching for answers. None came. No clever explanation. No aha moment. Just another big doughnut hole in an information string full of them.

Inhaling deeply, Mac filled his lungs to capacity, getting back in the game. Surrender wasn't a word he ever used, and as he held the breath, relishing the burn, he prayed the last time was the charm. He needed to connect with his dragon side like he needed legs to stand on. Letting the air go, he drew another lungful and released it.

Draw. Hold. Release.

Mac repeated the sequence over and over, using the breathing technique he'd learned in the navy. After a while, his heartbeat slowed. His body calmed. As the chaos in his mind receded, a sinking sensation grabbed hold and pulled him deep. A snick echoed as something unlocked inside him, releasing a flood of energy. The Meridian. Good

Christ. He'd found it, tapped into the electrostatic current that fed Dragonkind.

"Come on, beautiful," he whispered, nursing the fragile connection. "Stay with me."

His words swirled through the quiet, reminding him he was alone. Thank God. He didn't want anyone witnessing the train wreck if he failed again. Call it pride. Call it ego. Call it a severe allergy to ridicule. Whatever. It didn't matter, just as long as he caught hold of the magic and mastered the cloaking spell. The ability wasn't optional. If he couldn't cloak himself—go dark and invisible against the night sky—he couldn't fight alongside his brothers. And if he couldn't contribute as a warrior, he wasn't worth the space he occupied.

About the Author

Image © Julie Daniluk

As the only girl on all-guys hockey teams from age six through her college years, Coreene Callahan knows a thing or two about tough guys and loves to write about them. Call it kismet. Call it payback after years of locker room talk and ice rink antics. But whatever you call it, the action better be heart stopping, the magic electric, and the story wicked good fun.

After graduating with honors in psychology and working as an interior designer, Callahan finally succumbed to her overactive imagination and returned to her first love: writing. And when she's not writing, she is dreaming of magical worlds full of dragon-shifters, elite assassins, and romance that's too hot to handle. Callahan currently lives in Canada with her family and her writing buddy, a fun-loving golden retriever. She is the author of *Fury of Fire* and the upcoming novel in the Dragonfury series, *Fury of Seduction.*

Printed in Great Britain
by Amazon